THE MULTIPLE CAT

When Annabel Hinchby-Smythe is mistaken for a top interior designer and invited to redecorate a reclusive millionaire's London flat, she little realizes what the deception will lead to. Initially, she hopes that her entrée into Arthur Arbuthnot's secret world will provide her with titbits to feed to the gossip columns, and indeed his shabby mansion flat houses a motley and largely disagreeable group of relatives and hangers-on. Only Sally, a cat rescued from the streets, seems to have a place in Arbuthnot's affections, although she is loathed by everyone else.

As Annabel wrestles with the mysteries of material samples, the tension level within the cavernous flat rises. Family members are at each other's throats, lawyers come and go, and Arbuthnot's secretary succumbs increasingly to hysteria. Anything could happen, and does: the millionaire's body is discovered in his inner sanctum. The family are quick to cover up any suggestion that it might be murder, but Annabel is profoundly suspicious.

And then the bombshell drops: Sally is the main beneficiary of the will, and whoever looks after her controls the fortune. All too aware of what this means for the cat's life expectancy, Annabel spirits her away; the Arbuthnot entourage, however, are not to be thwarted, and soon any number of Sally lookalikes are being recovered by the greedy relatives.

Between posing as a designer, meeting the insatiable demands of Xanthippe's Diary, acting as a cat-refuge service, and solving a murder, Annabel Hinchby-Smythe has recourse to rather more martinis than usual.

The Multiple Cat is a funny and charming crime novel, which will appeal to cat-lovers and mystery-lovers alike.

THE MULTIPLE CAT

Marian Babson

HarperCollins*Publishers*

This novel is entirely a work of fiction.
The names, characters and incidents portrayed
in it are the work of the author's imagination.
Any resemblance to actual persons, living or dead, events or localities
is entirely coincidental.

Collins Crime
An imprint of HarperCollins*Publishers*
77–85 Fulham Palace Road, London W6 8JB

First published by Collins Crime 1999

1 3 5 7 9 10 8 6 4 2

A catalogue record for this book
is available from the British Library

ISBN 0 00 232681 7

Set in Meridien and Bodoni

Typeset by Palimpsest Book Production Limited,
Polmont, Stirlingshire
Printed and bound in Great Britain by
Caledonian International Book Manufacturing Ltd, Glasgow

1

Perhaps, if it hadn't been for that morning's flurry of bills cascading through the letter box, she would never have got involved. She stared unbelievingly at the telephone bill, midway between despair and fury. Couldn't that idiot who had rented her cottage pick up the telephone even once without dialling the International Exchange? Just look at the size of that bill!

Annabel Hinchby-Smythe closed her eyes, tossed back the remains of her martini and took a deep breath and then a deeper one.

Oh, the creature was probably honest enough and would pay the bill eventually. Meanwhile, however, she had to pay it herself or risk having the phone cut off – and he would expect to find it in working order when he returned from his trip to Italy.

Annabel frowned and absently poured herself another martini. It was just unfortunate that money was so tight at the moment. It seemed as though every company in her slim portfolio of stockholdings had issued a profits warning and notice of decreased dividends. The stock market appeared to be going through another of its periodic crises.

Furthermore, her lucrative little sideline of supplying items to the gossip columns appeared to have dried up. Either everyone had started behaving themselves, which was improbable, or they were lying exceptionally low. Also, most of her generation had sown their wild oats, reaped their whirlwinds and were now quietly breeding polo ponies in Argentina, raising sheep in Australia or – in one notorious case – writing poetry in a cloistered monastery.

Annabel drummed her fingers on her glass, setting the clear liquid rippling. Obviously, she needed to widen her circle of friends and acquaintances.

So it was just as well that she had agreed to attend that party being given by some highly dubious social climbers tonight. It was also fortunate that the opportunity to sublet her cottage had arisen at the same time that dear Dinah, who was taking a three-month cruise in the Far East to recover from the stress of recent events, had offered her the Cosgreave pied-à-terre in Knightsbridge. Lady Cosgreave could be benevolent – in her own way – or perhaps she considered it further assurance against Annabel's changing her mind about selling that very interesting story to the newspapers. So far, Dinah had done a sterling job at covering up the scandal.

Not that Annabel would dream of doing any such thing – and Dinah should have had more faith in her – but it *was* useful to have a rent-free Central London base while she collected rent on the short-term let of her own cottage.

That helped – quite a bit. Now, if only she could unearth a few juicy items to sell to the gossip columns . . . it had been so long since some of them had heard from her that they might be forgetting she existed – and that would never do.

The grandmother clock in the front hall chimed suddenly, startling her and reminding her that it was time to get changed for that cocktail party.

Initially, the party was disappointing. She had gleaned only one item she could sell on to a column and collected two leads to possibly developing stories she needed to keep an eye on. Nothing spectacular, though, nor even very interesting, just column-fillers for those dull days when nothing much was happening. On the other hand there seemed to be an awful lot of those days. She could not escape the feeling that the progeny of her own generation were a lot less enterprising, not to mention entertaining, than their parents and even grandparents had been.

It was borne in upon her gradually that a man on the fringe of her group was watching her intently and had been since she had been the centre of another group she had been regaling with a second – or perhaps even third-hand –

anecdote about Sybil Colefax, the famous between-the-wars society hostess and interior designer. After the laughter had died down and the group broke up and re-formed, he had followed her to stand on the edge of her new group, watching and listening.

Absently, Annabel wondered if she had picked up a stalker and, if so, whether the information would be of any value – or interest – to one of the gossip columns.

As this group broke up, the man finally made eye contact with her and moved closer to speak to her.

'You're an interior designer, I gather,' he said. 'I heard you talking about it. I've been thinking about doing up my place lately, but I keep putting it off because I never quite knew who I ought to get to do it. I wonder if you'd be interested in taking on the job, er, assignment?'

'Ummmm . . .' Annabel went through the pantomime of reluctance, although it was the best offer she'd had in months. 'Actually, I *am* rather busy just now . . .' She gave him an encouraging smile. How difficult could interior designing be? 'But I might be able to squeeze in a preliminary consultation. Er, my rates are rather high, you realize?' She tilted her head so that her diamond earrings flashed at him.

'Of course.' Gold glittered at his cuffs as he swept aside her demur. 'They would be. Anyone who worked with Sybil Colefax . . .'

'Mmmm.' How old did he think she was? His attitude was cheering, however. Numbers obviously meant little to him, whether in terms of money or years. She mentally doubled the amount she had thought of quoting; if he blanched, it could always be lowered.

He simply nodded, however, and handed her his card, then hesitated expectantly.

'Oh, I'm afraid I don't have my card with me,' Annabel said haughtily. 'This is a social occasion, after all.' She raised an eyebrow in faint reproof. (It was all coming back to her – those few occasions when she had seen interior designers in action in the homes of her friends: the customer is always wrong.) 'I wasn't expecting to do any business here.'

'Of course, of course . . . I'm sorry.' He was immediately

3

cowed, contrite and apologetic – all the hallmarks of the perfect client.

'It *is* possible,' she forgave him graciously, 'that I might be able to fit you in between two other clients. One is off to Bermuda for six months, so there's no desperate urgency about her country house . . .'

'I'd be most grateful if you could,' he said humbly. 'I'm sure you know how it is. One drifts along for ages thinking vaguely "I must do something about this place." Then, suddenly, the opportunity presents itself and you can't wait to get it done.'

'So many clients feel that way.' The Opportunity smiled graciously, working herself deeper into the part with every passing moment, while calculating rapidly. She could get to the library first thing in the morning and take out a selection of books on interior design, bone up on them over lunch and get the patter – not that he was likely to know the difference.

'You'll want to inspect the flat. Let me—' He retrieved his card and scribbled something on the back of it. 'This will get you in if I'm not there.' He hesitated. 'I'm afraid it's rather ghastly. I didn't realize how bad it was until Sally moved in – not that she's critical, she's too polite for that. But it's amazing the way you can tell what she's thinking.'

'Women *are* more sensitive to their surroundings,' Annabel agreed.

'All females are, I suppose.' He looked faintly surprised. 'I never thought of it that way before. Er . . . how soon do you think you might . . . ?'

'Perhaps I might find time to take a quick look tomorrow afternoon – lateish, of course, before I meet friends for dinner.'

As soon as she got back to Lady Cosgreave's flat, she reached for the telephone and dialled one of her sources. There was no point in doing all this homework without making sure that it was going to be worth the effort.

'Arthur Arbuthnot?' Xanthippe's Diary responded enthusiastically. 'The rumour is that Croesus is his middle name. You mean you've got something on *him?*'

4

'No,' Annabel admitted regretfully, noting that it sounded as though it would be very worth her while to keep her eyes open while she went about her new business. 'I, um, was thinking of entering a business arrangement with him and, since I'd never heard of the man, I thought I'd do a bit of checking. Make sure he's solvent . . . and honest . . . and all that.'

'No worries on the first score. Otherwise, I suppose he's as honest as any billionaire – if that's saying much. He's a bit of a dark horse, our Arthur. Nothing much known about him, dull as ditchwater. So dull' – the voice brightened – 'that there well could be something going on below the surface. You're sure you're not on to something?'

'Not really . . .' Annabel had a sudden doubt. Hadn't Arthur Arbuthnot said something about how shabby the place looked when seen through the eyes of the lady who had moved in? What lady? 'Anyway,' she added tantalizingly, 'it's far too early to say.'

'Remember,' Xanthippe purred, 'we'd pay *very* well.'

'If I find anything, you'll be the first to know,' Annabel promised.

2

The address was close to Regent's Park. Not, unfortunately, one of the lovely Nash Terraces, but one of the great Victorian mansion blocks set farther back from the park. Behind the wrought-iron-gate-protected glass-fronted door, the dark oak-panelled lobby was not exactly welcoming.

The man sitting behind the reception desk was even less so. He glared at her with such open hostility that she had to make an effort not to step back.

'I'm here to see Mr Arbuthnot,' Annabel said crisply, holding her ground. 'I'm expected.'

'Name?' It was a surly drawl. He knew who she was.

'Annabel Hinchby-Smythe.' There was no point in antagonizing him, he might be useful in the future, however unlikely it might seem. She gave him a perfunctory smile.

'Top floor,' he admitted grudgingly. 'Lift over there.'

As he pushed himself away from the desk to indicate the location of the lift, Annabel realized that he was in a wheelchair. One leg ended just above the knee. He could not be more than twenty-six.

So it was nothing personal then. He just hated the world. She couldn't blame him for that. Everyone did at some point in their lives. It was obvious that he had better reason than most.

The moment she was ushered into the dark gloomy hallway, Annabel knew that she was on to a winner. *Anything* anyone did to this dump would be an improvement.

Antlered skulls lined both sides of the long narrow corridor – which would not be so narrow if all those antlers were not branching out into the overhead space like perverted trees.

Just clearing them out would work wonders and then a lick of paint and perhaps a few pictures would transform the hallway into a more cheerful place.

There was a new lightness in Annabel's step as she followed the tall thin woman, who had not yet spoken a word to her, around the corner into a further long corridor, as gloomy and antler-ridden as the first.

The woman disappeared abruptly through a doorway on one side, without a backward glance and giving no indication as to whether or not Annabel was expected to keep following. Annabel began to get the feeling that she was not exactly welcome here.

Since all the other doors along the hallway were firmly closed, Annabel followed her reluctant guide into a small office where a large mahogany desk was placed in front of a window, so that its occupant could face the hallway. If the door remained open – and, somehow, Annabel got the feeling that it was never quite closed – everyone coming and going could be noted.

'I don't know why Mr Arbuthnot has bothered you,' the Broomstick-in-a-skirt said pettishly. 'There is nothing wrong with this flat the way it is. Is there, Wystan?'

For the first time, Annabel realized that someone else was in the room. He stood with his back to the window, his face in the shadows, and yet Annabel knew that he was looking at her. She stiffened as his gaze struck her like a jet of ice water and flowed down her body from face to feet. She felt that he was assessing her age, sex appeal and . . . possible child-bearing capacity.

'Now, now, nothing to worry about, Dora,' he said soothingly. 'The place could do with a bit of brightening up.'

She had obviously been judged and found wanting, negligible or, worse, perfectly safe. Annabel's face froze. This Wystan might not know it, but he had come perilously close to making an enemy. And she wasn't that fond of the Broomstick, either.

'If Mr Arbuthnot really feels the need to have something done,' the woman said coldly, 'we can get the painters in. Although I don't see why we should.' She looked at the dingy grey-green walls with complacency. 'Everything is fine just the way it is.'

The woman was a dark silhouette against the light of the window, dominating the room. Behind her, shadows swooped and fluttered as a pigeon landed on the windowsill.

'Get out!' She whirled and struck the windowpane a savage blow, sending the pigeon streaking off in terror. 'Flying vermin!' she muttered. 'Too much vermin around here already.'

'My appointment is with Mr Arbuthnot.' Annabel used her highest cut-crystal tones; for emphasis, she moved her hand so that her diamonds sparkled in the light. 'Perhaps you would be . . . good enough . . . to let him know that I have arrived.'

'I'll take her in.' Wystan, whoever he was, moved forward hastily, perhaps even nervously, as the Broomstick whirled to face back into the room, radiating fury and annoyance.

'Come along.' Wystan stepped between them. 'I know Arthur is looking forward to your visit, er, consultation.' He grasped Annabel's elbow tentatively and led her from the office.

'You mustn't mind Dora,' he murmured as soon as they were safely out of earshot. 'She's worked here so long she almost thinks the place belongs to her. Old retainer and all that, you know how it is.'

'Too tiresome.' Annabel forced an understanding smile to mask her dislike. Wystan was obviously the sort who perched on the fence, swaying first to one side and then to the other, depending on who seemed to be winning at the time. She had met that type before. Often, in fact.

'Means no harm,' he vouched improbably. The Broomstick would do all the harm she could – and delight in it, in the unlikely event that delight came within the scope of her vocabulary, not to mention her emotional range.

Wystan gave a perfunctory tap on the door at the end of the hallway and swung it open. 'Your decorator is here, Arthur,' he announced.

This was a room she would not dare touch – nor would she

be required to. Computer terminals hummed in every corner, flickering screens threw up and discarded images faster than the eye could focus on them, a constant procession of figures marched across other screens, a low-level susurration of irregular signals – probably a code, but quantum leaps beyond Morse – throbbed somewhere in the depths of all the high-tech apparatus.

The Heart of Empire, Annabel thought irreverently, but a business empire, overbearing, multinational and whispering of wealth beyond avarice. The diffident little Mr Arbuthnot was obviously far far more important than she had ever imagined. No wonder Xanthippe was so interested.

'Oh, splendid, splendid.' Arthur Arbuthnot rose and advanced, hand outstretched to greet her, but with the weight of empire still riding on his shoulders. 'I'm sorry. I intended to meet you at the door but' – he waved his hand about with an apologetic grimace – 'one gets so caught up in the daily grind that one loses track of time.'

'Quite all right,' Annabel cooed forgivingly, but she was not deceived. For a moment, before he began to speak, his face had been a cold robotic mask, as much a part of the machines as though he had been plugged into one of the electric outlets himself. Loss of humanity might be the price of being an emperor in the brave new electronic world.

'No, no, I should have . . .' Even now he could not quite make the transition to the human, flesh-and-blood world; he was much more comfortable interacting with machines. He never made the wrong move there.

'No problem at all, Arthur,' Wystan said soothingly. 'Dora and I were there to let her in. No harm done. Not as though' – the soothing tone tilted over into one less comforting – 'you'd pressed the wrong button on one of your computers and wiped out the Hang Seng Index.'

'Thank you, Uncle Wystan.' Arthur's voice was carefully neutral, but it was clear that he was displeased. There were some things one did not joke about. 'I appreciate your looking after my guest for me.'

'Be careful! Don't let her in!' the Broomstick shrieked suddenly from across the hall.

9

Annabel stiffened again. This was carrying antipathy too far. The woman must be mad. 'I'm perfectly able to see that you won't want this room touched,' she said coldly.

'Hah!' Arthur Arbuthnot made a sudden dive at her ankles and she barely repressed a scream. Were they all mad? And why hadn't she left a note telling someone where she was going? It could be days before she was missed and then no one would know where to begin looking for the body.

'Got her!' He straightened up triumphantly, clutching a squirming armload of dappled brown fur. 'She knows this is the one room she isn't allowed into,' he explained apologetically to Annabel. 'Cats are full of static electricity – that's why they aren't allowed near ammunition dumps or any sensitive areas.'

'Oh, yes, I see.' Annabel could feel her eyes widening. She looked at the array of mysterious machines crowding the room, at the cat, at the rather weird Arthur Arbuthnot and mentally began formulating excuses about too much work to take on any more, or perhaps a sudden summons to fly to some distant part of the globe to the help of an existing client. Money wasn't everything.

'And then there are all those little hairs flying about.' He gave the cat a friendly jiggle and it began purring. 'They can wreak havoc with delicate machinery. This is the only room barred to her so, naturally, it's the one she's determined to get into. There are moments when she makes me feel like Bluebeard.' He stepped forward, leading them out of the nerve centre of his empire, and closed the door firmly behind him. 'Shall we adjourn to the parlour? We'll be more comfortable there.'

'Of course.' Annabel followed him along the corridor, noting that the route was carrying them well away from the office where the Broomstick lurked. A shadow moved uneasily behind that half-open door, as though perturbed that the action was moving out of range of her sphere of observation. Annabel decided that it would be a delight to redesign the Broomstick's office, turning her desk around so that she faced the window with her back to the door. Venetian blinds over the window and quaint old Victorian screens blocking the door might also be a good idea. Poor Arthur Arbuthnot! Did he occasionally long for the happy bygone days of Machiavelli, when leaders could employ blind secretaries and deaf-mute personal assistants to carry out their orders?

'In here.' Mr Arbuthnot swung open a door at the end of the corridor, ushering her into what once must have been a grand drawing room with a magnificent view over the treetops of Regent's Park. Pity about the view inside the room. Still, it cheered Annabel.

Safely away from the faintly sinister humming lair of Future World, her spirits were lifting and this helped even more. Never had she seen a place so badly in need of redecoration. It couldn't have been touched since the 1890s, although an Art-Deco cocktail cabinet and a couple of uncomfortable-looking chromium-and-leather chairs gave mute evidence of a desperate attempt at modernization sometime around the mid-1930s.

'Do sit down.' Mr Arbuthnot began to wave her towards one of the chromium monstrosities, then realized his mistake and indicated a Victorian gossip-bench instead.

Annabel perched on one seat of the S-shaped contraption and found herself almost cheek-to-jowl with Uncle Wystan, who had taken the other half of the perch. She hadn't realized he was still with them.

'Er . . .' Neither, apparently, had Mr Arbuthnot. 'Was there something you wanted to see me about, "Uncle" Wystan?' This time, there could be no mistake: there was a certain ironic stress on the word 'Uncle'.

'Oh, um . . .' Uncle Wystan appeared rather confused, but gave the impression that this was a natural state with him. 'I, er, just thought you might like me to sit in on the session, give the benefit of my advice, perhaps. Artistic strain runs in my family, you know. My Aunt Etta painted watercolours, exhibited in the Royal Academy Summer Show every year up to the war, when they put her in the Camouflage Corps.' He sighed deeply. 'Ruined her technique, blighted a promising career.'

'I think I'll stick to professional advice.' Mr Arbuthnot spoke with elaborate patience. 'If you don't mind, Uncle Wystan.'

'Oh, certainly, certainly. Don't buy a dog and bark your-self, eh? Oh, sorry.' He blinked at Annabel. 'No offence intended.'

'None taken,' Annabel said graciously. Inwardly, she squirmed a bit. What if Mr Arbuthnot ever found out the truth about her professionalism?

'That's settled then.' Mr Arbuthnot looked pointedly towards the door. In his arms, the cat narrowed her eyes at Uncle Wystan, her tail lashing menacingly.

'Oh, er . . .' Faced with their combined disapproval, Uncle Wystan twisted around and struggled to his feet. 'I suppose I ought to go and find Zenia, although she told me—' He broke off unhappily, as though realizing that whatever he had been told was not for public consumption.

'*There* you are, Wystan!' The voice from the doorway cut across his discomfiture. If the glasses in the cocktail cabinet had been more fragile, it would have shattered them. The cat twitched her ears and emitted a protesting grumble.

'And there *you* are, Aunt Zenia.' Mr Arbuthnot had no need to turn around, there was a resigned note in his voice.

Annabel had a clear view of the woman in the doorway; carefully, she kept her facial muscles motionless. 'Uncle' Wystan was explained – and not as some late-arriving progeny of the Arbuthnot family. Aunt Zenia was of a suitable age to be an aunt to Arthur Arbuthnot, Wystan was clearly her superannuated toy boy, their union only slightly dignified by marriage. No wonder Wystan was younger than his 'nephew'. No wonder Mr Arbuthnot got that strange note in his voice when he addressed his 'uncle'. In years gone past, and without an obliging woman to support him, Wystan would have been a remittance man.

'Hmmmph!' The woman had been observing Annabel as closely as Annabel had been observing her, but with consider-ably less subtlety. The slightly bulging brown eyes blinked and dismissed her, turning to Arthur Arbuthnot. She was nearly as thin as the Broomstick, but it was a carefully sculpted, expensively maintained thinness, set off by a suit from the latest fashionable designer. Annabel could not quite name the designer, but she was certain that the price would have been in the four figures; she was equally certain that Wystan had not been the one to pay for it.

'I'd like to speak to you, Arthur,' Aunt Zenia said. 'I do wish you'd put that cat outside – you know how flying fur reacts on me.'

'You can always go back downstairs to your own quarters,' Arthur said mildly. 'Sally lives here and she can shed her fur anywhere she likes. This is her home.'

'I must speak to you, Arthur!' An impatient hand waved away any more of his protests. 'Perhaps Miss Thingee, here, can take the cat outside for a few minutes.'

'It's Mrs Hinchby-Smythe, actually.' Annabel bared her teeth at the revolting woman.

'Really?' The note of surprised disbelief was obviously intended to be insulting – and succeeded. Even Uncle Wystan looked embarrassed.

'I do apologize for my family,' Mr Arbuthnot said quickly. The look he gave his aunt left no doubt about what would have happened to her had she not been family. Unfortunately, one can't fire one's aunt.

'Quite all right,' Annabel said brightly. 'There's no need to apologize for family – everyone understands that you're not responsible.'

Zenia drew herself up but, before she could speak, her husband intervened hastily.

'Where's Neville? I thought he was supposed to be here today.'

If he had been trying to change to a more pleasant subject, he had evidently chosen unwisely. Mr Arbuthnot abruptly looked as though he had bitten into something sour.

'Are you expecting Cousin Neville, Aunt Zenia?' His voice was carefully controlled. 'I thought he'd settled in Manchester.'

'He still has his own room in my flat. He won't impinge on you in any way.' Zenia was quickly on the defensive, Annabel noted. Was there, perhaps, some difficulty about her son? Possibly, even, a scandal?

If so, was it one Xanthippe might be interested in? Apart from the lure of extra cash for any juicy little snippets,

13

Annabel would love to see Aunt Zenia in some sort of difficulty. She was already working up a strong dislike for the woman and would be prepared to bet that Zenia did not improve on further acquaintance.

In fact, there was no one in this flat she *did* like, apart from Arthur Arbuthnot and, possibly, his cat. The humans were a dead loss.

'What a beautiful cat.' Annabel smiled at the complacent tabby lounging in Mr Arbuthnot's arms.

'She is, isn't she? So beautiful she's made me take a new look at our surroundings.' Mr Arbuthnot stroked the cat's throat, eliciting a loud purr. 'I decided her setting ought to be worthy of her.'

Zenia had a nice line in snorts. She treated them to another.

Annabel choked back her own gurgle of amusement. So Arthur wanted his flat redecorated to set off not a woman he treasured but a cat.

'And I called her Sally,' he continued, 'because of the song. And because I found her in the alley, you see.'

'Yes.' Zenia's glittering eyes looked directly from the cat to Annabel. 'As you may have noticed, Arthur has a *penchant* for alley cats.'

3

'Here they are,' a voice said from the doorway behind them. 'We wondered where everyone was hiding.'

A young man advanced languidly into the room – or perhaps his tight designer jeans would not allow him to move more quickly – followed by a slightly older woman, who was beautiful but had something about her which betrayed that alley cats were, indeed, endemic in this establishment.

'Neville, dear!' His mother greeted him warmly, pointedly ignoring his companion.

'Tara!' Wystan's enthusiasm made up for his wife's indifference. 'Thought you were still in Mustique. Good to see you back. You're looking very – er . . .' A poisonous look from his wife stopped him dead. 'Er, very tanned, very fit.'

'Thank you.' Tara moved past him dismissively, heading for the real object of her interest. 'I brought you a little souvenir, Arthur.' She extended a closed hand, turned it over and opened it suddenly. A sparkling fish on a string bounced in midair. 'Actually, it's for Sally. What can one give to a man who has everything?'

A fond foolish smile spread over Mr Arbuthnot's face as Sally stretched out a paw and swiped lazily at the dangling fish.

'She likes it,' he said. 'Thank you, Tara. Thank you very much.' He took the toy from her and dangled it in front of Sally himself.

Zenia gave a sharp hiss of indrawn breath, glaring at Tara even more venomously than she had glared at her husband.

Interesting. Annabel made a mental note that the way to Mr Arbuthnot's heart was clearly through his cat. And if it annoyed Zenia, so much the better. It was obviously a lesson Tara had already learned.

A flicker of movement beyond the doorway caught Annabel's eye. When she turned her head, no one was there. Yet she had the impression that someone had been hovering outside, eavesdropping.

The Broomstick, probably. Unable to utilize her observation post at this distance, she had left it and followed them to make sure she wasn't missing anything.

How did Arthur Arbuthnot put up with it? An overbearing secretary, a ghastly family, these depressing surroundings – or was he too engrossed in his business empire and his billions to notice much about his immediate environment? No wonder he was so fond of his cat.

On the other hand, he had begun to make a start on at least one thing that needed attention: this gloomy flat. She herself was scheduled to be the new broom to sweep this clean. Did he have further plans for some of his other problems? And what about the lovely Tara? Was she Neville's special friend or Arthur's? What sort of setup was this?

Definitely a promising one from the gossip point of view, Annabel decided. Judging from the undercurrents swirling around Wystan and Neville, there was a scandal or two in the background and, unless she missed her guess, quite probably another one waiting to happen.

First, however, her own status here had to be confirmed. With elaborate unobtrusiveness, Annabel glanced at her watch and then at Mr Arbuthnot.

'Yes, quite.' He caught the unspoken message. 'I'll just finish showing you around and then you can send me your quotation.'

A loud snort from Zenia expressed her opinion of this. Her nephew looked at her coldly. 'Ah, yes, you wanted to speak to me, Aunt Zenia. Perhaps we could postpone it until —'

'I merely wanted to tell you that this whole project is ill-conceived and quite ridiculous. There is nothing wrong with this flat the way it is.'

Annabel permitted herself a small wince and closed her eyes briefly. It was a reaction she had once observed in an official of an auction house when confronted with an inferior reproduction of a famous painting.

'Yes, quite,' Mr Arbuthnot agreed. 'I think we're all well aware of your opinion by now, Aunt Zenia.'

And it wasn't going to change a thing.

'Personally, I think you're right, Arthur.' Tara weighed in on the winning side. 'This place could do with a complete redesigning. It's too fusty for words.'

'Not a bad idea, at all,' Neville also plumped for the winning side, albeit with an uneasy sidelong glance towards his mother. 'After all, if you didn't own the freehold, the terms of any lease would have insisted on your doing up the place every three years or so. It must be thirty-odd years since the old walls have seen so much as a lick of paint.'

It was an unwise move. His cousin ignored him, but his family would deal with him later. Wystan gave a strangulated throat-clearing noise of warning. Tara moved a little farther away from him. His mother turned dangerously and glared at him.

'Come along,' Mr Arbuthnot said quickly. 'This way.' He led Annabel through a door at the other end of the room, safely away from the hostilities.

He led her through room after dreary room of the vast cavernous flat, each room more depressing than the last. They had been kept clean and dusted, but it was obvious that no one ever lived in them, or even visited them occasionally.

Annabel had never considered herself particularly sensitive to atmosphere but, by the time they wound up in a small study next to the computer room, she felt badly in need of a martini or three.

No such luck here, though. Instead, she took a deep breath and looked around the study. It could have been lifted directly from a gentlemen's club. Built-in bookcases, leather armchairs, lamps and side tables with the morning newspapers and the week's run of the *Financial Times*. There was even a marble fireplace with a fire laid in it waiting to be lit. It was the most comfortable room in the flat and it was clear that Arthur Arbuthnot spent most of his time here when he wasn't working in the computer room.

'Well . . .' Mr Arbuthnot motioned her to an armchair, slumped into the armchair opposite and looked at her quizzically. 'You begin to see the size of the problem?'

She had the feeling that he was not referring solely to the outdated apartment. This feeling was reinforced when he asked anxiously:

'Are you willing to take it on?'

'Mmmm . . .' The hesitation was not entirely a bargaining ploy. When the offer was first made to her, she had not yet encountered the Broomstick and Aunt Zenia. Would the possible benefits be enough to counterbalance the aggravations? 'I'll think it over and send you my quotation and then you can think it over.'

'That won't be necessary,' he said quickly. 'I've already decided you're the designer I want. I simply said that to keep Aunt Zenia quiet.'

'Now that you mention it—' She decided to take the bull by the horns. 'I'd have to be assured that there would be no outside interference in my work.'

'You'll have a completely free hand. Any problems and you just come straight to me.'

'Well . . .' And, thinking of horns. 'For one thing, those revolting skull-and-antlers will have to go.'

'I knew you were the right choice,' he beamed. Even the cat seemed happy about it. 'Let me give you a retainer right now. You can have the tradesmen send bills direct to me as they're incurred. Here, hold Sally for a minute.' He stood up and thrust the cat at her.

Briefly, Annabel and the cat were nose-to-nose, blinking at each other. Then Annabel reached out and lowered the cat to her lap where it stood irresolute for a moment, then settled cautiously.

Distracted by the cat, Annabel did not see exactly what Mr Arbuthnot did next. When she looked up, the slanted end section of the window enclosure had swung aside revealing a deep, shelved compartment into which he was reaching.

The cat watched intently, then stirred restlessly. Annabel tightened her hold and tried not to gasp. The shelves were packed solid with sheaves of international currency. If this

18

was Mr Arbuthnot's petty cash, it was enough to stock a Bureau de Change for a lesser man.

'Stay there, Sally,' Mr Arbuthnot said. 'You've seen it all before.' In a swift motion, he closed the safe and moved back to Annabel. 'Sally knows all my secrets. She's the only one in this building I can trust.'

'Ummm . . .' Annabel was mesmerized by the sheaf of banknotes in his hand. He couldn't intend to give all that to her . . . ?

'I hope this will do for your retainer.' He extended it tantalizingly, then drew it back slightly. 'You understand' – a crisp commanding note sounded in his voice – 'I expect you to make other arrangements for any work you have on hand and begin here immediately.'

He looked at her with utter confidence, in no doubt that she would comply. He was obviously well aware of the over-powering effect of the sight of a large amount of cash and had used that fact to his advantage in the past. One of the reasons, no doubt, that he kept large amounts of cash on hand. It had not escaped Annabel's attention that there was still a great deal of English money remaining in the secret safe, as well as all the foreign currency. It must be nice to be able to take off for foreign parts when one wished without the need to bother visiting a bank.

'That's all right, isn't it?' Her silence appeared to unnerve him, he glanced irresolutely at the stack of banknotes. 'I realize that my family might make you think twice but, I assure you, they spend most of their time in their own quarters downstairs. If you'd like more money —?'

Danger money. The thought came to Annabel unbidden, startling her. *Aggravation money*, she amended. Aunt Zenia might be irritating and insulting, but it was overreacting to think of her as dangerous. As to the Broomstick . . .

'That will do – for now.' Annabel stopped him as he turned back towards the window. It was flattering to think that he trusted her more than he did his family, but she felt that she would rather not watch as he opened the safe again.

'Good.' He turned back and extended the money towards

her. The cat stretched out her neck to sniff at it, then drew back disdainfully. *All right for some!*

As offhandedly as possible, Annabel accepted the money and tucked it into her handbag, while appearing to pay more attention to the cat who was settling back on her lap. She wondered if she were fooling anyone.

'Sally likes you.' Arthur Arbuthnot sounded as though that was important to him.

'And I like her.' Annabel picked up her cue. 'She's a little darling, isn't she?'

'Indeed, she is,' he said warmly. 'I shall never know what she was doing starving in that alley. Except,' he added thoughtfully, 'that anyone can hit a bad patch in their lives.'

'They certainly can,' Annabel agreed fervently. Heaven knew she had hit more than enough bad patches in her own life. It had been difficult enough to have been born into the fringes of an aristocratic family with a bloodline good enough to get her presented at court, but without enough financial backing to fully finance her Season. Not that that mattered too much, times were already changing. Then she had met Young Hinchby – that first wild spring love, trailing in its wake the thrill of the engagement, the dream wedding and the happy-ever-after that had been blown to bits along with Young Hinchby in the skies over Korea while he was serving the last few months of his National Service. Good old Smythe had come along later, a lot later, bringing a quieter more mature love, but with a lot of laughter.

She glanced fondly at the twin diamonds on her left hand, smaller than Hinchby's diamond, but gleaming as brightly and also accompanied by a half-hoop diamond wedding band (Smythe was not to be outdone). They had found their dream cottage and settled in happily before a new photographic assignment had sent him to cover a small revolution in some obscure South American banana republic where he had aimed his camera at the wrong army at the wrong time. And that had been the end of Smythe and of another happy-ever-after. Men and their wars! Annabel had had as much as she could stand of both of them. She could not face that pain again, not that – at her present age – she was likely to be invited to. Yes, she had known bad patches with a vengeance.

Things were looking up again now, however. This interior-designing lark was a breeze – and Mr Arbuthnot *had* said that that delightfully thick wad of banknotes now reposing in her handbag was just the retainer, hadn't he? She stroked Sally enthusiastically and was rewarded with a throaty purr.

A sharp buzz startled Annabel. Mr Arbuthnot bent towards what had seemed to be a cigarette box on a nearby table and pushed a concealed button.

'Yes?' he snapped.

'Rio de Janeiro has just logged on.' The high resentful voice of the Broomstick filled the room. 'Your conference call can go through in five minutes. As scheduled.'

'Thank you, Miss Stringer. Is Luther here yet?'

'Not yet. He hasn't reported in all day. And he knows how important this is. It's *too* bad of him.' For a Broomstick, she had a whine of vacuum-cleaner intensity.

'He'll be here. You just take care of your end of things.' Mr Arbuthnot clicked down his switch, cutting off any further protests she might have made.

'You're very busy. I should leave now.' Annabel gave Sally a little push, but the cat remained solidly entrenched on her lap.

'I'll take her.' Mr Arbuthnot picked Sally up. Annabel's skirt rose with her as Sally dug her claws into the material, indignant at being disturbed.

'Sorry. Let me—' Together they disentangled the claws and Annabel stood.

'I'll be round tomorrow, if that's convenient,' Annabel said. 'I'll bring some colour charts and swatches . . . and perhaps do a few preliminary sketches.' She hoped that sounded sufficiently businesslike.

'Not too early,' Mr Arbuthnot said. 'I'll be working late tonight. Perhaps eleven o'clock.'

'Fine.' Annabel managed a smile, disguising the fact that she considered eleven practically the crack of dawn. She brushed at the cat hairs on her skirt, making a mental note to wear trousers, preferably brown, for the duration of this escapade.

Mr Arbuthnot opened the door for her and she nearly collided with a young man just outside, standing so close to the door that he might have been just about to enter . . . or eavesdropping.

'Mrs Hinchby-Symthe has agreed to take on the project, Luther. She begins tomorrow. You'll be seeing a lot of her and you're to give her every assistance. Mrs Hinchby-Smythe, Luther is my personal assistant. If you have any problems and I'm not around, bring them to Luther. He'll deal with them.'

Annabel shook hands perfunctorily with the earnest bespectacled young man as they murmured polite insincerities at each other. Behind the thick glasses, his glittering eyes told her that he was no more delighted to meet her than she was to meet him, that she was one more unwanted complication in a busy schedule and that the flat could stay the way it was for ever so far as he was concerned.

Another Broomstick. Only the gender was different. How did Mr Arbuthnot manage to collect them all? Of course, they were both probably very efficient at their jobs – and Mr Arbuthnot was so deeply involved with machines that he might not even have noticed any lack of human warmth in his associates, or perhaps he was more comfortable with them being that way. His family obviously provided more than enough emotion for his taste.

'We'll see you in the morning.' Mr Arbuthnot dropped Sally gently to the floor and went into his office.

'We'll coordinate' – Luther paused to assert his own authority – 'on details then. I'll need a clear idea of when you plan to move the workmen in.' With a curt nod, he followed Mr Arbuthnot into the office.

Workmen? Annabel walked slowly down the corridor, so abstracted that she failed to notice Sally close on her heels. Overhead, the antlered skulls seemed to loom menacingly. Perhaps there was more to this interior-decoration business than she had thought. Now that Luther had brought up the subject of workmen, it was obvious that Annabel could not

22

be expected to do everything by herself. Even taking down and disposing of the antlers would be a major project. As for painting walls, hanging wallpaper, putting up curtains and all the rest of it . . .

For a start, she should have counted those sets of antlers. Annabel halted and turned to look back down the corridor. At the far end, something fluttered and stepped back. She was being watched. Again.

Get used to it, Annabel. It was obviously going to be one of the unwritten Conditions of Employment. Annabel's eyes narrowed. There must be a way of taking care of that.

Something brushed against her ankles and she looked down. 'Sally!' She stooped and stroked the soft fur. 'What do you think you're doing?'

'She thinks she's going to go out.' Neville appeared behind her and swooped on the cat. 'It's a good thing you noticed her. Cousin Arthur would have been very upset if Sally followed you outside and got lost.' Something in his voice suggested that no one else would have been deeply concerned.

An almost palpable sensation of disappointment eddied down the corridor. It was enough to make Annabel wonder momentarily whether the place could be haunted. Then she realized the emotion had emanated from the Broomstick, who had been watching their progress with malicious glee, hoping that Annabel would get into trouble.

'I'll be more careful in the future,' Annabel promised, loudly enough to further disappoint the Broomstick. She wouldn't be caught that way again, but she wondered how many other little traps might be lurking for her to fall into. She smiled graciously at Neville and Sally and closed the door thoughtfully behind her.

Downstairs, the entrance hall was deserted, the commissionaire no longer at his post. Or did he only man it when visitors were expected? Neville had betrayed the fact that Arthur Arbuthnot owned the entire building and Annabel was beginning to suspect that the young man in the wheelchair was just a gesture towards the pretence that this was an ordinary block of flats.

Still more thoughtfully, she closed the outer door and

turned in the direction of Marylebone High Street, walking more quickly as her spirits lifted at the thought of the large amount of cash in her possession.

Time to do some shopping. She'd pick up an armload of decorating magazines, a bottle of gin and treat herself to a taxi back to Knightsbridge. Tonight she'd do her homework with the magazines and a bit of thinking. In the morning, she'd deposit the money in her bank account and then start work on the apartment.

4

After all that, the audience with a preoccupied Arthur Arbuthnot in the late morning was short and unsatisfactory. He seemed to have too many things on his mind to bother about making mundane decisions about colour schemes. Annabel was soon ushered out into the drawing room and left to her own devices, which meant beginning work – or appearing to.

She was amused to find that Sally had obviously appointed herself supervisor. The cat followed Annabel from room to room, sitting down and watching with great interest as Annabel wielded tape measure and notebook. With growing amusement, Annabel joined in the game, taking Sally at her own valuation.

'Would madam like the brocade or the velvet for the drapes?' Playfully, she dangled a swatch of each in front of the cat, who swatted at the rippling velvet.

'Oh, an excellent choice, madam —'

'You'll take your instructions from Mr Arbuthnot – and no one else!' The Broomstick appeared in the doorway behind them, quivering with indignation. She looked around, ready to do battle with the usurper. 'Where did she go?'

'Who?' Annabel widened her eyes with exaggerated innocence. 'I was just talking to the cat.'

'The cat?' Still deeply suspicious, the Broomstick turned her head from side to side, peering into the farthest corners of the room before dropping her gaze to floor level where Sally sat looking up at her. 'Do you mean to tell me you were using that tone having a conversation with that – that creature?'

I'd rather have a conversation with her than with you, Annabel thought. And it was not just because of the antipathy between them. She glanced down and met Sally's eyes, the unspoken agreement in them startled her. There could be no doubt that she and Sally were in perfect accord: the Broomstick was a Grade-A unmitigated pain in the —

'Were you looking for me?' a voice cooed from behind the Broomstick. Annabel suddenly realized who she had been suspected of consulting. Interesting. Was the Broomstick afraid that Tara was going to be in charge of things here in the very near future? And where did that leave Neville, who had appeared to be Tara's . . . um . . . escort, if nothing closer?

'I knew you were around somewhere.' The Broomstick did not bother to conceal her hostility. Again, an interesting point. Either she was so secure in her job (*she knows where the bodies are buried* was the phrase that sprang to mind) or Tara was not yet in any position to be a threat.

'And now you've found me,' Tara said smoothly.

'There is a message from Mr Arbuthnot.' If looks had any power at all, Tara would have shrivelled up and become a heap of smouldering ashes on the carpet. '*He* will be "delighted" to meet you in the downstairs lobby at twelve-thirty. I've made a reservation at Rules for one o'clock.'

'How kind of you,' Tara cooed.

The temperature had dropped at least ten degrees. Annabel looked at Sally with envy. Sally had retreated under the nearest chair, curled up and gone to sleep. Oh, lucky Sally. Unfortunately, Annabel couldn't do that, but she could do the next best thing.

'Excuse me—' She replaced her tape measure, swatches and notebook in her carrier bag and shouldered her way between the two quietly glowering women into the comparative freedom and open space of the long narrow corridor.

Pausing only to detach the smallest of the antlered skulls, Annabel rammed it awkwardly into her bag. Of course, it didn't fit. The long narrow skull slid into the bag, but most of the antlers reared out of it and the points nearest the skull bulged against the plastic, threatening to rip it apart.

No matter, it would have to do. She had a luncheon appointment of her own to keep and the antlered skull was vital to her plans. *Sprat to catch a mackerel*, Annabel told herself, stalking through the downstairs lobby and throwing the hovering young commissionaire a glare so challenging that he immediately found himself something to do behind the reception desk.

Mackerel . . . a very artistic mackerel. A late last night, faintly frantic telephone call to her American artist friend, back in the village where they both lived, had produced the lead.

Annabel had hoped that Leonora Rice might be able to join her in doing up Mr Arbuthnot's apartment – after all, paint was paint, wasn't it? But she had caught Leonora on the eve of her departure to set up her own exhibition in San Francisco and the best she had been offered was a substitute.

'So you're doing up the Arbuthnot apartment,' Leonora had said, with a strange note in her voice. There had been a long reflective pause. 'In that case, you might try Kelda. She'd be ideal – if she'd do it.'

'Why shouldn't she?' Annabel asked.

'Oh . . . artistic temperament . . .' There was definitely a false, perhaps even evasive, tone there.

'Well, you know her better than I do,' Annabel conceded. 'In fact, I don't know her at all. What makes you think she'd be so right for the job?'

'Oh, she would.' Leonora's voice firmed as she began to list her friend's qualifications. 'She supports her own painting by freelancing. She does a lot of set-designing for theatre and TV, so she knows all sorts of odd places to find interesting fabrics and furnishings. Furthermore, she's in her Georgia O'Keeffe phase right now – and skulls are hard to come by in London, so you've got a great bargaining point. If you promise her all those antlers, along with some cash, she ought to be tempted enough to take the job on, even though—' Leonora broke off. 'Or perhaps especially because—' She stopped again.

'She can have every last crumbling antler,' Annabel promised, scribbling rapidly in her notebook. 'Just tell me – Kelda who?'

'Just Kelda. That's all she uses. After all, you don't say Picasso who – or who Picasso – do you?'

'Actually,' Annabel admitted, 'I've never had occasion to say Picasso at all. Does she have a telephone number?'

27

'Of course . . .' Leonora hesitated. 'But give me time to talk to her first before you call her. I'll make her see sense about this. It could work out so well – for both of you.'

If she hadn't been distracted by pouring herself another martini, Annabel might have questioned the odd comments. As it was, she had written down the number and wished Leonora every success with her exhibition. Later, she had chanced her luck with the unknown Kelda, who had agreed to a discussion over lunch. She was on her way to that luncheon now.

It was love at first sight. Kelda and the antlers, that was. Annabel began to feel distinctly *de trop* as Kelda took the skull into her arms, crooned over it, stroked its antlers and generally made an exhibition of herself. Annabel shrank back in her chair – most unusually for her – and thanked her stars that they had met in such an out of the way watering hole. No one she knew was likely to venture into this place and witness her predicament. She hoped.

'How many more of these did you say there were?' Kelda suddenly switched from rapture to business. Her eyes were unnervingly shrewd within their kohl linings.

'Twenty-nine,' Annabel said grimly. 'The ancestral swine must have shot a whole herd of deer in his time – and those were just the trophies he kept.'

'Thirty . . .' Kelda gloated. 'And you're sure no one will object to my taking them away and . . . recycling them?'

'Play your cards right and they may even pay you to take them away. Just a joke,' Annabel added hastily as Kelda's eyes gleamed. 'And some of those skulls may not be in the best condition,' honesty compelled her to admit. 'They're pretty old.'

'Doesn't matter.' Kelda waved away the caveat. 'Plenty can be done, even with fragments. My sister is a florist, she can gild them and use them in flower arrangements. The really good pieces I can incorporate into my organic sculptures and the in-between stuff can be used as props and for stage settings.'

'You *are* ingenious.' Annabel began to see why Leonora

had recommended Kelda so highly. 'And what do you feel about perhaps doing a bit of painting? Ordinary wall painting, that is.'

'Nothing easier,' Kelda said. 'There are always a lot of kids hanging around the theatre ready to be helpful. I can round up a couple of them and have them wherever you want them. Of course, they may not be able to work *every* day . . .'

'What English workman does?' Annabel sighed, but her spirits were rising. As she had suspected, this interior-decorating business was a breeze. You just had to get your team in place and they'd do all the work while you swanked around and gave orders. 'Er, you *will* be coming along, too?'

'Don't worry. I intend to stand over them while they take down those skulls. I wouldn't want anything to happen to them.'

Annabel would have said that it was a century too late to worry about that, but smiled instead and nodded understandingly. There was no accounting for taste and Kelda had gone back to lovingly stroking the skull again.

Annabel averted her eyes and concentrated on her avocado, chicken and salad sandwich. 'Arthur Arbuthnot won't know the place by the time we get through with it,' she murmured optimistically.

'Arbuthnot?' Kelda raised her head and looked at her sharply.

'That's right. He's some sort of millionaire tycoon, I understand.' Something about the unnatural stillness in Kelda's face rang a warning bell. 'Do you know him?'

'I know . . . of him,' Kelda said carefully. 'He lives over by Regent's Park, doesn't he?'

'That's the one,' Annabel said, quite as though there might be several to choose from.

Kelda remained silent for so long that Annabel began to feel the stirrings of panic. Was the girl changing her mind? Had she encountered Arthur Arbuthnot (a dark horse, if there ever was one) before – possibly around the theatre – and not enjoyed the encounter? What was wrong here?

'Are you all right?' Annabel asked.

'Oh, yes.' Kelda pulled herself together with a visible effort. 'Yes, I'm fine. I was just thinking . . .'

'And you're still game?' Annabel pressed anxiously. 'You're going to take this on and continue in an . . . um . . . advisory capacity?'

'Oh, don't worry about that.' Kelda's eyes flashed with a sudden unnerving avarice. 'Who knows what else they might be throwing out? There are all sorts of possibilities. I wouldn't miss it for the world!'

When she saw the look on the Broomstick's face the next morning, Annabel decided that it had been worth all the hassle. Quivering with outrage, the Broomstick glared at the motley crew cluttering up the hallway she apparently regarded as her own and emitted several choking noises before she finally found her voice.

'What do you think you're doing?'

'Taking these down,' Kelda answered from the top of the stepladder where she was carefully detaching a skull-and-antlers from the wall, a task she judged too delicate to allow anyone else to do.

'Stop it! Stop it immediately!'

Sally had been poised on her hind legs, one paw on the bottom step of the ladder. She looked from Kelda to the Broomstick and appeared to be rethinking her position.

'Get down! Get down at once!' The Broomstick stretched out both hands, threatening to shake the stepladder and dislodge everyone and everything on it. Kelda shifted slightly and one foot swung loose; if she fell, she was going to kick out and ensure that someone's teeth came with her.

Sally prudently withdrew behind Annabel's ankles to watch future proceedings from that safe haven. Annabel backed up slightly, nudging Sally along with her.

'Get down, I said! At once!'

'Don't touch this ladder!' Kelda warned.

'What's going on here, Miss Stringer?' Arthur Arbuthnot appeared suddenly and Sally abandoned Annabel's ankles and ran to him. He stooped and picked her up with a soothing murmur, then his face froze as he turned to the humans. 'Is there some problem?'

'These people are tearing the place apart!' Dora Stringer turned to him accusingly. 'And just when you have all those important people arriving this afternoon.'

'Nothing to do with us.' Kelda clutched the skull protectively. She and Arthur Arbuthnot looked at each other briefly with mutual indifference. If they had ever seen each other before, they were consummate actors. 'You just go away and get on with it.'

'The effrontery!' Dora Stringer gasped, appealing to Arthur Arbuthnot. 'Did you hear the way she spoke to me?'

'Mr Arbuthnot—' Annabel decided it was time to take a hand. 'I was under the impression that you had promised me there would be no interference from your staff.'

'Quite right. So I did.' Mr Arbuthnot frowned at his secretary. 'And I meant it. I'm sorry you've been troubled. It won't happen again – will it, Miss Stringer? . . . Miss Stringer?'

'As you wish.' Dora Stringer abandoned her attempt to stare him down and turned away with an offended flounce. 'But on your head be it!'

Annabel arched an eyebrow at the departing back. Why on earth was the woman taking it so personally? One would think she had shot every last damned deer herself.

'I'm sorry about that.' Mr Arbuthnot was staring after Miss Stringer with an expression that boded no good for her. 'I'll see to it that it doesn't happen again.' He followed Miss Stringer down the corridor with a purposeful step.

'Well! What was that all about?' Kelda waited until the pair were out of earshot before speaking. 'Whose toes are we trampling on here, anyway? And why?'

'Good questions.' Annabel shrugged, again feeling the uneasy tingling at the back of her neck that suggested that other prying eyes were watching. This was no time to give Kelda any answers – not that she had any.

'Who knows? Let's get on with the work.' Annabel signalled to Peter and Paul, the teenagers who had appeared with Kelda and been introduced as her assistants – although

31

a certain facial resemblance gave reason to suspect that they were actually relatives, perhaps cousins. One of them stepped forward to receive the skull and lower it reverently to the floor while Kelda moved on to detach the next in line from the wall.

They worked well; she had to give them that. By the end of the afternoon there was a respectable (so to speak) pile of skulls in one corner, which Sally was ecstatically investigating.

Numbers of unknown and unidentified people had come and gone as they worked. Mr Arbuthnot was obviously not the semi-recluse she had imagined. It was interesting to notice that very few of the visitors looked happy as they came away from their audiences with the great man.

Something was obviously going on. Whether it might make an item for the gossip column or the financial pages was yet to be determined. *Eyes and ears open, Annabel*, she told herself cheerfully. This job might be a nice little earner in more ways than one.

Meanwhile, she surveyed the now-denuded hallway with satisfaction. It looked twice as large already. Even the discoloured patches where the skulls had been removed were less obtrusive than the spreading antlers.

'We'll wash down those walls tomorrow,' Peter, or perhaps it was Paul, assured her. 'Get them nice and clean, a couple of days to dry out and then you can tell us what colour you want them.'

'Excellent!' Annabel beamed on them.

Kelda, secure in her ownership of all the antlered skulls, beamed back. The boys nodded, unsmiling, but seemingly quite happy in the knowledge of a job well done and more to come in the morning. And, even better, payment at the end of the week.

Kelda piled their arms with the skulls and led them out of the apartment; she carried the largest and finest herself and was almost hidden behind her booty. It was to be hoped that she could see where she was going through the occasional gap.

Annabel lingered behind, half hoping to encounter Mr

Arbuthnot again. There were decisions he was going to have to make or, at least, be given the opportunity to make, although she suspected that fabrics and colour schemes were the least of his interests. But the gloomy apartment was silent, no whisper of life from any of its darkened rooms. All the earlier traffic had long since disappeared. Even the cat had vanished. She knew that she could not possibly be alone in the building, but there was nothing to prove she wasn't.

Except . . . that feeling of being watched by unseen eyes was back again. Hostile eyes.

Annabel swung around abruptly. No one there, of course. They were too fast – or too clever, watching from some secret vantage point. Perhaps one of those portraits so beloved in early films where, after the heroine had tiptoed trustingly down the hallway, the camera zoomed to a close-up of the portrait on the wall and the eyes blinked.

But there had never been a portrait in this hallway, only the endless antlered skulls. No human eyes could have hidden behind those curving empty eye sockets, nor was there a secret corridor running parallel with this one where a human body could lurk unseen. The grimy walls and innocent triangular patches were harmless. The menace emanated from some other source.

Annabel shivered and concentrated on practical matters. Pale lemon, she decided firmly. She would show Mr Arbuthnot various colour charts of off-whites and yellows, but she would guide him to pale lemon. Then the more traditional brass wall sconces interspersed with some cheerful watercolours would complete the transformation.

She could see it all in her mind's eye and, satisfied, turned to the challenge of the living rooms. Not that it appeared that anyone had done any living in them for generations. Some of the pieces of furniture were quite acceptable, however, and should be retained. The gossip-bench, for instance, although it could do with reupholstering in a better material. That was something else she would have to get Kelda to organize: swatches of material, wallpaper books, all that sort of thing.

Annabel looked around irresolutely. The apartment still seemed utterly deserted, no gleam of light showed from any of the closed doors along the business end of the flat. It was quite possible that everyone had gone somewhere else; she had already realized that there were several exits from the penthouse, some of the short flights of stairs leading directly into the private quarters below, which she had not yet had a chance to investigate and, given that Aunt Zenia was living there, she was unlikely to have the chance to investigate.

Oh, well . . . she pulled herself together. What was she standing around here for? It was not as though she were a guest leaving a party to which she had been invited and wishing to say a proper goodbye and thank you to her host. She was one of the hired help now and her comings and goings were of no concern to her employer . . . so long as she did her job.

She was crossing the lobby when someone shouted at her. She drew herself up and swung around to see the commissionaire waving her over. She glared at him for a split second before remembering that the man, although young, was not able-bodied. She could go over to him much more easily than he could come to her.

'Here—' He spoke between gritted teeth, obviously having noticed her initial reaction and interpreted it correctly. He did not want pity, nor to have others make allowances for him, but it was the situation he was trapped in for the rest of his life. He was finding it hard to learn to live with it.

'Here!' He almost threw the small heavy envelope at her. 'Arbuthnot left the keys for you. So you don't have to wait for anyone to open the doors.'

'Thank you.' So it had not escaped Mr Arbuthnot's notice that Annabel had been forced to ring the apartment doorbell four times that morning before the Broomstick deigned to answer it. The envelope was very heavy, with more than one key in it.

'The big one is for the street door,' he said, somewhat defensively. 'I can't always be here to let people in.'

'Of course not,' Annabel agreed.

It was so much noisier down here at ground level that Annabel realized the penthouse must be soundproofed. The street noises outside were loud and harsh, the roar of a motorcycle almost deafening as it pulled up outside and a helmeted messenger got off and approached the front door.

Although she was expecting it, the loud shrill of the bell made Annabel jump. Then there was silence. Across the wide expanse of lobby and through the grille on the door, the helmeted messenger and the young man in the wheelchair seemed to lock gazes. After a long moment, the messenger rang the bell again.

No one seemed in a hurry to open doors around here. Annabel wondered whether it were a matter of general policy or just bloody-mindedness on the part of the doorkeepers.

Just as the messenger raised his hand to ring again, the buzzer sounded sharply, releasing the door catch. The messenger took swift advantage, pushing the door open before it could relock, then hesitated, seemingly not anxious to approach the desk. He removed his helmet, suddenly looking young and vulnerable. Again his gaze crossed with that of the young man in the wheelchair; they were about the same age. He hesitated a moment longer, then moved forward slowly.

'Wotcher, Mark,' he said uneasily. 'You all right, mate?'

'Never been better,' Mark sneered, rolling back from the desk so that his stump could be seen. The unfortunate messenger turned a deep red; he clutched his helmet so hard Annabel was afraid it would crack and splinter.

'Got a delivery, have you?' Mark stared boldly at the parcel the messenger was carrying. 'Give it here. I'll see the old sod gets it.'

'Yeah, right.' The messenger held on to the package. 'Thing is, I've got orders to deliver it hand-to-hand.'

'You don't trust me?' Mark challenged him.

''Course I do. But I've got orders.' They faced each other implacably. It was an argument Mark was bound to lose; he was unable to stand up and physically wrest the package away from the other man.

'Fourth floor.' He contented himself with a shrug and another sneer. 'He's in the boudoir with his bint – and he won't thank you for bursting in on him.'

The messenger gave a nod that said maybe that was true – and maybe it wasn't – and turned away to the lift.

'Anything else you want?' Mark turned his attention back to Annabel, the fury smouldering at the back of his eyes told her that she would not be forgiven easily for having witnessed his defeat.

'Thanks for the keys,' she said. 'I'll see you tomorrow.'

'Mind how you go—' His mocking voice followed her as she hurried towards the door. 'I didn't – and look what happened to me!'

5

When she reached home, Annabel mixed herself a shaker of martinis, poured a generous one and told herself Dinah wouldn't mind at all if she had a quick rummage through the boxroom to see if she could find anything remotely useful to convey her growing accumulation of decorator's samples to and from the Arbuthnot premises.

At first glance, it didn't look too promising. There were a few old trunks which were far too large and cumbersome, even the child-size one. That child! It just went to prove how dangerous parenthood was – one never knew how the child would grow up. She shook her head and took another quick swallow before looking further.

A couple of battered leather briefcases, obviously the property of the late Lord Cosgreave, were too small. Suitcases were unsuitable, as were the plastic carrier bags piled in one corner, although Annabel seemed to recall reading that those in the legal profession, in a burst of reverse snobbery, had taken to using plastic carrier bags instead of briefcases to carry their papers to court. Wouldn't do for her, though.

Then she saw it. In the farthest corner. Good-sized, woven of thin slats of wood, sort of a cross between a trug and a small picnic basket, with the added advantage of a lid hinged in the middle, so that one could reach into one side or the other of it without disturbing everything it contained, it looked both chic and casual, the perfect compromise between looking too professional and looking as though one had no professionalism at all.

Annabel lifted the basket and blew off the dust. A good

wipe-down with a damp cloth and it would be ready for service. She carried it back to the kitchen.

There! It wasn't exactly gleaming, but it was not of a material that shone in any way. Thinking of which, she packed the paint charts and wallpaper samples in one side of it and the swatches of material in the other. Again, she noted the arrangement with approval, anything on either side of the basket could be concealed by just lifting the opposite side of the lid. That might be very useful . . .

Annabel crossed over to a cabinet where she had noticed a pewter flask, of the sort gentlemen carried to sports events so that they might ward off the chill, or restore themselves to a decent equanimity quickly and quietly if their wagered-on favourite should let them down.

She sniffed at it, rinsed it and then filled it from the martini pitcher. She screwed the lid and cup back on and then deposited it in the basket beneath the top swatches with a feeling of satisfaction. She was prepared for anything now.

She thought.

And she had been in such a good mood, too.

Even the non-appearance of Peter and Paul (they were starting their defections early) seemed unimportant. She accepted with a nod Kelda's explanation that they had another job to finish off first but would be back with Annabel as soon as possible.

Annabel had even been humming as she ruthlessly yanked down drapes which must have been *in situ* for generations, judging from the clouds of dust eddying out from them like a Saharan sandstorm as they hit the carpet – and that would have to go, too.

'You don't want those ratty old tassels!' Kelda swooped on the tarnished tasselled gold ropes, eyes gleaming. Beyond a doubt, she already had plans for them – and quality of that sort was almost unobtainable these days, certainly not at any price Kelda could afford.

'Oh, all right! Take them! No place for that old junk here!' Made reckless by a fresh infusion of decorating magazines last night (MINIMALISM RULES!; NO PLACE FOR CLUTTER!; A CLEAR VIEW

TO THE FUTURE; DON'T BE DAUNTED BY TRADITION) and with only a faint disquiet engendered by the back-of-the-book trailers for next month's editions (THE BABY AND THE BATHWATER; IF GRANDMOTHER TREASURED IT, PERHAPS YOU SHOULD, TOO; NEVER GIVE UP ON THOSE OLD FAMILIAR BYGONES), Annabel told herself that Mr Arbuthnot expected renewal, not restoration.

Of course, the best pieces would be kept. It had already been necessary to slap greedy hands away from several choice items but, on the whole, everything was progressing well.

Except for a strange uneasy feeling that would not go away. Annabel looked around, trying to pinpoint the source of her disquiet.

As had become usual, all doors except that of the room they were working in – and, of course, the Broomstick's – were closed. Occasionally, the Broomstick stalked down the corridor outside, sniffing disapproval, to answer the doorbell and usher yet another worried-looking stranger down to Mr Arbuthnot's office.

It had been a while since the last visitor had left, wearing the usual dissatisfied expression. The whine of the lift signalled the imminent arrival of yet another . . . Why did she think of them as supplicants?

This time the doorbell did not ring. Instead, there was the scrape of a key in the lock and the soft click of the door closing. No footsteps, not even those muffled by the carpet. After a moment, Annabel saw why.

The wheelchair rolled past silently, its occupant grimly intent on his mission, a large parcel in his lap. The parcel was bright with EXPRESS . . . URGENT . . . flashes. Someone intended Mr Arbuthnot to get it as soon as possible and Mark was going to oblige. He must consider it important, it was the first time Annabel had seen him move away from the reception desk. Usually, he piled any packages – even the ones marked EXPRESS or URGENT – on the edge of the desk and waited for the first person bound for the penthouse to take them up.

But that had been some while ago. Although Mark had remained with Mr Arbuthnot longer than might have been expected for a mere delivery, he had returned to his post at least an hour ago. There had been no more visitors since, although Annabel thought she had heard Wystan's voice at one point and Tara's at another. Presumably they had used the inner staircase.

It had been silent for some time now. No one was around – That was it!

'Where's the supervisor?' Annabel demanded.

'What? Who?' Kelda looked bewildered.

'Sally,' Annabel elucidated. 'She was here all morning, but I haven't seen her for ages.'

'Perhaps she got shut in one of the other rooms,' Kelda said indifferently. 'She's not here now.'

'Obviously not.' Annabel looked around again with increasing dissatisfaction. She had become accustomed to the friendly furry presence overseeing her efforts. There was a distinct feeling of something . . . someone . . . missing.

'Perhaps I'll just go and . . .' Annabel allowed the thought to trail off as she stepped out of the room and looked down the corridor, and looked at all the closed doors leading off it.

'Sally . . . ?' she called softly. 'Sally . . . ?'

'*Now* what is it?' Not softly enough. The Broomstick erupted from her office, as though she had just been waiting for an excuse to complain.

'Shhhh!' Annabel held up her hand, realizing as she did so that she was fuelling the woman's fury. But she thought she had heard something . . . a faint answering yowl.

'Don't you shush *me*, you – you—' Incandescent with rage, Dora Stringer stepped forward to block her path.

'Sally . . . ?' Annabel sidestepped her neatly and continued down the passage, no longer bothering to keep her voice low. 'Sally?' she called, pausing at each door and listening.

The plaintive yowl sounded closer. *Help*, it seemed to be saying. *Get me out of here.*

'Hang on, Sally,' Annabel said. 'I'm coming.'

'Wretched animal! Always nosing about where it has no business to be. No! It can't be in there! That's Mr Arbuthnot's office. The creature is never allowed in there.'

Nevertheless, the yowling was coming from behind that

door. More in deference to Mr Arbuthnot's sensibilities than to the Broomstick's, Annabel tapped lightly on the door and waited for a moment before opening it.

'Mr Arbuthnot can't be in there.' The Broomstick changed her tune, no longer able to deny the noises on the other side of the door. 'That miserable cat sneaked in – and heaven knows how much damage it's done to those sensitive machines.' There was a note of subdued glee in her voice. 'Now maybe he'll listen to me and get rid of it.'

Annabel pushed the door open cautiously. She could hear Sally complaining bitterly somewhere in the office.

'Here, Sally . . . Come, Sally . . .' she called.

Sally answered vociferously, but remained where she was.

'She's got herself caught behind one of the machines! Mr Arbuthnot will be furious!' Furious herself, Dora Stringer shoved Annabel to one side and barged through the door.

'Come out of there, you filthy little beast! Where are —?'

The scream was so piercing and sudden that Annabel recoiled. It seemed to ricochet from every surface, freezing her in her tracks, momentarily cutting off all coherent thought, almost deafening her. Annabel blinked and tried to pull herself together.

The scream went on and on, increasing in intensity. It was never going to stop. Sally's yowl rose in sympathy. The noise was unbearable.

One deals with hysteria by slapping the hysteric's face. Annabel fought with temptation and reluctantly won. She settled for pushing past Dora Stringer expecting, at the very least, to see total devastation, the precious computers a heap of smouldering wreckage. She was prepared to believe that Sally was relatively unhurt; no seriously injured animal could produce that amount of sound.

At first glance, everything seemed all right, the computers in place and undamaged, the work station in order.

'ARTHUR! ARTHUR!' The scream turned into a name. Dora Stringer hurled herself forward, falling on her knees beside a body lying on the carpet. 'ARTHUR!'

How had Annabel ever got the impression that the apartment was deserted? Suddenly people were converging on the scene from all directions, in varying degrees of distress and shock.

'*ARTHUR!*' Tara appeared in the doorway to the study and rushed to kneel at his other side. 'What's happened? Speak to me! Someone call an ambulance!'

Something about the way the eyes seemed to be glazing under the partially lowered lids made Annabel suspect that it was far too late for an ambulance. However, the formalities must be observed. She looked around for a telephone, but the only one available was connected to several other contraptions and she felt it would be safer not to disturb it.

Having crowded into the room, the others stood there frozen. Wystan stared down at his wealthy nephew's body in apparent amazement. Zenia moved closer to Neville, who abstractedly put an arm around her shoulders, although his speculative attention was centred on Tara.

'But – But—' Luther was shaking his head in denial. 'He had his annual medical checkup only a couple of weeks ago. There was nothing wrong with his heart. The doctor said he was in tip-top condition. For his age.'

'Wouldn't be the first time the quacks got it wrong,' Wystan said. 'I remember when old Buffy keeled over. Same thing – had got a clean bill of health only —'

'Wystan!' His wife glared at him. 'Shut up!'

Everyone shut up except Sally. Her wail rose and fell, as though she were mourning the man who had been her best friend. She hovered over one outstretched hand, nuzzling it and howling afresh when it did not move to pat her.

'Get away, you stupid beast!' Dora Stringer snatched at Sally, caught her around the midriff and hurled her across the room.

'You wouldn't dare do that if Arthur were still—' Tara broke off her protest, looking horrified at herself. She had nearly put the unthinkable into words and made it real.

'*Do* something!' Zenia demanded. 'Don't just stand there! Doesn't anyone know the kiss of life?'

They looked at each other blankly. Luther's face creased with distaste and he stepped back. Annabel was riven with guilt and inadequacy: why hadn't she taken that first aid course she had promised herself last summer?

'I'll try.' Kelda pushed forward and knelt by Arthur Arbuthnot's side, her body blocking their view of what she was doing. Several hearty thumps suggested that she was attempting heart massage.

'For God's sake, get a doctor!' Zenia snapped. 'Call an ambulance!'

'Yes, yes, of course.' Wystan started forward, then halted, staring uneasily at the complicated telephone. He extended his hand, then drew it back, looking down anxiously at Arthur Arbuthnot, as though the fallen tycoon might suddenly rise up and smite him for his temerity. 'Er . . . *any* ambulance?'

'Quite right – for once – Wystan.' Zenia was recovering from her initial shock. She stared at her supine nephew with a cold, calculating gaze. 'Ring Hopewell International Medications. They can be depended upon to do their utmost for . . . a majority shareholder.'

For the owner of their company. Annabel made the translation effortlessly. The Hopewell chain of private hospitals and even more private nursing homes was well known to anyone on the fringes of the gossip trade. Their discretion – some might say secrecy – was legendary. Whenever an aged relative, neurotic spouse, stressed-out (whether from drink or drugs) celebrity needed to disappear for a time, one could be fairly certain that the doors of one of the HIM establishments had closed behind them and would not be opened until they were back on their feet and presentable to the public once again.

'Erm, yes.' Wystan still looked unhappy. 'Erm, what's their telephone number?'

'Never mind, I'll call them myself. From downstairs.' Zenia started from the room. 'I'll want to have a word with them, in any case.' Wystan trailed after her, his face clearing now that someone else had taken the initiative. He did not look back.

Annabel desperately wanted to get to a telephone herself. It had just occurred to her that this was a first-class story for Xanthippe's Diary, possibly one that would wind up on the front page – and bring a tidy bonus.

'Go away!' Sally had begun creeping forward again, trying

43

to reach her beloved master. 'Away!' Dora Stringer stamped her foot and looked ready to kick out.

'I'll take her out of the way.' Annabel gathered up Sally, her excuse for getting out of there and to a telephone. 'I'll shut her in the study.'

Not being privy to her thoughts, no one moved to stop her.

'Come along,' Annabel whispered to Sally. 'You'll be safer with me.'

'How bad?' Xanthippe was all agog. 'Do you think he's dead?'

'Seriously ill, anyway. Perhaps in a coma,' Annabel qualified. 'See here, I can't talk now – they're all around me. I'll ring you from home tonight.'

'Find out everything you can,' Xanthippe directed. 'Meanwhile, I'll send a team over to doorstep. Don't worry, they won't know who the tip-off came from.'

'They'd better not!' Annabel replaced the receiver, then lingered, strangely unwilling to return to the crowded room where Arthur Arbuthnot lay. She glanced uneasily around the study, half afraid someone might have been lurking to overhear her telephone conversation.

But there was only Sally, prowling restlessly, obviously distressed and unhappy. What would become of her now, Annabel wondered. Apart from Mr Arbuthnot, there did not seem to be many cat lovers around this place.

Sally halted beside the window and sniffed at the side panel that Arthur Arbuthnot had swept aside to reveal his hidden hoard of cash. The panel appeared to be ajar.

Annabel moved closer, staring avidly at the panel. Sally stretched out a tentative paw and dabbed at it. What a good idea! Pawprints wouldn't show up the way fingerprints would and, even if they did, what could anyone do about it?

'Good girl, Sally,' she encouraged. 'Go ahead. See what's in there. It might be a mouse.' She caught her breath as Sally attacked the protruding edge of the panel with determination – and success. The panel swung open, revealing the contents of the cupboard it concealed.

Rather, the lack of contents. The cupboard was bare – or as good as – compared to the way it had been crammed full the last time Annabel had glimpsed it.

The thick stacks of currency had vanished. The dollars, pounds, Deutschmarks and francs were gone. The safe had been cleared out. Only a few meagre bills of mongrel devalued currencies remained.

Had Arthur Arbuthnot emptied it himself, perhaps distributing the money to all those strange characters who had been visiting him lately? Or . . . Tara had entered his office through the door from this study. Had she improved the shining hour herself?

If so, did that mean that Tara had known Arthur Arbuthnot was dead, or otherwise incapacitated? Had she, perhaps, discovered the body first and decided to help herself to all that nice untraceable cash?

Sally sniffed at the nearly empty shelves, lost interest and backed away. Voices rose in the other room as more people came out of shock and began arguing about what should be done next. In another minute, someone might decide to come into the study and see what was going on here.

Annabel nudged the panel with her foot, trying to edge it back to its original position. To her consternation, it sprang forward and snapped shut with a sharp little click. She had used too much force. And now there was no way to prove that it had ever been opened and left ajar.

But why should she need proof? It was not her problem. Presumably, whoever was inheriting might be understandably miffed to think that a large portion of cash had disappeared from the estate, but it had nothing whatever to do with her.

'What are you doing there?' a voice from the doorway demanded sharply.

Annabel stooped and swept up the obliging Sally before straightening up and turning to face Neville and Tara. And that was another interesting question: where had Neville been in those moments before Dora Stringer began screaming? In here with Tara? They were both looking beyond her – to the concealed safe. Was it her imagination that they seemed to relax as they saw that the panel was firmly closed?

45

'I'm keeping the cat out of everyone's way,' Annabel said coldly. 'Just as I said I'd do.'

'Sorry,' Tara apologized half-heartedly. 'I didn't mean to sound — We're so on edge. The shock. I still can't believe —'

In the distance a siren wailed. 'Ambulance,' Neville said tautly. 'I hope it's ours.'

From the office where Kelda worked over Arthur Arbuthnot, a muffled sobbing began. Somehow, it was unthinkable to connect it with Zenia. And Tara, Annabel noticed, was dry-eyed. Was the Broomstick the only one to mourn Arthur? Or was she possibly just mourning the loss of what must have been quite a good job?

A soft plaintive cry from the furry bundle in her arms made Annabel revise her opinion. No, Dora Stringer was not the only mourner.

Nor the only one worried about her job, Annabel suddenly realized. If Arthur Arbuthnot died – assuming he was not already dead – what was going to happen about the redecoration? Her only contract was verbal – and with Arbuthnot himself. Would that be binding on the heirs? On the other hand, it was only too likely that the heirs would have so many other more immediate problems that it would take them some time to notice that she was still around. Annabel made a quick decision to adopt a low profile and continue with business as usual.

'They're here!' Tara looked around helplessly as the doorbell pealed sharply. The ambulance siren had cut off directly under the window just moments ago.

'Are they?' Neville seemed equally at a loss.

'I'll get it.' Annabel started for the door, still cuddling Sally, who had begun trembling. She hoped the cat wasn't coming down with some illness.

'What's the matter? What are *they* doing here?' Mark blocked the doorway with his wheelchair, the paramedics immediately behind him.

'Mr Arbuthnot has had some sort of attack. In the office.' Annabel stepped back to let him roll past.

'Heart? Stroke?' Mark locked eyes with her momentarily before he moved. 'How serious is it?'

46

'Very, I'm afraid.' There was no point in denying it; he would see for himself soon enough.

He cursed briefly and spun past her. The paramedics surged after him. Annabel followed more slowly, not anxious to return to the scene, even with reinforcements.

'Stand back!' Annabel heard a new, authoritative voice order as she approached. 'Please, give us room to work. Give him room to breathe!'

To breathe? Was he still alive? Annabel reached the doorway just as Luther – the one most likely to respond to an order – began leading the reluctant exodus.

She stood aside to allow them to pass, then slipped into the office. Was Arthur really still alive? Perhaps that 'give him air' routine was one the medics used to clear away onlookers so that they could get on with their jobs.

Certainly, it hadn't worked with everybody. Kelda was still hunched over the body, continuing her first aid.

'That's all right, miss.' One of the medics gently lifted her away. 'You've done fine. We'll take over now.'

Seeming dazed, Kelda swayed on her feet. Was she going to faint? Annabel started towards her.

'So you got away!' Mark had wheeled his chair to Arthur Arbuthnot's side and was staring down at him, his face impassive but his fists clenched. 'You got away before I could —'

'All right!' Kelda snapped back to life. She darted forward, grasped the back of his wheelchair and whirled it around. 'They want us out of here – and they're right. If anything can be done, they're the ones to do it.'

But was there anything to be done, except carry the body away? Annabel felt Sally tense in her arms as the wheelchair swept past them and Kelda met her eyes with a commanding glance.

Like Lot's wife, Annabel could not resist a backward look as she followed Kelda and the wheelchair from the room.

The paramedics had begun working in silent unison, not allowing themselves to consider the possibility of failure. More heart massage, oxygen mask, IV feed attached; they began doing other more complicated things Annabel could not even identify.

47

So intent were they on their task that they did not notice what was immediately apparent to Annabel as they gently moved the still form in the course of their ministrations.

There was a small dark-red stain on the carpet in approximately the centre of the spot where Arthur Arbuthnot's shoulder blades had rested.

6

Instinctively, Annabel closed the door on the scene behind her.

'Don't ever do that again!' Ahead of her, Mark twisted round in his chair and glared up at Kelda. He caught at the wheels, trying to halt their progress. But Kelda was stronger than she looked and continued to propel the chair ruthlessly along the hall.

Until she had to stop, her way blocked by the others in front of her who had gradually slowed their steps until they stood motionless in a huddled group, abruptly aware that they did not know where they wanted to go or what they wanted to do. Caught in a fresh wave of delayed shock, they might have been clockwork figures, losing momentum and faltering into suspended animation as their mainsprings wound down. Worse, their mainspring lay broken, perhaps beyond repair, with no power ever to activate them again.

The doorbell shrilled abruptly and proved that they could move, after all. They swung to face the door, then froze again, as though afraid of what might be on the other side.

'I'll get it.' Dora Stringer moved forward, the familiar task seeming to give her a rush of confidence. She turned the knob and pulled the door open wide.

A flashbulb exploded in her face. She shrieked. Another flash, then another, the flashes forcing her back as the man behind the camera advanced into the hallway. Dora shrieked again and Tara added a yelp of her own, more the dismayed protest of a woman who realizes she has been caught not looking her best than a genuine sound of indignation.

'Stop that!' It was left to Zenia to explode with honest outrage. 'Who are you? What are you doing here? Get out!'

The man swivelled and the flashbulb exploded in *her* face.

'Wystan! Throw them out!'

'Erm, Luther—' Wystan immediately looked for reinforcements.

Sally wrenched herself from Annabel's arms, leaped to the floor and skittered down the hallway, racing for sanctuary from all the flashing lights and the shouting.

'And hurry!' Zenia snapped. The urgency in her voice reminded them that the door at the far end of the corridor might open at any moment to disclose the paramedics carrying out their grim burden.

'Is it true —?' A young woman stepped out from behind the bulk of the photographer. 'Is it true that Arthur Arbuthnot is dead?'

'Certainly not!' Zenia snarled.

'No comment,' Wystan, the weakest link, said unwisely, not realizing that no comment was tantamount to confirmation.

'Mr Arbuthnot has been taken ill,' Tara intervened smoothly. 'It's nothing serious. Overwork. His doctor is in attendance and he's resting comfortably.'

Most probably resting in peace. Annabel moved back a few steps, hoping the journalists would not notice her. She didn't think they'd recognize her, but she had visited the newspaper office a few times and one never knew. They looked suspiciously like the pair she had seen rolling over the photocopier, hilariously recording improper bits of their anatomies at the Christmas party last year. Unreliable types at the best of times; one could not trust their discretion. She retreated more rapidly and found herself outside a door just beginning to open.

'Don't!' She slipped inside and confronted the startled medics. 'Don't go out there! Not just yet.'

'Oh, good.' Neville had followed her. 'You've stopped them. Good thinking.' He gave her a nod of approval and she realized that she had inadvertently scored points with the family, although she had been more intent on escaping possible recognition than in sparing the family embarrassment. She gave Neville a weak smile.

'This way,' he directed the medics. 'There's a service lift. You won't have to carry him past the family and distress them.' He did not mention the waiting paparazzi. 'I'll go with you and make sure the way is clear. I mean, we haven't used the service entrance in some time. It may be locked, but I have the key.'

He opened the door to the study. 'Over there—' He indicated a door on the far side of the room. 'Tell Mother' – he turned back to Annabel – 'that I have everything under control here.'

The hubbub in the hallway seemed to have died down. Annabel edged the door open and looked out cautiously.

The photographer, the journalist, Luther and Wystan had all disappeared. Kelda had retreated along the hallway and was hovering beside the drawing room doorway, obviously ready to do her own disappearing act.

Aunt Zenia and the Broomstick had now turned their firepower on the unresisting Mark, who sat huddled in his wheelchair looking as though he might explode at any moment.

'. . . all your fault!' Aunt Zenia was seething. 'If you had been at your post, they never would have got in here!'

'And those are just the ones who found their way to the penthouse,' the Broomstick weighed in. 'How many others do you suppose might have got in and be sneaking through the building right this minute? We'll have to search the place and throw them out!' She sounded as though she relished the prospect.

'And what do you want?' She turned suddenly to glare at Annabel, who had come up behind them.

'Your son said to tell you' – Annabel addressed her answer to Zenia – 'that he has everything under control.' She paused and elucidated as Zenia frowned uncomprehendingly. 'They've taken . . . him . . . down in the service lift.'

'The service —? Oh, my God!' Zenia sprang forward. 'That fool, Wystan, told those paparazzi that he was going to throw them out through the tradesman's entrance because they're not fit to use the front door. They'll run right into each other! We've got to cut them off!'

'The backstairs! It's a slow lift and we might beat it.' Tara turned and sprinted down the hall.

'Stay here in case they come back,' Zenia directed Dora Stringer. 'I'll go down the main staircase. And you—' She glared at Mark. 'Take the lift and get back to your post!'

They all dispersed, leaving Annabel and Kelda staring at each other in the suddenly empty hallway. *Now what?* hung in the air between them.

'Ah, well,' Kelda shrugged. 'Back to business as usual.' She led the way into the drawing room, marched purposefully to a corner where a loose edge of wallpaper threatened to peel away from the wall, slid her fingernail along the weakness, prised enough away to get a grip, took hold and pulled violently. A great flap of wallpaper tore away, leaving a wide gash across the wall.

'Don't just stand there!' she ordered as Annabel gasped. 'Start stripping the wallpaper. They'll have to let us keep working then, even if it's just in this one room.' She clawed away another large strip.

'No, I'll do this wall.' She waved a hand, directing Annabel to the opposite wall. 'Take that one – and work fast. We want this place to look terrible before they have a chance to stop us.' She discarded the wallpaper on to the faded threadbare rug and kept tearing.

Annabel nodded and settled down to work on her own wall. Really, there was something almost therapeutic about this kind of destruction. One could begin to understand the pleasures of vandalism. After a while, the wall began to look better in its denuded state than it had when covered by that ghastly paper.

The pile of patterned strips in the centre of the rug grew to a satisfactory height before they paused for breath. No one would be mad enough to suggest that they go away and leave the room in its present state now.

With the silence no longer broken by the sound of tearing paper, it seemed to settle down around them oppressively.

'Quiet in here, isn't it?' Even Kelda seemed momentarily daunted.

'They've all got plenty to think about,' Annabel said.

'Yes, but you'd have thought someone would have come by and said something to us – even if it was only, "Get out!".'

Kelda was right. It was most unlike the Broomstick to miss such an opportunity for using her favourite phrase. There must be one hell of a conference going on somewhere. Downstairs, probably. Otherwise, there would certainly have been the sound of raised voices: this was not the sort of crisis any of them was likely to face with equanimity.

'They must be downstairs in Zenia's quarters,' she told Kelda. 'Unless,' a new thought occurred to her, 'some of them have gone to the hospital to be with—' But that was what a member of a normal family would do.

'Not them. Anyway, there's nothing they can do, is there?' Kelda was pragmatic. 'At least they got him out of here. Now their tame medics can get it recorded that he died in the ambulance. Or, better still, the private hospital. Then they won't have the police sniffing around here.'

'The police?' Annabel hoped she sounded more startled than she actually was. How much had Kelda seen? 'Why should the police be involved?'

'Sudden death – without a doctor in attendance. The police will want to know what happened. Especially to a billionaire. That means an autopsy, coroner's inquest—' Kelda seemed to notice that she was being entirely too knowledgeable and broke off, shrugging her shoulders. 'Who'd want to get caught up in all that? I don't blame them.'

'And this way . . . a doctor will be present.' Worse things had happened. Annabel remembered stories of dictators hitched up to medical machinery that kept their bodies technically alive for months and years. And there were other rich men who had died inconveniently and whose bodies had been transported by private jet to different countries in order to escape the complications of tax laws. As to what else might be covered up . . . she tried not to remember the dark stain on the carpet.

'They'll have a tame doctor who'll sign the death certificate without any argument. Then probably cremation. That would suit them just fine.' How had Kelda become so cynical in the comparatively few years she had lived? And had she also noticed the stain?

'Anyway,' Kelda shrugged again. 'It's nothing to do with us. We only work here.'

'Quite right,' Annabel agreed briskly. 'And I think we've done enough for one day. Let's tidy up and go home.'

Kelda nodded, shook open a black bin liner and began cramming in strips of wallpaper. Annabel watched her, still caught by a sense of uneasiness. Surely, someone should be coming to check on them after all this time, even if it was only the cat.

The cat! Where *was* Sally? Had she got shut into another of the rooms? And what was she shut in with this time? The thought would not go away.

'I'll be right back,' Annabel said abruptly. Kelda nodded indifferently; she hadn't really expected help in tidying up.

It was twilight and the dark corridor seemed to stretch into infinity. Annabel found herself tiptoeing, curiously reluctant to make a sound. She paused by each closed door, whispering the cat's name, rather than calling it out into the silence. Cats had superior hearing; surely if Sally were behind the closed door, she would hear and respond as she had done before.

Before . . . Annabel shuddered and moved more quickly, anxious to find the cat and . . . And . . . ? Why was she so concerned about the cat? Was it, perhaps, that those moments when Sally had looked so trustingly at her had engendered some sort of feeling of responsibility? Or was it those other moments – when cold eyes had stared down at Sally and feet had moved restlessly, as though to restrain a kick, now that her protector lay helpless – that had touched her own protective instincts? She told herself that she just wanted to make sure that Sally was all right before she left for the day.

She was at the end of the corridor, the door immediately ahead led into the study. (She'd think about that empty safe later.) The closed door on the right opened into the office. On the left, the door into the Broomstick's office was also firmly closed. Did the Broomstick have no further interest in what was happening outside now that her employer was no longer there to spy on?

Annabel hesitated, not sure which door to approach. Then a voice, low and urgent, 't . . . t . . . t . . .', it seemed to be insisting. What on earth . . . ?

Without knocking, Annabel silently turned the doorknob and inched open the door to the Broomstick's stronghold.

Sally crouched in the middle of the room, alert and quivering, ready to spring upon some unseen prey.

'Get it!' the Broomstick was urging. 'Get it! Go on, get it!'

Annabel stepped into the room. Now she could see the open window, the pigeon strutting along the windowsill, an insult and a challenge to any right-thinking cat with territory to defend.

'Go get it! Go on, get —'

'Sally!' Annabel shrieked as the cat gathered herself for the leap that would carry her out of the open window and – with or without the pigeon – down to the pavement six floors below.

'Wha —?' The Broomstick swung to face her. Sally, taking fright, bolted between her ankles and out the open door. 'What are you doing here?'

'I—' Annabel kicked the door shut behind her so that Sally couldn't get back in. 'I just came to say that we're leaving now. We'll resume work in the morning.'

'Indeed?' Dora Stringer arched a contemptuous eyebrow. 'Perhaps it would be as well if you waited for instructions as to when you might "resume your work".' She turned her back on Annabel, one hand swinging out almost casually to slam down the window.

But not before Annabel had seen the bread fragments scattered along the outside sill. Her eyes narrowed. It was only a few days ago that this woman had nearly cracked the windowpane, screaming, 'Vermin!', to drive away the hapless pigeons trying to perch on the sill. Now food was spread out invitingly, the window left open – and the cat was being urged to follow its natural instincts and pounce. With results that could only be fatal. No doubt about it, the Broomstick had deliberately tried to kill poor little Sally.

'I thought you said you were leaving.' The Broomstick turned and advanced, ready to sweep Annabel out of the room, out of the flat, out of their lives. A cold glint in her eyes defied Annabel to challenge her, to voice what she suspected.

Annabel retreated slowly, her mind working quickly, already suspecting a lot more than she had a minute ago. The woman would never dare try to harm Sally unless she was sure retribution could not descend on her.

'How is Mr Arbuthnot? Has there been any word from the hospital?'

'That's nothing to do with you!' Dora Stringer paused and seemed to regroup her thoughts. 'Luther is working on a statement to be released to the media shortly. Meanwhile, Mr Arbuthnot is doing as well as can be expected . . .'

. . . *of a dead man*. Annabel completed the sentence mentally. Arthur Arbuthnot was gone and his family and associates were fighting a rearguard action to conceal the fact until . . .

Until what? Until assets had been transferred? Until a Crown Prince had had time to seize the throne and make his position secure? Until a 'deathbed marriage' had been arranged and staged? They were scheming something. But the Broomstick was right – it had nothing to do with her. All she wanted to do was complete the decorating, collect the agreed sum and get out of there.

'. . . out!' The Broomstick completed some sentence Annabel had missed, but it was clear that they were two minds with but a single thought.

'Sorry I can't stay and chat any longer, but *some* of us have other work to do.' Annabel spoke with deliberate intent to annoy and she succeeded. She closed the door against the satisfactory spectacle of rolling eyes and a mouth that looked as though it were about to foam. This time she allowed her footsteps to sound heavily and defiantly as she marched down the corridor.

She found Kelda trailing a long strip of wallpaper for Sally to chase. They both stopped and looked up as she entered.

'Are you all right?' Kelda looked mildly anxious.

'Fine.' Annabel tried not to snap, no point in taking her annoyance out on Kelda. 'Let's get out of here.'

'Right.' Kelda rolled up the strip of paper and rammed it into the bin liner under Sally's wistful gaze. 'I'll load this stuff into the lift then.'

'Don't bother. Leave it for the cleaners. Just take your own things.'

'Right.' Kelda gathered up the sack bulging with her gleanings. 'Coming?'

'You go ahead.' Annabel could not have said why she was reluctant. 'I've got to get my things together. I'll see you in the morning. Meet me on the corner at ten. I think it will be better if we arrive together.'

'One argument instead of two. Good thinking,' Kelda approved. 'See you then!' She was out of the door, with Sally still looking wistfully after her.

Sally. Annabel looked down at the cat and began to realize why she had wanted to stay behind. What was to be done about Sally?

'Sally . . .' A voice called softly along the corridor, as though echoing her thoughts. 'Here, Sally . . . nice Sally . . . Come to Dora, Sally . . .' The voice was too sweet, insinuating, false. If Sally answered it . . .

Annabel wondered if Dora Stringer had opened the window again.

Sally looked towards the sound of the voice, then up at Annabel uncertainly. She moved over to brush against Annabel's ankles.

'Here, Sally . . . Where are you, you little beast? Sally . . . Come, Sally . . .'

Come and be killed. That did it!

'*Shhhh!*' Annabel bent and scooped up the soft furry body. It began to throb with purring.

'Shhhh!' Annabel warned again. She flipped open the lid of her basket, lifted out a wodge of fabric samples and lowered Sally into the basket. Sally blinked and began sniffing curiously at her new surroundings.

'Settle down.' Annabel pressed gently on her back and Sally obligingly folded her legs under her and yawned.

'That's right – go to sleep,' Annabel whispered, covering her with the fabrics. 'We'll get you out of here and safe with me for tonight. Tomorrow, we'll see what we can do with you.' The others were hostile or indifferent, but Tara had seemed to like the cat, even to the extent of bringing Sally a holiday souvenir. Or had she just been trying to curry favour with Arthur?

'Now just stay quiet . . .' Annabel lowered the lid, slipped the handles over her arm and left the flat at full speed. She noticed that she was tiptoeing again.

7

'You're in a good mood this morning,' Kelda said, as they took off their jackets and began unloading rolls of wallpaper from the carrier bags Kelda had brought.

'Must be spring,' Annabel agreed cheerfully, unable to confide the real reason. It was the relief because her initial fears about having a cat around the flat had proved groundless. Sally was the perfect house guest. After a preliminary exploration of her new surroundings, she had enthusiastically shared Annabel's cheese omelette. Later, she had accompanied Annabel to bed, where she curled up in a contented ball beside Annabel's shoulder and purred them both to sleep. This morning she had cheerfully breakfasted on slightly soggy cornflakes and settled down for a nap on the sofa. She was going to be no problem at all.

However, the fact remained that Sally belonged to Arthur Arbuthnot, or his family, and should be returned as soon as her safety could be ensured. Dora Stringer must not be allowed anywhere near her.

'Uh-oh.' Kelda lifted her head and listened. 'I knew this quiet was too good to last. Here comes trouble.'

Annabel nodded recognition of the footsteps grimly thumping along the hallway and was prepared when they reached the doorway.

'Good morning, Miss Stringer,' she said sweetly. 'What news of poor Arthur today?'

'*Mr* Arbuthnot,' Dora Stringer frowned severely, 'is still unwell.' She stamped across the room, picked up one of the rolls of wallpaper and unrolled it enough to see the pattern. 'No, no, no!' she cried. 'This won't do at all!'

'I beg your pardon?' Kelda blinked at her.

'This pattern is quite unsuitable.'

'But this is what Mr Arbuthnot chose.'

'Mr Arbuthnot was under the influence of *that woman!* He quite forgot the original intention was to remodel this room into a business reception room. Flower-sprigged wallpaper will not do at all!'

She spoke as though Arthur Arbuthnot was coming back to continue his plans for his business and his flat.

'Just a plain beige paint, I think, with dark-brown trim and dark-brown drapes in a rough weave. Plain and business-like.'

'But Mr Arbuthnot—' Kelda began to protest.

'Fortunately, I hold Mr Arbuthnot's power of attorney and have done for many years. It was often necessary for me to make on-the-spot decisions when he was away on business trips.' She took a deep breath and looked around the room with a proprietorial air, seeming to grow taller.

'So you see, all decisions are mine, now that Mr Arbuthnot is . . . not in a condition to supervise arrangements himself.'

She might be right. If Arthur Arbuthnot had had enough confidence in her to entrust her with his power of attorney, then she must be extremely knowledgeable about his business and who was to say that she might not have been left a sizeable share of it? Annabel reminded herself that she had walked in in the middle of the film, as it were. She had no idea of the prior loyalties or entanglements of these people. Dora Stringer clearly fell into the trusted-old-retainer category and it was obvious that she predated Luther, even though his job title was more impressive than hers. Those who held the titles were not always those who held the real power. It was probably better not to cross her . . . for the moment.

'If you want rough-weave drapes, perhaps you might like a textured wallpaper.' Kelda had evidently come to the same conclusion; she smiled winningly at Dora Stringer. 'Or use actual tweed material for the wall covering. It can be done quite easily, you know.'

'Don't think you could charge any more for that!' Dora

Stringer's eyes glittered menacingly. 'I know Arthur paid you enough to hang the walls with ermine!'

'Well, hardly!' Annabel protested. 'That was just a retainer. It by no means covers our fees and costs. Naturally, materials were not included; he hadn't even chosen them then.' No need to let the woman think she could get away with claiming they had been paid in full in advance.

'Don't think you're going to get away with that story—' A telephone began ringing in the distance and Dora Stringer was distracted. 'I'll deal with you later,' she said, starting for the door.

Annabel and Kelda scarcely had time to exchange a silent raised-eyebrow communication before Wystan came into the drawing room; he must have been hovering outside.

'Oh, good.' He looked around. 'You haven't started yet. I came to warn you not to begin until Zenia's talked to you. She has some ideas of her own and you don't want to waste time on work you'll simply have to undo. She's tied up at the moment, but she'll be along as soon as she can.' He gave them a nod and a wink and was gone.

'You know,' Kelda stared after him. 'People told me decorators had problems like this, but I didn't really believe them.'

'In this place, I'd believe anything!' *Except that Arthur Arbuthnot was still alive*, Annabel added silently to herself. She wondered how much longer the others could keep up the pretence while the very way they were all jockeying for position gave the lie to it.

'Oh, there you are!' Tara appeared in the doorway. 'I was hoping to find you here.' She walked into the room with a solemn stately grace, a lace-trimmed handkerchief clutched in one hand. 'I wanted to speak to you about the decorations.'

'Really?' Annabel exchanged a wry glance with Kelda.

'Actually, I intended to sit in on Arthur's original consultation with you, but I've been so busy since my return from my holiday . . .' She let the thought trail off before continuing more firmly, 'As Arthur's fiancée, I naturally expected to have a great deal of input on the choices made. After all, I'm the one who's going to be living here.'

That could be true. It might depend on Arthur Arbuthnot's

previous arrangements with the woman. (Somehow, Annabel did not feel that love had entered the equation – on either side.) A lot would depend on whether there had been a pre-nuptial agreement and/or whether Arthur Arbuthnot had made out a will in his fiancée's favour.

'Yes, that will do.' Tara inspected the proposed wallpaper and was in no doubt. 'After all, poor dear Arthur chose it himself to please me, didn't he?' She dabbed at dry eyes with the pristine handkerchief. Annabel wondered how soon she would exchange it for a black-bordered one.

'So you're satisfied with this wallpaper?' Annabel was anxious to get one firm decision on material already purchased.

'Well, I wouldn't say satisfied, but it will do . . . for now. I wouldn't want to go against Arthur's wishes . . .' Again the handkerchief came away from her eyes undampened. However, she managed a quaver in her voice.

'But—' Tara recovered briskly. 'I do think he hadn't a clue about drapes – they're all wrong. I see the whole as more effective if the windows are sort of swathed . . . with sort of swagged bows . . . do you see what I mean?'

'Sort of,' Annabel said limply. If these were the kind of instructions she was going to have to cope with, life was going to get increasingly difficult.

'Chocolate box!' Kelda snorted.

'Exactly!' Tara turned to her, pleased. 'Something completely feminine and charming.'

'A slightly formal boudoir.' Annabel took a deep breath and tried to get into the spirit of it, wondering why the concept seemed vaguely familiar. Someone had mentioned the word before – and in connection with Tara.

'That's it! I was sure you'd understand. I'm not completely sure about the furnishings.' Tara gave the chairs a well-deserved dismissive glance. 'But we can talk about those later. I know Arthur has already paid for everything —'

'Not everything! Not by a long shot!' Where had everyone got the idea that Arthur had showered untold gold on his interior decorator? 'Just a retainer and enough for initial expenses. The rest —'

'Tara! You're here.' So was Neville and he did not appear pleased to see her.

'Neville.' The smile Tara gave him was something less than radiant; she wasn't exactly delighted to encounter him, either. 'I was just discussing plans for the flat with the designers.'

'Yes, yes. It will all have to go, of course.' He frowned at everything in sight. 'Loft living – that's the thing these days! Open plan, height, light and space. We'll knock down the walls between most of these rooms, then break through the floor to the flat below, remove most of the floor – just keep enough around the sides to transform into a gallery area – perhaps take back the plaster to the brick foundation wall.'

'But doesn't your mother live in the flat below?' Annabel could not quite believe what she was hearing. Did he plan to evict his own mother to facilitate his grandiose schemes?

'Oh, I'll take care of her,' he replied ambiguously. 'She won't have to worry about anything, you'll see. I've got lots of plans for this building.'

'You might wait until it's yours!' For once, Tara allowed her claws to show.

'Bound to be,' Neville said blithely. 'Arthur had – has – too much sense to leave it to Mother; it would let us in for two lots of inheritance taxes eventually. Much better to skip a generation and let the business flow forward unimpeded. I've got plans for the business, too.'

'I'm sure Arthur wouldn't think much of them,' Tara said.

'Wouldn't he?' They exchanged a look they obviously thought inscrutable and he turned to Annabel. 'What do you think?'

'I think I'm getting a headache,' Annabel said faintly.

'Oh, you needn't worry,' Neville said. 'We'll get some proper builders in to take care of the structural alterations.'

'Planning permission!' Kelda broke in triumphantly. 'I'm sure you'll need planning permission for changes like that. It could take years.'

'We'll see about that,' Neville said smugly. 'Meanwhile, I have no objection to your carrying on for the moment. Just don't spend too much money. It will all be temporary.'

'I wouldn't be too sure of that.' Tara's eyes narrowed.

'Remember' – she said with peculiar emphasis – 'Arthur has his own plans. You shouldn't forget that.'

'There are lots of things we should remember.' Now Neville's eyes narrowed. They regarded each other with cold speculation. 'For instance, that little agreement we've had in place for some time.' Neville moved closer and put an arm around Tara's waist. She froze.

'This is neither the time nor place to discuss anything.' Tara moved away.

'Just the point I was making.' He followed her to the door. 'I suggest we adjourn to a quiet spot for a full and frank discussion.' There was unexpected steel in his tone; Tara was not going to enjoy the discussion. They left without another word.

'What price being a fly on the wall for that little confrontation?' Kelda looked after them.

What price, indeed? Possibly a very good one from Xanthippe. Unfortunately, one had to be a bit clearer about the facts before reporting them. Again Annabel wondered just how true it was that Arthur Arbuthnot had intended to marry Tara; the woman could claim anything if she knew Arthur would never be able to deny it.

Annabel's first impression had been that Tara was Neville's girlfriend, yet he had cheerfully stepped into the background when Arthur was around. And what was the basis of the 'little agreement' he had mentioned? Was it perhaps that Tara would marry Arthur and – in the fullness of time, it was to be hoped – become a rich widow, at which point she would then marry Neville and bring the estate back into the family? If she still wanted Neville by that time. Unless he had some hold over her . . .

'Has Wystan spoken to you?' Zenia appeared abruptly, looking around the room.

'Everyone has spoken to us,' Kelda muttered. Not surprisingly, it went over Zenia's head.

'Very well,' she said. 'Then you know I don't think much of the wallpaper Arthur chose.'

'Practically no one does.' Kelda was in rebellious mood. Again, she was ignored.

'I want Regency stripes,' Zenia said, in a tone that brooked no argument. 'Pale gold. I'll want to see a wide selection of samples and swatches. Everything must be exactly right.'

'But this is what Mr Arbuthnot chose.' Kelda, for some reason, seemed disposed to argue. 'And Tara likes it, too.'

'She would.' Zenia sniffed. 'Arthur was – is – always too easily satisfied.' She turned to glare at Annabel. 'I suppose you think I'm being unreasonable.'

'Not at all,' Annabel murmured. After Neville's ideas about refurbishing and updating, anything that didn't involve demolition and a flying trapeze paled into insignificance.

'Good.' Zenia turned her hostile gaze to the bare walls. 'I won't pretend I don't disapprove of this ill-advised plan of Arthur's but, since you've started, you might as well finish. Especially as I understand you've been paid in advance.'

'That is not true!' Annabel felt her hackles rising. 'Only the initial cost of consultation and some of the materials has been paid in advance. You will receive our invoice for the balance after the work has been completed.'

'We'll see about that!' Zenia turned on her heel and stalked out, leaving an aura of impending lawsuits in her wake.

'I wish I hadn't given up smoking,' Kelda brooded. 'God, how I need a cigarette right now.'

'Have a drink instead.' Annabel rummaged around in her basket and pulled out her flask. 'I knew this would come in useful. Here—' She poured into the flask top that doubled as a cup and handed it to Kelda. For herself, she took a swig directly from the flask. These were desperate times, need was urgent, and there was no time to waste trawling through the flat in search of a glass. Apart from which, she had no wish for further encounters with any of its inhabitants.

'That's better,' Kelda sighed, holding out her cup for a refill. 'I'm almost relaxed now. Arbuthnot is dead, isn't he? He must be, or they wouldn't be carrying on like this. Do they all imagine they're going to inherit?'

'Don't relax too much.' Annabel caught the sound of another set of approaching footsteps.

'Good God!' Kelda heard them, too. 'Who else is left?'

'Good morning.' Luther slithered into the room. 'Getting on well, are you?'

'That depends,' Annabel said warily. 'What do *you* want done here? Stripes? Flower sprigs? Zigzags . . . ?'

'Really, I couldn't care less.' Luther looked carefully around the room – at baseboard level. 'It's nothing whatever to do with me. I'm simply looking for dear little Sally. I haven't seen her all day. Has she been in here?'

8

Sally!

Instant guilt. Annabel hoped her flaming face might be blamed on the gin. She had forgotten all about the cat. So had everyone else. Luther was the first to come looking for Sally.

Strange, she had not pegged him as a cat lover.

'I haven't seen her today,' Kelda said. 'The last time I saw that cat, she was sniffing around the bin liners with all the stuff we were throwing out. That was last night.'

'*What?*' Luther paled; he looked desperately towards Annabel.

'That's right,' Annabel confirmed. 'Sally was definitely nosing around those rubbish bags. Perhaps she thought there was something to eat in them.' That much was true. Annabel snapped her mouth shut and forbore to add what she and Sally had done after that.

'Oh, no! This is terrible!' Luther stared around wildly. 'You don't think —?' His voice rose to a squeak. 'She couldn't have crawled into one of those bags and been thrown out with the rubbish?'

'Why don't you ask Miss Stringer?' Annabel suggested. 'She might know something about it.'

'Dora always hated Sally.' Luther shuddered. 'From the very first moment Arthur brought the poor little stray into his life, that miserable – Er . . .' He cleared his throat sharply. 'Thank you. Perhaps I *will* go and see if she knows anything about . . .' His voice faded away as he slid out of the room and drifted down the corridor towards Dora Stringer's office.

'These damned flasks are always too small!' Annabel shook it impatiently. The thing was empty already.

'I move we adjourn to the nearest pub,' Kelda voted sensibly. 'We might even get something to eat there.'

'Very good idea. Brilliant, in fact.' Annabel replaced the flask under the pile of swatches and closed the lid of her basket. 'Let us away.'

'But it's not just Dora, you know.' Unexpectedly, Luther's head popped round the door again. 'They *all* hate poor dear little Sally. If you find her, you must bring her to me. Otherwise, I can't answer for her safety. Jealousy is a terrible thing!' His head disappeared again.

'Out!' Kelda grabbed Annabel's elbow and propelled her forward. 'Quick! Before any more of them come back.'

'What are you doing down here?' They were halfway across the downstairs lobby when Mark challenged them. 'You're supposed to be working.'

'Even the hired help gets a lunch hour,' Kelda said. 'If you don't, perhaps you ought to join a union. If you do, why don't you join us?'

'Oh, very funny.' Mark laughed; it was not a pleasant laugh. Kelda acted as though she did not hear it and continued to regard him gravely.

'Go to your lunch, then. Don't wait for me.' He was suddenly savage. 'I don't eat with traitors!'

'Who are you calling a traitor?' Kelda reacted immediately – to Annabel's relief. For a moment, she had been afraid that her own connection with Xanthippe might have been discovered.

'You tried to save the old bastard! Don't deny it – I saw you!' His mouth twisted in more of a sneer than a smile. 'But you couldn't do it, could you? He's dead, at last.'

'You can't know that!' Kelda fought against the very conclusion she had reached earlier herself. 'It hasn't been admitted – I mean, announced – yet.'

'It doesn't have to be. Look around you – everybody is walking on air, already planning how they're going to spend the money. They're so happy, I wouldn't be surprised if they hadn't finished him off themselves.'

'You'd better not get caught making remarks like that,' Kelda warned. 'They could sue you.'

'For what – my wheelchair?' He pushed viciously at the desk, propelling himself away from it.

'Mark!'

Annabel hadn't realized that one of the panels behind the desk was a swinging door. Mark crashed through it and was gone.

'There's a nice-looking little pub around the back.' Annabel carefully did not appear to notice that Kelda's eyes had filled with tears as she took her arm and led her out of the building. 'It should be quick, cheap and cheerful.'

'Why not?' Kelda blinked and raised her chin, but was still following her own train of thought. 'Do you think it's possible that Mr Arbuthnot could have been murdered? Or do you think that Mark is just trying to stir up trouble?'

'Why should he want to do that?'

'He hates them all; he blames them for his accident. Mark used to be a motorcycle courier – one of the fastest and best. So Arthur Arbuthnot used him a lot. About two years ago, he got a call to make an urgent delivery of documents. It was a cold rainy night, but Arthur Arbuthnot made a big song and dance about how important it was and promised him a bonus if he got there in less than half an hour. So Mark took chances, skidded on a turn and—' Kelda shrugged. 'And now he's like that.'

'Really?' Annabel tried to work out how many opportunities Mark and Kelda had had for exchanging confidences. It seemed to her that they had barely spoken to each other – until just now. 'How do you know all this?'

'We've . . .' Kelda avoided her eyes. 'We used to know each other . . . before . . . Oh! Here we are. How charming!'

'Relentlessly.' The Bower had lush window boxes, over-crowded colourful hanging baskets and rustic wooden seats outside mullioned windows. So had a lot of other pubs in London. Kelda wanted to change the subject. Annabel decided to let her get away with it . . . for the moment.

'Inside or outside?' Then she shivered as an unexpectedly chill wind swept around a corner. 'Perhaps inside.' Annabel answered her own question. 'We can sit by the window and look out.'

They collected gin and tonics and sandwiches and carried them to a window table before realizing their mistake.

'Perhaps this wasn't such a good idea,' Annabel admitted.

'It isn't the greatest view in the world,' Kelda agreed.

Across the narrow street, the rear of Arthur Arbuthnot's building was not so imposing as the front. The ground-floor level was almost obscured by the high wooden fence enclosing the areaway. It was obviously refuse collection day, for an array of black bin liners and garbage bins were piled along the foot of the fence.

'Not at all salubrious,' Annabel mused. 'At least we'll escape any smell from them.' Now that she noticed, none of the outside tables were occupied, although the pub was doing a brisk business inside.

'Houses with Queen Anne fronts and Mary Ann backs, that's what they call them,' Kelda said. 'Not that there's much Queen Anne anywhere, it's plain ugly Victorian – How odd!'

Caught by her sudden change of tone, Annabel followed her gaze. Luther was closing the areaway door behind him and looking uncertainly at the heaps of rubbish awaiting collection. After a moment, he advanced cautiously and bent over. He appeared to be talking to himself – or, perhaps, to one of the bulging black bin liners.

'What on earth does he think he's doing?' Kelda wondered.

Apparently receiving no reply, or dissatisfied with the reply he got, Luther moved on to one of the garbage cans. He lifted the lid and peered inside, his nose crinkling but his lips still moving. Again, there seemed not to be the response he hoped for. He replaced the lid and nudged another bin liner with his foot.

'I'd say he was looking for something.' Annabel was riveted. She watched raptly as Luther picked up one of the bin liners by its knot and shook it, testing its weight and possible contents.

'You told him—' Light dawned. 'Kelda, you said the last time you saw Sally, she was nosing around the bin liners. He must think she got inside and was carried out with the trash. He's looking for her.'

'But why?' Kelda shook her head as Luther lifted the lid of another garbage can, picked up a stick and prodded its murky depths. 'He doesn't even like that cat. I've seen him stamp his foot to frighten her out of the room. In fact, I'd have said he hated her.'

'That was my impression, too.' Annabel frowned. There was the throb of a heavy motor advancing inexorably from the far end of the street. The sound seemed to drive Luther into a paroxysm close to hysteria. He hurled himself into the midst of the bin liners, nudging with his feet, picking up and shaking, his mouth working frantically.

'Sally . . . Sally . . .' They could hear his desperate cries inside the pub now.

The garbage truck rumbled closer. A couple of workmen ambled along in front of it. They were looking at him curiously.

Luther looked up and saw the men watching him. He dropped the sack he was holding and bolted through the door in the fence, slamming it behind him.

The men looked at each other and shrugged their shoulders, then began heaving sacks into the revolving maw at the rear of the truck.

'Well!' Kelda said. 'What do you think of that?'

'I think I'll have another gin and tonic,' Annabel said. 'And not so much tonic with it, this time.'

'Cold chicken all right with you?' Annabel asked needlessly. Sally had begun purring the instant the scent from the parcel Annabel was unwrapping reached her.

'Yes, I thought it might be.' The warm furry pressure on her ankles was curiously heartening after the long day. It was very pleasant to come home to such an enthusiastic welcome.

Poor Arthur Arbuthnot. No wonder Sally had meant so much to him. His poisonous relatives almost certainly had never evinced such warmth towards him. Even now, their main concern was not his untimely demise, but the amount they stood to gain from it.

Had Mark any basis, except spite, for his suggestion that one of them had killed Arthur?

Not that it would surprise her. She had more than half suspected it herself when she saw those traces of blood on the carpet beneath Arthur's body. But then so much had happened so quickly and been so confused. And ever since, the door to the computer office had been locked, even though Luther spent most of his time working in there, so she had never been able to get back in and take a closer look at the condition of the carpet.

At her feet, Sally chirruped anxiously, reminding her that she was very hungry and that chicken smelled awfully good.

Sally! Sally had been in the office, a silent witness to whatever had happened. A witness who could never testify. But, possibly, one who could yet instil feelings of guilt and uneasiness on the murderer by the accusation in her eyes.

Was that why the Broomstick had tried to kill her? Why Luther was searching for her so frantically?

'*Mmrrryaah?*' The eyes were hopeful and trusting as they looked up at Annabel. '*Prryaah?*'

'All right, all right, I'm hurrying!' Annabel poured out a martini from the pitcher in the fridge and divided the cold chicken with Sally, but kept the potato salad for herself as Sally reacted to it with a disdainful sniff. She carried them into the living room and sank into an armchair but, before she had time to put her feet up on the matching footstool, the telephone rang.

'Annabel! I expected to hear from you long before this!' Xanthippe complained. 'What have you been doing?'

'Eating.' Annabel took another bite.

'For days? You haven't been dealing with other columnists, have you? Not trying to get an auction going, or anything? I would react very badly to that, Annabel. Very badly indeed.'

'I never thought of such a thing.' The obvious regret in Annabel's voice seemed to convince Xanthippe.

72

'Just as well. We have other sources, you know.'

'Have you really?' Annabel's voice was frigid. She set her plate down on the floor by her feet and sat up straighter to deal with this barely concealed threat. 'Then perhaps —'

'Oh, but you're the best,' Xanthippe placated hastily, aware that she had gone too far. 'You're the one on the inside. We're looking to you for all the gory details. Now that it's official.'

'Official?'

'The flash just came over the Press Association line. It should be on the late-night newscast and all the papers will have it in the morning. Arthur Arbuthnot died this afternoon.'

Died this afternoon. Did he, indeed?

'Annabel, are you still there?'

'What? Oh, yes. I was just thinking . . .' Annabel reached down for her plate to continue eating. Her hand encountered a small furry head. 'Oh, you little rat!'

'Really, Annabel! There's no need to be rude!'

'No, no, not you. I was just talking—' Annabel suddenly realized that it might not be wise to admit to custody of a purloined puss. Not to a national columnist.

'I mean, I just . . .' She faltered. Sally had raised her head and was giving her an injured look. That plate had been placed on the floor, clearly an invitation to partake of its contents. How was she to know that Annabel had not finished with it?

'I'm sorry,' Annabel said. 'I just wasn't thinking.' She was unused to sharing her home with a cat; she would have to be more careful in future.

'All right.' Xanthippe forgave her graciously. 'I've been called worse. But you can't fool me, you were thinking, you still are. Thinking what?'

'Isn't there a law that says a person isn't allowed to profit from a crime they've committed?'

'Crime? What crime? Murder?' Xanthippe pounced gleefully. 'Annabel, you're on to something! You think Arthur Arbuthnot was murdered!'

'No, no,' Annabel said quickly. 'Nothing of the sort. It was just a passing thought.' She didn't sound convincing, even to herself.

'A likely story!' Xanthippe jeered. 'Come on, Annabel – give!'

'There's nothing to give. Nothing solid, nothing anyone could prove. Nothing . . .'

'Annabel, Annabel,' Xanthippe wheedled. 'If you've got suspicions, that's good enough for me. You know you've got a nose for scandal. Just keep nosing around, let me know what you find. Off the record, if you like, just as background material. We won't use any of it.' Now Xanthippe was the one who sounded unconvincing.

'You're right there on the spot, Annabel. You'll see things. You'll hear things. There'll be a bonus, Annabel, a good one, if we get a story out of this. Even if it's only suicide —'

'No.' Annabel was sure of that. 'It wasn't suicide.'

'Then stay with it. Find out —'

At Annabel's feet, Sally finished the last shred of chicken and looked up at her speculatively.

'That's all there is right now,' Annabel told her firmly.

'All right, then keep in touch,' Xanthippe said. 'And I mean close touch. Ring me tomorrow – whether you have anything to report or not.' She rang off abruptly.

'So . . .' Annabel replaced the receiver slowly. 'What do you think of that?'

Sally obviously thought that she could be more comfortable. She gathered herself and sprang into Annabel's lap where she curled up and began purring again.

When Annabel entered the lift in the morning, it was already occupied by a short man with a worried look, who was carrying an imposing briefcase. As she entered, he appeared to make a conscious effort to smooth out his expression; summoning even more effort, he managed a wintry smile. Above it, his eyes were cold and assessing.

Annabel curved her own lips briefly, no more anxious for polite conversation than he seemed to be. She had seen briefcases like that before; they portended no good.

He allowed his forefinger to hover over the top button

and gave her an inquiring glance. She nodded. He pressed the button and the lift glided upwards.

The Broomstick was waiting when the lift doors parted. The man stepped back to allow Annabel to precede him.

'Oh, you needn't bother about *her!*' the Broomstick snapped. 'She's just the decorator.'

'Interior designer,' Annabel corrected icily.

'Now, Dora,' the man said. 'Now, now.'

'You're late!' Dora turned her firepower on him. 'They're all here waiting for you.' She eyed the briefcase greedily.

'I' – he checked his watch – 'am precisely on time.' He wasn't going to let Dora get away with anything, either. 'Possibly the others are early.'

'I'll show you to the study,' Dora urged him on impatiently.

'I know the way.' He was not to be hurried. He nodded to Annabel with more warmth than he had yet shown and set off down the hallway at a leisurely pace. Dora fussed along ahead of him, darting forward then coming back, like a sheepdog with a recalcitrant charge.

At the end of the hallway, he stopped and looked back. Seeing that Annabel was still in sight, he nodded to her again, but she had the impression that he wasn't really noticing her. He appeared to be looking for something else, or perhaps measuring the distance back to the lift.

He and Dora rounded the corner and disappeared. Annabel was still staring after them when she became aware that Kelda had been lurking in the shadowed door during the exchange.

Realizing she had been spotted, Kelda stepped forward and stared bitterly down the hallway. 'What does that rotten little twister want now?'

'You know him?'

'He's the Arbuthnot hatchetman. Solicitor,' she clarified, in answer to Annabel's puzzled look. 'Lawyer, whatever you want to call him. Whenever there's dirty work to be done, Pennyman's the one who does it, waving his papers around to prove it's all legal, upright and above board. What he does may be legal – but it isn't right!'

'You do seem to know him.' Annabel felt a mounting disquiet. It was becoming increasingly obvious that Kelda was no stranger to this establishment. They might not know her, but she certainly knew them.

'I should,' Kelda said. 'He was the bastard who came to Mark in hospital and told him he had no right to sue Arthur Arbuthnot because it wasn't Arbuthnot's fault that he, Mark, had taken reckless chances in doing his job. He told Mark that, if he tried to sue, Arbuthnot would defend – and he had more money to pay legal fees than Mark did. And then he said that Mark wouldn't be able to get legal aid to sue because—' Kelda's voice quivered between rage and tears.

'With Mark lying right there in the bed, he told him he wouldn't get legal aid because . . . because he hadn't a leg to stand on!'

'Oh, dear,' Annabel murmured. 'That was tactless. I suppose it was such a cliché that it just slipped out before he thought.'

'He knew what he was saying!' Kelda was unforgiving. 'Mark was helpless – and he was rubbing it in. Then he made Arbuthnot's counteroffer: Mark would always have a job with him and be looked after. It was the least he could do – but it made Mark feel like a charity case. He accepted the deal – he had to, but he's hated himself and Arbuthnot and everybody else in sight ever since.'

Her eyes bright with unshed tears, Kelda whirled abruptly and marched back through the doorway to the drawing room.

Well! Discretion, Annabel decided, was called for. It was not a quality that had ever loomed large in her life, but Kelda obviously needed a bit of time to pull herself together. She had probably said far more than she had intended to, but the words had come spilling out once she had started. There was doubtless more to come and more questions to be answered but, for the moment, Kelda needed to be alone.

Besides . . . Annabel found herself drifting innocently down the hallway. Somehow, she was on tiptoe again. She pulled the tape measure out of her basket; such a useful thing, a tape measure – it provided both a badge of office and a measure of invisibility. An explanation for being anywhere at any time.

She turned the corner and was surprised, but cheered, to see a streak of light marking the study door. Someone hadn't closed it properly. The murmur of voices could be heard beyond it.

Annabel moved closer and studiously bent to measure the distance from the floor to the light fixture beside the door.

9

Just her luck, Annabel thought. All the way down the corridor and around the corner, she had been able to hear an unfamiliar male voice droning on in a monotone. Now that she was close enough to distinguish words, the voice had stopped and there was complete silence in the study. It seemed that she had missed whatever was going on. Or had she?

'I don't understand —'

'You can't be serious!'

'No! No! It's impossible!'

Suddenly, there was uproar. Shrieks, shouts and the occasional indignant phrase breaking through. Annabel began backing away slowly, poised to turn and run if the door opened any wider. She would hate to be caught eavesdropping.

'I suppose this is Arthur's idea of a joke!' Zenia's voice rang out loud and clear, absolving Annabel of any possible accusation of eavesdropping. She must have been audible three blocks away.

'How could you let him do this to us?' Tara was turning on the lawyer, plaintive, but with a strident note in her voice.

'Mr Arbuthnot had a perfect right to do whatever he wished with his estate. Such a bequest is not unknown.' There was reproof in the lawyer's voice. Also, it seemed to be moving closer. Annabel retreated a bit farther.

'I'll want a copy of that will.' Neville's voice was closer, too. It sounded as though he were following the lawyer to the door. 'My own solicitor will want to take a close look at it.'

'A not unreasonable request.' There was a rustle of papers.

'It's a bit complicated to take in all at once. I would, however, draw your attention to clauses nine through to thirteen. You will wish to study them carefully.'

'Naturally, we intend to contest.' That was Wystan, trying to sound in command of the situation.

'As you wish. It would be most inadvisable, however. Mr Arbuthnot took that contingency into consideration. You will find that anyone who contests the will stands to lose any bequest already made to him . . . or her.'

In the long and thoughtful silence that followed, the door opened and Mr Pennyman paused in the doorway for his parting shot.

'Unfortunately—' His voice edged closer to elation than regret. 'Most unfortunately, I have an important meeting in Edinburgh this afternoon, so I can't stay to discuss this further with you. I'll be back on Monday. You will have had time to digest all the implications by then. I haven't time now but, since I am the trustee, I will wish to meet the, um, "heiress" and attempt to ascertain her preference for a guardian.'

'But—' someone began to say, and broke off with a gasp, as though suddenly kicked.

'I'm sure we understand each other,' Mr Pennyman said smoothly. He turned and set off down the hallway at a brisk pace that threatened to break into a sprint at any sign of pursuit.

Annabel flattened herself against the wall, realizing, with reluctant admiration, the cleverness he had shown in coming to the family to read the will rather than having them assemble at his office. He had obviously expected trouble and it was easier for him to make his escape here than it would have been for him to try to clear a cluster of hysterical, squabbling legatees out of his office.

Mr Pennyman cast an anxious backwards glance over his shoulder at discovering that the lift was not waiting and opted for the stairs, taking them at a breakneck pace. He was wise not to linger; already voices were rising again in the study and the rustle of turning pages sounded like dry winter leaves flying down the street before a gathering storm.

'Where is he?' Zenia appeared in the doorway, obviously the first to recover. 'He can't leave us like this! I want to know—' Glancing over her shoulder, she stepped into the hallway and pulled the door shut behind her. A crafty look spread over her face.

'Sally . . .' she cooed. 'Here, Sally . . . nice Sally . . . come to Auntie Zenia, Sally . . . Sally . . .' She moved forward and headed for the nearest doorway with a determined tread. 'Sally . . . ?'

Behind her, she left chaos.

'I can't believe it!' Tara's voice soared above the others, perilously close to hysteria. 'I just can't believe it! After all we were to each other —'

'Oh, yes?' Neville's tone was nasty. 'And just how much "all" was that?'

'I served that man for thirty years . . . I gave up any chance for a life of my own . . .' One had to feel sorry for the Broomstick, even though one did think that she had been a fool.

The diamond rings on Annabel's hand seemed to gleam sympathetically. Dora Stringer was now learning belatedly the lesson Annabel had learned a long time ago. The one about not putting your faith in the princes of this earth. No matter how truly princely they might be, they were mortal. They had a nasty habit of dying – and then where were you?

'I don't know what you're complaining about.' Wystan's voice had never sounded so sharp. 'He's left you a nice little nest egg. Not like poor Luther, who's got scarcely anything.'

'Oh, I don't mind,' Luther said unctuously. 'I haven't been working for him very long, comparatively. I'm touched that he remembered me at all.'

'Well, I mind!' Neville snarled. 'Do you realize he's left me less than he left to that miserable broken-down motorcycle jockey downstairs? And I'm his own blood kin!'

'The old boy always felt a bit guilty about poor Mark,' Wystan said. 'One can understand it, but it's a pity he didn't consider his Aunt Zenia's feelings —'

'Arthur wasn't to know he'd predecease his aunt.' Tara

was roused to a feeble defence; she didn't sound as though her heart were in it. 'After all, she's older than he was.'

'Yes, well . . .' Wystan seemed to take that as a personal criticism, as well as a reminder. She was older than he was, too. 'Where *is* Zenia? She hasn't come back.'

'That's right!' There was the sound of the door being wrenched open so hard it hit the wall. 'Where is she? What's she doing?'

Suddenly, everyone burst into the hallway. Annabel was caught. Casually flourishing the tape measure, she bent and took a careful measurement of the distance between two imaginary points. Anyone could see quite clearly that she was far too absorbed in her work to have been paying one bit of attention to anything that might have been going on in the study. She hoped.

'Have you seen Zenia?' Tara demanded.

'Zenia?' Annabel blinked vaguely, wondering how much she dared deny. 'I think she went past a few minutes ago. She seemed to be looking for the cat.'

'I knew it! I knew she was up to something!' Tara started forward. 'If anyone is to take care of dear little Sally, it should be me. Zenia doesn't even like her – and she'd have been *my* cat after I married Arthur. I'm sure that was what he was thinking about.'

'Mmmm . . .' Wystan watched her hurry away purposefully. 'Perhaps I ought to . . .' He seemed to fade into the distance.

Neville stood there dithering, obviously unable to decide whether to follow his mother or his girlfriend. He turned to the others. 'Has anyone seen the cat this morning?'

'I had more to worry about this morning than that bloody cat!' Dora Stringer said bitterly.

'Me?' Annabel was startled to find Neville waiting for a response from her. There flashed into her mind so vivid a picture of Sally settling down on her sofa with a contented purr just before she left the flat that she was almost afraid the others could see it, too.

'Sally wasn't around when I got here,' Annabel said, arranging the truth as meticulously as a politician.

81

'No,' Luther agreed. 'Sally wasn't here this morning. I'm afraid I can't remember when I last saw her.'

But he had been looking for her. Desperately. Only yesterday afternoon, Annabel had watched him rootling among the rubbish bins in the back alley, calling the cat. *Very* anxious to find the cat.

One did not have to be a mathematical genius to add up the way the family were behaving and to reach the conclusion that Arthur Arbuthnot had left most of his fortune to Sally, his cat. It had happened before, it would undoubtedly happen again. Eccentric millionaires did do things like that – not that Arthur Arbuthnot would have had to be particularly eccentric to prefer his cat to his poisonous relatives.

Luther must have known what was in the will; that was why he had been searching so frantically for Sally. What else did he know? He was looking suspiciously smug. Too smug. Annabel wondered just how much he was going to inherit. Even if it wasn't enough to retire on, he was still in a very good position. Young enough to continue making his way in the world, and a stint as Arthur Arbuthnot's personal assistant on his CV would be made doubly impressive by the fact that he had neither resigned nor been fired, but had lost his position solely because of his employer's demise. Yes, Luther was the best placed of any of them for onward-and-upward progress.

Unless, of course, he had been the one who killed Arthur Arbuthnot. That would be certain to discourage any future employer.

'Sally . . . Sally . . .'

'Here, kitty, kitty, kitty . . .'

'Come on, Sally . . . Good girl, Sally . . .'

The plaintive calls resounded from various quarters of the apartment as the hunt intensified. The original urgency was giving way to panic.

'Where is the hell-forsaken beast?' Neville demanded. 'Where can it have got to?'

'If you ask me—' Even now, the Broomstick could not keep the grim satisfaction out of her voice. 'The wretched creature has gone back to whatever alley it came from.'

'Who asked you?' Neville snapped, quite forgetting that he had.

'Well, now,' Luther murmured complacently. 'If she's run away and lost herself, that would be most unfortunate. Most unfortunate indeed, as things stand.'

'What do you mean?' Neville regarded him with justifiable suspicion. Luther appeared to be enjoying himself far too much, in his own quiet way.

'It looks as though Sally has disappeared.' Luther's glasses flashed a spark of light as he turned to Neville with an unpleasant smile. 'Wouldn't it be ironic if you had to wait seven years before she could be officially declared dead and the estate redistributed?'

By late afternoon, the hunt had spread to the lowest reaches of the building. The searchers had spent an inordinate amount of time in the lower part of the flat, unable or unwilling to believe that Sally would not have gone to ground in the bedrooms or kitchen.

'Here, Sally . . . dear Sally . . .'

'Come to Auntie, darling . . .'

'Get out here, you filthy little bastard!'

Annabel's initial feeling of guilt had disappeared when she overheard a number of stray remarks which left no doubt as to Sally's fate when and if she were found. At best, the poor innocent would be torn apart as everyone squabbled over her custody. At worst . . .

'A dead cat can't inherit.' Neville and his mother had paused for a quick consultation while they waited for the lift. 'We're the closest of blood kin. No cat – and everything would revert to us.'

No, the only recourse was to hold on to Sally until she could deliver her safely to Mr Pennyman on Monday and let him take over from there.

'These people are crazy!' Kelda exploded, reappearing in the drawing room after a break for lunch. 'Do you know what they've just done to Mark? Made him get up out of his wheelchair – all the way out. So that they could check it over. As though he might have been sitting on the cat – like it was a cushion and he hadn't noticed it was there.'

'Incredible,' Annabel murmured soothingly.

'I hope they never find it! I hope they have to wait for ever for the estate to be settled! It would serve them right!'

'And what about Mark?' Annabel watched as Kelda stormed around the room, picking up brushes and putting them down, moving pots of paint, frowning and miserable. 'Will he want to wait that long?'

'Mark has waited long enough already! Do you know —?' Kelda slammed down a roll of wallpaper. 'The old bastard left him the exact amount he was going to sue for! That just goes to show, doesn't it?'

'Show what?' Annabel deftly removed a pair of scissors before the twitching hands could close on them.

'He felt guilty. Mark was right – it was all Arbuthnot's fault and he knew it, even though he kept denying it. If he'd only given Mark the money in the first place, everything would have been so different. We could have —'

Outside, the lift doors clattered and a triumphal shout blasted down the hallway.

'GOT HER! FOUND THE LITTLE BLIGHTER! HERE'S OUR SALLY, SAFELY HOME!'

Annabel was through the doorway and into the hall before Kelda had time to raise her eyebrows.

Uncle Wystan was almost jogging down the corridor, still crowing his triumph. Bouncing in his arms was a large placid tabby, who bore no resemblance to the dainty Sally, except for the mottled tiger fur.

'Oh, well done!'

'Splendid . . .'

'Where did you find her?'

The others converged from every direction, exuding relief and exultation. They crowded round Wystan and his captive, reaching out to touch the cat. Then they gradually fell silent.

'Um, are you absolutely sure, old man?' Neville was the first to voice disquiet. 'She looks a bit, um, tatty.'

'Isn't it bigger than Sally?' Tara frowned critically. 'And there's something wrong with its mouth.'

She was right, Annabel saw. One long sharp incisor protruded at an angle, twisting the cat's lip and giving it the appearance of leering.

'Coat's a bit rough at the moment, that's all,' Wystan assured them. 'After a night out on the tiles, you might not look your best, either. Er, that is, I mean—' He broke off, suddenly aware of extreme tactlessness.

'I don't think that's Sally,' the Broomstick said slowly. 'There's something different about her.'

'But close . . .' Luther studied the cat admiringly. 'Very, very close. If Sally doesn't come back, it just might work.'

'Of course this is Sally,' Wystan insisted, tousling the cat's already tousled fur. 'Just look at the way she responds.' A loud purring had started. 'She knows us, all right. She knows she's home.' He bent and deposited the cat lightly on the floor. 'Just watch – she'll go straight to her food bowl.'

The cat lifted its head and sniffed the air, then seemed to come to a decision. It sauntered away from them. It was heading in the right direction, but . . .

'Wystan, you fool!' Zenia screamed. 'That's not Sally! That's a – a – a Salvatore!'

The cat swivelled its head and regarded them genially, as though acknowledging its name. When it swung away again, they all saw what Zenia meant.

'It's a male,' Neville said. 'No doubt about it.'

Tara giggled abruptly, shrilly, teetering on the verge of hysteria. The Broomstick snorted in disgust and turned away.

'Ooh, ah.' Wystan looked after the cat in dismay. 'I hadn't noticed. The fur – The markings are so nearly right.'

'Very close indeed,' Luther affirmed. 'Without the real Sally, you still might just get away with it.'

'Nonsense!' Zenia snarled. 'If there's one thing certain, it's that that bloody cat was a female.' A calculating look crept into her eyes. 'Of course, we might just . . .'

'Hmmm, I see what you mean.' Neville was clearly a chip off the old block. 'I didn't exactly get the impression that old Pennyman was a keen animal lover. I'd be surprised if he pays any attention to them at all. After all, they don't show up in court often, either as plaintiffs or defendants.

He probably can tell a cat from a dog but, other than that, I doubt that he'd know one cat from another.'

'Even so,' Tara said. 'Someone else might.'

Salvatore seemed to sense something unpleasant in the atmosphere. He sat down abruptly, turning to face them, his tail tucked tightly around his body.

'We have until Monday,' Zenia calculated rapidly. 'And there are plenty of veterinarians around. Just a few minor adjustments and . . .'

Salvatore began to look worried. He stared from one human to the other, but seemed to shrink as they stared back impassively. A stray cat was accustomed to the indifference of the world around him, wary of the random malice of bullies who would harm him, but ever hopeful that somewhere, sometime, some friendly stranger might rescue and adopt him and bring him in from the cold.

'It would have to be a vet from well outside the city,' Neville said judiciously. 'A country vet with a large practice, too busy to ask questions and with no time to read the newspapers or watch television . . .'

'Exactly,' Zenia agreed. 'It should be quite simple. A snip here and there . . . and that tooth would have to go . . .'

Salvatore looked beyond them and met Annabel's eyes.

Annabel shuddered involuntarily. It was as though she had just intercepted a cry for help.

'Bit hard on the poor old boy.' Wystan demurred momentarily, then succumbed as his wife's stony gaze fell on him. 'Still, all for the best, I daresay. Win some, lose some – he'll have a good home now.'

'A short life, but a merry one,' Luther murmured.

'Not all that merry,' Neville laughed nastily, 'after he's seen the vet.'

Again, Annabel was conscious of an imploring look from the cat. She hoped the others hadn't noticed it.

They hadn't. They were all staring down at the cat, but without seeing it as a being in its own right. To them, it was nothing but a necessary pawn in their game.

Salvatore shifted uneasily and lowered himself to a crouch. His eyes scanned the territory beyond the forest of legs surrounding him. He had obviously been having second thoughts about his new friend, Wystan, and was about to make a dash for freedom.

'I don't know about this,' Wystan frowned. Salvatore looked at him hopefully. 'Even if we get the poor old boy done right away, won't it still show by Monday? I mean, won't the scars be, er, raw? Noticeable?'

'Don't be absurd, Wystan,' Zenia said crisply. 'You can't imagine Mr Pennyman is going to inspect the cat closely enough to notice anything like that. The beast is the right size, shape and colour; we'll tie a pink bow around its neck and no one will be able to tell the difference. Certainly not a solicitor who has no interest in cats to begin with.'

'You may be right,' her husband admitted.

'Of course I'm right! Now, about that vet . . .' Zenia turned away, frowning thoughtfully.

'My cousin in Bedfordshire has a jolly good vet,' Tara said. 'She's always going on about how wonderful he is. Of course, he specializes in horses, but that's all to the good, he wouldn't pay much attention to a cat, either. I could ring her and she'd make an appointment for us. We could pop the cat into a box and drive down this afternoon.'

Salvatore abandoned hope. He launched himself forward, dived through a gap between Neville's ankles, and scurried down the hallway, his paws barely touching the floor.

10

'Stop him!' . . .

  'Get him!' . . .

  'Head him off!' . . .

  'Close the doors!' . . .

  'Don't let him get away!' . . .

The confusion of shouted orders led to everyone moving at the same time, colliding with each other as they rushed to follow the cat, block exits, and recapture their victim.

Annabel backed quietly into the drawing room, bumping into Kelda, who was close behind her.

'Do you think we should try to help?' Kelda asked.

'Help *them?*' Annabel shot Kelda a look of such distaste that Kelda immediately backtracked.

'Or, at least, show willing,' she qualified. 'We don't actually have to do anything, just seem to be on their side.'

'And are we?' Annabel asked icily. She knew whose side she was on – and it was not the side of people who were prepared to mutilate an innocent cat while overlooking the possible murder of their benefactor.

'Well,' Kelda said uneasily. 'Luther could be right. It might tie up the probate of the will for ages if they can't produce the, um, main beneficiary.'

Which meant that Mark would have to wait a long time for the money to start his new life. And so, possibly, would Kelda.

'Go ahead, if you want to,' Annabel said. 'I have quite enough to do right here. Speaking of which' – Every good general knows the best defence is an attack – 'where are those assistants of yours? Peter and Paul – I thought you had them lined up to do the donkey work for us. What's happened to them?'

'Oh ... er ... yes ...' Kelda had started for the door, but paused and turned back uneasily. 'Umm, I didn't have a chance to tell you, but we'll have new helpers tomorrow. The boys had a sudden rush job at the theatre, so they're sending along a couple of friends to take their places.' She sent Annabel a look as pleading as Salvatore's. 'Please, just don't say anything. Anything at all.'

'All right, all right,' Annabel said impatiently. As Peter and Paul had not appeared since they had cleared the hall of antlers, their presence did not figure greatly in her life. 'Just as long as there's somebody to do the heavy work.'

'Guard the stairs!' Outside, the sporadic shouting erupted. 'If it gets outdoors, we'll never find it again!' There was a bellow and a thud.

'Stop playing the fool, Wystan!' Zenia was in no mood to suffer fools gladly. 'Get up and get on with it!'

'I tripped,' Wystan whined. 'I might have dislocated something. I've got to rest a minute.'

There was an explosive sound of disgust, heralding Zenia's arrival in the drawing room. She looked around slowly, frowning at Kelda and Annabel. She seemed disgusted with them, too.

'Is there anything we can do?' Kelda asked nervously.

For a moment, it didn't appear that Zenia was going to answer; her gaze travelled slowly around the room at floor level. When she raised her head, her eyes were colder than usual.

'Find that cat!' she ordered. 'And bring it to me. To *me*, do you understand? Don't let any of the others get it!' Her eyes bored into them, as though trying to hypnotize them to her will, then she turned on her heel and stalked from the room.

'Brrr!' Kelda shivered. 'I feel sorry for that poor cat if it falls into her hands.'

'As well you might,' Annabel said darkly.

'Perhaps we shouldn't help them.' Kelda hovered, irresolute. 'But Mark ...' She thought a moment. 'Maybe I can look as though I'm trying to help – but I don't actually have to *do* anything.' That settled to her satisfaction, she took off after Zenia.

Annabel sighed and slumped against the wall.

'*Phwerrr* . . .' A tiny little voice seemed to echo her relief.

'What?' She looked around cautiously, but not at floor level. The sound had come from much nearer to her ears.

'Where are you?' she whispered.

There was no answer. That one small mewl had been as instinctive and involuntary as Annabel's own sigh. But Salvatore was back on guard now and lying low. But where? The room was stripped and bare, except for the pile of wallpaper rolls in one corner, waiting either a change of decision (for the moment, pale-yellow Regency stripe had won) or the arrival of the new helpers to hang it – whichever came first. No hiding place there.

Annabel held her breath, listening to the silence in the room. She could faintly hear the rush of traffic in the road below, the wail of a siren in the distance, the hum of the wind rounding the corner of the building. Then she heard it: a faint susurration of fur brushing against a rigid surface, as though someone was changing position slightly.

'Gotcha!' She crossed to the window in two strides and looked behind the half-folded shutters.

Scrunched unhappily between the windowpane and shutter, Salvatore looked up at her, half defiant, half pleading.

'You're all right,' she said. 'It's only me.' *And I'm going to get you out of here.* She closed her lips over the sentence, afraid someone might hear her talking in an empty room and come to investigate.

Her thought seemed to convey itself to Salvatore. He stretched his neck forward and gently nuzzled her hand. The little snaggle tooth brushed against her fingers, the sensation was not unpleasant. The tooth obviously didn't bother him, he had learned to live with it comfortably. He was a perfectly healthy, happy cat. At least, he would be happy again once he got out of here. It was unthinkable that those ghastly people should be allowed to mutilate him to serve their own purposes.

'Come along.' She slid her hand under his body and tried to lift him free of the shutters. He didn't help, but he didn't try to hinder, either. He went limp, as though he had resigned himself to whatever fate had in store.

Annabel felt the weight of almost too much responsibility. But what else could she do? Salvatore trusted her and she could not let him down. Nor could she return him to the streets, where they might find him again. After all, what was the worst any of them could do to her if they caught her making off with the cat? Fire her, that was all. And it would be no hardship to be rid of this place.

'Shhh-shhh . . .' she crooned, opening the lid of her basket and lowering Salvatore into it, draping a swathe of dotted muslin over him. He wriggled uncomfortably and she burrowed beneath him to rescue her flask. And that wasn't such a bad idea.

She unscrewed the cap and raised the flask to her lips for one quick swig before continuing their escape.

'I say, have you seen —? Oops! Sorry!' Neville stood awkwardly in the doorway, staring with fascination at the flask.

'Yes?' Annabel eyed him coldly, lowering the flask. No point in pretending it wasn't there. She screwed on the cap, rather wishing she had been ladylike enough to have poured her martini into that first, and replaced it in the basket, which gave her the opportunity to check that Salvatore was completely concealed by the material. He was. She shut the lid and faced Neville haughtily. 'What was it you wanted?'

'Oh, er . . .' From the wistful expression on his face, a chance at the flask for himself would not have come amiss. 'I was looking for Tara. I, um, don't suppose you've seen her?'

'I have not seen anyone – although I have certainly *heard* everyone!' Annabel drew herself up and passed the back of one hand across her forehead in what she hoped was a suitably distraught manner. 'The noise levels around this place have been appalling and quite unacceptable!

How is one expected to be able to create in such a mad-house?'

She stooped and picked up her basket, balancing it carefully and hoping Salvatore would not do anything to give them away.

'I can't work in such chaos! In the unlikely event that anyone should be looking for me, I shall be at home, composing myself for the morning when my new assistants will be here. And I trust the rest of you will have yourselves under control by then!'

As she had hoped, the artistic temperament card had been the right one to play.

'Of course, of course. I'm terribly sorry.' Neville backed hastily out of her way, allowing her to sweep from the room.

Fortunately, the lift was waiting at the end of the corridor and she did not break stride or look back as she jabbed at the button and whisked inside the instant the doors opened wide enough.

She thanked her stars to find the entrance hall deserted; not even Mark sat at his post. Taking no chances, she charged through, looking neither left nor right, swung through the front door and across the pavement and hailed a taxi, sinking into the seat nearly as limp with relief as poor Salvatore.

Never had the front door of Lady Cosgreave's flat looked so welcoming. Annabel stepped inside gratefully and deposited her basket on the floor. Salvatore had been getting increasingly restless during the long taxi ride and now he ventured a soft, *'Meerroww?'*

Sally, who had come to greet her, promptly abandoned Annabel's ankles and turned to investigate the basket. *'Mmmmrrraa?'* she inquired, in her turn.

'Mrraaah!' The lid popped open suddenly, startling Sally. She skidded to a safe distance away and crouched, watching.

Annabel tensed. She had not given sufficient thought to whether or not the cats would get on together. She seemed to remember something she had read in the distant past to the effect that the best way to break up a cat fight was to throw a glass of water over the combatants. But a lot of fur could fly before she got to the kitchen and back again with the water. She wondered whether emptying the flask of martinis over them would have the same result.

She needn't have worried. Salvatore's head rose slowly above the rim of the basket and turned unhurriedly, surveying this new territory. Then he tilted his head ceilingwards, sniffing the air.

Annabel found herself inhaling deeply in sympathy. She had never noticed before how thoroughly Lady Cosgreave's expensive Parisian scent had permeated the atmosphere. Her own lighter, less expensive but deeply loved, floral scent floated on top of it. And heaven alone knew what secret feline messages were drifting out from the lovely Sally.

Salvatore lowered his head and looked around again. It was a dwelling place of females. Friendly females. His muscles seemed to relax and his facial expression became an affable leer.

Salvatore, you lucky devil, he seemed to be saying to himself, *you've landed in a tub of butter.*

He shook himself, smoothing his fur down, and leaped out of the basket. After twining appreciatively around Annabel's ankles, he sauntered over to Sally. They regarded each other solemnly for a moment, then stretched out and touched noses delicately. They seemed to commune silently, then Sally, flirting her whiskers, rose and stretched luxuriously and led the way into the kitchen.

Annabel trailed after them, feeling slightly superfluous. They were going to get along beautifully. Perhaps they had known each other back in the old days in the alley.

After one questioning glance at the complacent Sally, Salvatore hurled himself at the bowl of dried cat food with an eagerness that betrayed his hunger. Wystan must have captured him as he had been foraging for his next meal among the dustbins. Sally looked on benevolently, secure in the knowledge that a more appetizing meal would soon

93

be on offer now that Annabel was home. She tilted her head at Annabel expectantly.

'Sautéed chicken livers on toast, I thought,' Annabel responded. 'The toast is for me, of course.'

Salvatore lifted his head from the bowl momentarily and gave a loud purr of approval. Somewhere, there had been a word he recognized, or perhaps he had tuned in to the image in Annabel's mind of chopped onions and chicken livers sizzling in the frying pan – and the further image of most of them being divided into two saucers and set down on the floor.

Annabel removed the tub of chicken livers from the fridge and checked that they had thawed during her absence. They had been neatly cleaned and trimmed before being frozen, so they were all ready for cooking. What a pity that Lady Cosgreave's hospitality hadn't extended to retaining her excellent housekeeper for Annabel's term of residence. On the other hand, perhaps that was just as well. She would not like to have to explain just what she thought she was doing to a disapproving housekeeper, especially since she wasn't sure she knew that herself.

Salvatore had licked every last crumb from Sally's bowl. He looked at Annabel and, obviously realizing that it was going to be a little while before anything more was forthcoming, took a stroll around the kitchen and then headed out into the hallway. Sally padded after him.

'That's right, give him the guided tour,' Annabel grumbled. 'It would be a shame if he missed anything.'

Sally paused and looked over her shoulder at Annabel, seeming to smile in agreement.

Agreement! A cat! She was going out of her mind. She *had* gone out of her mind. She was personally responsible for removing a cat worth unknown millions of pounds from its lawful – very lawful; in fact, it presumably owned the premises – abode. She had also catnapped Salvatore, who was worth, perhaps, fifty pence on a good day – although he didn't look as though he'd had many of those lately, so perhaps she needn't worry unduly about him.

There was no doubt about it, she was completely and

utterly out of her mind. She hoped that would be a viable defence, when and if she were caught.

Annabel opened the fridge and poured herself a martini from the waiting pitcher, then snatched up an onion and began to chop it furiously.

11

Annabel awoke in the morning to discover two pairs of small eyes blinking at her fondly, two soft furry bodies pressed against her own, one on either side.

'Good morning, little chums,' she said, then felt slightly foolish, but only for a moment.

Sally stretched out her neck to plant a delicate kiss on Annabel's cheek. Salvatore extended a protective possessive foreleg to lie across her ribcage. The sound of gentle purring intensified. Good morning? It was a splendid morning.

Annabel felt ridiculously happy; in another minute, she would begin purring herself. Wouldn't it be nice to spend the morning lying here contentedly, playing with the cats and not worrying about anything else in the world?

The world! Suddenly, it all rushed back to her. Her little chums had been illicitly acquired, her employer had most probably been murdered, her principal outlet for gossip tips was pushing for more information than she was willing, or able, to supply, and her financial situation —

Annabel sat up abruptly, tumbling the cats away from her and threw back the covers. The purrs changed to a duet of protest.

'Sorry about that,' Annabel apologized, feet sliding into her slippers. 'Who's for breakfast?'

The word was recognized and instant forgiveness ensued, with furry bodies twining around her ankles as she drew back the curtains and sunshine flooded into the bedroom. An omen for a good day, she hoped.

She led the parade into the kitchen, where generous dollops of last night's leftovers sent the cats into a state of bliss.

She smiled down at them. There was a pet shop nearby, she must make a small detour on her way to or from Regent's Park and pick up a little treat for them. Perhaps a catnip mouse . . .

The telephone interrupted her pleasant train of thought.

'What are you doing there?' The voice ringing down the line was loud, indignant, haranguing – unmistakably the Broomstick's. 'You ought to be here! Controlling your workers! They're tearing the place apart. They've only been here ten minutes and they've already broken a window. You should be sued!'

'Workers —?' But the Broomstick had slammed down the telephone. Belatedly, Annabel remembered that Kelda had said something about new helpers starting work today. She stabbed out Kelda's telephone number, but there was no answer.

A deep foreboding settled over her. She returned to the kitchen only long enough to refill her flask with the martini mixture from the pitcher in the fridge. If the day continued the way it was going, they would be needed. So much for hopeful omens.

Kelda and the Broomstick were both waiting to intercept Annabel as she stepped out of the lift. Mark must have notified them of her arrival downstairs.

'I insist that you get rid of these people immediately!' Dora Stringer confronted her head-on. Behind Dora's back, Kelda was making frantic signals that Annabel could not interpret.

From farther down the hallway, a great pounding and banging was going on. Far too much noise when the main job to be done was to hang some wallpaper.

'I locked them in the antechamber,' Dora Stringer pronounced righteously. 'Before they could do any more damage.'

There was something disquietingly familiar about the raised voices coming from behind the locked door. Annabel held out her hand, palm upwards, directly in front of Dora Stringer. After a long moment, the woman dropped the key into it.

'Keep them under control!' she demanded, retreating with hands on hips to watch from a safe distance.

'Stand back!' Annabel called. 'I'm opening the door.'

There was an abrupt silence, during which they could hear the scrape of the key turning, then the door was wrenched open from the other side, pulling Annabel off balance.

'Let me at her! I'm going to kill her!'

'No, you're not! I am!'

Annabel was jostled aside as two demented figures burst from their imprisonment and charged towards the Broomstick.

Annabel took a considered step backwards and thrust out her foot. The man went sprawling, catching the woman as he fell and taking her with him.

'Disgraceful! They're probably drunk, too!' The Broomstick surveyed the melee with grim relish. 'They should be dismissed immediately!'

'I'll deal with them, thank you,' Annabel said crisply. As she had suspected, they were the journalists who had forced their way into the building a few days ago. Xanthippe's minions. And now they were back, masquerading as part of the decorating team. Annabel gave her own minion a withering glare.

'I'll explain,' Kelda said frantically. 'Just don't—' She broke off. To finish the sentence would be to give the game away to the listening Broomstick.

'They're only temporary,' Annabel assured Dora Stringer, baring her teeth at her, then turning the bared teeth warningly on Kelda and on the two suddenly subdued paparazzi, who had belatedly remembered their cover stories. 'We just got them in to do the rough work.'

Sudden disquiet flared in the watching eyes. 'Now, wait a minute—' the woman began.

'They're going to take up the carpet,' Annabel said firmly. 'Then scrub the floor – and possibly sand it. Don't worry, they're going to be too busy to get into any more mischief.'

'Er . . .' Kelda said nervously, as disquiet turned to naked horror in the watching eyes and lips began to mouth silent threats.

'Either that, or they can leave now.' Annabel was certain that they would rather do as she said than go back and face Xanthippe. In this case, the devil they didn't know was better than the devil they did. It was probably untrue that Xanthippe drank the blood of victims who had failed her, but it had been many a long day since anyone had cared to put it to the test. These two weren't going to.

'Very well.' Dora Stringer capitulated suddenly, turning on her heel. 'I have more to do than stand around here supervising the pathetic inadequates who work for you. On your head be it, if we have any more trouble from them.'

They watched her stalk down the corridor and disappear into her office, then three pairs of eyes turned to regard Annabel warily. Annabel stared back implacably.

'Umm . . .' Kelda ventured. 'I don't think you've met Cindy and Sid. They're . . .'

'I know who they are,' Annabel said coldly. 'And I know *what* they are.'

'So what are you going to do about it?' Sid challenged her directly.

'I'm not – you are. You can start in the far corner, move carefully and try not to raise too much dust. The carpet—' she answered their uncomprehending looks. 'Roll up the carpet – and watch out for the carpet tacks.'

'You're joking!' Cindy gasped.

'Not at all. The Victorians were very keen on carpet tacks. Most of them must be quite rusty by now.'

'Annabel—' Kelda tried to intervene. 'I don't think —'

'So I've noticed!' Annabel's look sent Kelda backing away.

'Wait a minute.' Cindy's eyes narrowed. 'Don't I know you? I've seen you somewhere before.'

'That's right,' Sid agreed. 'Didn't we doorstep her a couple of years ago? What was it . . . ? Yeah!' He snapped his fingers. 'The Black Widow! They got you after you offed your fourth husband. How come you're out so soon? I thought they put you away for a good twenty years.'

'Very funny,' Annabel said. 'Now get started on that carpet. And after that you can scrub down the walls.'

'Annabel!' Kelda wailed. 'You're making a terrible mistake.'

'She sure is.' Sid rummaged in something that looked like a lunchbox and brought out a small camera. 'You just sort her out while we get on with it.'

'Given up the photocopier, have you?' Annabel stared pointedly at the camera. 'What a pity. You were doing some very . . . innovative . . . work on it. I believe I still have a few copies. What did you do with the rest of them – send them out as Christmas cards?'

'What?' Sid let the camera slide back into the lunchbox. 'Who are you?'

'Shall we say . . . a friend of the management? Your management. Have you shown them your interesting experiments? They could give new meaning to Page Three.'

'I've changed my mind,' Cindy announced abruptly. 'I don't want to throttle that old bitch down the hall any more. This one is top of my list now.'

'Business first,' Annabel said briskly. 'Playtime afterwards. Now, get at that carpet!'

She waited until they had reluctantly stooped to the task, then turned to Kelda. 'And you – I'll speak to you in the study. Come along!'

They had barely reached the study when Wystan appeared.

'Oh, erm, I was just looking for Zenia,' he said unconvincingly. It was probably Zenia who had sent him up to see what was going on.

'You won't find her here!' Annabel swung to face him, not bothering to adjust the laserbeam glare that had been piercing Kelda; he quailed as the full force of it struck him. Kelda took the opportunity to retreat a few steps.

'Oh, no? Erm, perhaps not.' He twitched visibly, evidently torn between facing a furious Annabel or an implacable Zenia. 'Just the same,' he added more firmly, obviously coming down on the side of not further annoying the woman he had to live with. 'I think I'll just look around a bit.'

'As you like.' Annabel turned back to block Kelda's escape route. That young woman had a great deal of explaining to do before she was allowed to get away.

'Ah! Right!' Realizing that her attention was diverted, Wystan slid away.

'As I was saying before we were interrupted—' Annabel advanced on the hapless Kelda. 'How much? How much did they pay you?'

'Not a lot,' Kelda quavered. 'Hardly anything, really.'

'How much?'

'They haven't actually paid me anything yet.' Kelda tried to look pathetic. 'It was only a promise.'

'How much?'

'Five hundred pounds,' Kelda admitted.

'Chicken feed,' Annabel sneered.

'Per day,' Kelda defended. 'For every day they're allowed free access to the premises.'

Annabel drew a deep breath. That was beyond anything Xanthippe had paid her . . . to date. Either Xanthippe was counting on this as a big international story, or Kelda had hidden depths as a negotiator. In fact, there was quite a lot about Kelda that might repay a closer look . . .

'I say—' Uncle Wystan reappeared in the doorway. 'That female in there looks strangely familiar. Haven't I seen her before?'

'Not knowing the range of your female acquaintanceships,' Annabel quelled him, 'I couldn't say.'

'Ah! Well!' He retreated backwards. 'It was only a thought. Can't be sure. Can't be sure at all.'

'I think they're from out of town,' Kelda said impulsively. She caught Annabel's eyes. 'But I can't be sure,' she echoed.

'Always difficult,' he sympathized with her. 'So many of these females look alike nowadays. Practically in uniform. Hard to tell them apart.

'Not you, of course,' he assured Kelda anxiously, as though afraid he might have offended her. Nor you,' he assured Annabel. 'Different generation entirely —'

Annabel raised an eyebrow.

'I mean—' He worked his mouth violently, like a man who had suddenly and inexplicably found his foot in it again. 'Well, still looking for Zenia!' He turned and bolted away.

'I'll help you look!' Kelda dodged past Annabel and bolted after him.

Annabel let her go; she would deal with that young lady later. The first priority must be to keep the Arbuthnot heirs from realizing that the paparazzi were in their midst. They would then have the perfect excuse for cancelling the decorating contract. Instantly. And with extreme prejudice. The Broomstick would take care of that.

Annabel shuddered and determined to keep her unwilling helpers so busy that they had no time for prying and spying. She went back to the drawing room and looked in on them.

Sid was propped up against the wall, groaning. The carpet was in the middle of the room, half rolled up. Cindy was kicking ineffectually at the carpet, trying to roll it along.

'That's no good,' Annabel said crisply. 'You've got to put your back into it.'

'You!' Sid turned to face her, wincing. 'This is all your fault. I've gone and done me back in.' He rubbed the small of his back, wincing some more.

'Sid hasn't lifted anything heavier than a camera in years,' Cindy said accusingly. 'You're killing him.'

'That would be too much to hope for!' Annabel regarded them both coldly. 'If you're not up to the job, you can always leave.'

'Not until we've got our money's worth.' Cindy pouted belligerently. 'That other one' – she obviously meant Kelda – 'promised us we'd have a free hand.'

'The promise wasn't hers to make. In any case, I can't see what you hope to gain by this. Nothing is happening here now. Arthur Arbuthnot is dead. It's all over. The parade's gone by.'

'We have information otherwise,' Cindy smirked.

'Yeah,' Sid agreed. 'We've got a friend at court in here somewhere. The tip-off is that there's a big story breaking.'

With a guilty start, Annabel realized that they were talking about her. Xanthippe had sent them here to follow up on her own carelessly dropped hint about murder. Something she was powerless to prove and unable to investigate – and which might not even have happened. Had Xanthippe told Cindy and Sid what they should be looking for? At any rate, they did not appear to know the source of the tip-off – and Annabel intended to keep it that way.

'If you're planning to hang around here until something happens,' Annabel said, 'you're in for a long wait. Meanwhile, I suggest you finish rolling up that carpet and stand it up in the corner over there.'

'Now, wait a minute—' Sid began.

'What's going on here?' Zenia stepped into the room. 'Who are these people?'

'Temporary help. The others are down with flu. If these two don't work out, we won't have them back tomorrow.' Annabel watched with grim satisfaction as Cindy and Sid stooped to the carpet and began pushing it energetically.

'They don't look very expert,' Zenia said critically.

'They'll learn.' Annabel tried for a diversion. 'Have you seen your husband? He was in here looking for you a few minutes ago.'

'Really?' Zenia shrugged indifferently but, after a narrow-eyed look at Cindy, who was displaying an inordinate amount of cleavage, moved off in the direction of the Broomstick's office.

'Whew!' Sid straightened up and wiped his brow. 'Wouldn't like to meet her in a dark alley!'

'I don't even want to see her around here,' Cindy said.

'You could always leave,' Annabel tried again.

'Oh, no, we've got too much to do around here.'

'Quite right – and you'd better finish with that carpet now. That's all you're going to accomplish today.' *If only*, Annabel thought, *she could get another look at that other carpet, the one in Arthur Arbuthnot's office. A close look.*

'Oh, I dunno.' Sid rubbed his sleeve over a large button on his shirt. 'Haven't done too badly – so far.'

'Sid's got the latest in spy cameras,' Cindy said proudly. 'No one even knows he's snapping them.'

'Got a great one of the old boy in the doorway.' Sid rubbed the lens again. 'Looked like a stranded trout.'

'You'll be the ones stranded if you're reported to the Press

Council. That doorway is very identifiable. They'll have you dead to rights on flouting the privacy guidelines.'

'Nobody pays any attention to those things any more,' Cindy said. 'They're out of date.'

'Already?' Annabel was disbelieving. 'But it's not that long ago that they came into force.'

'Not much force there. How they going to police them? Oh, maybe we have to tiptoe around the kiddies,' Sid conceded. 'But this lot are old enough to look out for themselves.'

'They're not doing too good a job of it.' Cindy grinned maliciously. 'Not when they've got a mole under their roof feeding the Spider.'

Annabel tried to look suitably puzzled; as though she had no idea that Xanthippe, sitting in the midst of her web of gossip and waiting for the first tentative vibrations at the edge of the web to tell her that another victim had been enmeshed, was often referred to as the Spider. She tried to look as though she had never heard of Xanthippe at all.

Was Cindy looking at her speculatively?

'Be that as it may,' Annabel said sternly, 'if you don't work properly, you have no excuse for being here.'

'Right! That's done!' Sid gave the carpet a final turn, heaved it upright and stood it in the indicated corner. 'Now maybe you might be a bit more helpful for the money we've paid and give us something to do in one of the other rooms. Some place nearer to the action.'

'Not much action around here,' Cindy grumbled. 'We'll have to make do with background stuff, general shots of the layout and people involved. Have it all on hand when the story breaks.'

'You haven't paid *me* anything – and there is no story.' Annabel was getting into her new role of double agent. Deny everything and disarm the suspicions of these two, while quietly continuing to feed whatever developed – well, most of the developments – to Xanthippe. In fact, Xanthippe was the perfect role model for aspiring double agents —

'What's that?' Cindy asked sharply.

'What's what?' Sid looked around.

'I thought I heard a cat.' Cindy motioned for silence. 'There it is again. Listen!'

'Oh, no!' Annabel moaned. 'Oh, God, no!'

12

One of the cats must have crawled into her basket before she left the flat. Was it possible that she had not noticed the extra weight and had unknowingly carried the poor innocent back into the field of danger?

Only too possible, she decided glumly. The weight of the basket varied from day to day, depending on how many swatches and sample books she loaded into it.

But . . . surely she had filled the basket right up to the brim this morning? She recollected now that she had had to slip her flask lengthwise along the side of the basket, taking up the last iota of space. In that case . . .

The cat sounded closer now. It was coming this way. Annabel turned towards the door, forgetting that it was unwise to turn her back on her unwilling helpers. With her cold gaze elsewhere, Sid made a dash for freedom.

He collided with Tara, who was passing the doorway at that moment. Sid went sprawling on the floor, Tara was knocked back against the wall and dropped what she had been carrying.

'Get the cat!' she shrieked. 'Don't let her get away!'

But the cat wasn't going anywhere. It marched over to the prone Sid, glaring at him, and proceeded to tell him exactly what she thought of his rudeness and clumsiness.

'Sally!' Annabel gasped – and then looked again. Not quite, but a closer match than Salvatore. The world was full of tabby cats. This one was definitely female, dainty, petite, with a touch more white in her markings – and very opinionated. Her opinion of Sid was not favourable and she was letting everyone know it.

'She's got your number, all right,' Cindy chuckled, looking down at the scolding cat.

'*Now* what?' The Broomstick burst out of her office and advanced upon the scene. She appeared to barely restrain herself from kicking Sid as she passed him. Annabel sympathized with her, for once. She was beginning to feel a growing desire to kick Sid herself.

'I found Sally!' Tara announced triumphantly. She scooped up the scolding cat and cuddled it. 'She knew her Auntie Tara and she came to me straight away, didn't you, darling?'

The cat touched noses with her delicately and chirruped agreement. Then she looked down at Sid, who was scrambling to his feet, and added a few more comments, obviously disparaging. Annabel could not help but agree with her.

'Noisy creature!' The Broomstick radiated disapproval from every pore. 'Can't it shut up for even a minute?'

The cat looked at her curiously. It was a very young cat, Annabel realized, just out of kittenhood and into feline adolescence, quite a bit younger than Sally. It was quite obviously someone's pampered pet, well-fed, well-groomed, happy and trusting, unaware that the world could present any dangers, or even problems. Annabel wondered where Tara had found her – and where her owner might be.

'She's a sassy little thing,' Tara agreed. 'Aren't you, Sassy? I mean, Sally! Sally!'

'Probably a bit of Siamese blood in there somewhere,' Cindy said. 'They talk a lot.'

The Broomstick sniffed and turned to glare at Cindy. 'Don't you have work to do?' she demanded. 'If you've finished, you can leave the premises. We don't need workmen underfoot wasting time drinking cups of tea.'

'Chance would be a fine thing,' Sid complained. 'I haven't seen a cup of tea all day.'

'There's plenty for them to do.' Kelda appeared suddenly, intent on protecting her – or, rather, their – investment.

'Yes, indeed.' Annabel's grim tone let them know that

their relief was premature. 'They're going to wash the walls down now.'

'Hold on, hold on,' Sid bleated. 'It's lunchtime. Time for a sandwich and a pint of beer at the pub. We're entitled to a break.'

'We can send out for sandwiches,' Annabel said. If they ever got out, they might not come back – and certainly not in any state to do any work.

'I won't have them drinking in here!' the Broomstick snapped.

'I wouldn't dream of allowing it,' Annabel assured her, with the complacency of one who had already arranged her own supplies. 'He can have his cup of tea now.'

For good measure, the cat added her opinion.

'You can just shut up!' Sid shouted at the cat, the only being who had no power to control his fate. 'I've 'ad enough of you!'

'Now you've frightened her,' Tara protested, cuddling the cat, who had shrunk back against her. 'There was no need for that.' The cat grumbled agreement.

'Quiet, now,' Tara frowned. 'I told you, you're all right.'

The cat voiced her growing doubt.

'Doesn't that creature ever shut up?' The Broomstick glared at it.

'Don't you know?' Dangerously, Cindy caught the slip and challenged her. 'I thought the cat belonged here. You ought to be used to it.'

'I take care of Sally most of the time,' Tara said. Annabel noticed that her hand had slipped upwards and tightened around the cat's throat, ready to choke off any more sounds. 'Miss Stringer deals with the business side of things.'

The explanation had a double-pronged effect, Annabel noted with reluctant appreciation: it excused the Broomstick's blunder and, at the same time, it reinforced Tara's argument that she should be given custody of the cat. Arthur Arbuthnot had intended his cat to reside with someone it could love and trust.

The cat appeared to be having second thoughts. It wriggled uneasily and twisted round to look up at Tara, as though sensing a certain lack of enthusiasm in the people around her. She began to voice a question which was – quite literally – choked off.

The cat began to struggle in earnest, alarmed by the no longer friendly pressure on her throat.

'Now stop that!' Tara's grip tightened. The cat reacted instantly and instinctively.

'OOOOOOW!' Tara dropped the cat and stared incredulously at the thin line of blood welling up from a deep scratch along her forearm. 'That monster scratched me!'

The cat dashed down the hallway, uttering loud complaints of her own.

'Not all that fond of you, it seems,' the Broomstick said, with her usual grim relish.

Tara shot her a venomous glance and turned away but, before she could pursue the cat, there was a triumphant shout from one of the other rooms.

'Sally! Sally's back!' Neville came into view, holding aloft the cursing, spitting, captured cat.

'Back?' Cindy and Sid were paying far too much attention – especially for a pair of itinerant decorators. 'Back from where? Where's she been, then?'

'I believe you wanted your lunch.' The Broomstick eyed them without favour. 'I suggest you go and get it. Now!' She met Annabel's eyes and added implacably. 'All of you.'

Annabel knew when it was time for a strategic withdrawal. It was obvious that the family intended a Council of War. She could probably pick up the gist of it later. Meanwhile, it would not be a bad idea to accompany Cindy and Sid and make sure that they returned to do some more work.

She made only one mistake in her calculations: she met Sassy's worried eyes before she left.

Lunch was silent and sulky; they were the quietest table in the Bower. Sid disappeared into his pint of beer. Cindy slipped away to make a series of telephone calls, huddled in a corner with her mobile phone and nibbling on a sandwich. Kelda was almost too nervous to eat for fear of imminent criticism from Annabel, who was holding her fire waiting for a more opportune – and private – moment.

The atmosphere enveloping them all was still fraught when they returned to the apartment. Except for Sid, who was exceptionally relaxed. He must have managed to get his mug refilled, perhaps more than once, without being caught; he was humming a bawdy song under his breath. Too bawdy to be reprimanded for, because one would have to admit to knowing the words. One simply had to tighten one's lips and thank heaven he wasn't hanging wallpaper this afternoon.

The apartment seemed curiously deserted. Annabel found herself listening for the sound of a cat, but there wasn't a meow or a purr to be heard. Had they silenced Sassy already? Or was she sleeping? Possibly Tara had carried the cat down to Arthur Arbuthnot's quarters, into which she appeared to have moved since her fiancé's demise, the better to establish her claim to all or part of the estate. In possession of both cat and living quarters, Tara was increasingly a force to be reckoned with.

Except that she didn't have the cat. Not the real Sally. She had an unwitting imposter, who was quite probably named Sassy, the name Tara had let slip. A good name for a talkative cat. But, most unfortunately, that talkativeness could be an irritating trait to someone who did not know or understand cats. There was every reason to suspect that Sassy's days would be numbered, once the estate was safely in her custodian's possession.

Annabel fought off a feeling of impending doom. There wasn't room in the Knightsbridge flat for another cat. There wasn't. And, even if there were, how could she take such a talkative cat into protective custody? Sassy would announce her presence every step of the way out of the building.

No, this one would just have to take her chances. How much danger could she be in at the moment? The family had to have a live cat to present to Mr Pennyman on Monday – and had to keep it alive until the probate process was finished and the estate distributed. After that . . . ?

Uneasiness held Annabel in its grip and would not let her

go; it crawled along her spine and tickled the back of her neck. She looked around restlessly, went to stand in the doorway and listened intently.

Was there a faint mewl coming from behind one of the closed doors at the end of the corridor?

'I'll be right back,' she told the indifferent Cindy and Sid. 'I just want to check a few points with Dora Stringer.'

Kelda gave her an anxious look, but made no reply. Cindy and Sid met each other's eyes and turned to regard Kelda with some animosity.

As Annabel moved away, she thought she caught the faint echo of '. . . our money back . . .'. But that was Kelda's problem. Kelda had got herself into this and she was going to have to take the consequences.

Unusually, Dora Stringer's door was closed. Surely, she couldn't have lost all interest in what was going on outside? Or was it possible that she wanted some privacy for herself?

Gleefully, Annabel gave a perfunctory tap on the door and flung it open. 'Sorry to disturb you—' she began and stopped.

The office was empty. No Broomstick caught reading a romantic novel, or painting her toenails a lurid red, or even tippling from Arthur Arbuthnot's private stock. Ah, well, these disappointments come to us all.

A flutter of wings caught her attention as a pigeon alighted on the windowsill. The window behind the desk was wide open.

Sassy!

Annabel rushed to the window, frightening the pigeon back into the sky, and leaned out, terrified of seeing the small furry body lying on the pavement below.

The body she saw was much larger.

Annabel reeled back into the room, trying to choke off a scream, not very successfully. Her high-pitched strangled wail brought the others running.

'Oh great!' Cindy and Sid shouldered her aside to lean out of the window themselves. There was a series of clicking sounds, then Sid drew back into the room.

'You do it?' He focused on Annabel, who raised her hands to shield her face. 'Don't worry – she had it coming.' He turned to Cindy. 'Deal with this. I've got to get down there before the cops arrive.'

Screams and yelps of outrage along the corridor announced that the others were arriving and that Sid was crashing into them on his way to the lift. A plaintive sustained yowl was Sassy's disapproving contribution to the proceedings.

'Don't say anything,' Cindy said quickly. 'I want to get their unprompted reactions. I'll interview you later. Don't talk to any other media. This is our Exclusive. We'll make it worth your while. We might even get you off.'

'Don't be ridiculous!' Annabel snapped. 'I didn't do it. You know there wasn't time, we've been together all day.' When did it happen? How long had Dora Stringer's body lain there? It was on the quiet side of the building, around the corner from the main road. There wouldn't have been many passers-by.

'Pity. The deal could have been lucrative – for us both.' Cindy lost interest in her and turned to watch as the others swarmed into the office.

Where had they all come from so suddenly? They had obviously all been together. Neville was carrying Sassy, Tara clung to his arm. Zenia and Wystan were right behind them and Luther brought up the rear with a curiously smug expression on his face. Whatever they had been plotting obviously suited him right down to the ground.

'What is it? What's the matter?' Zenia glared at the two women standing by the window. 'Who was making that dreadful noise? Why?'

In the distance, there was the rising and falling shriek of an approaching siren and Annabel noticed for the first time that Kelda was missing. Had she called the police and were they arriving so soon? Her paparazzi friends wouldn't like that.

'Where's Dora?' Zenia was suddenly, sharply aware that someone else was missing. 'Why isn't she here? She was supposed to be getting those figures together for—' She broke off, realizing that Cindy was gesturing towards the open window with a strange expression on her face.

Sassy gave a muted strangulated wail. Annabel saw that Neville had his thumb and forefinger circled round her muzzle, holding her mouth shut. Sassy kept trying to pull her head away, twisting and squirming.

Zenia crossed to the window and leaned out. Her face was grim when she withdrew and turned to look at the others.

'That's Dora?' It was a question without hope of a contradiction. 'What happened?'

'I don't know,' Annabel said. 'The office was empty when I came in to ask her something. The window was open. I looked out and . . .'

Sassy gave another eerie wail.

'Too bad she didn't take that cat with her,' Zenia said. She looked from the cat to the open window. A scheming look came into her eyes.

Annabel could read her thoughts as clearly as though she were speaking them: *If we could show Pennyman the cat's body and say that Dora took it with her when she jumped, they couldn't blame us for it and we'd get the estate without any more nonsense.*

The telephone on the desk bleeped suddenly, startling them all, issuing a summons for a woman who was now beyond answering it. They stared at the telephone, reluctant to touch it.

'Hello?' Unexpectedly, Wystan moved forward, a step ahead of Luther, and murmured into the phone. 'I'm sorry, I'm afraid Miss Stringer isn't available at the moment. May I take a message?' He listened without expression. 'I see. Yes. I'll have . . . someone . . . get back to you later.' He looked shaken as he rang off, as though he had suddenly realized what he had said, as though the reality of the situation had just forced itself upon him.

When the telephone rang again, almost immediately, he made no effort to reach for it, but allowed Luther to take the call while he walked over to the window and leaned against the frame, breathing deeply.

'Right, Mark, we know,' Luther said quietly. 'Yes, awful. No, everyone's here. Yes,' he sighed heavily. 'Yes, I suppose you can send them right up when they arrive. Oh – ring

113

through first, of course, and give us a bit of warning.' He replaced the receiver slowly and looked at the others.

'Were you talking about the police?' Zenia demanded. 'Has some interfering busybody called the police?' She glared directly at Annabel.

'When would I have had the time?' Annabel fought back. 'I'd only just discovered the – what had happened – when you all came rushing in. You've been with me every moment since.'

'None of us knew anything about it,' Cindy said. 'There wasn't a sound – until Annabel screamed. Someone outside must have called the cops. Somebody who saw her go out the window . . . or found her on the pavement. You can't just leave a body sprawled on the pavement.'

'Indeed?' Zenia's face said that the only correct thing to do about a body sprawled on the pavement was to kick it into the gutter. None of this nonsense about ambulances and police.

'*Aaarrrrooooooeeeeoow*!' Sassy squirmed free of Neville's restraining hand and sent out a heartfelt yowl.

'Shut that beast up!' Zenia transferred her murderous gaze to the cat; another body she would like to see kicked into the gutter.

'Sorry, Mother, she's a slippery little thing. Here now – stop that. Ouch!' Neville yanked back his hand and Sassy leaped to the floor and darted down the hallway.

'Get her!' Zenia commanded. 'Lock her up somewhere! There'll be strangers in and out of here this afternoon. We don't want to lose this one, too.'

Too? Cindy's lifted head and narrowed eyes showed that the odd phrasing had not escaped her. Why such a fuss about the cat? There was more of a story developing here every minute.

Sassy's plaintive wail could be heard loudly, its meaning plain: she didn't like this place, she no longer liked these people, she wanted to go home. Home – did they hear her? – home! Now!

Annabel couldn't have agreed more.

The others looked towards the sound with varying degrees

of irritation. Sassy had been a popular substitute for Sally – until the moment she opened her mouth. Now she was rapidly losing every bit of popularity she had had.

'Doesn't it ever shut up?' Neville echoed his mother's complaint, frowning at the bite mark on his finger. 'Do you think —?' A more pressing concern occurred to him. 'Do you think I might need an anti-rabies shot? The thing bit me to the bone.'

'Oh, don't be so silly!' Tara's patience snapped. 'You're barely touched – she didn't even draw blood! It was just a little nip. And English cats don't have rabies! If you're afraid of her, I'll shut her in the study myself.' She started off after the cat, calling, 'Sa-ally . . . It's all right, Sally. Auntie Tara will take care of you.'

The telephone rang again. Luther picked it up. 'Already? Right. Thanks, Mark.'

'They're on their way?' Neville twitched. 'Up here? Now? Why?'

'They'll have questions.' Luther shrugged. 'Probably they'll want someone to go down and identify the body. All the customary things. A woman has died, they can't just ignore it.'

'What questions?' Wystan looked to his wife unhappily. 'What can we possibly tell them?'

'Poor, dear, *tragic* Dora!' Zenia swept them all with a basilisk look, clearly issuing orders. 'She always seemed so sure of herself, so efficient, so in control. How were we to know that she would feel that she could not bear to go on living without Arthur?'

13

Sally and Salvatore came running to welcome her as she turned the key in the lock, swung the door open and stepped into the Knightsbridge flat. Their little noses were working overtime, twitching and sniffing, their eyes focused on her basket, they both began to purr.

'I stopped to pick up a roast chicken,' Annabel told them. 'I can see I made the right choice.' She hoped there was enough for all of them, but she didn't particularly care. Right now, a martini and a couple of aspirins were as much as she felt able to face.

The cats followed her into the kitchen and watched her set the basket on the table. She opened one side of the hinged lid, gently lifted out the unconscious Sassy and laid her on the table beside the basket. Both cats leaped up to investigate.

'If you wake her, you'll be sorry,' Annabel warned them. 'She's pretty noisy. I had to spike her milk with my martini to knock her out so that I could smuggle her out of the flat. I do hope you're all going to get along together, there's nowhere else I could take her.'

Salvatore raised his head and beamed at Annabel, his affable leer becoming more affable than ever. Another pretty little female *and* a large roasted chicken. He head-butted Annabel's arm fondly. What a splendid establishment this woman ran!

Sally wasn't so sure. She circled Sassy's still form cautiously and ignored the blandishments of roast chicken. She seemed profoundly uneasy and, with every sniff at the recumbent form, she became more unsettled. She gave Annabel a questioning look.

'I wish I knew,' Annabel said wearily. 'I wish I knew what you want to know – and I wish I could explain it to you and be sure you understood. But right now it's all too much for me.'

Hoping she wasn't being foolish in turning her back on the cats on the table, she went to the fridge to pull out the martini pitcher and pour a generous one into the chilled glass. When, after a long swallow, she turned back to the table, the situation seemed to be settling down.

Sally was industriously washing Sassy's face. Salvatore was dividing his attention between the two females and the carrier bag in which the roast chicken still reposed. He met Annabel's eyes and his loud purr rasped out hopefully.

'Yes, yes,' Annabel said. 'I know you must be hungry. But, if you think you've had a long day, you should have seen mine.'

It had been an endless afternoon; she took another gulp of her martini. The police questioning had been repetitive and tedious. Fortunately, she and her team had been able to alibi each other, thanks to her determination not to let them out of her sight. When, at last, the police had dismissed them in order to concentrate on a determined questioning of the family, Annabel no longer had fears that her team would desert her. Their story had come alive, so to speak, with the Broomstick's death, and it would take dynamite to keep them away from the premises now.

Annabel had delayed her departure until the others had left and the police were fully occupied with the family. Then there had been the problem of getting Sassy to safety. Finding her saucer of milk and doctoring it, then standing over her while she drank it and, still mumbling, fell asleep. The harrowing long tiptoe down the hallway, hoping no door would open suddenly or that Sassy would wake and start talking again, had taken more out of her nervous system than she cared to acknowledge. The outside world had never looked so good.

Salvatore head-butted her again, a bit tetchily this time,

reminding her that she was awfully slow about carving the chicken.

'Sorry,' she apologized. 'I was lost in thought.' She wrestled with the clingfilm swathing the chicken until it gave way suddenly, smearing her hands with grease.

'Ooops!' Absently, she began licking her fingers. Salvatore thrust himself forward urgently. He might be a rough diamond, but he was a gentleman – no lady need ever lick her chicken-greasy fingers when he was around. Allow him! The rasping tickling little tongue made her laugh aloud and brightened her spirits immeasurably.

Sally abandoned the semi-comatose Sassy and strolled over to see what was going on. She found a grease blob on the table and tidied it up. Both cats, Annabel noticed, were inching their way closer to the large fragrant chicken.

'Thank you, that's enough.' She pulled her hand back and gently pushed both eager heads away. 'Just you wait a minute. I don't want this chicken torn apart. We'll serve it in a civilized manner.'

Two heads turned towards her in injured dignity. They wouldn't dream of having it any other way. Little pink tongues swiped across anticipating lips. For an instant, sharp little fangs gleamed disconcertingly.

'Yes, yes, I'm hurrying,' Annabel placated. She tried to fend off the eager cats while briskly carving off large chunks of meat. Every once in a while, she directed a slice on to her own plate; it was her supper, too.

It was amazing, the way they could eat and purr at the same time. Smiling at the two happy cats, she reached out for a nibble from her own dish and encountered a sleek little head.

'That's my plate!' she protested.

'*Mmmrrumph-uumph!*' Revived by the scent and taste of the succulent chicken, Sassy was not above speaking with her mouth full. '*Grrr . . .*' she added, for good measure, just in case anyone was thinking of trying to take that chicken away from her.

Sally and Salvatore looked up briefly, but returned to their meals when they saw there was not going to be a fight.

'Sorry to disappoint you,' Annabel murmured, 'but there's enough for all of us. That's why I got the largest one they had.'

Sassy came up for air, blinked and shook her head. Despite the chicken, she was clearly not a completely happy cat. She shook her head again, possibly it was aching.

'Bit of a hangover?' Annabel was sympathetic. 'Sorry about that, but I had to keep you quiet. If they'd caught us, you'd never have got out of that house.' *Not alive, that is.* Still uncertain about how much cats understood, Annabel felt it was more discreet not to worry Sassy with that unpleasant possibility.

Worry Sassy? Annabel, what are you thinking about?

On the rare occasions when her conscience surfaced, it took on the voice of her old nanny, disappointed in her and disapproving of any scheme she had in mind. *It's all very well to save the cats, but a woman died this afternoon. There was no one to save her.*

And no one would want to, Annabel answered her nanny-conscience rebelliously. But the seed had been planted.

Perhaps that's the saddest thing of all. No friends and no future, once the only employer who'd put up with her died. No wonder she chose suicide —

'NO!' Annabel said out loud. The cats looked at her askance. Nanny disappeared back into the deepest recesses of Annabel's mind, where she usually lay dormant. 'NO!'

No, the Broomstick was not the sort to kill herself just because Arthur Arbuthnot had died. Especially not since he had left her a tidy inheritance. Dora Stringer would not have to look for another employer, she could have retreated to a country cottage, gone on a trip around the world, or done whatever she wanted to do. She would not have chosen to dive out of the window.

It was Zenia who had proposed the suicide theory to the police, backed immediately by her husband and son. Even Tara had been quick to agree that a poor distraught secretary with, possibly, a secret passion for her employer, might have taken such a desperate step in a moment of temporary insanity. Luther had charitably suggested that it was equally possible that Dora might have been leaning out of the window for a breath of air – or possibly to chase the pigeons away – and overbalanced and fell. Misadventure, was his summing up of the situation.

They were all lying. Did the police realize that?

Why should they? They had no reason to connect the two deaths in any sinister manner. A man had died; his spinster secretary had committed suicide. These things happen.

Only someone who had been there from the beginning, who had been on the scene when Arthur Arbuthnot had . . . collapsed . . . was in a position to think the unthinkable.

Murder . . . double murder. Someone had stabbed Arthur Arbuthnot in the back and left him dying in his office. Someone had pushed Dora Stringer out of that window. Undoubtedly the same someone. Someone familiar, someone trusted, someone able to get close enough to the victims to . . . to make them the victims.

Kelda had not been out of her sight for more than a moment all afternoon. The thought rose to the surface of Annabel's consciousness, bringing with it a rush of relief. She now acknowledged the suspicion that had been nagging at her for days.

Kelda had rushed to administer first aid to the fallen tycoon. Kelda – who worked surrounded by the potentially deadly tools of her trade: sharp chisels, sharper knives and blades of all sizes, wallpaper shears, scissors . . .

Kelda – who hated Arthur Arbuthnot for the way he had treated Mark. It would have been so easy for her to have slipped a knife in and out of his back while she heaved his body about under the guise of trying to save his life . . .

A gentle insistent head-butting against her arm and a querulous murmur of complaint from her other side, brought Annabel back to the present. She looked down into Sally's eyes, bright, sad, old as time.

Sally had been witness to the first murder, taking the sudden opportunity to slip into the forbidden territory on the heels of the killer. A witness who could never identify or testify against the killer.

120

Sassy began to complain afresh, looking down at Annabel's erstwhile plate; her complaint seemed to have something to do with the fact that here was all this lovely chicken and she didn't feel well enough to finish it. She shook her head unhappily.

Salvatore was instantly at her side. Another damsel in distress – how fortunate that he was on hand to assist. He gave her a reassuring lick, lowered his head over the plate and made short work of the chicken.

Sassy did not appear to find this entirely satisfactory. She muttered something that did not sound quite ladylike, but did not seem able to take the matter further.

'Go and lie down,' Annabel advised her. 'Sleep it off and you'll feel a lot better.'

It was Sally who was the first to yawn, give herself a quick wash of paws and face – just a lick and a promise, really – and curl up into a soft purring ball of fur.

Salvatore cleaned every plate and looked around hopefully.

Sassy voiced one final tirade, but her heart wasn't in it. Flicking her ears and muttering uneasily, she hunched down, tucked her tail tightly around her body and closed her eyes. Even so, the discontented muttering continued.

Annabel had absently begun pulling shreds of meat off the chicken carcase and nibbling them as she observed the cats. Now, as she paused with a chunk of chicken just torn off, she felt a gentle tug and looked down to find Salvatore pulling at the other end of the chunk.

'It *is* good, isn't it?' She relinquished it to him and bemusedly pulled off another chunk which, somehow or other, he also got. His deep throbbing purr encouraged her to spoil him. She gave him another chunk and then another.

'This is the last one,' she said finally. 'I can't stand here and hand-feed you all night.'

He didn't see why not. He rubbed his head along her hand coaxingly and she softened.

'Well, perhaps just one —'

The doorbell pealed sharply.

Annabel froze. Who on earth —? She wasn't expecting

121

anyone. She didn't want to see anyone. Some stranger must have pressed the wrong button by mistake.

Annabel ambled over to the closed-circuit-TV screen above the entryphone and was horrified to see Tara waving frantically at the camera. She recoiled as though Tara could also see her. The doorbell rang again, Tara began exaggeratedly mouthing something at the camera. Sassy lifted her head and gave an unhappy little mew.

She couldn't let anyone in here! Annabel stared unbelievingly at the screen as one of the other residents came along, inserted his key in the lock and stepped back, beaming, to allow Tara to precede him into the entrance hall. Men! There were notices on every floor warning residents that they should not admit anyone into the building who was not known to them personally. It seemed a pretty face was introduction enough. If burglars came in pairs of pretty females, some men would undoubtedly help them carry their loot down the stairs and hold the car door open for them.

Meanwhile, Tara was on her way up. Was it possible to pretend she wasn't home? Too late, Annabel realized that she had not drawn the curtains. Tara would have seen the lights and known that she was here.

Annabel gathered up the startled cats and bundled them into the bedroom, tossing them on the bed. Sassy raised her voice in protest and Annabel hastily rearranged them: Sassy on the bottom of the pile, the other two on top of her.

'Keep her quiet,' she pleaded, and tossed the quilt over them as a further muffling measure. She closed the door firmly behind her, wishing that it had a lock, and also that there was not an inch gap at the bottom where the carpet had flattened down. How much sound could escape through that?

The inner doorbell shrilled. Annabel caught up the cats' dishes and dumped them in the sink, then advanced slowly towards the door, looking around. Was there anything else that might give the game away?

'Annabel! Annabel!' The doorbell and then a persistent

knocking reinforced the call. 'Annabel! I know you're in there! It's me, Tara. Let me in!'

Were the cat hairs terribly noticeable? Possibly not to someone who was not looking for them. But what about the frayed material at the end of the sofa where someone had sharpened little claws too enthusiastically? Again, possibly not – unless to eyes searching for evidence.

'Annabel! Annabel!' The voice sharpened imperiously. 'I *must* talk to you. Let me in!' The bell rang again, the knocking intensified and an indignant muffled howl sounded from the bedroom. This was no place for a cat with a hangover.

'Just a minute—' Annabel called. 'I'm coming!' Desperate measures were needed. She flew into the kitchen, sloshed some milk into a saucer and recklessly added gin. The cats looked up expectantly as she entered the bedroom.

'Here!' She set the saucer on the floor beside the bed, caught up Sassy and put her on the floor beside the saucer, dunking her nose into the potent contents. 'Hair of the dog – if you'll pardon the expression.' She paused to make sure that Sassy was lapping it; with any luck, it would put her back to sleep. Sally and Salvatore leaped to the floor and began circling the saucer with interest, ever alert for new gourmet experiences.

Annabel closed the bedroom door firmly again, shook herself, and gave a final sweeping glance around the sitting room.

'Annabel! Are you all right?'

'Sorry.' Annabel crossed and opened the door with an innocent expression. 'I'm afraid you caught me in the loo.'

'Oh!' It was the only explanation that was both acceptable and too awkward to pursue. 'I'm sorry. I should have – I mean, how was I to – Er, sorry.' Thoroughly wrong-footed, Tara advanced into the sitting room and changed the subject. 'How charming.'

'Yes, isn't it? Not quite my taste but' – Annabel played her trump card – 'I'm subletting from Lady Cosgreave

123

so, of course, I can't change anything. Dinah is so sensitive.'

'Of course,' Tara agreed cordially. Her cool assessing gaze swept the room and dismissed everything in it. 'You would have done it up so much better.'

'I'd like to think so,' Annabel murmured modestly, wondering just what Tara was up to. At least she did not appear to be in search of missing felines; despite her words, she was showing no real interest in her surroundings.

'Oh, but you would!' Tara gazed earnestly into Annabel's face. 'You're so clever – and so talented. I can't wait to see Arthur's pokey old apartment when you've finished with it.'

'How kind of you to say so.' Annabel had always been wary of flattery and this was being laid on with the proverbial trowel.

'No, no, you deserve it. You've already done wonders with the place.' Uninvited, Tara sank down in a corner of the sofa and placed her handbag beside her feet, clearly settling in for a long stay.

Already listening for any betraying sounds from behind the bedroom door, Annabel discovered a new worry: the catnip mouse the cats had been playing with was lying temporarily abandoned between the sofa leg and Tara's handbag. The instant Tara looked down, she would discover it.

'How about a drink?' Annabel asked urgently. 'What would you like?'

'Why, thank you.' Tara seemed a bit startled at the fervency of the invitation. 'Whatever you're having will be fine.'

'Martinis,' Annabel said firmly, adding, 'I make them rather strong, I'm afraid.'

'I don't think I'll mind that.' Tara gave a little shudder and leaned back against the cushions. 'This has been quite a day.'

'It certainly has,' Annabel agreed. 'Why don't you just close your eyes and rest a moment? I'll be right back with the drinks.' She waited until Tara had obediently closed her eyes before going into the kitchen. With any luck, Tara wouldn't move for a few minutes, she looked completely exhausted. That must have been quite a session with the police. But why should Tara come to see her right now? Surely, anything could have waited until morning.

There was one generous measure left in the pitcher. Annabel poured it for Tara and filled her own glass with water. This might be a moment when she needed all her wits about her.

'Here we are.' As she handed the drink to Tara, she gave the catnip mouse a brisk kick. But she misjudged the force of her kick and saw the mouse go skittering under the sofa and come out the other side. She heard the faint thump as it hit the bedroom door.

'Oh, thank you.' Tara took a sip and shuddered. 'Delicious,' she lied. 'Umm, do you think I might have a bit of ice in it?'

'I'll get some.' Annabel was used to this reaction, practically everyone she knew insisted on watering down their drinks; at least, they did when she had mixed them. 'Wimps' was the word that sprang to mind.

Although perhaps Tara shouldn't be included in that category. Despite her request, the level of liquid in her glass had descended noticeably when Annabel returned immediately with two ice cubes in another glass.

'Oh, thank you.' Tara seemed surprised when Annabel tipped them into her glass, perhaps she had forgotten her request. 'Actually, this, um, rather grows on one the way it is.'

'I've always found that,' Annabel agreed absently, wondering how long Tara intended keeping up the social chit-chat before coming to the point.

Tara appeared to be in no hurry. She looked around the room again, more carefully this time, and Annabel flinched as her gaze rested on the shredded upholstery on the arm of the wing chair, where sharp little claws had been sharpened even more. She would have to do something about that before Dinah returned and saw it.

125

And hadn't Dinah muttered something about no pets being allowed under the terms of her lease or Dinah would risk forfeiting the lease? It didn't bear thinking about and Annabel tried to put it out of her mind.

'What did the police have to say?' Annabel attempted to jolt Tara out of the trance she seemed to have fallen into.

'Police?' Tara looked so vague she might never have heard of such an organization.

'Police,' Annabel insisted. 'You know. All those strange people in dark-blue uniforms who were milling around the place when I left.'

'Oh. Yes.' Tara took another sip. 'The police. They were really very understanding . . . eventually. These things happen. They must see so much of them, poor dears. A terrible job, really, but they've gone now. I think they're satisfied. They haven't sealed up any of the rooms, or anything. That was what I wanted to tell you. It's all right to come back to work as usual in the morning.'

'Is it?' Annabel looked at her coldly. That message could quite easily have been conveyed over the telephone. 'It may have escaped your attention, but tomorrow is Saturday.'

'Exactly! That's why I wanted to see you tonight.' Tara faced her triumphantly. 'Saturday is when you designers trawl the street markets for all your exciting finds, isn't it? Oh' – she cut off any protest Annabel might be about to make – 'I know you have your favourite suppliers and they give you special discounts and all that, but the real profit is in the little things you can pick up in street markets and junk shops, isn't it?'

Annabel opened her mouth, but nothing came out. She was beginning to feel a bit dizzy.

'So I thought you might be willing to let me trail along with you tomorrow—' Tara finally got around to the purpose of her visit. 'I'll be very quiet and won't interfere with your bargaining. I'll just listen and learn. And, maybe, you could indicate some of the things you want for the flat and I could buy them myself – and resell them to you later.' She paused and watched Annabel intently to see how she would respond to this proposal.

'At a profit, I presume.' Annabel found her voice, although it was a weak one. She had never had any intention of trawling street markets or bargaining with suppliers; she had planned to leave all that to Kelda.

'Naturally,' Tara said expectantly. 'You can't tell me it isn't done all the time. One of my friends collected a nice little nest egg from the interior designer when her husband had his offices completely renovated. There's nothing wrong with it, it's just business.'

'Er . . . quite,' Annabel agreed cautiously, her stunned mind trying to cope with this unexpected development. 'The only thing is' – she extemporized wildly – 'I'm going away for the weekend. Visiting friends in the country. Early train in the morning. I won't be doing any shopping at all, just relaxing and unwinding. Perhaps we could do something Monday.'

'But the best street markets are on weekends,' Tara protested. 'Besides, there's the appointment with Mr Pennyman on Monday. He wants to meet the cat.'

The cats! Annabel had forgotten them completely. Automatically, she checked the bedroom door – and froze in horror.

The door was still closed, but a little dappled brown paw had snaked out beneath it and was raking the carpet, trying to capture its catnip mouse. If Tara turned around and saw that –

'Perhaps Tuesday, then?' Annabel offered, watching a tiny claw connect with the mouse's nose and then pull the toy sharply up against the door. Surely it was her imagination that the toy made a soft thud as it hit the door?

'Tuesday . . .' Tara mused. 'That's really not very satisfactory.

Abruptly, Annabel realized that, depending on the decision of Mr Pennyman and the responses of the family, Tara might no longer be part of the entourage on Tuesday. There was an underlying suspicion that she certainly wouldn't be if Zenia had anything to do with it. If she was unacceptable as a spouse for Zenia's nephew, she was twice as unacceptable as a future daughter-in-law. Perhaps Tara couldn't be blamed for attempting to feather whatever nest she still possessed.

'Oh, dear.' Tara gave a deep sigh. Suddenly she looked small and forlorn. 'I *had* hoped we could come to some arrangement.' She set down her glass and leaned forward to pick up her handbag. In another moment, she would stand and turn to face the door – the bedroom door, as well as the door to the foyer.

The telephone shrilled suddenly, startling them both. Even the little paw was withdrawn quickly, abandoning the catnip mouse to its fate. There was a waiting silence, broken only by the persistent ringing of the telephone. Instinctively, Annabel felt that it boded no good.

'I don't suppose it could be for me,' Tara prodded delicately. 'Although I did mention that I might drop in on you . . .'

Trapped, Annabel crossed to the telephone and lifted the receiver. 'Hello?'

'It's about time!' Xanthippe's strident tones set her ears ringing. 'What the hell are you playing at? Why haven't you called me? Why haven't –'

'Sorry, wrong number.' Annabel broke the connection, but did not replace the receiver; she set it down beside the cradle and turned back to Tara. 'Wrong number.'

'Oh?' Tara raised an eyebrow. 'How tedious for you.' She looked at the unreplaced receiver. 'Do you get many of them?'

'Too many,' Annabel said promptly. 'Once they start, they keep coming. Wires crossed, or something. The only thing to do is to put the phone out of action for an hour or so. That discourages them.'

'I see.' Tara looked as though she were seeing a manifestation of some hitherto unrecorded eccentricity.

Behind her, the little paw slid out from under the door again and began groping for its catnip mouse.

'Look—' Annabel said desperately. 'Suppose I ring my friends and tell them I'll catch an afternoon train? That will give us the morning. We can do Camden Passage and perhaps Portobello Road.'

'Oh, wonderful!' Tara's face cleared.

'It will mean an early start,' Annabel warned. 'I'll meet you at the Angel tube station at seven a.m. Outside, if it's a fine day; inside, if it's raining.'

'Seven?' Tara gasped.

'And that's a bit late.' Looking beyond Tara, Annabel saw a second brown paw appear beneath the bedroom door, at such an angle that it had to be another cat joining in the game. And was that a faintly complaining mew in the background? 'The dealers all get there at the crack of dawn.'

'I suppose they do.' Tara's eyelids flickered – had she heard that mew?

'Sorry.' Annabel cleared her throat, giving a credible imitation of a cat's cry, and remained standing. 'Well, you'll want an early night, if you have to get up so early in the morning,' she hinted strongly.

'Yes. Yes, you're right. I must be going.' Tara stood and seemed to hesitate.

'Yes, you must. I mean, such an early start. Sorry, but it can't be helped.' Annabel closed in behind her, preventing her from turning around, and herded her towards the door.

As Tara moved ahead, Annabel saw the cluster of brown cat hairs clinging to the fawn silk skirt. Too late, Annabel remembered that Salvatore loved to curl up in the corner where Tara had been sitting.

Annabel stretched out a hand – and withdrew it quickly. To brush off the hairs would be to call attention to them. She could only hope that they fell off on Tara's way home. Or that Tara would assume that she had picked them up somewhere in the Regent's Park flat, where Sally had resided long enough to leave little souvenirs of her presence.

'I'll see you in the morning,' Tara said, as Annabel opened the door for her. 'The Angel at seven.'

'That's right! Good night!' Annabel did not care if she

seemed to slam the door upon her departing guest with undue haste. She leaned against it limply for a moment, then pushed herself away and headed for the kitchen and a well-earned martini.

14

Annabel might have been able to ignore the alarm clock in the morning – the temptation was strong – but she could not ignore the cats. Salvatore immediately prowled over to investigate the thing making strange noises which suggested something birdlike and edible might be hiding inside and promptly knocked it to the floor where it continued to tweetle. Sassy raised her head and began a dialogue with the strange object, scolding and berating it and finally dropping to the floor to join Salvatore as he began batting it about.

Only Sally seemed to feel that it was all too much effort; she snuggled closer to Annabel and went back to sleep.

'Sorry,' Annabel said, dislodging her, 'but I'm afraid it's time to rise and shine – for me, at any rate.' Sally gave a perfunctory purr and rolled into the warm hollow left by Annabel's body. The other cats followed Annabel into the kitchen.

Sally had come a long way from the alley, Annabel reflected, glancing back at the sleeping cat, now serenely confident that there would always be food available with no need to rush and compete with the other cats for it.

Salvatore, on the other hand, was still new enough to the experience to be enchanted by it. He hurled himself against Annabel's legs, twining in and out around her ankles, purring loudly as she filled his food dish. Breakfast! And he had had dinner last night! What a world of luxury this was! And he was thriving on it, Annabel noticed, his coat was smoother and shinier, his eyes brighter, even his little snaggle-fang seemed whiter and not quite so protruding. No doubt about it, Salvatore was flourishing.

Sassy advanced to her own dish and examined it critically, then voiced a complaint. She sniffed at it, which brought further dissatisfaction. She looked at Annabel accusingly and made a few pointed comments. When nothing happened, she reluctantly sampled the offering, then launched into a tirade.

'I'm sorry, I know it's not what you're used to – but I don't know what that is.' Annabel stooped to caress the indignant little creature. 'I wish I did.'

Sassy leaned into the caress for a moment, closing her eyes briefly, then opening them again and looking up. She let out a small wail of distress as she saw Annabel's face rather than the loved one she wanted.

'I know, I know,' Annabel soothed. 'You're someone's darling pet and you miss her – and she must be frantic wondering what's happened to you. Damn that selfish Tara —'

Tara! She had nearly forgotten that she was supposed to be meeting Tara and it was quarter to seven already. She'd have to skip her own breakfast, but she could pick up the No. 19 bus in Sloane Street and it would carry her direct to the Angel. The route went through the heart of the West End but, at this hour of the morning, there shouldn't be much traffic. With luck, she wouldn't be terribly late and, if there were any delays, Tara would just have to wait. Serve her right if she did. Too bad it wasn't pouring.

Annabel looked sadly at the forlorn little feline, callously catnapped to serve Tara's selfish ends. The other two cats had been waifs and strays, but such a pretty and rather spoiled little madam would never have been allowed to stray far from her doting owner. Tara had probably picked her up in the Regent's Park area, perhaps even lifted her off her own doorstep.

'*Mmmrr . . . rrreoow . . .*' Sassy gave herself a little shake and slowly began to nibble at her unsatisfactory breakfast, still mumbling complaints.

'I'll do my best to get you home,' Annabel promised her.

Tara was waiting behind the glass entrance of the tube

station, although it wasn't actually raining, just grey and a bit misty. She had the anxious expression and large empty shopping bag of the hopeful bargain-hunter.

Annabel relaxed a little. Perhaps Tara was genuinely intent on exploring the possibilities of earning something extra on the side, or perhaps even looking into a new career as an interior designer.

Or possibly – a more disquieting thought came to Annabel – Tara was the killer and wished to find out how much Annabel knew or suspected about the recent deadly events she had, if not quite witnessed, been in close conjunction to.

That new suspicion made for a slightly less than auspicious start to their expedition.

'We turn along here,' Annabel directed, neatly sidestepping so that Tara was beside her rather than a couple of steps behind her. She realized that she did not want to turn her back on anyone from the highly suspect group that had surrounded Arthur Arbuthnot.

Idiot! Idiot! Annabel silently berated herself. She had been so caught up in rescuing the cats that she had allowed herself to keep forgetting that there was a sinister reason for their plight. It was highly unlikely that the deaths of Arthur Arbuthnot and Dora Stringer had been accidental; even less likely that they were unconnected. Someone had been responsible – and that someone might be here with her right now, watching for an opportunity to make her the third victim.

Had she carelessly condemned herself to a jolly morning's shopping with a murderess?

The first wave of early-risers were thronging the passageways, bright and alert for bargains. Surely she was safe in the midst of such a crowd. Only . . . their attention was centred on the stalls and all the enticing wares on display. They weren't wasting any attention on the passing throng – they *were* the passing throng and, after they had passed, a body could be found lying in a dark corner and no one would have noticed a thing.

Except, Annabel cheered up slightly, for the stallholders.

They were keeping sharp eyes on everyone, alert to the ever-present threat from shoplifters. While they smiled and chatted with prospective customers, they watched the people beside and behind their punter. It was the oldest trick in the trade to distract a stallholder with the prospect of a large sale while a cohort quietly lifted valuables from the other end of the stall. No, they would be keeping watch; they would see and register any sinister movements or strange behaviour.

Of course, by the time they got out from behind the stall and into the passageway, a person could be dead. It didn't take long to shoot a gun or wield a knife – and the shock of witnessing such an event held spectators motionless in shock for seconds, long seconds during which a killer could escape. And it was well known that subsequent descriptions never agreed.

'Over here!' Tara had no qualms about turning her back to Annabel. She wormed her way between a group of French tourists and a gaggle of Italian tourists to stand transfixed before a window full of ornate items of furniture. 'Look at that! Isn't it divine?'

Unsure of what she was being called upon to admire, Annabel gazed without enthusiasm at the entire display. 'Ummm,' she said noncommittally.

'Oh, yes.' Tara nodded wisely, interpreting her response. 'One should never seem too interested, should one?'

'You're learning,' Annabel said, quite as though it had been her intention to teach that lesson. She could now see that Tara's admiring gaze was fixed on a large glass-and-inlaid-wood cabinet at the back of the window.

'Don't you think,' self-preservation compelled her to add, 'that it would be better to concentrate on small, easily portable objects today? We can always come back for the big stuff later.'

'Oh . . . I suppose you're right,' Tara agreed reluctantly.

'I am.' Annabel nudged her away from the window and the tempting – but enormous – items with relief. If this whole thing fell through – as well it might, depending on what happened on Monday – she did not wish to be left with an oversize, overexpensive Edwardian cabinet on her hands.

'What about' – Tara brightened – 'jewellery?'

'Small enough,' Annabel agreed. 'Portable enough, but . . .' She dashed Tara's hopes. 'A bit hard to justify as *objets d'art* for an apartment, wouldn't you say? More for personal adornment only, although I have seen some earrings big enough to use as curtain pulls.'

'Yes . . .' Tara relinquished the idea with a sigh and allowed herself to be led over to a stall piled with bobbles, bibelots and small statues.

This time Tara was unenthusiastic, while Annabel pounced on a spray of wooden roses, carved in full bloom and gilded. If they proved unsuitable for the flat, she could always give them to Dinah. The price was right, too; so right that she was afraid to haggle, in case it had been mispriced. Perhaps it had fallen off a lorry, part of the spoils of a burglary. That was always a hazard of street markets. However . . .

Several stalls later, Annabel was just getting into her stride when Tara caved in.

'Can't we stop and have a cup of coffee?' Tara's voice took on a fretful note. 'I didn't have any breakfast. We had to meet so early, there wasn't time.'

'I suppose we can take a few minutes out.' Annabel was glad that Tara had raised the subject first. Her own stomach had been complaining softly for some time. 'That looks rather a jolly café over there.'

Annabel managed to acquire one of the sidewalk tables by dint of shamelessly staking out a young couple who were nearly finished and standing beside their table, staring at every mouthful they consumed. In no time at all, they had hurriedly choked down the last bit of croissant, gulped a final mouthful of coffee and departed hastily.

'That's better.' Annabel sank down into a chair that was still warm and pushed the dirty crockery to one side of the table as a strong indication to the waitress that the present occupants had not been the ones to dirty them. She looked around with approval, she really ought to do this more often. Perhaps, if she carried on with this interior-decorating lark, she would.

The pavements were thronged with happy, jostling crowds,

all enjoying the mild weather and the vast array of goods on display. Local people and tourists, young and old and –

Annabel twisted around in her chair, caught by a movement at the edge of her vision. A wheelchair. Of course, there would be wheelchair-users among the crowd – and a good thing, too. As many places as possible had wheelchair access these days, but the pavements were still the most accessible of all. But ... wasn't there something disquietingly familiar about that barely glimpsed figure in that wheelchair? And why had he disappeared so quickly when she turned?

Tara had begun rummaging in her shopping bag, trying to rearrange the bulky and knobbly objects she had been buying so enthusiastically, caught up in the Saturday-morning madness that can be contagious in street markets.

'Oh, dear,' Tara said. 'I hope I don't need another bag.' She pulled out a silver candelabra, already sliding free of its newspaper wrapping, twisted the paper tighter and slid it upright along the side of the bag.

'Much better to keep to one bag,' Annabel agreed. 'Lumber yourself with too many bags to carry and you risk losing some.' She watched Tara's frantic efforts to arrange everything more compactly with a pleasant feeling of complacency. She had managed to avoid buying anything but the carved roses herself, while scoring Brownie points because Tara assumed that she was holding back on the bargains to give Tara a chance.

'Damn!' Tara pulled a brass Art-Nouveau picture frame from the depths of the shopping bag, dislodging other parcels on its way. Tara pushed them back frantically, not noticing that a pale blue strip of suede was still caught in a protruding curlicue. Tara stuffed everything down indiscriminately, looking exhausted and uncomfortable, grimacing as she noticed that her hands were grimy and streaked with black where the newsprint had rubbed off on them.

'The ladies' room is inside at the back,' Annabel told her helpfully. 'I spotted it while we were waiting for the table.'

'You're sure you wouldn't like to go along first?' Tara offered anxiously as the waitress bore down on them.

'I'll stay and watch the shopping and order for you. Coffee? And those Danish pastries look awfully good.'

'Would you?' Tara was properly grateful. 'Coffee and Danish would be fine. Thanks so much.'

'Not at all.' Annabel waved her away, trying to look benevolent and not as though she had no intention of risking her unguarded cup of coffee in any proximity to dear Tara who, so far as she was concerned, was guilty until proved innocent.

Annabel gave their orders and the waitress departed briskly. And while she was thinking about things being unguarded . . . Annabel glanced around casually to make sure that she was unobserved, then, even more casually, leaned over and peered into Tara's shopping bag.

Yes, there along the side was the thin, pale-blue suede strip she had noticed earlier. A curious item for Tara to be carrying around but, equally, something that could have easily been overlooked in the stress of coping with more urgent considerations.

Annabel slid her hand down into the shopping bag and snaffled the blue suede band, coiling it neatly into her palm before withdrawing her hand.

She was just in time. When she looked up, both Tara and the waitress bearing a tray with their order were converging on the table. She opened her handbag and thrust the band into its depths – no time to investigate her prize. (She hoped it wasn't just a discarded Alice band, but surely Tara's head was bigger than that.) She pulled out a handkerchief and blew her nose loudly, then looked up with a feigned start of surprise.

'That was quick!' She pushed her handkerchief back into the handbag, hiding her ill-gotten gain with it.

'Was it?' Tara smiled vaguely and resumed her seat. The waitress set coffee and Danish before them and bustled off to another table.

'Mmm . . .' Tara wasted no time in taking a sip of her coffee and sinking gleaming white teeth – which suddenly seemed a bit fanglike – into the luscious apricot-topped pastry. 'I needed this.'

'You're sure you're not getting overtired?' Annabel asked solicitously. 'You're looking a bit pale.' She knew she was on a safe wicket there. Even in this day and age, no young woman minded being thought pale and, by implication, interesting.

'I *am* a bit tired,' Tara admitted. 'I haven't been sleeping well lately. So much has been happening. So much to worry about . . .'

'A very upsetting time,' Annabel sympathized. 'Two deaths, coming so close together. And,' she added slyly, 'the police involved now. There'll have to be an inquest on Miss Stringer, I suppose. Too awkward for you all.'

'That woman was nothing but trouble!' Tara snapped. 'It's just like her to kill herself in a way that leaves everybody with more problems than ever. Why couldn't she have just gone off and jumped into the Thames, if she had to do any jumping?'

'It could have been an accident,' Annabel pointed out. 'As Luther said, she might have leaned out of the window for some reason and overbalanced.' Annabel carefully refrained from any mention of the word 'pushed' – in her opinion, a more likely explanation.

'Oh, what does it matter?' Tara slumped in her chair. 'She's dead – and she took a lot of the secrets of Arthur's business with her. There are probably some foreign accounts we'll never be able to trace now. Luther was training up well, but he still had a lot to learn.'

'Actually, I was thinking more of the emotional toll on all of you,' Annabel said. 'I was just working there and I've found it fairly shattering. But you knew these people personally. It must be —'

'Arthur, yes.' Tara's eyes clouded briefly. 'Oh, I know what people think – and it's true it wasn't a great wild romance like first love or, even, infatuation – but we had something going and it might—' Tara broke off and her face hardened.

'Anyway, that's finished,' she said bitterly. 'And I'm not going to pretend I was devastated by Dora Stringer's death. It's too bad, of course, but she never liked me or approved of me, so you can't expect me to care about her. If she had been able to, she would have ruined everything between Arthur and me.'

Annabel nodded. That had been the way she summed up the situation, too.

'If only that bitch had died first – and Arthur not at all!' Tara slammed her cup down into its saucer. 'It would have made all the difference!'

This was so manifestly true from Tara's point of view that, with that plaintive cry, she removed herself from Annabel's list of possible killers.

If Tara had been going to kill anyone, she would have chosen Dora Stringer, and possibly Zenia, thus clearing away the main opposition to her marriage to Arthur Arbuthnot. And he, most certainly, would still be alive.

Poor Tara. Everything had been within her grasp – and then had been abruptly snatched away. Annabel decided that she now even forgave Tara for her treatment of Sassy. The cat hadn't been harmed, after all, and the poor woman couldn't be blamed for trying to hold on to what had almost been hers.

'Well.' Annabel drained her cup and set it down. 'Shall we return to the fray? Do you want to carry on here or would you like to sample Portobello Road?'

'This has been so kind of you—' Tara darted a shrewd glance through half-closed eyelids. 'And it's fascinating. But – what about you? I know you have a train to catch.'

So Tara was just as anxious to get rid of her as she was to see the last of Tara. Good. That simplified matters.

'Actually' – Annabel glanced at her watch – 'if we were to pack it in now, I could get an earlier train.'

'Of course,' Tara agreed warmly. 'I have a few other things to do myself. Tomorrow is going to be a Hell Day.'

Equally relieved, they beamed false smiles at each other and looked around for the waitress.

'Amazing, the way they disappear when you want them,' Annabel said.

'Never mind. We'll just leave the money on the table.' Tara reached into her bag and brought out a multicompartmented billfold. 'Let me do it. You've been so kind, showing me the ropes.'

'There!' A sudden flicker of movement at the edge of the pavement caught Annabel's attention. 'Did you see that?'

'What? Where?' Distracted, Tara turned to look in the direction of Annabel's pointing finger. 'I don't see anything.' Automatically, she dropped a banknote beside her coffee cup.

'They might accept that here' – Annabel looked at the money – 'but I doubt if you'd get a good rate of exchange for it.'

'Oh!' Tara hastily snatched up the American twenty-dollar bill she had tossed down. 'Wrong compartment! I haven't had a chance to get to a bank and cash in my currency left over from Mustique. Things have been so frantic!' She replaced the bill with a ten-pound note and seemed ready to rush off.

Fortunately, the waitress arrived to give her change and they departed to wave down the nearest taxi.

'Your train—' Tara said.

'No, no. You take this one,' Annabel said expansively. 'I'll get the next one. There's no shortage of taxis here on a Saturday morning.'

'Well, if you're sure . . .' Tara murmured, diving into the taxi before Annabel could change her mind.

'Positive!' Annabel slammed the door on Tara and stepped back with a sense of freedom sweeping over her. She did not have to catch a mythical train, the rest of the day was her own. She stepped back from the kerb, waving until Tara's taxi was out of sight, and breathed a deep sigh of relief.

The relief was momentary. A disruptive movement of the crowds thronging the pavement made her turn. The stream of pedestrians was parting to allow passage to a wheelchair, then closing in again behind it.

But not so swiftly that she hadn't caught a glimpse of its occupant.

As she had suspected earlier, it was Mark. His departure told her that it had been Tara he was following. Now that

Tara was gone, he had no interest in anything Annabel might do.

What *was* Mark's interest in Tara? Was it his own idea to follow her or had he been instructed to do it? Perhaps by Zenia, or even Neville, both of whom had good reason to mistrust her.

Annabel shuddered suddenly and was caught by a faint sense of panic. What was she standing here for? She had wasted enough time this morning, she ought to be home feeding the cats.

15

There was a long jagged scratch on the outside of the door to the flat and flakes of paint were missing, as though someone had tried to force entrance during her absence.

Annabel blessed the sense of alarm that had sent her hurrying back to check that the cats were safe. So immediate had been the sense of peril that she had taken a taxi after all.

The door was still firmly closed and there was silence on the other side of it. As she tried to insert the key in the lock, she saw small bright scratches around the keyhole where someone had obviously tried his or her luck with the keys they already possessed before getting down to trying brute force.

Had she disturbed the intruder at work? There had been a sense of disturbance in the air when she arrived. She had not bothered to muffle her footsteps and there had been a faint echo from the far end of the corridor by the emergency staircase. Had she heard, or had she imagined, the whisper of the fire door closing?

It was a battle to force the key into the damaged lock. Annabel had nearly despaired when, abruptly, the lock yielded and the doors swung open . . . into an empty foyer.

'Sally . . . ? Sally . . . ?' Annabel called. From the back of her mind rose the vision of Luther tiptoeing amongst the dustbins, also calling. 'Salvatore . . . ? Sassy . . . ? Sally . . . ?' Automatically, she slammed the door shut behind her and fastened the safety chain. When she turned back, all three cats were lined up watching her with interest.

'Oh, thank heavens! You're all right?'

As though to reassure her, they crowded forward to mob her ankles. There was a brief pleasant interlude before Sassy began to complain again. Salvatore flicked his ears and hunched his shoulders, acquiring the look of a henpecked male who has heard it all before and is damned if he'll listen to it again. Sally gave Sassy an impatient look and moved off towards the kitchen.

Sassy mumbled several comments at them under her breath, then looked up at Annabel and emitted a long plaintive yowl.

'All right, all right.' Annabel bent and scooped her up, carried her into the drawing room and settled down in a corner of the sofa. 'I think I have something here that belongs to you,' she told Sassy, opening her handbag.

Sassy went into hysterics at the sight of the pale-blue suede collar with the name SASSY in tiny brilliants. She flung herself at it, pawed at it, and tried to get her head into it, even though it wasn't buckled into a circle, all the while chattering wildly.

'That's what I thought,' Annabel said. 'In fact, I was pretty certain. Just a minute—' She tried to restrain the overexcited Sassy while she reached for the telephone.

The other two cats wandered back to see what was going on, the new pitch in Sassy's voice evidently alerting them. They watched with interest as Annabel fended off Sassy while dialling the number engraved on the little silver disc attached to the collar.

'Hello?' A woman's voice answered on the third ring. 'Hello?'

'*Mmmmrrreeeeooow* . . .' Sassy heard the beloved voice and tried to climb into the telephone.

'I have someone here who'd like to speak to you,' Annabel announced, somewhat unnecessarily, as Sassy was already making herself quite clear on that point. She not only wanted to speak, she wanted to go home.

'Sassy! Sassy!' the voice screamed joyfully. 'Where are you?'

'Knightsbridge, actually.' Annabel won possession of the

143

phone again. 'She's perfectly safe and well, but home-sick.'

'Knightsbridge?' The voice was startled. 'How did she get way over there? We live in Regent's Park.'

'Who knows?' Annabel was not going to admit that she did. 'Perhaps she got into a car or on a bus and wound up over here.'

'Where? Where is here?' The woman was insistent. 'What's your address? I'll come and collect her immediately. In fact, I was offering a reward —'

'Not necessary,' Annabel broke in. 'I'm only too glad to restore her to her proper owner. I'm sorry I couldn't do it sooner, but she got separated from her collar and it was only by sheer luck that I found it.' She gave the woman her address.

'Please let me speak to Sassy again,' the woman said.

'Certainly.' Feeling slightly foolish, Annabel held the tele-phone to Sassy's ear.

'Darling,' the woman trilled. 'Mummy's coming right away. Be a good girl and stay where you are. Mummy will be there as fast as she can.'

Sassy responded with excited chirrups and purrs. She seemed to understand what had been said. She marched over to the door and sat down expectantly, still chirruping.

'Well.' Annabel looked down at Sassy thoughtfully. 'That's your problem solved. Now what do I do with the rest of you?'

The telephone rang, startling them all. Sassy leaped up and pranced over to the table, chattering with renewed hope. Annabel looked at the telephone uneasily, debating the wisdom of answering it. There was no one she wished to talk to right now. Why not just let it ring?

Because Sassy would not allow it, that's why. She began berating Annabel for her slowness in answering. After all, it might be for her.

She could be right. Annabel picked up the phone before remembering that she had given the woman her address but not her telephone number. 'Hello . . . ?'

There was silence at the other end of the line.

144

'Hello . . . ? Hello . . . ?' Was that a faint uneven breathing she could hear? 'Hello . . . ?'

Sassy shoved closer and added a few comments of her own. Annabel hastily covered the mouthpiece with her hand and pushed the cat away.

There was a final explosive breath – almost a snort – at the other end and the click of the receiver being replaced, then the dial tone. Annabel replaced her own receiver more slowly.

Wrong number? Heavy breather? Or something more sinister? The interrupted prowler calling to see if the coast was clear and he could return to make another attempt at forcing entry?

Had Sassy's voice carried over the line and thrown the other person off stride? Or told them what they really wanted to know? Annabel looked at Sally and Salvatore with renewed favour. Thank heaven for cats who could keep their mouths shut.

Annabel was under no illusions as to why anyone would want to break into the flat. Obviously, she hadn't been so clever as she'd thought – or the others hadn't been so stupid. Someone had recollected her ever-present basket and connected it with one – if not all – of the missing cats.

Who – or rather, which faction – was stalking her?

Had Tara been detailed to lure her out of the flat so that Neville could try to repossess Sally? Or had Mark learned that they were doing the street markets this morning and kept them under observation so that Kelda could attempt a raid on the flat?

The clumsy try, leaving a damaged lock and all those scratches on the paint, was the work of a bungling amateur. Which could describe anyone in the Arbuthnot ménage – and why not? Outwardly respectable, upper-middle-class people might be moderately expert at tennis, bridge or golf, but breaking and entering was not usually numbered among their accomplishments. They were bound to fumble a bit on the first attempt.

The first? Did she really think there would be others? She considered the question coldly for a moment and decided that the answer was: probably. They might not have been sure there was a cat on the premises prior to that silent telephone call, but someone was certain now.

'You've blown the gaff,' she told Sassy resignedly. 'Now we're for it.'

Sassy looked at her blankly, then strolled away to resume her vigil by the door. It was nothing to do with her; she was as good as out of here. Just as soon as Mummy arrived.

'It's all right for some,' Annabel muttered. 'But we're stuck here and you've given the game away.' She looked around, with some vague idea of barricading the door with the sofa overnight, in case the would-be intruder tried again. It was obviously impossible to rely on the locked front entrance – there might as well be a 'Welcome Burglars' mat displayed. She had seen for herself just how easy it was to gain access thanks to an obliging resident.

For a female, that is. A toss of the hair, a roll of the eyes, a charming pout – and the unregenerate sexists in this building would roll out the red carpet. The finger of suspicion swung towards Kelda again.

On the other hand, a man brandishing some sort of spurious identification could pass himself off as a plumber or electrician answering an emergency call. He might even be carrying a case containing the tools he had used to try to break open the door. A case in which a cat could be concealed and carried away.

It was growing darker outside, rain clouds had been gathering slowly and determinedly, forging themselves into an overall deep grey ceiling which was about to open up and release the deluge. Even as she noticed this, the first heavy drops splattered against the windows.

Did that mean she ought to put on the lights and draw the curtains? Rather, first the curtains, then the lights, so that no one could look up and see that she was home – she had been caught that way last night.

Perhaps not just yet. There was movement in the street below. A Range Rover had turned into the street and was driving along slowly, as though the driver were trying to read the block numbers through the rain.

Across the room, Sassy suddenly turned her head and looked towards the window.

There was one parking place on the other side of the street and the Range Rover pulled into it. Sassy left her post and came to join Annabel at the window, chattering excitedly.

'Yes, I think so, too,' Annabel said. Together, they watched as the Range Rover door swung open and a tall thin woman hopped out, holding what looked like a collapsible cat carrier over her head to protect her hairdo from the worst of the downpour. She darted across the street and up the steps to the apartment block. A few seconds later, the doorbell rang.

'*Mmrrraaah!*' Sassy streaked across the room, shrieking to Annabel to follow and be quick about it.

The buzzer sounded again and, with only a perfunctory glance at the tiny TV screen, Annabel pushed the lock release, then watched the woman dive through the door and disappear into the hall.

Sassy scurried back and forth between Annabel and the door, uttering urgent little cries. The other two cats had moved some distance away, Annabel noticed, and were observing the scene from the shelter of the kitchen doorway.

When the inner doorbell sounded, Sassy leaped forward, nearly tripping Annabel, and yowling excitedly.

'Sassy! Sassy, darling!' No less excited cries came from the other side of the door. 'Here I am! Mummy's here!'

Annabel managed to wrench the door open and stood back. Sassy hurled herself forward, leaped for the hem of the tweed skirt and clawed herself upwards and into the waiting arms. The nylon cat carrier hit the floor as Sassy filled the woman's arms. The woman and cat purred and cooed at each other, lost in a world of their own.

Annabel cleared her throat, there seemed to be a lump in it. She closed the door behind them and bent to pick up the carrier, which shook itself out into a flat-bottomed bag which might have been used for sports equipment were it not for the fine mesh at one end. A cat could settle down and watch the world go by when she was being carried along in this. Annabel nodded approval.

'I can't thank you enough!' The woman remembered her suddenly and swung to face her, still clutching Sassy. 'I was so worried. I was frantic. I thought I'd lost her. I'm so grateful. Are you sure I can't give you the reward?'

'I wouldn't dream of taking anything,' Annabel said firmly. 'Just seeing Sassy back in her rightful place is enough for me.'

'Oh—' The woman looked beyond Annabel and her smile grew even wider. 'You have cats of your own. Of course, you understand.'

'They're not exactly—' Annabel began, then let it go. Sally and Salvatore were not to be explained. 'Can I offer you a drink?' she suggested instead.

'You are kind, but I'm driving and I really must get back, if you don't mind. My husband has been so worried, too. He can't wait to see Sassy again.'

'Quite all right,' Annabel assured her. 'Here, let me help—' Sassy did not want to abandon those loving arms long enough to allow them to put her into her carrying case. Annabel unzipped the case and held it open while the woman lowered Sassy into it. There was a slight tussle as Sassy protested.

'Now be a good girl, Sassy,' the woman told her, 'and we'll soon be home.'

Annabel pushed Sassy's head down firmly and zipped the bag shut. Sassy immediately began complaining loudly.

'Thank you again,' the woman said. 'If there's ever anything I can do for you, just call me.'

'That's all right,' Annabel said. 'It was my pleasure.' She did not add that a great part of the pleasure was seeing the last of Sassy and knowing that there was going to be some peace and quiet around here now. She suspected she was not the only one to feel that way; a quiet sense of satisfaction seemed to radiate from the other cats as they watched Sassy depart.

Annabel went over to the window to pull the curtains. The rain had settled down into a tropical downpour and she watched the woman run across the street and leap into her Range Rover. Even from this distance, she could hear Sassy's voice, and even after the door had slammed.

The motor roared to life, the headlights flashed on and the Range Rover moved forward, swung out, seemed to dither a moment, then made a U-turn and drove off.

Seconds later, another car, small, dark and inconspicuous, also started up, moved forward and duplicated the U-turn. This one did not put its headlights on. It slid silently in the wake of the Range Rover until the big vehicle turned into the main road. Then the smaller headlights lit up and the car followed the Range Rover out into the mainstream traffic.

'Well . . . what do you think of that?' Annabel drew the curtains, no longer sure that it was necessary.

The cats looked up at her, their bright eyes twinkled affection, but they kept their opinions to themselves and moved off towards the kitchen.

Annabel knew what she thought: the driver of the second car had been her intruder, lurking in his vehicle, hoping she would leave the flat again and give him another chance to break in and begin his interrupted search.

It was someone after Sally, of course. Someone who suspected Annabel of harbouring her. Someone who, hearing Sassy's loud cries as she was carried across the road and unable to differentiate one cat from another, now believed that Annabel had passed Sally on to a friend to hide. That was why he had abandoned his surveillance. He was going to follow that poor woman home and try to get the cat away from her.

And that would be a fight worth seeing. No one was ever going to part Sassy from her mistress again. Not only that, but Annabel had the strong impression that the woman lived in the sort of establishment that came equipped with high-tech security equipment and probably guards.

Just the same . . .

She still had the telephone number. Should she ring the woman and warn her? Or was she overreacting? It was quite possible that the dark car belonged to some innocent party, who was just happening to pull out at the same time and copied the U-turn because it looked like a good idea. Annabel told herself sternly that she had no real reason to think that the car intended to follow the Range Rover – nor, given the level of competence displayed thus far, to think that it had any hope of succeeding.

Annabel adjusted the drapes so that no chink of light would show, and turned away from the windows, becoming aware of the cats watching her hopefully from the kitchen doorway.

'You're hungry, I suppose,' she said, as they fell in on either side of her and escorted her to the fridge. 'I was going to buy some tins of cat food for you, but I was being watched, so it wasn't safe.' She opened the freezer section and rummaged inside. 'You'll just have to take pot luck.'

Frozen cauliflower and broccoli florets, peas, corn, a half leg of lamb – it would take for ever to defrost. However, she transferred it to the fridge, it would do for tomorrow's dinner, since she was planning to hole up here for the rest of the weekend.

With a guilty pang, Annabel realized how thoroughly she was depleting Dinah's supplies; she'd have to replace them before she left. That was why she was trying to go lightly on those delicious one-serving homemade meals the housekeeper had left prepared for Dinah. The odd chop, steak or roast could be easily replaced; she didn't fancy the thought of doing a lot of heavy shopping to restock the freezer. Although that venison stew looked awfully tempting – and the cats would probably like it, too.

'Ah, this should do!' She straightened triumphantly, clutching a large packet of prawns. 'I'll try to pick up some cat food for you later—' She broke off, not just at the sudden realization that there wasn't going to be much of a later, not after Monday, but also because the cats had looked at each other and were now regarding her with what she could swear was amusement.

For a moment, she put herself in the cats' position and

recognized the joke: she was apologizing for serving them large luscious prawns instead of tinned food.

Salvatore ambled over and head-butted her ankles fondly. He loved a woman with a sense of humour.

16

Sunday – and she'd promised herself that it would be a peaceful day of rest. After opening the door to take in the newspaper, Annabel pulled up the drawbridge mentally, safe in her borrowed castle for the day. She stretched out on the sofa, dissecting the paper, discarding the Appointments, Sports and Children's sections, and settled down for a good read. The cats were having a game with their catnip mouse, the aroma of roasting lamb was beginning to permeate the air and, outside, it was still raining, the sort of steady persistent downpour that added to the contentment of those who were comfortably inside their dwellings with no need to venture out that day.

A sudden gust of wind slammed rain against the windows. The cats stopped playing and went to investigate. Annabel was suddenly aware of just how precarious her safe haven might be. If anyone were to look up, the cats could be seen from the street below.

'No!' Annabel fought free of the theatre section and dashed over to pull them back out of sight. 'Don't do that!' She peered out through the curtain of rain, which was obviously having a dampening effect on anyone who might have considered lurking below. The street was deserted.

'Why don't you take a catnap?' She carried the cats over to the sofa and deposited them on it, then stretched out again herself. Sally curled up where she had landed and obligingly went to sleep. Salvatore inched upwards until his head rested on her shoulder and closed his eyes in bliss. Annabel absently nuzzled the top of his head with her chin and went back to the theatre pages, wondering if the new play previewing this week was going to be worth the effort of getting to an early performance. The cast was good, but the playwright was unknown.

The sudden buzz of the downstairs doorbell startled them all.

'Now what?' Disentangling herself from cats and broadsheets, Annabel stumbled over to check the entryview screen. No one she knew, but the young woman's face was partially obscured by the oversized flower arrangement she carried.

A quick check out of the window revealed a genuine florist's van outside the building and Annabel judged it safe to push the lock release. A few moments later, she was opening the door to receive the arrangement, which was even more enormous than it had looked on the screen.

'Have a nice day!' the messenger burbled and dashed away – so quickly that, for a paranoid instant, Annabel wondered whether the flowers were booby-trapped.

Gingerly, Annabel managed to get it over to the table, it was almost too awkward to carry and the fact that the cats had come to investigate and were underfoot didn't help. She set it down and stepped back to survey it, finally sighting the small white square nearly concealed in the lower foliage.

'A MILLION THANKS

FROM

SASSY AND HER MUMMY'

Turning the card over, Annabel whistled with surprise at the name engraved on the other side. The lady could, indeed, afford to give a million of anything; between them, she and her husband owned a large chunk of Canada.

An additional scribbled message assured Annabel, once she had deciphered it, that Sassy's mummy was eternally in her debt and could be called on at any time.

'That may be useful,' Annabel murmured thoughtfully.

Salvatore leaped up to investigate and disagreed; it wasn't edible. Sally joined him and sniffed delicately at a few blooms so exotic that Annabel could not even put a name to them, but seemed to approve. They circled the arrangement, then Salvatore decided to give one of the flowers a second chance. He nipped off a petal, chewed thoughtfully, then spat it out in disgust. He had been right the first time. He strolled to the edge of the table and leaped over to the bookcase, settling full length along one of the not-too-crowded shelves, his tail dangling off the edge.

Sally took another turn around the flower arrangement, still sniffing, until she decided which bloom she favoured and curled up beneath it with a yawn. It was nap time again.

Annabel yawned in sympathy and decided that the cats had the right idea. A nice little snooze was just the thing on a day like this. The sofa was calling . . .

First, though, she went over to check on Salvatore; his position on that shelf looked rather perilous. If he rolled over, he would be on the floor. Perhaps she ought to move some of those books, so that he had the shelf to himself.

'Sorry to disturb you,' she said, reaching over him to remove some books, 'but you'll be more comfortable when I finish.'

Salvatore lifted his head and opened one eye halfway, giving her the benefit of his affable leer. She could do anything she wanted. He closed his eye again and allowed her to slide him to the back of the shelf, purring his thanks.

Annabel deposited her armload of books on the side of the table Sally wasn't using. They were a mixed bag of bestsellers out of the mists of time. Probably Dinah's husband had been the book buyer in the family, biography and adventure figured largely.

One of the books caught her attention, triggering a nagging irritation that she had ignored in the press of more urgent events. She removed the book from the pile and brought it over to the sofa, where she stretched out and looked at it with grim satisfaction. She knew just who this book ought to go to – one could only hope that he would get the message.

Reach For the Sky was the biography of Douglas Bader, the pilot who had lost both legs, got himself fitted with artificial ones and learned to walk again. No moping around in a wheelchair feeling sorry for himself for *him*. He had even taken to the sky again, fought in the Battle of Britain, been shot down over occupied France, and escaped from his blazing aircraft, ironically enough, by leaving his hopelessly trapped artificial leg behind. Not surprisingly, he was captured by the Germans, who, in one of the more honourable incidents in that deadly conflict, communicated with London, where arrangements were made for a replacement leg to be parachuted down for him.

Yes, indeed, it might be very salutary for Mark to read this story. The young so often assumed that no one else had ever had the troubles they faced, that they were alone in an uncharted wilderness without a compass.

Annabel hadn't realized she had fallen into a doze until she was rudely awakened. *Damn!* She should have unplugged the telephone before lying down. She contemplated not answering, instinctively feeling that this disturbance of her peace on a quiet Sunday afternoon boded no good. She had no desire for another session with the heavy breather. On the other hand, if she did not answer, he might appear in person, thinking the flat was empty. The thought brought her to her feet.

'Annabel!' The long wait for an answer had not improved Xanthippe's temper. 'What are you doing there?'

'Having a quiet Sunday. At least, I was.'

'Wasting your time, you mean,' Xanthippe corrected. 'Why aren't you with the Arbuthnots?'

'Why should I be?'

'Because they're cremating Arthur Arbuthnot.'

'On a Sunday?' Annabel was startled. 'Isn't that unusual?'

'The rich are different, Annabel. You should know that by now. Hopewell run their own crematorium in tandem with their medical establishments. And if the Arbuthnots want to order a cremation on a Sunday, none of the hirelings is going to quibble about the day of the week. They know which side their bread is buttered on.'

Yes, hirelings would – and not only those on the lower levels. There had been rumours that certain doctors at Hopewell clinics had been struck off the register of various countries because of an excessively casual attitude towards reporting such things as gunshot wounds, communicable disease and, of course, knife wounds.

'So the cremation is just a family affair.' Annabel pulled her attention back to the immediate situation. 'Very private. Why am I not surprised?' She should have guessed this would happen. Annabel remembered now the strained look on Tara's face when she mentioned that today was going to be a 'Hell Day'. This must have been what she was referring to.

'Where are your doorsteppers?' Annabel sailed into the offensive. 'Cindy and Sid. Aren't they there?'

'Too identifiable,' Xanthippe said. 'If they blow their cover showing up there, they won't be able to work at the flat again.'

'You think they work, do you?' But the riposte was automatic, the full implications of the situation were becoming apparent: the family were disposing of the evidence. A cremated body could not be exhumed and examined at a later date when enough suspicion of foul play had surfaced to call for police intervention.

'We're losing the story!' Xanthippe snapped. 'What are we going to do?'

'Difficult, isn't it?' Annabel sympathized. 'But I don't see what could be done, even if we attended the service. It isn't like a wedding, you know. The minister isn't going to say, "If anyone can show just cause why this body should not be cremated, let him speak now or for ever hold his peace", or whatever.'

'*Tchah!*' Xanthippe made an explosive little sound of annoyance. 'I wish you'd try to be serious, Annabel.'

'Oh, I'm very serious,' Annabel assured her, and she was. Someone was going to get away with murder. The murder of a man she had known and liked. Oh, undoubtedly he had been difficult and overbearing in his relations with other people, but he had been all right with her. Perhaps, if she had known him longer, she might have discovered his harsher side, but it seemed unfair and unjust that someone should be able to kill him and then destroy the body so that he escaped all consequences.

On the other hand, how much could the body have betrayed? The private medical institution had obviously been able to keep Arthur Arbuthnot in some semblance of life for several days on their high-tech machines. Would that have been long enough for any knife wound in his back to have healed naturally? It was possible, Annabel supposed, which would make it even more unlikely that the police would be able – or willing – to do anything.

Of course, there was still Dora Stringer's body. No one was going to worry too much about her. But a push wouldn't show up in any autopsy – not even a sudden and violent push – unless she had bruised easily. And even then, a bruise or two would prove nothing —

'Annabel? Are you still there?'

'Just thinking,' Annabel said.

'And —?'

'And nothing, I'm afraid. Nothing we can prove, nothing we can do, nothing . . .' Annabel glanced at her watch: four-thirty-five. 'In any case, the cremation must be over by now. You've left it a bit late to call, haven't you?'

'I've just got in and found the information on my answering machine. I couldn't call earlier. I'd hoped you would have been there.'

'Who left the message?'

'I think it was Cindy.' Xanthippe hesitated. 'The voice was rather blurred, not a good line, probably on her mobile, but it was a woman's voice. It must have been Cindy.'

So much for the other source of information about the Arbuthnots Xanthippe had claimed she had. Annabel had suspected she had been bluffing, now she was sure. There was no other mole in the Arbuthnot ménage – at least, not one that Xanthippe was aware of.

'Annabel? Don't do that!'

'Do what?'

'Go off into those long silences when I'm trying to hold a conversation with you.'

'Sorry.' Now that she knew it bothered Xanthippe, Annabel made a mental note to do it more often. 'Just thinking.'

'Thinking what? What are you going to do?'

'I'm going to have a peaceful Sunday – what's left of it. Goodbye.' Annabel replaced the receiver and strode over to pull the plug out of its socket. There! She should have disconnected the phone much earlier.

That done, she stood irresolute for a moment, looking around the room as though she might find some answer. The cats were awake and alert again. They looked at her with interest.

'Oh, Sally,' she sighed. 'If only you could tell me what you know.' Sally blinked back at her, inscrutable.

'Oh, well,' Annabel said. 'What do we do now?'

The cats were in no doubt. As one, they leaped to the floor from their respective perches and marched kitchenwards.

We eat.

17

Kelda and Mark were deep in conversation behind the reception desk when Annabel arrived in the morning. Close together, heads bent, they looked almost furtive. Their conversation was too low to be overheard. Pity, it might have been interesting.

'I'm glad you're both here.' Annabel noted the way they jumped apart guiltily. They had obviously been too absorbed in each other to notice her approach.

'I have something' – Annabel reached into her basket and brought out the Bader biography – 'that I think you both ought to read.' She set it down in front of Mark emphatically. 'Especially you,' she told him.

Kelda started back with a strange mewling cry. Mark glared at both of them and cleared his throat loudly. It seemed the Bader story was not unknown to them; perhaps it had already been the subject of some discussion.

'What do you think you're playing at?' Mark demanded. His face was turning quite red.

'Mark, please—' It was a strangulated cadence that did not sound quite right. Kelda tried again. 'Please. Annabel is only trying to be helpful.'

'She's not helping *me*. Go on, clear off!' He waved Annabel away. 'Go upstairs and meddle with *them*. Leave me alone!'

'Perhaps you'd better go up,' Kelda said pleadingly. 'I'll follow along shortly. I just want to have another word with Mark.' She put a tentative hand on his shoulder, as though to calm him.

'Don't be too long,' Annabel said, just to exert some

authority. She was pleased to notice that they had not returned the book.

Upstairs, there was muted chaos. Cindy and Sid were trying to look fully occupied while lurking in the doorway of the drawing room.

'Aren't you wanted anywhere else?' Annabel demanded crossly. 'Or are you planning to take up residence here?'

'Look who got up on the wrong side of bed this morning,' Sid jeered.

'What a surprise,' Cindy said. 'The right side is probably pushed up against the wall.'

Take it whence it comes, Annabel. She contented herself with giving them a look which should have struck them to the floor, but it merely glanced off their rhinoceros hides, and turned away. There was too much at stake today to worry about unruly minions. Except, they weren't really minions – they were paparazzi and dangerous.

'Anyway, we *are* working.' Cindy brandished a dripping paintbrush defensively.

'Mmmm,' was as much as Annabel would commit herself to. She didn't know all that much about it, but she had the vague impression that one didn't start painting the skirting boards before one had done anything to the walls.

'Did Kelda tell you to do that?' she asked.

'She's been too busy to talk to us today,' Sid said. 'Makes you wonder what she's up to, doesn't it?'

Actually, it did, but Annabel wasn't going to admit that. Fortunately, no one in England was ever surprised at discovering that their workmen were completely incompetent and had done a bodged job. Dismayed, yes; surprised, no. Whoever inherited the place, via the lovely Sally, would just have to sort it out later.

Certainly, no one around here was going to worry about anything so mundane at the moment.

'Since you've started on your natural habitat – the woodwork – you might as well do the door now,' Annabel said, closing it firmly behind her. With any luck, they might paint

160

the door shut and be stuck inside. Reluctantly, Annabel banished a tantalizing vision of two skeletons being discovered several decades from now and pulled her attention back to business.

This was a day to lurk in whatever shadows she could find, as close to the study as possible. Annabel carried her basket down to the very end of the corridor, removed the tape measure and notebook, knelt and hunched over, trying to make herself as small and inconspicuous as possible. If she remained below eye level, obviously absorbed in her work, it was just possible that everyone would be too intent on their own concerns to notice her.

She hadn't long to wait. She felt the vibration of their tread shudder along the floorboards before she looked up and saw them. She hadn't expected Mr Pennyman to bring a colleague with him, but it made sense, given the circumstances. Safety in numbers, and all that. Poor Mr Pennyman had obviously learned his lesson in that first session of dealing with Arthur Arbuthnot's heirs en masse. He couldn't be blamed for wanting someone along who would be on his side.

But it upset the vague plan Annabel had made. She had wanted to intercept Mr Pennyman for a private conversation, before he dealt with the family. There was no chance of that now.

Also, Luther was there in the lead, opening the study door and ushering them inside. 'You're a bit early,' he said. 'I'll tell the others you've arrived.' He closed the door firmly and went back down the hallway, so deep in some thoughts of his own that he hadn't even noticed Annabel.

The others appeared almost immediately, but stood huddled in a defensive group at the far end of the hallway, seemingly bracing themselves before advancing on the study.

Uncle Wystan was in the middle of the group, carrying what looked like a large jewel box. Zenia and Tara suddenly flourished handkerchiefs.

Annabel's nose wrinkled as a sudden whiff of onions eddied towards her. Odd, the kitchen was in the basement

161

and no cooking smells had ever reached the upper floors before.

'"Forward the Light Brigade",' Cousin Neville gave the order.

Tara dabbed gently at her nose and gave a loud sniff.

'No need to overdo it, old girl,' Wystan said.

With measured tread, Uncle Wystan advanced solemnly, the others falling into step behind him. Luther brought up the rear, stepping forward at the last moment to throw open the study door, still with that look of abstraction. They all marched into the study.

Annabel hurled herself forward and managed to shove a corner of her notebook into the opening in time to prevent the door closing completely. The smell of onions was stronger than ever.

Annabel slid the notebook out of the aperture and pushed the door open a little wider. Now she had a partial view of what was going on, as well as being able to hear everything.

'I am the bearer of sad tidings,' she heard Wystan announce, just before he stepped into view to set the jewel box down on the library table in front of Mr Pennyman.

'Poor, dear little Sally—' Tara murmured, breaking off with a tearful sniff.

'These things happen,' Neville said.

'Sad, very sad.' Wystan swung the lid of the box up and they all crowded round to look down at its contents.

'Most unfortunate,' Mr Pennyman agreed. 'How did it happen?'

'She got out when we weren't watching,' Tara said. 'We were shattered when we discovered it. We looked everywhere for her, but we couldn't find her. Then . . . then . . .' She dabbed at her eyes, at her nose, with her handkerchief.

Mr Pennyman coughed and stepped back slightly as a wave of onion scent threatened to overwhelm him. Tara was overdoing it, indeed. Annabel could feel her own eyes smarting. At this rate, the whole group would soon be racked by onion-induced grief.

'In the street.' Neville put his arm around Tara comfortingly. 'By the kerb, actually. Poor little thing must have been hit by a car. Accident. These things happen.'

'So you said.' Mr Pennyman gave him a shrewd look. 'Pity you couldn't have found her sooner. While she was still alive.'

'We can only be thankful that poor Arthur isn't here to see this day,' Wystan said. 'It would have killed him.'

'If Arthur had been alive, it wouldn't have happened,' Zenia pointed out. 'It was his death, and then Dora's, that upset the household routine so much. People coming and going, leaving doors open. The police and, of course,' she added venomously, 'the decorators.'

'It really wasn't our fault,' Tara protested tearfully. 'We tried our best to find her. We looked everywhere.'

Mr Pennyman's companion had moved forward and was frowning down into the jewel casket. He bent over and reached inside, seemingly prodding the body, then straightened up.

'You can keep looking,' he said. 'This isn't Sally.'

Some instinct made Annabel step aside a split second before the door swung wide and Luther slipped out of the study. He took off down the corridor at a jogging pace, looking neither left nor right, an aura of determination surrounding him.

'What?'

'Of course it is!'

'How do you know?'

'Forgive me,' Mr Pennyman said. 'I should have introduced my, er, associate, earlier. This is Mr Tilbury, Arthur's – and Sally's – veterinarian.'

The casket lid fell with a snap that reverberated through the sudden silence.

'Oh, thank heavens!' Tara recovered first. She tucked her handkerchief into her handbag with an air of relief. 'Then perhaps we can still find Sally alive.'

'We can hope,' Wystan said unconvincingly. 'While there's life, there's . . . that is, if she *is* still alive.'

Zenia's explosive snort had nothing to do with the onion

163

slices in her own handkerchief. 'I just hope you know what you're doing!' She glared impartially at her husband, at Mr Pennyman and at the veterinarian; it wasn't clear which one she was addressing.

Mr Pennyman cleared his throat, a vague noncommittal sound, playing for time, promising nothing. Mr Tilbury looked at him, then at the others, and waited for further elucidation.

'Annabel – get out of the way!' The command came from behind her, and Annabel whirled around to find Kelda and Mark poised to roll into the study as soon as she stopped blocking their way. Mark had a small carrying case in his lap.

'Don't say anything,' Kelda warned. 'Keep out of this! Just let us pass.'

Annabel could feel her eyes widening as she stared at the wire-mesh end of the case, there was soft furry movement behind it. She stepped aside automatically, allowing Mark to sweep into the study, Kelda immediately behind him.

'Ah!' Mr Pennyman looked at them without surprise. 'And what have we here?'

'Sally,' Kelda said, when Mark did not respond quickly enough. 'It's Sally. She always liked Mark and she came to him for protection after Mr Arbuthnot died.'

'Indeed?' Mr Pennyman became blander than ever. 'Well, suppose you let us have a look at the little lady?'

'Right.' Mark fumbled with the latch and finally opened the mesh door. When nothing happened, he reached inside and seemed to engage in a slight struggle. A severe bout of foul language issued from the case and Mark dragged a protesting tabby from its depths. Once out, she shook her bristling fur back into a semblance of smoothness and looked around warily.

'Oh, I say!' Wystan choked. 'That's a bit much! Abducting our cat like that.'

The cat wasn't a bad match. If Annabel had not been in close proximity to the real Sally for the past few days, even she might have been fooled. People to whom the cat had been nothing more than an annoyance underfoot were more easily duped. They regarded the cat – and then Mark – with varying degrees of hostility.

'Sally, darling—' Tara started forward and the cat shrank back.

'That isn't Sally.' Zenia sounded as though she spoke more from hope than from conviction.

'No.' Mr Tilbury stared at the one white paw which did not match up with Sally's markings. 'I don't believe it is.'

'A good try,' Neville sneered at Mark. 'But not quite good enough. Anyone in the family would know that isn't Sally.'

'How could it be —?' Luther stood in the doorway, cradling a cat in his arms. 'When I have Sally right here?'

The world was full of tabby cats! Annabel reeled as she realized what this did to her plans. How could she show up with Sally now? No one would ever believe her. They'd think she was just another chancer. She'd be laughed out of court, out of town. And poor little Sally would never come into her rightful inheritance.

'You slimy, double-crossing creep!' Neville snarled at Luther.

'Fascinating!' Mr Pennyman had steepled his fingers and was gazing over them, as though looking down on an alien world of Lilliputians. 'How Arthur would have enjoyed this.'

This cat was a winsome little creature and, unlike the other, obviously happy and comfortable in familiar arms. Also, it was a perfect double for Sally. Annabel wondered how long it had taken Luther to find her – and how long he had had her.

'I always took care of Sally when Mr Arbuthnot was busy,' Luther said. 'Didn't I, sweetheart?' He lowered his head to hers and she rubbed against his chin with a fond purr. Yes, she knew him well, loved and trusted him. In fact, she was his cat; it was doubtful that she had ever encountered Arthur Arbuthnot in all of her short life.

'These others—' Luther gave the family a scornful, dismissive glance. 'They never cared for Sally at all. Not until they thought they could use her.'

How long had Luther been plotting this? And which had

come first, the cat or the plot? It was obvious that he had known the major dispensations in Arthur Arbuthnot's will. Had he deliberately gone looking for a cat that would be Sally's double, or had he found the cat first and then realized he could replace Sally? Was that why he had been searching so desperately among the dustbins? If he had found Sally then, would he have done away with her and replaced her with this cat so obviously devoted to him and who would run to him, given a choice of owners?

But ... however clever the scheme, it could only take effect after Arthur Arbuthnot was dead and, in the normal course of events, Arthur could have lived another couple of decades. Moreover, although the stakes were high, the outcome couldn't be guaranteed. Would Luther really have murdered Arthur Arbuthnot on the off-chance that he could swap cats and thus control the financial empire? Did he imagine that the family would stand by quietly and allow him to get away with it?

'That cat is ours!' Zenia advanced on Luther with deadly purpose. 'Hand it over!'

The cat shrank back against Luther for protection as Zenia reached out to snatch at it. Luther took a step backwards and half turned, presenting his shoulder to Zenia and sheltering the cat.

'That's right!' Neville moved forward on Luther's other side. 'Give it here!'

'You really had better, old boy,' Wystan weighed in. 'You know you can't possibly get away with keeping it.'

'Sally has the right to choose which of us is to be her guardian.' Luther faced them all with steely determination. 'It says so in Arthur's will.'

By this time, Annabel had been drawn forward irresistibly and was now standing inside the study with her back against the wall. Only the faintest flicker of Mr Pennyman's eyelids showed that he had noticed her. No one else had.

'He meant one of us – not you!' Zenia was incandescent with fury.

'Possession' – Luther smirked – 'is –'

'We'll see about that!' Neville snarled.

'Tilbury,' Mr Pennyman interrupted with quiet authority, 'what's your opinion?'

'Closer, much closer. In fact, possible.' Mr Tilbury went up to Luther. 'Let's have a better look at you ... Sally.'

The little cat cocked her head and watched him approach. No doubt about it, she was a man's cat and her name was definitely Sally. But then, it would be, wouldn't it?

Luther held on to his cat protectively, making soothing little noises deep in his throat as the veterinarian stroked and prodded. Luther was human, after all, Annabel decided. Wherever he had found the cat and whatever plans he had made for her, the bonding had worked both ways, he really cared about her.

'Hmmm ...' Tilbury was probing between her shoulder blades with a thoughtful expression. 'Let me just ...' He stooped and opened a small satchel, bringing out something that looked to Annabel like one of the early hand-held hair dryers.

'It's all right, Sally,' Luther assured his little pet. 'It won't hurt you.' He glared at Tilbury sharply. 'Will it?'

'Not a bit.' Tilbury moved his gadget up and down the length of the cat's spine, from between the ears to the tail, several times, then switched it off and looked over to Mr Pennyman.

'No.' He scratched Sally's ears. 'You're a beautiful, healthy little cat with a sweet nature —'

Luther snuggled the cat a little closer, preening.

'But you're not the right Sally,' Tilbury concluded.

'I always knew you were a crook!' Neville snarled at Luther. 'I'll see to it you never get another job in this town!'

'Oh?' Luther laughed out loud. 'Who do you imagine would listen to you? I've already had several approaches, not to mention offers from New York, Frankfurt, Paris and Vancouver.' He laughed again. 'And none of them ever heard of *you*.'

'We'll see about that!' Even to himself, the reply must

have sounded pretty feeble for, still fuming, Neville looked around for someone else to vent his rage on.

'And you—' His gaze fell upon Annabel. 'You're fired! I'll see to it that you never decorate another flat for the rest of your life!'

'That's all right with me.' Annabel smiled sweetly. Neville would never know how little terror his threat held. 'I was thinking of retiring, anyway.'

'As you can afford to,' Zenia said coldly, 'considering the amount of non-declarable cash you've made away with.'

'Now wait a minute!' Annabel was not prepared to let that pass. There had been too many nasty suggestions about the size of her remuneration. 'Mr Arbuthnot only paid me a basic retainer which isn't going to cover —'

'I'm not referring to that!' Zenia cut her off. 'I'm talking about all the cash you helped yourself to from the safe in his study!'

Mr Pennyman cleared his throat, an unassuming sound that, this time, somehow spoke volumes about false accusations, slander, defamation of character and long expensive lawsuits.

Zenia closed her mouth abruptly.

That safe! By a great effort of will, Annabel kept herself from glancing in its direction – which would surely be taken as an indication of guilt. Suddenly all the snide insinuations began to make sense. The Broomstick had been the first, with her flat statement that Annabel had been paid enough to hang the walls with ermine. Was that what she had believed when she had checked the safe and found it empty? That Annabel had been given – or had taken – the contents of the safe?

But perhaps the Broomstick had found out, or suspected, differently later. That could be why she had died. One forgot, blinded by the vast total of the entire estate, that there were those to whom the hundreds of thousands worth of domestic and foreign currency stashed away in the safe was an amount worth absconding with.

Annabel opened her mouth to point this out, but was forestalled.

'I don't see the difference.' Kelda looked from Luther's Sally to her own nominee and voiced her grievance. 'They both look alike to me. I'm sure *we've* got the right Sally. You didn't even try her out with that thing you've got.'

'Oh, very well.' Tilbury approached the cat in Mark's lap. Unlike Luther's Sally, this was not a happy cat. It bristled its fur as Tilbury drew closer and hissed warningly.

'All right, all right, this won't take a minute.' Tilbury ran the scanner over it and frowned in surprise. 'Well!'

Annabel edged closer. She could see movement on the tiny visual display screen of his instrument.

'Not Sally,' he said, 'and definitely not Arthur Arbuthnot's, but, as soon as I can call her up on my central registry, I can tell you who she does belong to.'

'I told you it wouldn't work!' Mark snapped at Kelda. 'This was all a waste of time and effort. All those stupid excuses you gave for borrowing —'

'Or perhaps you already know the owner,' Tilbury said.

'She's a friend of mine.' Kelda admitted defeat. 'The cat looked so much like Sally . . . I told her I wanted to use it as a model for a different kind of picture than the ones I usually paint.'

'But what would you have done if the cat had been accepted as Sally?' Annabel was too curious to keep quiet. 'You wouldn't have been able to give it back then.'

'We'd have come to some arrangement.' Kelda shrugged. 'I would never have bothered if I'd known she'd had the damned thing booby-trapped.'

'Microchipped, actually,' Tilbury corrected. 'More and more owners are having it done these days, thank goodness. Then if the pet gets lost and separated from its collar, it can still be identified and returned to its owner.'

'And Arthur Arbuthnot had Sally microchipped?' Annabel felt giddy with relief. The real Sally could prove who she was.

'Arthur insisted on it, before I even had a chance to suggest it to him. He didn't want to risk losing Sally; he said she was too good a cat to go back to that alley.'

169

'In that case' – Annabel turned to Mr Pennyman – 'I have something to tell you.'

'Ah, yes,' he said without surprise. 'I rather thought you might have.'

18

There were too many people here, Annabel thought resentfully. And most of them self-invited.

Bristling with mistrust, Zenia and Neville had stalked in and glared around the Knightsbridge drawing room. Wystan trailed unhappily in their wake. A strangely subdued Tara sank into the corner of the sofa she had occupied on her last visit and seemed to detach herself from the proceedings.

Kelda stood protectively behind Mark's wheelchair, while Luther lounged against a wall and watched. Annabel still wasn't sure what they were doing here – or what they had done with their respective Sally candidates.

Messrs Pennyman and Tilbury looked at Annabel expectantly.

Annabel looked back at them, momentarily blank. Although she would have liked a drink herself, she was damned if she was going to offer one to any of these interlopers. They had pushed their way in here and she was not going to appear to ratify their presence. They were pests, not guests.

'Let's get this over with,' Zenia said brusquely. 'Where is this cat you claim is Sally?'

The entrance doorbell buzzed . . . and buzzed . . . and buzzed . . . urgently and persistently. It was not going to stop until someone was admitted. With a sinking heart and a gloomy conviction that she knew who it was, Annabel crossed to the window and looked down.

'There she is!' Cindy spotted her. 'Let us in! Annabel! Let us in!' The doorbell settled down to a long steady buzz.

'What are they doing here?' Zenia demanded. 'They haven't done something dreadful to the flat, have they? You should never have left them there unsupervised.'

'Ignore them,' Annabel advised, raising her voice above the buzzing. Doorsteppers, Xanthippe had called them – and the doorstep was where they belonged.

'They won't go away,' Kelda warned.

'Then you go down and deal with them!' Annabel lost what little patience remained. 'And stop them ringing that doorbell!'

'I think they've stuck a pin in it. It will fall out eventually.' It was clear that Kelda did not intend to miss anything that was happening up here.

'That's not Sally!' Wystan said suddenly, as Salvatore sauntered into the room to see what all the commotion was about. 'It's the other one, the chap I found. Here, old chap, come and say hello.' He snapped his fingers encouragingly.

Salvatore lifted his head and curled his lip, giving Wystan a *Have-we-met?* look, and detoured around him to sniff at Mark's wheelchair.

'Silly woman, made off with the wrong cat,' Wystan chortled, not noticing that he'd been cut dead.

'So did you,' his wife reminded him. Something in her tone implied a deeper meaning.

'If we might proceed . . . ?' Mr Pennyman frowned at his watch. 'I take it there is another cat? A female one?'

'Sally . . . ?' the veterinarian called softly. 'Sally . . . you can come out now. We're all friends here.'

Sally knew better. Or possibly she hadn't heard his voice above the maddeningly insistent buzzing.

'Can't anyone stop that racket?' Zenia complained.

'Oh, right!' Abruptly galvanized into action, Wystan went over to the entryscreen and yanked with suppressed violence at the wires. The entryscreen went blank, but the buzzing stopped.

Silence . . . beautiful silence. Everyone seemed to breathe more easily.

'That's better, eh?' Wystan blinked diffidently at them.

'Sorry about any damage,' he apologized to Annabel. 'We'll pay for it of —'

'Wystan!' Zenia cut across his apology. 'She can pay for it herself. She's made off with enough to —'

Mr Pennyman cleared his throat again.

Something hit the windows sharply. Cindy and Sid must have found some pebbles, or perhaps they were throwing coins. It was to be hoped the windows did not break. Broken wires were bad enough.

'Sally . . . ? Sally . . . ?' Tilbury was not to be distracted by minor problems. 'Sally . . . ?'

Annabel was the first to spot the tiny nose poking around the corner. Salvatore saw it next and went over to give it an encouraging lick and to usher his friend into the room.

Just inside the doorway, Sally stopped and looked around. Her ears flattened and her fur began to rise, her tail brushed out.

'All right, Sally, it's all right, girl,' the vet soothed. 'Come over here and let's look at you.'

Sally had to pass Tara, Zenia, Wystan and Neville to reach him. Her fur rose higher at every step until she looked like a fur football.

'That isn't Sally, either,' Wystan said. 'It's one of those fancy breeds, Persian, Angora, whatchamacallem.'

Sally turned her head and spat forcefully in his direction.

'That can't be Sally.' Tara had started to hold out her hand to the cat; she changed her mind and drew it back. 'She never behaved like that.'

Neville took a step backwards. Whoever she was, he didn't intend to tangle with her.

'Here we go.' Tilbury ran his scanner over Sally. Salvatore reared up on his hind legs to sniff at it. 'Oh, you want to try it, boy? All right, then.'

Annabel hadn't realized she was holding her breath until she released it when the vet said, 'No, no chip in you.'

'And the other cat?' Mr Pennyman queried.

'Oh, yes, definitely our Sally.'

'But she looks nothing like—' Zenia began to protest and

173

stopped. Sally's fur was slowly falling back into place and she looked more Sallylike with every passing moment.

'Definitely,' the vet said again. 'Her chip is in there.'

'Oh, good,' Tara said. 'Now we can take her home. Where she belongs.'

'I think not,' Mr Pennyman said. 'I believe we'll take her with us. We wouldn't want any more . . . accidents.'

'I don't know what you mean,' Zenia said frostily.

'Possibly he refers to the cat in the jewel casket, the one you tried to pass off as Sally, deceased.' Luther spoke in the rational detached tone of a good personal assistant explaining a difficult problem to a faintly dimwitted employer.

'That cat was dead when we found it!' Neville protested. 'That's why we thought it was Sally.'

'That's right,' Tara agreed. 'We'd never kill a cat.'

'What about a human being?' Suddenly, their sanctimoniousness infuriated Annabel beyond recall. 'It's too bad someone didn't feel that way about killing Arthur Arbuthnot.'

Mr Pennyman raised an eyebrow, but did not clear his throat. She was not his client.

'How dare you!' Zenia whirled to face her.

'What do you mean?' Wystan had gone pale.

'And Dora Stringer,' Annabel added, with a sense of fatality. In for a penny, in for a pound.

'Are we to assume that you have some basis for these allegations?' Mr Pennyman inquired.

'If you mean absolute proof, no.' Annabel could feel the tension dissipate in those around her and regretted that she had tipped her hand so soon.

'Proof notwithstanding' – Mr Pennyman looked at her consideringly – 'you would not, I trust, make these, er, suggestions without feeling that you had justification for them. Apart from, er, female intuition, that is?'

'How about a bloodstain on the office carpet?' Annabel was emboldened by the possibly irrational suspicion that Mr Pennyman was on her side. Unlike the others, he appeared to be willing to consider the possibility that his late client's demise might not have been unassisted. 'A bloodstain – right where Arthur Arbuthnot had been lying.'

174

'Ridiculous!' Zenia snorted.

'I saw it, too,' Kelda said.

The room went very quiet.

'There *is* a stain on the carpet,' Luther agreed. 'I noticed it when I was working in the office. Of course, I'm not an expert. I couldn't tell you whether it's blood or coffee. But, doubtless, someone will be able to.'

'The proper testing can be arranged.' Mr Pennyman steepled his fingers again. 'But is that what we really want?'

'Certainly not!' Zenia snarled. 'We are not going to stand by and see our lives disrupted on the word of a drunken gin-soaked madwoman!'

Mr Pennyman cleared his throat.

'She *does* carry a flask,' Neville said. 'And to work, too.'

'So might you!' Annabel snapped. 'If you had to deal with people like yourselves!'

'This is all so pointless—' There was a quaver in Tara's voice. 'It can't be true. Who would want to murder Arthur? He wasn't a bad sort. And no one has gained by it. Except the cat.'

'I think we can take it as read,' Mr Pennyman said drily, 'that Sally did not stab her master in order to inherit.'

A fresh shower of coins hit the main window sharply. A long crack appeared.

'Money is at the root of it,' Annabel said. 'Not inheritance. Just plain money. All that ready cash in the safe. I didn't take it – but someone did. Someone in this room.'

'I always told Arthur he was a fool to keep that much money on the premises! It was an open invitation to burglars – and the untrustworthy!' Zenia's pointed gaze raked Mark and Luther, then turned to Annabel, just in case she thought anyone was fooled by her protestations of innocence.

'There must have been a few hundred thousand there, if one added up the value of all the various currencies,' Neville said. 'The woman has a point.'

The others had gone very quiet. More coins hit the main window and tiny cracks began to radiate outwards from the large one. The window wasn't all that was close to breaking.

'You—' Annabel looked at Tara. 'You had a lot of foreign money in your billfold on Saturday. Is the American dollar really the currency they use in Mustique?'

'Dollars are good anywhere,' Tara said defiantly. 'Anyway, I might go to New York next.'

'Planning your getaway?' Annabel was unsurprised.

'Oh, now stop right there!' Wystan decided to intervene. 'You can't think Tara had anything to do with it. If you ask me, it was' – he took a deep breath – 'Dora Stringer! Yes, Dora! She was in a position of trust. She must have been quietly skimming off small sums for years.'

'Certainly, Arthur was deeply concerned about something he had discovered recently,' Mr Pennyman said slowly. 'That was why he made out a will in Sally's favour. It was never meant to be anything more than a temporary measure, until he got to the bottom of what was going on.'

'That was my understanding,' Luther concurred. 'In fact, I was detailed to spread the word about the will – just in case anyone thought Arthur might be worth more to them dead than alive. But I never had time to begin letting the news leak out, as we had planned. He died so suddenly. But I find it hard to believe that Miss Stringer —'

'Dora,' Wystan insisted. 'Arthur caught the poor old girl in the act and she killed him and cleared the safe. Then she . . . she found she couldn't live with herself – and without him. So she – Well . . .' He trailed off, looking at them unhappily. 'Not a pretty story . . . and not one we'd want to have the tabloids get hold of . . .'

'You're right, Wystan,' his wife said. 'This is the sort of thing one must keep in the family.'

'Exactly.' Wystan nodded glumly. 'After all, poor Dora was practically a member of the family. Been with us all these years . . .'

'If that was the case, then a lot of money should have been found with Dora Stringer's effects,' Annabel pointed out. 'Was it? I think not. Whereas, I know for a fact that Tara was in possession of, literally, a bundle.'

'Leave poor old Tara alone,' Wystan said, with feeble gallantry 'Nothing to do with her.'

Tara had begun chewing on a fingernail.

'That was a truly masterly reconstruction of possible events,' Mr Pennyman conceded. 'But may I suggest that, as they say, only the names have been changed to protect – in this case – the guilty?'

'Maybe Tara wouldn't mind if we searched her room,' Kelda suggested. 'If she's innocent, she won't have anything to hide.'

'Now that is too much!' Tara surged to her feet. 'Are you going to stand there and let them say things like that about me?' She looked, interestingly, to Wystan for support, before looking to Neville.

'It might not be a bad idea.' Zenia had not missed that look. 'I think I'll lead the search party myself.'

Mr Pennyman did not clear his throat. There was a long silence.

'I'm not going down alone,' Tara warned.

'Steady on.' Neville stepped forward. 'No need to panic.'

'Dora,' Wystan insisted stubbornly. 'It was all poor old Dora. One of life's tragedies —'

'Oh, shut up, you fool!' The words were Zenia's, but the voice was Tara's. It appeared that Wystan eventually had that effect on everybody.

'Don't you call my husband a fool, you slut!' Zenia snapped.

Mr Pennyman still did not clear his throat. He watched with as much interest as the cats, whose heads were turning from combatant to combatant.

Something heavy hit the window and the glass pane shattered, spraying glass across the room.

Any stray cat knows what it means when the rocks start flying. Salvatore took to his heels and skittered across the room for the safety of the kitchen. Sally wrenched herself free of the vet and dashed after him.

'I'll call him anything I like!' Tara's fragile composure also shattered. 'Fool! Thief! *He* gave me the money. With Arthur dead, our original plan was ruined, so we were going to run away together. He'd do anything to get away from *you!* But I never thought he'd – He swore Arthur was dead when he found him. So it made sense to clear out the safe and —'

'Ah, yes.' Mr Pennyman nodded sagely. 'Such an excellent reconstruction that it could have been done only by someone who was actually there. And trying to throw the blame on someone else.'

'Wystan!' Zenia gasped.

Wystan, of course, Annabel realized. Who else would have been quite so inept at breaking and entering? And that sudden disconcerting flash of violence when he ripped out the entryphone wires had betrayed a side of his character usually kept well concealed beneath that weak bumbling exterior. A side that would allow him to lash out savagely at anyone who had trapped him.

'Murderer!' Tara's voice rose to a scream. 'You killed Arthur! You couldn't wait until I got access to his money. You went to that safe again – and he caught you stealing. You! You killed him!' She burst into sobs.

'Erm . . . self-defence,' Wystan offered. 'He went for me. He was going to kill me . . . injure me. In a very nasty mood . . .' Wystan was trapped now. His face still held the neutral, faintly apologetic expression familiar to it, but his eyes moved rapidly, assessing the situation he was in, searching for a way out.

Annabel told herself that she should have suspected 'Uncle' Wystan earlier. Just because a man is a buffoon, it doesn't mean he can't be a villain.

'Pennyman!' Zenia ordered. 'Do something!'

'Quite right, dear lady,' Mr Pennyman murmured soothingly. 'We will institute divorce proceedings in the morning.'

'Never mind divorce,' Zenia snapped. 'I want him hanged!'

'One does understand. Unfortunately these things are never quite so simple. Apart from the fact that we no longer have the death penalty, I fear that there is insufficient evidence for the Crown Prosecution Service to mount a viable case. They don't like to undertake prosecutions without "a realistic prospect of conviction", as they put it.'

'But he just confessed,' Zenia flared. 'You heard him!'

'Self-defence,' Wystan said. 'Self-defence, that was all I admitted. Arthur threatened me, was getting violent, went for me. I was afraid for my own life. I snatched up the letter-opener—' Wystan broke off abruptly, as though suddenly realizing that he was admitting too much.

'Mind you—' A crafty look came over his face as he decided to try to change the subject. 'It wasn't just the money Arthur was upset about. I think he was beginning to suspect about me and Tara. So long as he thought she favoured Neville, he was prepared to be a bit tolerant because they were both young. But he and I were closer to the same age, so jealousy played a big part in his fury.'

Not to mention outrage over the fact that Wystan was his aunt's husband. It would not be surprising, Annabel decided, if Arthur really had grown angry enough to threaten the man who was stealing his woman as well as his money.

'And I suppose Dora Stringer was trying to kill you, too?' Luther was coldly disdainful. 'Not that one could blame her, if she was.'

Wystan nodded slowly, as though realizing that he had just been given, however inadvertently, another out. 'That's right. Poor old Dora, quite demented. You know how she was about Arthur – unhealthy, really. Got it into her head that I'd taken all that money. You know how she was—' He turned to Annabel for support. 'She accused you of taking the money first.'

Annabel stared him down coldly. He would get no sympathy from her.

'Ah, well . . . Dora went mad, quite mad,' he said. 'Somehow she realized I'd . . . had to act in self-defence against Arthur. She went for me. I thought she was going to kill me. I was standing in front of the open window at the time – and she just flew at me. Naturally, I stepped aside to escape her. I never thought – It was an accident. You must see that.'

'You can testify against him!' Zenia swung to face Tara, still trying. 'You're his accomplice. They'll go lightly on you, if you turn Queen's Evidence.'

'I'm no one's accomplice!' Tara drew herself up. 'He

179

duped me, just as he duped you. I have no evidence to give. I know nothing about anything. In any case' – her eyes grew shifty – 'I may not even be in the country at the time of any trial.'

Annabel placed a mental bet with herself that Tara already had an outward flight booked – and not necessarily to New York.

'You heard him – all of you!' Zenia looked from one to another desperately.

'Self-defence.' Wystan would not now be budged.

Annabel wondered if anyone else had noticed that he was edging, almost imperceptibly, towards the door.

'I'm not going to say anything more until I have a solicitor present.' He glared at Mr Pennyman. 'A good one!'

'I don't care what anyone says—' Zenia also glared at Mr Pennyman before transferring the glare to her husband. 'You'll pay for this – and it will be the first thing in all the time I've known you that you *have* paid for anything!'

'I won't stand here and be insulted any longer!' Clutching at a precarious dignity, while moving rapidly, Wystan crossed to the door and wrenched it open, breaking into a run as he gained the main hallway.

At first, Annabel thought he had taken the wrong turning. Then she remembered the fire stairs. Wystan had good reason to know where they were located. It would not be the first time he had used them.

The others had followed her out into the hallway and were staring bemusedly at the still swinging fire door when it happened.

They heard the rush of pounding feet, the shouts, the screams – the crash. The silence.

Then they heard the solitary footsteps hesitantly mounting the stairs. The fire door opened slowly.

'I'm sorry.' Cindy stood there, staring at them dazedly. 'I think somebody better call an ambulance. Maybe two.'

'Why?' Kelda started for the fire door.

'I wouldn't go down there,' Cindy said. 'It's pretty bad.'

'What happened?'

'We were running up the stairs. We were almost at the

top when that weedy old boy came running down, taking the stairs two or three at a time. He and Sid – Sid is a big man. When they hit bottom, he was on top. Sort of. You could do them more damage trying to untangle them. Call an ambulance and leave it to the experts.'

Zenia and Tara pushed past her and rushed through the fire door. Then Zenia started screaming.

'I told her it was pretty bad,' Cindy said, slumping to the floor.

'Another martini?' Annabel smiled with favour on Mr Pennyman; he was the only one who had not asked for ice.

'I might easily be persuaded,' he agreed. 'You mix, as I believe they say, a mean martini, dear lady.'

'I shouldn't even be in charge of a wheelchair after a couple of these,' Mark said. Annabel caught Kelda's look of pleased surprise – it was obviously the first time Mark had made a joke about his situation. Things could only get better.

Mr Tilbury took another cautious sip of his and tickled Sally's ears. She was curled up happily in his lap.

'Do you think we ought to ring the hospital and get the latest report?' Kelda asked.

'What latest? "Resting comfortably" is all they ever say.' Annabel was pragmatic – and too comfortably unwinding after the hectic day to want to get involved further. 'Tara and Zenia are under sedation, with Neville standing by. Cindy has been treated for shock and is watching over Sid and all his broken bones. And Wystan —'

'I don't believe we'll have to concern ourselves with Wystan,' Mr Pennyman said. 'His condition is grave – and I believe he has lost the will to live any longer.' He sighed. 'Even if he were to escape prosecution, his future would be bleak. I suppose it's all for the best.'

'And so little Sally cops the lot.' Luther shook his head bemusedly. 'By default.'

'Not quite,' Mr Pennyman smiled. 'Arthur Arbuthnot laid careful and intricate plans, just in case. There will be a suitable redistribution of the estate in due course.'

'How can you do that?' Luther was alert. 'Are they going to be able to contest the will, after all?'

'The will was, shall we say, a false front, intended to be set aside in certain circumstances. I am the executor of a secret trust which Arthur set up at the same time he made the will.'

'I didn't know anything about this!' Luther gulped the dregs of his martini indignantly.

'You were not intended to. That's why it was a secret trust,' Mr Pennyman smiled indulgently. 'The general public doesn't realize secret trusts can exist, but they do. Their use is rare, but not unknown. They ensure that the testator's wishes can be carried out secretly, without anyone knowing. That was why Arthur set his up.'

'Then the cat doesn't inherit?' Luther began to laugh immoderately. Perhaps Annabel had mixed those martinis a bit too strong. 'All that fuss – and for nothing!'

'Oh, Sally will do quite well, when all is said and done. She'll live in the lap of luxury – but she won't be able to cast the deciding vote at any board of directors meetings.'

'Live where?' Annabel wanted to know. 'With Zenia? Tara? Neville?' They all seemed unlikely candidates for taking the best care of her.

'Possibly, Mr Tilbury will have that honour.' Mr Pennyman steepled his fingers at the veterinarian. 'Arthur wanted to be sure Sally had the best possible care always. Mr Tilbury is well placed to provide that, if he agrees. She will, of course, come to him with a substantial legacy of her own, enough to endow an animal hospital which, I believe, is what Arthur had in mind.'

'It isn't as though Sally will be in a boarding cattery, or anything like that,' Mr Tilbury assured Annabel earnestly. 'She'll live in my house, be my house cat, won't you, luv?' He rubbed her ears and Sally purred up at him. Yes, definitely a man's cat; she would be happy in his house.

One couldn't argue with that. Annabel poured another round of drinks and sank back into her chair. Salvatore sat hopefully at her feet, still slightly uneasy in the presence of someone who carried the scent of a veterinarian's surgery.

'Er, if I may ask —?' Luther looked at them. 'What are you going to do about that stray? You only took him to get him out of the way before the family managed to kill him, didn't you?'

'Do?' Annabel bent and scooped Salvatore into her arms, holding him tightly. He was another good cat who had been through more bad patches than most, but not any more.

'Do?' Salvatore looked up at her, pleased and gratified as he sensed her intentions, then he relaxed against her limply, moulding himself to her contours and began to purr loudly.

'When you have an appointment for us—' She looked over to Mr Tilbury. 'I'd like to have him microchipped. After all, Salvatore is *my* cat now.'

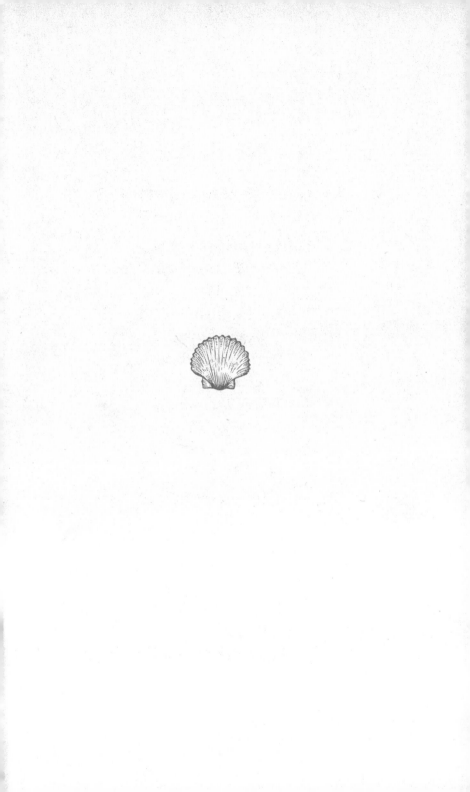

MYSTERIES *of* MARTHA'S VINEYARD

MYSTERIES *of* MARTHA'S VINEYARD

Waves of Doubt

NANCY MEHL WITH SHAEN LAYLE

Guideposts

New York

This book is dedicated to my incredible daughter-in-love, Shaen Layle (Mehl). My son Danny had to wait a while to find her, but God was faithful, even moving him from Kansas to Missouri so they could meet. After searching for years, Danny met Shaen online the first week after he relocated. They'd both been through "waves of doubt" wondering why they hadn't been able to find the *one*. But look what God has done! Not only are they perfect for each other, Shaen has become the daughter I never had. And now, God has used me to open a door she's longed to find for many years.

Please, if you have a dream, whatever it may be, stay patient. Trust God. He will not only answer your prayers but will bless the lives of many other people through His grace and love. He has a good plan for your life!

I am so thankful for this faithful, godly woman, and I could never thank her parents enough for raising such an extraordinary person. This book is also dedicated to Bryan and Darlene Pogue. Thank you for allowing us to be part of your family. We are truly blessed.

CHAPTER ONE

Priscilla took a deep breath, grabbed the folder, and got out of her car, taking a moment to smooth her wrinkled blouse and capris. Then she began walking toward the lovely house. She was struck again by the beauty of its gorgeous Queen Anne craftsmanship, both solid and delicately ornate at once. Situated just outside of Tisbury, it was surrounded by trees, hard to see from the road, and very isolated. Priscilla had heard rumors that Virginia Lawrence was thinking about selling, but she had no idea if the gossip was true. She'd only met the elusive historian once before today, when she'd set up the lecture. Priscilla's cousin, Joan Abernathy, had recruited her to snag Virginia for the summer series at the library.

"You're so much better with people than I am," she'd said. "I'm sure she'll agree to speak at the library if you ask her."

Priscilla considered herself much too tactful to point out that a past unfortunate comment, made many years ago by Joan at a History Tea sponsored by the museum, had driven a wedge between the two women. Joan never shared the actual comment, but it must have been a doozy to produce such a longstanding rift.

As Priscilla approached the front door, it suddenly swung open. Virginia Lawrence stood there in all her peculiar glory. Bright red hair in a shade not actually seen in nature was piled high on top of her head. The mound of hair, obviously a wig, tipped so precariously to one side that Priscilla worried it would topple over. Virginia's eyebrows, drawn on with black pencil, arched on her forehead, making her look permanently surprised, and her hot pink blush formed two perfect circles on her cheeks. One hand extended from underneath her red cape, which was a fashion accessory worn by the unconventional historian on all occasions, regardless of the weather. June on the Vineyard usually ranged in the 70s or 80s, but no matter how hot it got, Virginia's cape stayed in place.

"Is that it?" Virginia asked in her nasal voice. She pointed at the folder Priscilla held in her hands.

"Yes, it is," Priscilla said with a smile.

Virginia swung the door all the way open. "Please bring it in."

Priscilla suddenly felt as if the folder she had brought was the guest, and she was nothing more than a delivery driver carrying precious cargo. She followed her hostess into a large living room decorated with furniture and artwork that matched the style of the house. It was tastefully done, which surprised Priscilla. Virginia looked sadly out of place in the gracious room.

"Have a seat," the elderly woman said, waving her hand toward a rose-colored brocade couch. "Would you like some lemonade?" A pitcher and two glasses waited on a silver tray placed on a carved mahogany table in front of the couch.

"Thank you," Priscilla said as she took a seat. "That sounds nice."

At that moment, a large Irish setter came galloping into the room. He ran right up to Priscilla and sat down in front of her.

"Magnus, don't bother the woman." Although Virginia's words were a rebuke, her voice was gentle. It was clear the dog was special to her.

"He's not bothering me," Priscilla said. She stroked the soft fur on the setter's head. Magnus rewarded her with a sloppy smile. "I have a dog too. His name is Jake."

For a moment, the elderly woman's self-important expression slipped, and a softness came into her eyes. "I don't know what I'd do without Magnus," she said. "He's my best friend." As if suddenly remembering she had a guest, she cleared her throat and poured two glasses of lemonade.

"We've had a lot of interest in your lecture," Priscilla said, taking the glass held out to her. "I think we'll have peak attendance."

Virginia stared at Priscilla as if cucumbers had suddenly sprouted from her ears. "Of course we will. I have quite a following. I assumed you knew that."

Although Priscilla suspected the featured topic of Nancy Luce was the main reason for interest in the lecture, she had to admit that the whole town was buzzing over the fact that Virginia might actually make a public appearance after all these years. Though she'd lived on the island most of her life, Virginia was notoriously reclusive. And yet, Nancy Luce held a great deal of local fascination in her own right. The quirky historical figure known as the "Chicken Lady," Luce lived her entire life at her farmhouse near the head of Tiah's Cove in West Tisbury. She cared for her parents until they died, and she raised animals, including the chickens she named and loved. She was a folk artist, poet, businesswoman, and writer. Some considered her to be the first female entrepreneur on the island.

Priscilla raised the glass of lemonade to her lips, giving herself a moment to regroup. She almost gasped at the sourness of the drink. In addition to her reclusiveness, Virginia was also known as a tightwad. It appeared sugar was on her list of luxuries. Priscilla put the glass on the table and forced a smile for the starchy woman. Magnus, who seemed to have grown tired of staring at Priscilla, lay down on her feet.

"Would it kill you to use a coaster?" Virginia pointed a scarlet fingernail at Priscilla. "I assume you weren't raised in a barn. Though, coming from Kansas…" She trailed off, one eyebrow raised.

Priscilla shot Virginia another tight smile and looked for a coaster. Not finding one, she placed her napkin underneath her sweating glass. She looked longingly toward the front door.

She exhaled slowly in an attempt to steady her nerves and picked up the folder. She opened it and carefully withdrew a small journal. "Here is the most recent discovery—Nancy's diary. Mildred told me it was found in an attic in an old house in West Tisbury."

Virginia sniffed. "As the preeminent scholar of Nancy Luce's life and accomplishments, I truly believe I should be the keeper of her legacy. I have said this to Mildred Pearson many times, to no avail. Why that woman has been entrusted with the care of the East Shore Historical Museum is beyond me." She took the diary from Priscilla.

Priscilla withdrew the rest of the folder's contents—letters and photographs, all encased in plastic sleeves. "Here are some pictures of Nancy and her chickens." She put the pictures in front of

Virginia, who picked up the photos as if she were touching something sacred.

"Teeddla Toona, Levendy Ludandy, and Otte Opheto," Virginia said in a breathless tone.

"Excuse me?" Priscilla asked with alarm. Was Virginia having a stroke?

Virginia glared at Priscilla. "The names of some of her chickens. Don't you know anything about Nancy Luce?" She shook her head. "Really, if you want to work with people like me, you need to educate yourself." She sighed deeply, obviously pushed to her limits having to deal with a moron like Priscilla.

"I may not know the names of her chickens, but I know she was a very independent lady who made a name for herself because of her creativity and resilience. Like you, Virginia." Priscilla tossed her another smile even though it hurt. "I'm glad you'll be able to use these artifacts for your lecture. Mildred will meet you after the presentation tonight to pick them up. She asked me to remind you that they are on loan from the New England History Museum in Boston and should be returned in pristine condition." Priscilla stood, which took some talent since she had to regain the use of her feet. Thankfully, Magnus cooperated and scooted over. "I really must be going, but I'll see you this evening at the library."

Virginia pushed herself up from the sofa, trying not to trip over her dog. "I—I really do appreciate the chance to view these items before tonight. I will most certainly incorporate them into my lecture, and I'll guard them closely until this evening. You have my word." She stuck her hand out. "Thank you, Priscilla."

Priscilla shook Virginia's hand, wondering what had happened to make her soften her stance. Maybe she wasn't quite as obnoxious as Priscilla had assumed. "You're welcome, Virginia. I'm really looking forward to tonight."

"Of course you are, dear. I hope I can bring a spark into your dull existence."

Priscilla turned and headed for the front door and freedom. "Your home is beautiful," she said, attempting to fill the awkward silence.

"Yes, it is," Virginia said. "I'll miss it."

Priscilla turned to look at her. The rumors must be true. "Miss it? Are you leaving?"

Virginia nodded. "I've actually sold the property. I'm moving to Boston. I'm ready to leave this dreary little town behind me. *My kind of people* live in Boston, and I want to be a part of something bigger. I'm sure you understand." She gazed at her beautiful garden through the large windows that lined one side of the room and sighed. "It seems there are fewer and fewer cultural opportunities on the island. Be sure you take in *Murder by Moonlight* this Saturday night. My nephew, Douglas, is putting it on at the Playhouse, you know, and I'm the major sponsor. You won't want to miss it."

Priscilla nodded. "My cousin, Trudy Galvin, has a starring role. She's very excited about it. Loves the play."

"Of course she does. It's very good. I hope she has some talent. I would hate to see Douglas's play destroyed by amateurish hacks."

Priscilla swallowed hard. "I'd better go. I'll see you tonight." She almost ran out to her car. When she got inside, she gripped the steering wheel and waited until her pounding heart began to beat normally.

She spent the rest of the afternoon helping Mildred and Clara, the head librarian, prepare for the lecture. They decorated the library's largest conference room with poster-sized excerpts from Nancy's diary and black-and-white portraits of her beloved chickens. Linen-covered tables lined the perimeter, offering a catered spread of delicious-smelling treats from Candy Lane Confectionery. The display nearest Priscilla held a new confection from Candy—rosewater petits fours—studded judiciously with cranberries. They smelled heavenly, and Priscilla's mouth watered.

But this was no time for treats. They still had to put the chairs in place. Judging from the registration list, the room's 112-person capacity was going to be stretched to its limits. Priscilla worked until she was starting to perspire a little and had to fan the collar of her blouse to cool herself off. She was surveying their work when she heard someone call her name.

She looked up to see Joan striding purposefully toward her.

"Hi, Joan. What are you doing here so early? The event doesn't start for another forty-five minutes."

"Tell that to the mob of people waiting out front. There's even a news crew here." She rolled her eyes. "They probably think they're going to get a rare interview with the town's Havisham."

Priscilla grinned at Joan's reference to the mad Miss Havisham from Dickens's novel, *Great Expectations*. There were definite similarities between Virginia and the wildly eccentric character.

Joan glanced around the room appraisingly. "We're going to need more seating."

Clara led the women to another room that held a few more chairs. Priscilla, Mildred, and Joan had just set them up when Clara opened the door and let the crowd in. Priscilla was surprised to see Dr. Eve Pennywhistle, Virginia's chief rival for the coveted title of the Vineyard's number one historian. Virginia and Eve disliked each other intensely, but there was Eve slipping into a chair on the back row. She certainly didn't look happy.

Priscilla was also intrigued to see several women in long white dresses enter the room. The women in white. She'd heard about them from Mildred. A group dedicated to keeping Nancy Luce's legacy alive. Frankly, Priscilla found them odd. Their devotion to the long-deceased "Chicken Lady" seemed more than a little eccentric.

A few minutes later, Priscilla's cousin Gail walked through the door. Joan went over to meet her, and they took their seats on the third row, saving a seat for Trudy, who was in rehearsals at the Playhouse. She'd promised to come as soon as she got out.

Mildred sat down in the front row, probably so she could keep a close eye on the Nancy Luce items. As soon as the lecture was over, she planned to return them to the museum.

Priscilla smiled to herself as she scanned the room, watching for Gerald, her handsome Coast Guard captain. He finally showed up at six, just when the lecture was supposed to start. But where was Virginia?

At ten minutes after six, Priscilla started to perspire in earnest. Sweat, actually. The news crew was getting antsy. If Virginia didn't show up soon, they would probably leave. Five minutes later, Priscilla left the buzz of the crowd to call Virginia. She found an empty hallway and pulled her cell phone out of her purse. She didn't expect Virginia to still be at home, but what if she had taken ill at the last minute? Priscilla didn't have a mobile number for her and suspected she didn't own a cell phone. The landline rang and rang, until it finally clicked over to an answering machine with a crabby-sounding recording of Virginia deriding telemarketers and solicitors, followed by an ear-piercing beep.

"Hello? Virginia? It's Priscilla Grant. You have quite a large crowd gathered at the library. I was just—um—checking to make sure you weren't ill or something. Please call me back." With a sigh, Priscilla ended the call. If Virginia didn't show up, what on earth was she going to say to all these people? Although she'd tried to ignore them, some of the skeptical comments from the audience had reached her ears.

After several more calls to Virginia's house with no success, the reality of the situation hit Priscilla. Virginia wasn't coming. It was possible she'd changed her mind, but mere hours earlier, she'd seemed genuinely interested in leading the lecture.

In her gut, Priscilla knew something was wrong. Virginia wasn't here.

And neither were the museum's artifacts.

CHAPTER TWO

I can't believe Virginia didn't show." Joan tossed a sympathetic glance at Priscilla.

The news crew had packed up their equipment shortly after six, and the patrons cleared out soon after that. To Priscilla's dismay, they'd also cleared out Candy's mouthwatering dessert displays. Only crumbs remained. A bite of something sweet would sure ease Priscilla's frazzled nerves right now. But no such luck. She felt like a deflated party balloon.

Trudy, always the effervescent optimist, gave Priscilla's shoulders a squeeze. "I'm sure there's a reasonable explanation. Maybe Virginia got sick at the last minute?"

"Or maybe she just flaked out." Joan shook her head. "I'm sorry, Priscilla. I feel responsible. I'm the one who pushed you into this. It seemed like a good way to mend fences."

"It's all right, Joan. You didn't force me into it," Priscilla reassured her cousin. "I just don't understand it. When I met with Virginia this morning, she seemed excited about the lecture. Grateful for the opportunity. It just doesn't make sense."

"Priscilla, this is a real problem," Mildred said. The museum curator had been wringing her hands for the last thirty minutes. "You need to get those artifacts back. The New England History

Museum loaned them to us in good faith, and they're to be returned at the end of next week. Period. When I gave them to you, you promised me Virginia would return them. The only reason I handed them over was because I trusted you to make certain nothing would go wrong."

"I know, Mildred. I'll get them back. I'm sure it's just a misunderstanding."

A short, wiry man with a mustache strode toward the group of women. Virginia's nephew, Douglas, who was living with her temporarily while he produced his show at the Playhouse, looked beside himself with worry. Priscilla knew he'd tried to call his aunt several times.

"Any success getting through to your aunt?"

"No." He shook his head. "I don't know what could have happened."

"I hope she didn't fall," Trudy said, a worried expression on her face. "Maybe she couldn't get to a phone."

"I'm heading back to the house," Douglas said. "I need to check on her."

Priscilla glanced at her cell phone once again to make sure Virginia hadn't tried to contact her while they'd been talking. No missed calls. "Is it all right if I meet you there in a few minutes, Douglas? I just need to clean up a few things here first."

"Don't worry about it." Joan waved at the mess. "I told you, I feel responsible. I'll help Clara clean up. You go."

"Joan, you're a gem. Thank you." Priscilla gave her cousin a smile.

"Why don't you let me drive, Priscilla? You seem upset," Trudy offered. "We can come back and pick up your vehicle later."

Priscilla released a sigh and felt the tension in her shoulders release. She really was blessed to be surrounded by such wonderful family. Now she just had to find out what had happened to Virginia.

Her throat was tight with worry as Trudy drove to Virginia's house, the car's headlights illuminating the dense forest around them. She clutched her hands in her lap. What if Virginia really had been hurt? Or there had been a break-in? The remote house seemed to be a perfect target for burglars.

In front of them, Douglas's turn signal flashed. "Turn left here," Priscilla directed. Trudy obediently angled her car to follow Douglas's vehicle up the winding drive. It was difficult to see in the violet shadows of twilight, but the house finally appeared.

Trudy let out a tiny gasp as she exited the car. "It has turrets! And look at the fish-scale siding!" Then she covered her mouth with a fist, as if her words had run away with her.

"It's okay. It is lovely." Priscilla smiled tightly. She struggled to shake off images of Virginia, sprawled on the floor with a sprained ankle—or worse—inside that beautiful house.

"Ready, ladies?" Douglas showed them up the front steps, and after a shuddering breath, unlocked the door and pushed it open.

"Aunt Virginia?" His shoes echoed on the hardwood floor as he crossed the hall to the great room where Priscilla and Virginia had sipped lemonade.

No answer.

He called again, a little louder. He was met with ringing silence.

He poked his head back into the hallway, where Trudy and Priscilla waited by the mahogany and pitch-pine staircase. "Well, she didn't trip on the steps at any rate." Douglas looked relieved, but his voice was still shaky. "And I don't see signs of forced entry, at least from the front. So, that's good."

Priscilla had to agree. Everything was perfectly in place, from the copper umbrella stand to the blue-and-white Oriental vases flanking the entry table. With so many delicate pieces on display, it seemed something would have been broken if a scuffle had taken place.

"Where is Magnus?" Priscilla asked. She'd expected the exuberant dog to meet them when they came in.

"He's in a back room," Douglas said. "My aunt puts him up when she leaves the house."

Sure enough, Priscilla could hear faint barking from the rear of the house. "Maybe we should fan out and give the whole house a once-over," she said. "Would that be okay with you, Douglas?"

"Of course. I'll take the upstairs. You two could search down here. Just please be careful." As if to illustrate his point, he grabbed a particularly spiky umbrella from the burnished holder and held it in front of him like a machete as he ascended the stairs. "And please don't let Magnus out," he said as he disappeared from sight.

Priscilla couldn't help but think his actions were rather theatrical. As soon as he was out of earshot, she caught Trudy's eye, and they both burst into giggles.

"An umbrella might do some damage, I guess."

"He looks like he's about to jump out of his skin, poor man."

Priscilla wasn't sure it was appropriate to laugh under the circumstances, but after the tension of the last few hours, some break in emotion felt necessary.

"You check the dining room and kitchen, and I'll search the rest?" Priscilla asked.

Trudy nodded and tiptoed off. Priscilla combed the great room once more, as well as the formal sitting room and a bathroom. On a whim, she stepped out into the cool garden, with its beautiful plants and pleasing décor. A path of paver stones gleamed in the moonlight. All looked pristine and ordinary.

There was no evidence of a struggle. No reason to think there had been an accident. It was as if Virginia had vanished into thin air. But Priscilla couldn't shake the feeling that something was off. She didn't have time to dwell on it though.

Trudy shouted. Whether she had been attacked or found something unpleasant, Priscilla didn't know, but she hurried back inside, her heart pounding in her ears. Douglas's eyes were wide as saucers as he scrambled down the staircase.

"Trudy! Are you all right?"

"I'm fine!" Trudy called, and Priscilla felt a whoosh of relief. "I think I found something."

Douglas and Priscilla entered the kitchen to find Trudy hovering over a note pinned down by a butterfly paperweight on the kitchen counter.

Douglas pulled at his mustache in a gesture of anxiety. "What does it say? Is she all right?"

"I don't know," Trudy said. "I can't quite make out the handwriting. It's hard to read."

Priscilla glanced at the note to see an ocean of scrolled letters. It looked as if it had been dashed off quickly by someone in too much of a hurry to be neat. "I see something about the island. Maybe Oak Bluffs?"

Douglas pushed in. "Let me read it. I know my aunt's handwriting." He squinted for a few seconds. "It looks like, 'Dear Douglas, I just couldn't bring myself to speak at the library tonight. I'm sorry to let everyone down, but my nerves wouldn't allow me to appear in front of all those people. I'm leaving for a few days to travel the island—maybe Oak Bluffs. Maybe Edgartown. A little fresh air and time to finish research for my book will do me good.'"

"But where are the artifacts?" Priscilla asked. "Does she mention them?"

Douglas shrugged. "I don't know. Let me finish reading." He hunched over the paper again. "Let's see—'Please tell Mildred at the East Shore Historical Museum that I have sent the Nancy Luce items back to her by courier. She should have them by sometime this evening.'"

"Ah, well, there you have it." Douglas shrugged. "I'm sorry. My aunt has been reclusive for a long time. I guess the lecture was just too much for her. I'm certain she's fine. When I checked her bathroom I noticed that many of her toiletries are gone. I also checked the garage. Her car is gone. She's probably staying somewhere on the island. She'll come home when she's good and ready." He rolled his eyes. "That's just how she is."

Trudy's brows knit together as she looked at Priscilla. "Maybe you should call Mildred to see if the courier has arrived yet."

Priscilla fumbled for her phone. She called the museum, but no one answered. Then she tried the library, but Clara told her Mildred had already left.

"There's nothing in the note to indicate which courier service she used," Priscilla said after she disconnected. "The artifacts could be anywhere."

Douglas sighed loudly. "My aunt has a problem using the phone book. I know it sounds silly, but she was always looking at one listing and dialing a different number. She's tried ordering pizza from a car repair shop and flowers from a chiropractor. Argued with the poor man for almost ten minutes, determined he was going to give in and bring her the fresh flowers she wanted."

That news certainly didn't help quell the nervous butterflies in Priscilla's stomach. Where in the world were the artifacts?

CHAPTER THREE

Saturday morning Priscilla woke up with a slight headache. She knew it came from worrying about the missing museum pieces. Douglas had promised to call every courier service in the area to see if he could find out which one his aunt had contacted.

The possibility that the artifacts were floating around the island somewhere, maybe even in the hands of someone Virginia had accidentally called, was the reason Priscilla's sleep had been restless at best. She sat up and swung her legs over the side of the bed. She stayed there a moment, thinking. Why wouldn't Virginia deliver the items to the museum herself before she took off? Was she so embarrassed by her last-minute attack of nerves that she put the precious artifacts at risk? No one valued them more than Virginia. It didn't add up.

Douglas had told Priscilla several times that his aunt had a propensity for disappearing on a whim. Priscilla had heard this from other people and believed it to be true. But Virginia had seemed so excited about the lecture. Priscilla hadn't sensed any hesitation in her attitude when they talked at Virginia's house.

Priscilla's dog, Jake, raised his head and looked at her out of one eye.

"Yeah, I'm getting up," she told him.

He immediately jumped off the bed. He was already waiting for Priscilla in the kitchen by the time she came in. His enthusiasm for food always made her laugh. She got out the dog food and poured it in his bowl. While he chowed down, she made coffee and heated up some cinnamon rolls she'd made earlier in the week.

After breakfast, she got dressed and grabbed Jake's leash. Priscilla looked forward to their morning walks. Except during really cold winter days or when it rained. On those occasions, they liked to stay close to the cottage. When she opened the door, she found that the Vineyard had produced a truly beautiful June day. She and Jake walked past the lighthouse that had been on the Latham property since 1852. Priscilla never got tired of looking at it. Down through the years, its bright beam had meant salvation for many ships at sea. And now it had rescued her as well. After the death of her husband, moving to Martha's Vineyard had brought her renewed hope. A new life. One that she loved.

Jake tugged on the leash, pulling her toward the cliffs. The seagulls that dipped and swept past the side of the cliff had changed from Jake's antagonists to his friends. He barked happily at them as they flew by, their eerie cries filling the air.

Priscilla stopped at the edge of the cliff, and Jake sat down beside her. Together, they looked out on the ocean that washed in and out, creating a constant whooshing sound that caused Priscilla's spirit to grow quiet. It was balm for her soul. Priscilla felt she and Jake were sharing a moment together that meant something to each of them. Jake, a dog lost and found, and Priscilla, a Kansas farm gal whose life had started over again in this beautiful spot. After several minutes, Priscilla broke the silence.

"Let's go, boy," she said gently.

Jake looked up at her with one of his doggy grins, which made her laugh. They turned and headed back to the cottage.

After getting Jake squared away, she was preparing to leave when the phone rang. It was Douglas. "I've called every courier service on the island, Priscilla. I hate to tell you that none of them admits to receiving a call from my aunt yesterday."

Priscilla stuttered from shock. "Are—are you sure?"

"Yes, I'm so sorry. I have no idea what happened. I'm afraid those Nancy Luce items could be anywhere. And I have no idea where my aunt is. If I could locate her, I'd be able to ask her about it. But as it is..."

Priscilla exhaled slowly as she tried to wrap her brain around Douglas's news. "I understand, Douglas. Thank you for trying to find them."

She'd just hung up the phone when it rang again. It was Trudy.

"Are you okay?" she asked when Priscilla picked up.

"No." Priscilla told her about the call from Douglas.

"Maybe the artifacts will turn up," Trudy said.

"Maybe. I'm also a little worried about Virginia."

Trudy sighed loudly. "You would be. That woman leaves you in the lurch, and you're concerned about her?"

"I'm confused, Trudy. Why would she take such a risk with Nancy Luce's artifacts? They were precious to her."

"What if she didn't?" Trudy asked.

"I don't understand…" Priscilla realized what Trudy was hinting at. "You mean, what if she lied? What if she took them?"

"It's possible, Priscilla."

"I realize Virginia has an ego the size of Texas, but I've never heard she was a thief. Have you?"

"Well, Joan told me Virginia was accused of plagiarism once, but the charges didn't hold up, and it turned out to be the other way around. I guess some wannabe historian tried to steal Virginia's thunder."

"Wannabe historian? Are there a lot of them out there?"

"Sure there are. Historians are important people…in some circles. I guess if you're into history, stealing someone else's work could be seen as pretty serious."

"I guess."

"What are you doing today?" Trudy asked.

"I'm thinking about going by the police station. I want to talk to Chief Westin."

"So you *do* think she might have stolen that stuff? Wow. If I ever get nicked for theft, I hope it's for something worth more than a bunch of old papers and pictures that belonged to a woman who made tombstones for her chickens."

"Oh, Trudy. First of all, you'll never get *nicked* for stealing." Priscilla paused a moment. "I'm not going there to accuse Virginia of anything. I want Chief Westin to help me find the artifacts. And Virginia. Make certain she's okay."

"Look, I'm rehearsing for the play this morning. Why don't we meet for lunch afterward?"

"I thought you rehearsed at night."

A frustrated sigh came across the line. "According to Douglas, we're not 'breathing in the spirit of the play.' I have no idea what that means. I'm breathing just fine. Or I would be if he wasn't getting on my last nerve."

Priscilla laughed. "Okay. Why don't we meet at the Nautilus? I'm in the mood for one of their great salads."

"Sounds good. Will twelve thirty work for you?"

"Perfect. After the police station, I need to go by the museum and talk to Mildred. If she's still speaking to me, that is."

"Yikes. I don't envy you. I had no idea a human being's face could turn that red. I thought she was going to stroke out right there in the library. Is there any chance someone brought the Nancy Luce stuff back?"

"Not much. If none of the courier services delivered them, I don't know who would do that. Besides, Mildred would have called me if she'd received them. I have no idea what to say to her. I'm hoping that when I tell her I went to the police she'll feel better."

"I don't think she'll feel better until you put those artifacts in her hands."

"You could be right, but I'm going to try to mollify her if I can."

"Good luck," Trudy said. "Would I be a disloyal cousin if I told you I'm glad it's you and not me?"

"No," Priscilla said. "You're just an honest cousin. I can't fault you for that."

Trudy said goodbye and hung up. Priscilla stared at the phone for several seconds, wondering if her visit to Hank would help bring this nightmare to an end. She really wasn't sure he could do anything, but he was a smart man. The idea of having him on her side made her feel better.

Priscilla said goodbye to Jake and jumped in her SUV. She rolled the windows down so she could enjoy the summer air. It was in the 60s and would climb into the 70s later in the day. But right now, the temperature was perfect.

By the time she pulled into the police station parking lot she had rehearsed what she wanted to say to Hank several times. She was certain he'd be willing to help her find Virginia.

She pushed the door of the police station open and found Gabrielle Grimes manning the main desk.

"Well hello, Priscilla." Gabrielle pushed her thick glasses back up on her nose. "How are you?"

"Pretty good, Gabrielle. How are you?"

"Can't complain. Things have been pretty quiet lately."

"Is he in?"

Gabrielle nodded slowly, her expression guarded. "Just a moment." She picked up the phone on her desk and pushed a button. "Priscilla Grant is here, Chief. Do you want to see her?"

Her question seemed more like a warning than a query. But Hank obviously replied in the affirmative, because Gabrielle said, "Okay, Chief. I'll send her in." She put the phone down and gestured toward the door behind her.

Priscilla smiled and walked past her into the hallway that led to Hank's office. She knocked on his door and heard him call out, "Come in!"

When she opened the door, she found him hunched over his desk, a pile of papers in front of him.

"Priscilla," he said, his eyes narrowed and his face tight. "I've got a lot of paperwork that needs to get done today. What can I do for you?"

It was obvious the chief was under pressure. Priscilla hated to add to his stress, but she had no choice. She heaved a sigh and took a seat.

"I need you to help me find some artifacts that have gone missing from the New England History Museum," she said. "On loan to our own museum."

"The museum was robbed? Why am I just now hearing about this? Why hasn't Mildred called us?"

"Well, they didn't go missing from the museum. They were loaned to Virginia Lawrence, and she was supposed to return them last night during her lecture. But she didn't show up. She left a note saying she sent the artifacts back to the museum through a courier service. However, they never arrived. I'm really concerned because Douglas told me Virginia has a habit of accidentally calling the wrong numbers from the phone book. She might have picked a nearby number instead of a courier service."

The chief frowned. "I'm not sure what you want me to do."

"I guess I'm worried about the missing items...and Virginia. She was really looking forward to the lecture last night. It doesn't make sense that she just suddenly disappeared."

Hank frowned at her. "So, what's the crime? I take it you have no proof Virginia has these..."

"Artifacts."

"I know, thank you. These artifacts."

"No," Priscilla said, feeling a little defensive. "I don't have any proof, but the artifacts are gone, and so is Virginia. Something's not right."

"I'm sorry, Priscilla. It sounds to me like Virginia left on her own accord, and she sent these items back to the museum through a courier service. There's no telling how long it might take them to make a delivery. They could be running behind. There's no crime here. Nothing I can do."

"But those items from the museum are valuable, Chief. Can you at least keep an eye open for them? And for Virginia?"

Hank stood to his feet. It was obvious he was ready for Priscilla to leave. He took a deep breath and let it out. "Look, I'll spread the word. Tell my officers to let me know if they hear anything about these missing museum pieces. And we'll watch out for Virginia. But I can't do anything more than that. Not at this point."

Priscilla stood up and offered her hand to the cranky police chief. He shook it and gave her a small smile.

As she left his office, she was pretty sure the smile came from Hank's relief that she was leaving.

So now what? The artifacts were missing, and Priscilla was responsible for them. Somehow, she had to find them. With Hank's help or without it.

CHAPTER FOUR

Priscilla walked out of the station and stood on the sidewalk for a few minutes. She was disappointed in her meeting with Hank. She could only hope things would go better with Mildred. Just to make sure, she stopped by Candy's to pick up some crème horns—Mildred's favorite—as a token of apology. The sweet-smelling treats filled Priscilla's car with a sugary aroma, and her stomach growled. Lunch with Trudy couldn't come quickly enough.

The short drive to the East Shore Historical Museum did Priscilla good. The temperature had climbed from the early morning, but the breeze that whooshed through her open windows still felt pleasant and light. A little fresh sea air cured a lot of woes.

It helped that she felt hopeful about receiving a positive reception from Mildred. The woman had had time to calm down and, after all, she and Mildred had grown close over the last couple of years, bonding over the heartache of widowhood and the promise of new seasons of life. Priscilla had even gifted Mildred with her cat, Hiacoomes.

With a lighter heart and higher hopes, Priscilla stepped out of her SUV and opened the door of the museum. Mildred waited a few feet away wearing a beautifully ruffled Victorian bodice over a plum-colored gown. Her gray hair was pulled into a tight bun, making her look every inch the severe schoolmarm.

Priscilla gulped. "Good morning, Mildred. I brought crème horns, if you have time for a visit."

The caretaker didn't smile. "Good morning, Priscilla. Please come in."

Priscilla clutched the bag of treats and stepped across the threshold as a tiny bell chimed her arrival.

Mildred headed toward the back of the museum, where the kitchen was located. "Would you like a cup of coffee?" she asked over her shoulder. Her skirts rustled as she walked.

"I don't think I'll take one today. I've been drinking more iced coffee this summer," Priscilla said. Perhaps she was imagining Mildred's disapproving look at the doorway. The older woman had invited her in for coffee. That was a positive sign. Although maybe she was just interested in the pastry.

In the kitchen Priscilla slipped into a chair at the large rectangular table. Mildred popped a pod into the Keurig for herself and, after it brewed, sat down at the table. She eyed Priscilla's small handbag.

"I see you've come empty-handed. I'd hoped you'd located the Nancy Luce artifacts."

Priscilla sighed. "I haven't, Mildred, but I will." She rushed to explain. "I left the library last night and went to Virginia's house."

"And?" Mildred raised an eyebrow and took a sip of her coffee.

"And she wasn't there." Priscilla explained about the note, Virginia's reluctance to attend the lecture, and her plan to take some time to do research on the island.

Mildred shook her head. "But I don't understand. You did deliver the items, correct?"

"Yes, I did. Virginia left a note saying she'd changed her mind about the lecture. She claims she had the artifacts sent back here through a courier. I don't suppose anyone has contacted you about them?"

Mildred took another sip of her coffee and narrowed her eyes. A long pause hung heavy in the air before she spoke. "Don't you think if I'd heard something, I'd tell you?" She frowned at Priscilla. "I'm not sure what peculiar brand of tomfoolery is going on here, but the artifacts have to be somewhere. They didn't just disappear into thin air."

"I'm just as confused as you are, Mildred. I assure you." Priscilla gulped nervously. "Douglas Lawrence called every courier service in the area looking for them. Every one of them denied receiving a call from Virginia. Frankly, I have no idea where they are." Priscilla blinked back tears. "I'm so sorry about this. I trusted Virginia to bring them back. Obviously, that was a mistake."

"I don't know if you understand the gravity of this situation, Priscilla." Mildred set her cup down. "My reputation is on the line. If those artifacts are not returned, this museum could get shut down. I—" The older woman bit off her sentence before finishing it, but Priscilla knew what she meant. If the museum shut down, Mildred would be out of a job.

Priscilla knew widowhood had been a tough transition for Mildred. She needed work to give her purpose. And she'd run the museum for so many years, it was probably a large part of her own identity. She'd kept it afloat for so long, constantly beating back the threat of low funds and waning public support. Knowing how important this place was to Mildred made Priscilla feel even worse. She had to find those artifacts. In the end, she alone was responsible for their return. She'd promised to bring them back, and she had to follow through.

Mildred shook her finger at Priscilla. "You must find them, Priscilla. There will be serious trouble if you don't."

"I understand." Priscilla stood. "Goodbye, Mildred."

"Goodbye, Priscilla."

Priscilla walked outside to her vehicle. She opened her car door, and the sugary scent of crème horns still lingered, even though she'd left the bag in the museum's kitchen with Mildred. Priscilla couldn't help but think the situation must be dire. Mildred hadn't even touched the pastry.

"It sounds like you've had a rough start to your day." Trudy tucked a strand of platinum-blond hair behind one ear and gave Priscilla a sympathetic look. Priscilla had just filled her in on the details of her morning errands, and her cousin, as expected, was comforting. Just because it was expected didn't make Priscilla appreciate it any less though. Trudy was a keeper.

Priscilla nodded and took a long sip of her sweet tea. Even though the tourist season wasn't quite in full swing yet, the Nautilus Café was still substantially busier than it had been at the end of spring. She and Trudy had somehow managed to snag a corner booth, where they could talk privately without much fear of being overheard.

Glancing around at the restaurant's calming beachy décor, Priscilla felt herself begin to relax. The Nautilus was like being inside a particularly cozy sailing vessel, its planked walls dotted with shells, nets, and anchors. The impression was made even more pronounced by the lapping ocean practically outside the door and the fishermen at the dock unloading their morning's fresh catch.

"I think what bothers me most is that Mildred didn't seem as though she gave me the benefit of the doubt. She acted like I was keeping the artifacts from her on purpose."

Trudy reached over and patted Priscilla's hand. "I know it's terrible to feel as if your character is being questioned."

Priscilla wondered if Trudy was remembering the time her husband, Dan, soft-spoken and gentle as he was, had been suspected of being mixed up in a missing person case. In that situation, Dan's name was eventually cleared, and the missing man, a drifter on a houseboat, had been found, safe and well. Priscilla could only hope things would turn out as positively for her. When word got around that the Nancy Luce collection was missing, what would people think? Since it was her job to oversee the transfer, would they blame her for the loss?

"So, what are you going to do?" Trudy asked. "About the missing artifacts, I mean?"

Priscilla shrugged. "I guess the only thing I can do now is try to find Virginia and sort out this whole mess. Though I have to admit, I have no idea where she could be. Her note didn't exactly narrow down the options."

"It has to be a misunderstanding." Trudy stirred the lemon wedge in her water glass with her straw and looked thoughtful. "How old is Virginia anyway? Do you think she might have been confused when she wrote that letter?"

Priscilla raised an eyebrow. "She's not much older than we are, and if you're suggesting she's having memory lapses..." She trailed off, but Trudy got the gist.

"Oh, right. And we're spring chickens, so that idea is obviously silly." Trudy tried another angle. "Is it possible that Virginia's lying? Could she have stolen the letters and photos and taken off?"

"It's possible, but what reason would she have for stealing them?"

"Cash?" Trudy pursed her lips. "I'm sure there are shady buyers out there who'd pay quite a bit to get their grubby hands on primary resources."

"I didn't get the impression Virginia was hurting for money. She just sold her property here, and with its location and historic value, I'm sure it brought a tidy sum. Besides, I don't think Nancy Luce is famous enough to make her personal property that valuable. Of course, with the discovery of the diary, it's probably worth more now than it was previously. I can't believe it would bring more than a couple thousand dollars if it went to auction though."

"Then maybe Virginia just wanted to keep the items in a personal collection. You know, just act like they disappeared, and wait until the fuss died down? You did say she was excited to look them over when you visited."

Priscilla shook her head. "That would be pretty bold, even for Virginia. I guess anything's possible, but I have a gut feeling something else is going on. I don't know why. I really need to think about it more and figure out how to locate Virginia. She's the missing piece of the puzzle, and nothing is going to make sense until we find her."

"Well, I'll do my best to help you, though I'm pretty stumped too." Trudy brightened. "Hey, maybe we should brainstorm a list of places to look for her. I have plans this evening, but tomorrow after church, we could get out and get some fresh air? See what we can find?"

Priscilla nodded. "That sounds like a great idea. And for right now, maybe we can just try to enjoy lunch?"

"Agreed," Trudy said.

Priscilla's mind kept spinning though. Would she be able to find Virginia and set things right? Or was she going to lose her friendship with Mildred? The thought of that made her want to cry.

CHAPTER FIVE

Priscilla struggled to empty her mind of confused thoughts and choose a dish from the menu. Everything looked good. Her stomach rumbled again. It was definitely time to eat. If nothing else, her morning of confrontation had worked up an appetite.

As if on cue, their waitress appeared, clad in a smart black apron. Her blond-streaked hair was pulled back in a loose ponytail, and her name tag read *Julie*. She pulled a pad and pen from her apron pocket. "Are you ladies ready to order, or do you need a few extra minutes to look over the menu?"

"I think we're ready." Priscilla took one last glance at the list of salads. Something fresh and light would sit easier on her churning stomach than rich seafood or a heavy sandwich. "I'd like the Boston salad with chopped almonds and lemon vinaigrette, please."

"And I'll take the Bibb lettuce salad with tomatoes and bacon," said Trudy.

Julie smiled. "All right, we'll get those right out." She headed back to the kitchen with their order.

Trudy sighed wistfully. "That salad is the closest thing to a BLT I can think of. I'm going low-carb, and it's been tougher than I thought."

Priscilla smothered a laugh. Trudy bounced in and out of diet plans, trying a new one every few months. Priscilla suspected it had as much to do with Trudy's exuberance in testing new trends as it did her desire to lose weight. She had to say, she couldn't fault Trudy's methods though. Her cousin looked fabulous and svelte.

In no time at all, Julie returned with their food. The salads looked delicious. Priscilla and Trudy said grace and dug in.

"Who needs bread anyway?" Priscilla said with a smile.

Trudy paused a beat before wailing, "Me!" She speared lettuce and a cherry tomato on her fork. "But I suppose I can live without it for a while. At least I'll be able to fit into my dress for Rachel's wedding."

Rachel's wedding.

Priscilla couldn't believe her little girl was getting married. It seemed like only yesterday she was putting Band-Aids on her daughter's skinned knees, taking her to kindergarten, helping her with math homework. Now her darling girl was all grown up and starting a new chapter of her life. The whole thing felt surreal.

"How's the planning going?" Trudy asked.

Priscilla answered honestly. "Good, I think." She took a thoughtful bite of her own salad. The bright lemony dressing had been a good choice, summery and refreshing. "Rachel and A.J. have taken most of the work on themselves. You know young professionals. They've got a sense of pride." She grinned. "I'm getting frequent updates, but I wish they'd give me more to do."

"Did you get a mother-of-the-bride dress yet? If you haven't, we could go shopping together." Trudy's eyes practically sparkled, and Priscilla imagined there was nothing Trudy would like better than a girls' day shopping spree.

"I did find an outfit. It's the most beautiful skirt suit with brocade detailing. Very elegant."

"Oh." Trudy looked crestfallen. "And you have jewelry and everything?"

Priscilla thought for a moment. "Now that you mention it, I am looking to replace a piece of jewelry I lost. I had a cameo brooch that Gary's mother gave me at our wedding. It was passed down to her from her mother, and her mother before that. I wanted Rachel to have something from Gary's family to wear at the wedding."

"For her something old or her something borrowed?"

"Yes, or her something blue. The background of the cameo was the most beautiful blue agate." Priscilla sighed. "The idea was that a piece of her father would be there. Of course, I don't know, she may not want it at all. Especially if it isn't the real thing. I'd like her to at least have a choice though, and it would ease my heart to have a replacement. We could start the tradition fresh. I just can't seem to find anything quite the right style in any of the jewelry shops I've visited."

"Have you checked antique stores?" The idea was so simple, Priscilla felt silly she hadn't thought of it herself. If any place carried vintage jewelry, it would be an antique shop. Trudy pulled her smartphone from her polka-dotted handbag and checked the time. "Why don't we go now? I'm done with play practice for the day, and I don't have anywhere to be for a while."

Priscilla felt a little worn out after her busy morning, but Trudy had been so kind to listen to her ramble over lunch, and a girls' outing did sound like fun.

They split the lunch bill and headed toward downtown in Priscilla's SUV, where the majority of Vineyard Haven's antique shops were. It took a while to find an empty parking space, but they finally snagged one, even if Priscilla did have to parallel park, which she wasn't fond of.

Trudy fed the meter quarters, and they started walking north. The first shop they came across had an intricate display in the window featuring a summer scene with antique bicycles and an elaborate vintage picnic. The sign swinging above the door read *Acorn Antiques, Proprietor Lucille Basham.*

"Want to try here?" Priscilla asked.

"Sure," Trudy agreed.

The shop was quiet as they entered and vaguely musty-smelling. A display case of vintage jewelry caught Priscilla's eye right away, but to her disappointment, there were no cameos.

Trudy paused in front of a garden-themed booth, every nook and cranny filled with birdbaths, decorative paver stones, and intricate mosaic tiles. Grapevines had been artistically twisted with twinkling lights and silk flowers to form a roof over the display, giving the effect of a glowing outdoor pergola.

"Isn't this beautiful? Oh, Priscilla, you should buy this for your garden!" Trudy bounced up to a weathered sundial and clapped her hands. "This would be perfect in that empty spot right next to the rosebushes Ida put in."

Priscilla laughed. "You are the queen of impulse buys, Trudy. And how would I even get that home? I'm pretty sure I would break my toe if I tried to lift it into my vehicle."

Trudy's eyes twinkled. "I'm sure Gerald would be happy to help you with it." Though Priscilla blushed, she didn't argue.

"I'm sure I could rope him into it. We're actually going out to dinner later this evening." Gary would be surprised if he knew how many times a week Priscilla ate out. She and Gary had been homebodies when they'd been married; they'd eaten most meals at home, in true meat-and-potatoes style.

But Priscilla's relationship with Gerald was different than it had been with Gary. With Gary, she'd been a young bride, full of fanciful ideas about the future. She'd had a lifetime of memories and a daughter with Gary, and a piece of her heart would always be with him.

But her future? She hoped her future was with Gerald. And even if the dynamic was different with him, it made sense, because she was different too. The Vineyard had changed her and shaped her in new and surprising ways.

Wiping sudden moisture from her eyes, Priscilla bent her head over the sundial to shield her face from Trudy's view. Now that she was looking at the ornament up close, she had to admit, it was striking. She ran her hands along the base and marveled at the detailed vine pattern carved into the pedestal. The dial on top was meticulously created as well, delicate Roman numerals etched into the tan stone face. The piece was truly a work of art. Trudy was right. Priscilla could envision it sitting in her yard among her blooming roses and hydrangeas.

"How much is it? I can't look."

Trudy flipped the tag over and winced. "Sorry, I should've looked at the price first. It's pretty expensive."

"I'd have to give it some thought, Trudy."

Trudy clapped her hands as if a sudden idea came to her. "Well, you won't have to. I tell you what, Priscilla. I'm getting this for you. Consider it a mother-of-the-bride gift."

Priscilla scoffed. "Trudy, that's ridiculous."

"Why should the bride have all the fun? The mother's the one who put in the hard work raising her. You deserve a little treat too."

"I'd hardly call something like this a little treat."

"Well, a big treat then. Please? I know it sounds silly, but we weren't in each other's lives for so many years. I missed out on a lot of birthdays and anniversaries and celebrations. So this is like all those gifts wrapped up in one. That makes sense, right?"

Her cousin looked so hopeful, Priscilla didn't have the heart to argue. She sighed. "All right. Thank you, Trudy. You've got a heart of gold. And hopefully a wallet of gold too."

Trudy grinned. "I'll worry about me. Now you just have to figure out how to get this thing home."

CHAPTER SIX

A little before seven, Gerald's car pulled up to the cottage. Priscilla glanced in the mirror on the wall and checked her hair. Then she carefully looked over her brightly colored summer dress. It was something Trudy had encouraged her to buy. Priscilla wasn't really a dress person, but the cute blue-and-yellow frock had called to her. With a push from Trudy, she'd purchased it. Priscilla sighed. Trudy and her impulse buys. Priscilla hoped this time her impulse was the right one.

With help from the employees at the antique store, they'd gotten the sundial in the back of Priscilla's car. Now she hoped Gerald would be willing to help her get it out.

When she heard his knock, her heart leaped with happiness. She opened the door to find Gerald smiling down at her. Then his eyes widened.

"Priscilla, you look...beautiful. I mean, you always look nice, but tonight..." He nodded approvingly. "You'll be the prettiest woman in the restaurant."

Priscilla felt her cheeks turn warm at his compliment. She loved the recent change from friendship to dating. It was exciting, yet, at the same time, comfortable. She was glad they'd spent so much time getting to know each other. It had built trust between them.

"I'm glad you find me so fetching," she teased. "Because I'm getting ready to ask you a favor."

He gave her a quick bow. "Anything for you, my lady."

She laughed at his antics. "I'm glad you're so willing. Maybe you'd better wait until you hear what I need you to do."

"Tell me now while I'm still stunned by your beauty."

Priscilla laughed again and pointed at her SUV. "Trudy talked me into buying something this afternoon. I need you to help me get it out of my car."

"Manual labor, huh? I'd hoped for something more exciting. Like fighting a lion or rescuing you from pirates."

"You're incorrigible, you know that?"

Gerald winked at her. "I'm aware. Let's take care of this and go to dinner. I'm starved."

Priscilla grabbed her purse, said goodbye to Jake, and locked the front door. Then they went over to her SUV. When Priscilla opened the back, Gerald looked inside and groaned.

"Wow. It looks heavy."

"It is," Priscilla said. "I can get someone else to—"

"Now wait a minute," Gerald said, raising his hand like a cop stopping traffic. "Don't count me out yet. I'm not that old." He studied the sundial for a moment.

"There's a tarp underneath it," Priscilla said. "I used it to pro- tect the floor of my car. Maybe you should cover the sundial with it. It might be easier to handle and will help to keep your clothes from getting dirty."

"Good idea," he said. He lifted the dial a few inches and pulled the tarp out from underneath it. Then he wrapped it carefully and turned to Priscilla. "Where is this going?"

Priscilla pointed at the small garden she'd been working on. "Over there. I thought it would look good next to the roses." She frowned. "Why don't you let me back the car up a little closer? I should have—"

Before she could finish her sentence, Gerald grabbed the sundial, pulled it out of the car, and carried it over to the garden. After setting it down exactly where Priscilla had indicated, he straightened up. When he turned around, she noticed a frown on his face. She hurried over.

"Did you hurt yourself?" she asked. Why hadn't she just hired a professional to move the stupid thing? Why had she let Gerald injure himself?

He laughed at her worried expression. "I'm fine. It wasn't so bad." He bent over to look closer at the sundial. "This is really interesting. Where did you get it?"

Priscilla told him about the antique store.

"I know the one you mean. I've found a few treasures there myself." He stood back and looked over the garden. "It really adds something, doesn't it?"

She noticed his rather pensive expression. "Are you sure you're all right?" she asked.

"Positive. It's just that...For some reason this sundial looks familiar. Maybe I saw it in the store."

"Maybe." Priscilla took his arm. "Let's get going, Hercules. You deserve a good meal."

Gerald laughed. "I agree."

They got into Gerald's car and headed toward the restaurant. They'd decided on the Colonial Inn and Restaurant, a favorite of Priscilla's. Gerald loved it too. The owner, Tilly Snyder, made sure his favorite booth was available whenever he wanted it. A spot next to the windows where they could gaze out at the harbor. The ornate restaurant featured white linen tablecloths and silver accessories. In the evening the lights went down, and candles on the tables provided a romantic ambiance.

As they pulled up in front of the Inn, Priscilla gasped at the hanging baskets adorning the huge front porch of the old building.

"Tilly has outdone herself," she said. "She's a great cook, a smart businesswoman, and an incredible gardener. Is there anything she can't do?"

"She can't be Priscilla Grant," Gerald said softly. "And that's the best thing anyone could be."

Priscilla leaned over and met his lips. Their kiss was sweet and lingered a few seconds. Finally, she pulled her head back. "Food. Now," she said.

He nodded. "Agreed. Let's go."

Gerald got out of the car, then went around and opened the door for Priscilla. She stepped out and hooked her arm through his, and they went inside the restaurant. It was crowded, which was normal for a Saturday night. Priscilla was happy to see Tilly acting as hostess. It didn't happen often. Tilly liked to be free to visit with her patrons. Her dark gray hair was swept up and held in place with a beautiful vintage hair pin. Her long dress was made of satin and lace. Small pearl buttons on the front set off the gorgeous outfit. Tilly had her own style, and she wore it well. When she saw Priscilla, Tilly hurried over and wrapped her in an enthusiastic hug. The aroma of violets reached Priscilla's nose. It was Tilly's favorite scent.

"I've got your table ready," she said with a smile. "Follow me."

They trailed behind the elderly dynamo. Sure enough, she led them to Gerald's booth. A vase of flowers had been placed on the table and, in the middle, there was a candle set inside an etched glass bowl. The flame flickered and danced. It was breathtaking. And perfect.

Gerald waited while Priscilla sat down. The soft music in the background added to the air of romance. The tension she'd had since Virginia disappeared eased a bit. Gerald slipped into the other side of the booth while Tilly called a waitress over to them. Priscilla thanked the kind restaurant owner and ordered a glass of iced tea from the waitress, who told them she'd be back for their order.

"I'm so glad we picked the Inn," Priscilla said. "Everything is so lovely tonight."

"Including you," Gerald said with a disarming smile.

Priscilla returned the smile. She loved seeing the romantic side of Gerald. Dating someone she loved made her feel young again and brought back something she'd thought was gone from her life.

They looked over the menus. When the waitress came back, Priscilla asked for the blackened salmon, and Gerald selected a steak. As the waitress walked away, Gerald asked Priscilla about Rachel.

"Is everything coming together for the wedding?"

Priscilla smiled. "I think so. There are so many things to do, but Rachel and A.J. are handling them well. They're having fun taking care of all the details." She sighed, then said, "I would never tell Rachel this, but I'm really bothered about one thing."

"What's that?" Gerald asked.

Priscilla leaned down and picked up her purse. She pulled out her wallet, removed a picture, and handed it to him.

"What a handsome woman," he said. "Who is she?"

"Gary's mother. I wish she was here to see Rachel walk down the aisle."

"I'm sorry," he said. "You've told me about her, but I think this is the first time I've seen her picture."

Priscilla took the photo from him and pointed to Gary's mother's dress. "Do you see the brooch she's wearing?"

Gerald leaned in and looked closely. "It's a cameo, isn't it?"

She nodded. "It belonged to Gary's great-grandmother. It was passed down to each woman in his family when she got married. Since Gary was an only child, it came to me. You can't tell from the photo since it's black-and-white, but the brooch has a blue agate background. It was to be the something blue."

"So the piece was passed to you? And you'll give it to Rachel?"

"I can't find it, Gerald. It's gone missing. I think it was lost somehow during the move. I've looked everywhere. I'm afraid it's gone for good." She sighed. "I haven't told Rachel yet. I dread telling her."

"I'm truly sorry, Priscilla. Maybe you can find something else that belonged to Gary's family?"

She shook her head. "That was the only piece of jewelry from the Grants that I had." She sighed. "I have a string of pearls. I'll let Rachel wear those as her something borrowed. As far as the brooch, I'll just have to tell her the truth. She loves that brooch. She'll be heartbroken."

Gerald picked up the picture again and stared at it carefully. Then he handed it to Priscilla, who put it into her purse again.

"So, any sign of Virginia?" he asked.

Priscilla shook her head. "Tomorrow, after church, Trudy and I are going to search for her. She mentioned in her letter that she might head to Oak Bluffs or Edgartown."

"That's a pretty large area to cover," Gerald said. "Do you know where she likes to stay in those towns?"

"Joan had some suggestions. She used to know Virginia pretty well. Until they had a falling out, I guess." Priscilla took a sip of her tea. "Would you like to come with us?"

"I'd love to, but I can't. I'm having lunch with Aggie. Just the two of us. We don't get to spend much time together without the kids and Nick. I love being with all of them, but spending time with my daughter is really special."

"I completely understand," Priscilla said. "Please tell her I said hello."

"I will. I'll call you tomorrow night, and we can set something up for next week. Do you think seeing you every day is too much to ask?"

Priscilla laughed lightly. Then she looked up and gazed into his eyes. "Not for me," she said quietly.

Tomorrow she would have to face the problem with Virginia. Tonight belonged to her and Gerald.

CHAPTER SEVEN

The next day after church, Priscilla drove over to Walt's, her favorite burger place, to meet Trudy for a quick lunch. They ate cheeseburgers and fries and then set out in her SUV for Edgartown.

"Any idea where to look?" Trudy asked.

Priscilla signaled a left turn. "Joan remembered a couple of places Virginia used to go when she wanted to get away to work on a book." She nodded at her purse on the floor at Trudy's feet. "I wrote them in my notebook. Can you get it out?"

Trudy reached down to get the purse. "What's this?" she asked, pulling out the picture of Gary's mother. "Is this who I think it is? And is that the brooch you were talking about yesterday?"

Priscilla frowned. "Yes, it is. I thought I put that back in my wallet." She shook her head. "I must have been distracted."

"By a good-looking Coast Guard captain?"

Priscilla laughed. "Probably." She sighed happily. "It was a perfect evening, Trudy. So romantic. The restaurant was lovely, the food delicious, and the company…" She winked at her cousin. "Well, you know."

"Hey, I've been married a long time. Not sure I do."

Priscilla snuck a quick look at her cousin. "I'm sure you and Dan have romantic moments."

Trudy shook her head slowly. "Dan is so busy with work there's not much time for 'romantic moments.' He's not big on going out, you know. I mean, we do. But he usually can't wait to get home to his squids and barnacles." She laughed. "Not that he has any in the house. Yet. Sometimes I think if I suddenly turned into a mermaid I'd be more interesting to him."

"Well, of course you'd be more interesting," Priscilla said dryly. "Since mermaids don't actually exist."

Trudy laughed again and waved her hand at Priscilla. "Just ignore me. Typical marriage frustration. I'm sure you and Gary went through times when he wasn't the most romantic."

"Of course. We had a farm to run. But every once in a while we'd take time out for ourselves. True, those times got further and further apart as time went on. Every married couple goes through it, Trudy."

"I'm sure you're right," Trudy said with a sigh. "Now, back to our search." She flipped open Priscilla's notebook. "So where are we going first?"

"There are two B&Bs that Virginia frequents in Edgartown. Let's try those first."

"I doubt they'll tell us if Virginia is staying there."

"I realize that," Priscilla said, "but Virginia's car isn't hard to spot."

Trudy giggled. "A pink Cadillac. Not too many people have them."

"I would say that's a safe bet."

The two women laughed. Priscilla was so glad Trudy was with her. A boring day had turned into a fun expedition with her cousin.

They talked and laughed all the way to Edgartown. When they got to town, they visited both the B&Bs on Priscilla's list. They were surprised to find that the owners didn't mind telling them Virginia wasn't there. Although both owners said they hoped she'd visit again, Priscilla and Trudy got the impression their invitations weren't heartfelt. Virginia must have been a rather difficult customer. Priscilla asked both owners if they knew any other places in Edgartown Virginia might go. They both named the same restaurant. It seemed it was a favorite of Virginia's. They followed the directions given to them by the B&B owners and found a charming French restaurant set in an old house. Unfortunately, it wasn't open until five thirty.

"We could drive to Oak Bluffs and then come back here later to check it out," Trudy said.

"You just want to eat here," Priscilla said.

"Well, I wouldn't say no to a good French dinner."

Priscilla shook her head. "I have the addresses of a few more high-end B&Bs and hotels where she might be. Let's spend our time looking for her car. If we don't find it, we can be fairly certain she's not in Edgartown. That means we don't need to worry about finding her here."

"All right. But we could have had a fabulous French meal," Trudy grumbled.

"We'll drive back here sometime in the next few weeks and have dinner, okay?"

Trudy immediately brightened up. "That sounds great."

After they'd spent another hour driving around town, there still wasn't a trace of Virginia. On a hunch, Priscilla drove to the library, but it was closed.

"Let's go on to Oak Bluffs," she said. "I don't think Virginia's here."

"All right, but could we get some coffee? I didn't get my usual four cups this morning."

"Four cups?" Priscilla looked at her, aghast. "That's a lot of coffee, Trudy. Is that good for you?"

Trudy grinned. "It's not only good for me, it's a necessity. Now, can we look for a coffee shop?"

Priscilla couldn't help but smile. "I guess I could use a boost too. There's a really cute place just down the street from us. Big selection."

With Trudy's agreement Priscilla drove to Toccopuro Coffee, a charming shop that served the best iced coffee Priscilla had ever tasted.

After carrying their coffees to the car, the women headed to Oak Bluffs. But the results were the same. No trace of Virginia anywhere. Finally, Priscilla decided it was time to go home.

"This is useless," she told Trudy. "We're not going to find her this way. I'm really afraid something has happened to her."

"But she took her car, Priscilla," Trudy said. "That doesn't sound like someone who's been injured or kidnapped."

"Maybe," Priscilla said. She thought for a moment. "What do you think of Douglas?" she asked finally. "You've spent time with him in rehearsal."

"He's really into his play," Trudy responded. "I mean, it's like an obsession. He told us some big shot from New York would be in the audience when we open Saturday night."

"Do you think Douglas would hurt Virginia?"

Trudy was quiet as she considered Priscilla's question. Then she said, "No, I don't. There's no reason for it. She's already given him the money he needs for the show. Besides, he's very solicitous of her, Priscilla. Seems to really care for his aunt. They've only got each other, you know."

"No, I didn't know that. I wonder who gets Virginia's money if she dies."

Trudy's sharp intake of breath made it clear she'd gotten the message. "Douglas."

"Right. I think we need to look at him a little closer."

"I . . . I just don't see him as someone who would hurt his aunt," Trudy said slowly. "But I get your point. It makes me feel a little weird. About being in his play, I mean."

"Oh, Trudy. It's just a suspicion. Don't take it so seriously. He's probably not involved at all."

"I hope not."

They rode in silence the rest of the way to Tisbury. Priscilla was lost in thought about where Virginia might be when she realized they were close to the cemetery. "Let's swing by the West Tisbury Village Cemetery."

Trudy's eyebrows arched in surprise. "Why do you want to go there? That place is spooky."

"It's just an idea. Nancy Luce is buried there. I just want to check since we're so close."

Trudy agreed, but Priscilla could tell her heart wasn't in it. Actually, the cemetery was a beautiful place, full of old tombstones and memorials. She doubted Virginia was there, but since they'd looked everywhere else, she figured stopping by couldn't hurt.

They pulled up to the cemetery and parked. Priscilla opened her door and started to get out before she realized Trudy hadn't moved. She turned to look at her. Trudy was staring straight ahead, a strange look on her face.

"Trudy, are you coming?" Priscilla asked.

"I...I don't like cemeteries," she said softly.

"Oh, Trudy. There's not anything here that can hurt you. Most of these people have been dead a long time. They're not going to jump out of their graves and grab you."

Trudy sighed. "I know that. It's just...Well, Dan watches those zombie shows."

Priscilla burst out laughing. "Zombies? Seriously? In West Tisbury? They wouldn't dare. Village officials would never allow it. They're very strict about that kind of thing."

Although Trudy tried to keep a straight face, she lost the battle and laughed. "I'm sure you're right." She smiled at Priscilla. "Sorry. Those stupid shows get under my skin. I wish he'd quit watching them."

"Have you told him that?"

"Well, no."

Priscilla let out a sigh of frustration. "Maybe it's time for you and Dan to have a talk, Trudy. About more than his TV choices."

Trudy nodded. "I know." She straightened her back and ran her hand through her hair. "I'm coming."

Priscilla smiled as her cousin got out of the car and joined her. Trudy could be a little narcissistic from time to time, but in the end, she always came around.

"I'm not sure where Nancy's grave is," Priscilla said as they walked through the rows of tombstones, many from the 1700s and 1800s. Priscilla noticed quite a few decorative ornaments scattered throughout the grounds. Probably bought by relatives of the deceased. Angel statues, small benches, special vases, paver stones in and around the graves, and figurines of things that must have meant something to a lost loved one. She stopped at one grave surrounded by paver stones with shells and abalone. They were beautiful, but it looked as if whoever was placing them hadn't finished. One area was still bare. She also noticed a lovely statue, a figure of a girl holding flowers. It was enchanting. Priscilla wondered if it was a likeness of the person who had passed away.

As they searched the names on the tombstones, they came upon an elderly man standing in front of one memorial.

"Excuse me," Priscilla said. "I'm sorry to interrupt you, but do you know where Nancy Luce is buried?"

"She's over there." He pointed to a spot a few rows away. "You'll know it by the chickens on her grave."

"Chickens?" Priscilla said, a little alarmed.

The elderly man chuckled. "Not real chickens. People bring statues, figurines. Place them next to the tombstone."

Priscilla breathed a sigh of relief. She had nothing against chickens, but they could be somewhat antagonistic. Nancy Luce may have loved them, but Priscilla wasn't in the mood to battle a horde of aggressive birds today.

She glanced at the gravestone he stood in front of. It read *Marian Sweetwater Born: 1939, Died: 2015.* Next to that was *Elias Sweetwater: Born: 1937, Died:.* There was nothing written next to the word *Died.* She wondered if the man standing next to her was Elias Sweetwater.

He pointed at the gravestone in front of him. "My wife," he said. "I come here when I can. Just to be near her." He looked at Priscilla. "You probably don't understand that."

Gary was buried back in Kansas. Priscilla had wished many times he'd been buried here, near her. "I understand more than you know." She stared at him for a moment. "I'm sorry, but have we met? You seem kind of familiar."

The old man chuckled. "No, I don't think so. I tend to remember beautiful women."

Priscilla laughed. "I think you're right. I'd remember a charmer like you."

The man smiled, and Priscilla thanked him for his help. Sweetwater seemed like the perfect name for the charming old man.

As she and Trudy walked toward the place the man had indicated, they realized he wasn't the only person in the old cemetery.

Standing around a grave, which Priscilla was certain belonged to Nancy Luce, stood four women in long white dresses.

"It's those *women in white*," Trudy whispered loudly. "We can't go over there. It's obvious Virginia's not here."

"I realize that, Trudy, but I want to talk to them. See if they might know anything about Virginia."

Trudy took a deep breath and let it out slowly. "I knew coming here was a mistake." She grabbed Priscilla's arm. "Come on. Let's get this over with."

As they got closer to the grave, an elderly woman with gray hair pointed at them. "That's her," she shouted. "The woman who lost the diary."

The entire group turned to stare at Priscilla with rather menacing expressions.

At that moment Priscilla wondered if Trudy was right. They shouldn't have come to the cemetery. She looked around to see if anyone else was there, but the cemetery was empty. Even the old man was gone.

CHAPTER EIGHT

You!" Another of the ladies left the group to aim an accusing finger at Priscilla. Her long gown swished around her ankles as she moved closer. "You are betraying the memory of Nancy Luce!"

Priscilla had no idea what the woman was talking about. She had barely stepped foot inside the cemetery and hadn't even touched Nancy Luce's grave. How could she possibly be offending anyone? She was taken aback but stood her ground. "I think you have me confused with someone else."

"This is just like a horror movie," whispered Trudy. Trudy was obviously still thinking about Dan's zombie shows. Normally, Priscilla wasn't a scaredy-cat, but the surreal effect the women in white made, silhouetted against the dreary gravestones, creeped her out.

"No." Another woman, this one a bit younger, with shining, black hair wrapped in a crown of braids, said, "We know exactly who you are, Priscilla Grant." At the sound of her name being spoken so familiarly by a complete stranger, Priscilla couldn't help but shudder, despite the warm temperatures. "We saw you at the library," the raven-haired woman continued. "You were in charge of the lecture Virginia Lawrence was supposed to give."

"And," continued another woman, this one petite with a flowing mass of coppery curls, "you were in charge of keeping the artifacts safe. Including her newly discovered diary. Shame on you, and shame on Virginia Lawrence. She'll pay for disgracing the name of Nancy Luce!"

"Then you have the audacity to disturb Nancy Luce's final resting place after what you've done." The silver-haired woman stooped low over the grave and lovingly adjusted a ceramic figure.

Priscilla squinted closer to see what the object was and realized it was in the shape of a chicken. In fact, now that she studied the grave, she noticed a tidy cluster of objects at the base: tiny decorative hens, little baskets filled with glass eggs, and even a laminated photocopy of Luce herself, with her trademark saucer-eyed stare and her checked kerchief looped around her head. It was an eccentric, cobbled-together memorial to Nancy Luce and her beloved pets. Priscilla felt a hysterical bubble of laughter rise up in her and fought to quell it.

"That's actually why we're here." Trudy's voice came out as little more than a squeak. "We're looking for Virginia. Have you seen her?"

"We were supposed to see her the night of the lecture." One of the women glared disapprovingly at Priscilla. "If you want her, you'll have to find her yourself. I can tell you she hasn't been home since Friday night."

Priscilla wondered how the women knew Virginia wasn't at her house. With its remote location, it wasn't as if you could swing by it easily. Unless, thought Priscilla with a start, the women had been watching Virginia and keeping tabs on her from afar. She made a mental note to scope out Virginia's house herself. She had no intention of trusting these women to tell her the truth.

Priscilla fought the urge to hold her hands up in a surrender pose. "We're sorry we bothered you. Please let us know if you hear of Virginia's whereabouts. We'd really like to speak with her."

None of the women gave an affirmative or negative answer but stared at Priscilla and Trudy as they got into their vehicle and drove off.

"That was weird," said Trudy, from the cocoon of the SUV, rubbing her hands along her arms. "I've actually got goose bumps. What's going on with those ladies anyway?"

"I don't know," said Priscilla. "But we need to find out."

Monday morning was cloudy with a light but gloomy drizzle of rain.

After the past few days of dead ends and strained relationships, the bad weather matched Priscilla's melancholy mood. She read her Bible, took Jake for a quick walk, and got dressed. She'd arranged to have all three of her cousins over this morning for brunch. She planned to make omelets with a variety of fillings, cut up some fruit, and squeeze some fresh orange juice. The one thing she didn't have on hand were pastries and muffins, but a quick trip to Candy's would soon fix that.

She tried to push the thought out of her mind that the last time she'd visited Candy's was when she'd picked up crème horns for

Mildred. Mildred hadn't called her to inquire about the whereabouts of the still-missing artifacts yet, but Priscilla could feel the tension in the air and knew she soon would. The thought put her on edge.

After securing Jake in the house, Priscilla drove to Candy's. She shook raindrops from her umbrella and stepped in the front door. The bad weather clearly wasn't keeping patrons away. A mix of locals and tourists crammed the small space. Priscilla muscled her way to the counter and smiled at Candy Lane's welcoming face.

"Priscilla! What can I get for you? More crème horns?" Candy, the owner of the shop, was always cheerful, and her bright mood lifted Priscilla's spirits a little.

"No, no crème horns today." Priscilla explained about the brunch she was putting on for her cousins, and Candy leaped into action, expertly boxing up blueberry muffins and orange scones.

"Oh, my. I think this should take care of us for the month, Candy. How delicious everything looks." Priscilla could smell the fruity, sugary pastries through the box, and her mouth watered.

"Happy to help, and it's always a joy to see you, Priscilla." Candy's melodic voice reminded Priscilla of a songbird.

Grinning, she paid for the pastries and took the box Candy offered. She was turning toward the door when she saw something that made her breath catch in her throat.

Tucked away in the front corner of the shop was the back of a familiar man, immersed in conversation with a lovely blond woman. Their heads were close together, and they were murmuring quietly. The woman looked so elegant, her hair pulled back in a smooth chignon, and when the man said something that made her laugh, she tossed her head back and playfully swatted at his hand. They looked every inch an ordinary couple in love, except for one problem.

The man was Gerald.

Normally, Priscilla wouldn't have thought a thing of it. Gerald was the steadiest, most reliable man she had ever met. No one would ever suspect him of two-timing or cheating or whatever it was people called indiscretion these days. There had to be a reasonable explanation. She and Gerald had shared such a wonderful, romantic evening on Saturday. He had seemed so focused on her and so committed. Priscilla decided to walk over and say hello to Gerald and the woman he was with. As she approached, Gerald looked up and saw her. His eyebrows shot up, and he looked surprised. Maybe even a little nervous.

"Hello," Priscilla said when she reached their table.

"Uh...Hello, Priscilla," Gerald said, stuttering a bit.

She waited for him to introduce the woman sitting beside him, but to her surprise, he didn't.

Gerald blinked several times and cleared his throat. "I forgot to ask you about the missing artifacts at dinner the other night. Have they turned up?"

Priscilla shook her head. "Nothing yet."

She stood there, waiting for an introduction that never came. Finally, she said, "Nice to see you." Then she turned and fled.

She walked to her car on shaky legs. This was ridiculous. Why had she left so abruptly? And why was she concerned about Gerald's motives? He'd acted so oddly. Was it possible the mysterious woman had something to do with the Coast Guard? Gerald's work occasionally required confidentially. Perhaps that was what was going on here. Priscilla shook her head to clear it of unsettling thoughts and drove home to get ready for her cousins. After a much-needed cuddle in the armchair with Jake, she unlocked the front door, then got out her skillets. She took eggs from the refrigerator and started cracking them into a bowl.

"Mmm, it smells good in here." Trudy, always early, appeared in the kitchen. Spying the bakery boxes on Priscilla's counter, she clapped her hands. "And you swung by Candy's too. I would say perfect, but I'm still eating low-carb. Those pastries smell divine."

Priscilla busied herself with whisking the eggs.

"Any reason why you look like you're about to murder those helpless eggs?"

"No, not really." Priscilla wanted to tell her cousin about seeing Gerald, but she didn't know how to begin. She was normally steady and calm, and lately, she had been neither.

"Something has to have happened to turn your eyebrows into thunderclouds." Trudy smiled. "Come on, Priscilla. You can tell me. Maybe I can help."

Trudy was right. Her cousins had supported her through thick and thin. Priscilla turned from the stove and paused before speaking. "I saw Gerald this morning. At Candy's."

"And? That usually makes you happy."

Priscilla bit her lip. "He was at a table in the corner. With a beautiful blond woman."

Trudy laughed. "Oh, Priscilla, you have to be joking. Gerald is in love with you. There's no way he would be seeing another woman."

Priscilla shook her head, trying to shake the thought away. "I'm sure you're right. Seems I've been wrong about a lot of things lately." She thought of Trudy telling her about her troubles with Dan. Those two had such a wonderful marriage, and if things were unsettled on their home front, maybe no one was safe.

Trudy's voice softened. "Everything will be okay. It's just some kind of misunderstanding."

"What kind of misunderstanding?" Gail entered the room.

With a sideways glance at Priscilla, Trudy explained. "Priscilla saw Gerald at Candy's with another woman."

"A beautiful blond woman," Priscilla corrected.

"Oh, nonsense." Priscilla felt marginally better when Gail dismissed the situation with a wave of her hand. "Gerald is crazy about you. You have nothing to worry about."

"Thanks." Priscilla dabbed at her eyes. Noticing Gail's questioning look, Priscilla gestured toward the now-cooking omelets, piled with fillings. "It must be the onions."

Joan was the last of the cousins to arrive. She helped carry out the food and drinks to a patio table Priscilla had set up in the garden. After saying grace, all four women began eating, though true to her low-carb diet, Trudy had only one small bite of pastry and then contented herself with her western omelet and a tiny serving of berries.

Joan took a second helping of omelet and gave a small, happy sigh. "I can't believe it's still cool enough to sit outside this late in the morning."

"It helps that it's been overcast today," Gail said. "But you won't be able to get the full effect of Priscilla's new sundial without the sun."

Joan smiled. "I heard Trudy's been acting like King Midas lately. Knowing the storm geek Gail is, she bought her an antique barometer the other day."

Gail held her hands up. "I'm not going to be one to look a gift horse in the mouth. Be patient, Joan, and you may be the next recipient of Trudy's generosity."

"Oh, you two." Trudy tossed a wadded-up napkin at them. "I just care about you all. I'm thankful for my cousins. And my sister." She gave Joan a one-armed hug, then hopped up from her chair. "Now let's go see Priscilla's new toy. I'm sure it looks magnificent, sun or no sun."

The group walked to the far edge of the garden, where the sundial sat beside a cluster of brilliantly blooming roses.

Gail cast an admiring glance at the garden ornament. "This really is beautiful. It must have cost a fortune."

"It had a bit of a price tag with it," Priscilla said. "I tried to talk Trudy out of it, but she wouldn't take no for an answer."

"It was worth it." Trudy grinned. "Doesn't it just look perfect in Priscilla's yard? Like it was tailor-made for the space?"

Gail nodded her agreement. "Has Ida seen it yet? She'll be drooling with envy." Ida Lee Jones occasionally helped Priscilla out with landscaping, and much of the work done in Priscilla's yard could be chalked up to Ida's keen eye and helpful hands.

"No, not yet." Priscilla smiled. "I may have to tell her about the treasures Acorn Antiques has though. She'll want to snap up some pieces for her own place."

Joan, the garden connoisseur of the group, hadn't said anything yet, and they all looked at her, waiting for her reaction. Priscilla was surprised to see a guarded, almost wary, expression on Joan's face. "What do you think of the sundial?" Priscilla asked.

Joan didn't answer immediately. She seemed to be weighing her response. Finally, she said, "I was working on some family genealogy in a local cemetery, and I'm sure I saw this sundial. It's very old and has a distinctive design." She turned to look at Priscilla. "I hate to say this, but I believe this sundial is stolen."

CHAPTER NINE

Priscilla stared at her cousin, her mouth open. "Stolen? It came from Acorn Antiques. There's no way it's stolen."

Joan sighed and looked at her cousin as if she were simple. "Antique store owners aren't perfect, Priscilla. They can be fooled."

"Why do you think it's hot?" Trudy asked.

"Several things have gone missing from local cemeteries, not only here, but in surrounding towns. A friend of mine had a statue of an angel taken from her husband's grave."

Priscilla suddenly felt sick to her stomach. When she'd gone into the back room of the antique store, she'd noticed a stone angel sitting on a shelf. Could that be stolen as well? Could her sundial actually belong to someone else? Someone who had used it as a way to honor a loved one's final resting place?

Priscilla stared at the sundial she'd been so crazy about. Suddenly, it didn't seem as attractive as it had before. "I want to find out more about the thefts before we call anyone and report this as stolen property. I believe you, Joan, but I don't want to move too quickly before I'm sure."

Joan shrugged. "I think that's wise. This might not be the missing sundial. We should be sure before we accuse anyone. I like

Acorn Antiques. Shop there myself. I would hate to be wrong and cast a shadow on their reputation."

"Let's finish up, and then we'll go to the West Tisbury cemetery," Priscilla said. "I'd like to talk to the people who run it." She pulled her phone out of her pocket and took several pictures of the sundial. She prayed it wasn't stolen. As they walked back to the table, she tried to put her concerns on hold so she could enjoy the rest of her brunch with her cousins, but it was difficult. The sundial wasn't the only thing she had on her mind. No matter how hard she tried, the memory of Gerald with the attractive blond woman kept creeping into her mind. She was certainly younger than Priscilla. Could she have been wrong about Gerald? Was he capable of deceiving her?

As she forced down the last bite of omelet, she realized that down deep inside, she couldn't believe he was the kind of man who would tell her he loved her while he was seeing someone else. His meeting had to be about something innocent. She wondered if she should ask him, but she couldn't come up with a way to do that without it seeming as if she didn't trust him. She had to quit worrying about it. She had enough to concentrate on for now. Where was Virginia? And where were the artifacts?

"Any news on Virginia?" Gail asked, as if she were reading Priscilla's mind.

"No. Trudy and I looked everywhere for her. No sign. We visited every single place we thought she might have gone. I'm really worried."

"I don't see why you're worried," Joan said dryly. "Virginia thinks only about Virginia. She's taken off with the Nancy Luce stuff, leaving you in the lurch. Typical Virginia."

"But why would she take it?" Priscilla asked.

"Maybe she wanted more time to go through the diary," Gail said.

Priscilla thought about that. Could that be it? Was Virginia just buying time so she could carefully study the diary? Could this be about research for one of her books? "If that's what's going on, it's really selfish," Priscilla said.

"That would be Virginia," Joan said. "The most selfish person I've ever known."

"Which begs the question," Priscilla said. "What was it you said that caused such a rift between the two of you?"

Joan didn't respond. Just shook her head.

"You tell her, or I will," Gail said, grinning. "I mean it. Time it came out into the open."

"It's just so stupid," Joan said. "And childish. I can't believe I said it. And I can't believe she got so offended."

"Tell us," Trudy said. "Come on, Joan. Spill it. I've wondered about that for a long time."

Joan sighed, took a sip of coffee, and then put her cup down. "Okay," she said finally. "We were at the last book signing she ever did on the island. Lots of fans gathered around. She was so egotistical, I felt she needed to be taken down a notch."

"What did you say?" Priscilla pushed.

Joan sighed. "She was bragging on the new pink Caddy she'd just bought. I said..." She blushed and cleared her throat. "I made an announcement that she would be doing her signature makeovers for anyone who was interested after the signing. I might have even implied that it was quite an accomplishment to sell enough makeup to win a pink Cadillac. Everyone heard me."

"Oh, Joan," Priscilla said. "How could you..." She didn't finish her sentence before all three of her cousins broke out in giggles. Even though she fought it, Priscilla joined in. She was dismayed to think what a makeover by Virginia might look like. "Oh dear," she said, once she could control herself. "That's awful."

"But really, really funny," Trudy said, breaking out in a new round of laughter.

"Well, at least I understand why you pulled out of working on her lecture," Priscilla said, chuckling.

"Yeah, but she was so embarrassed she quit showing up in public," Joan said. "Not my finest hour. I'm not proud of what I did."

"Speaking of that pink Cadillac," Gail interjected, "Clara Lopez over at the library told me she saw Virginia's Cadillac on Saturday afternoon. The day after she disappeared. She was headed out of town."

Priscilla almost dropped her fork. "When did you hear this?" she asked.

"I was helping Sara in the bookstore on Saturday. Clara came in. She'd just seen her. I planned to tell you, but I thought you knew she'd left town. I didn't think it was all that important."

Priscilla tried not to look upset, but she couldn't believe Gail had held on to that information for two days. "At least we know she's okay," Priscilla said. "She really did take off on her own. She hasn't been kidnapped or anything."

"No one would be crazy enough to kidnap her," Joan said under her breath. "It'd be like *The Ransom of Red Chief.*"

Priscilla decided she'd call Hank later and give him that information. It ruled out foul play. Even though she should feel relieved, for some reason, she couldn't shake the feeling that something was wrong. No matter what Joan said, Priscilla couldn't see Virginia as the type of person to steal valuable artifacts belonging to someone she idolized. She seemed to truly appreciate that the museum had decided to loan them to her before the lecture.

The women finished up their brunch and then headed over to the cemetery. When they got there, Priscilla noticed Trudy craning her neck and looking all around. "What's the matter?" she asked.

"Just making sure those weird women aren't here."

Priscilla chuckled. "No, the women in white aren't in the cemetery. They really upset you, didn't they?"

Trudy nodded. "They're really creepy, Priscilla. Who worships a woman who made tombstones for her chickens? It's nuts."

Priscilla laughed. "Nancy Luce was more than just the Chicken Lady. Still, it's certainly strange, all right."

The women made their way into the cemetery where they noticed a large group of people gathered around Nancy Luce's grave. Some tourists were taking selfies, trying to get the grave in the background. Priscilla watched as a middle-aged woman picked up one of the ornamental chickens and held it up, while a man, possibly her husband, took her picture. Her actions caused a chain reaction. Other people in the group picked up the figurines and had their pictures taken as well. Priscilla almost said something, chiding them for disturbing Nancy's gravesite. But before she could do anything, the group moved on to another grave. It appeared they were taking a tour. An older man began talking, telling them about the gravestone they stood around.

Standing with her cousins, Priscilla noticed a guard standing near the cemetery's office. Some cemeteries on the Vineyard had guards because of celebrity gravesites. Priscilla was the first to reach him. He was a large, burly man who didn't look very friendly. He seemed surprised to be approached by a group of women.

"Excuse me, sir," Priscilla said. "We heard there have been some thefts from this cemetery. Do you know anything about that?"

He eyed her suspiciously. "Yeah, I know about it. What's your name, and why are you asking?"

Priscilla took out her phone and pulled up the pictures of her sundial. She held the phone so the guard could see the screen. "My name is Priscilla Grant. Does this look familiar to you? Is it among the objects stolen?"

The guard's already stern expression deepened. Rather than answer her questions, he pulled out his own phone and repeatedly tapped the screen. Before Priscilla could figure out what he was doing, he spoke into his phone.

"This is Dudley Farmer. I handle security for the West Tisbury Village Cemetery. I've got a Priscilla Grant here. She's the one who has the stolen sundial from our cemetery. Please get here right away."

CHAPTER TEN

Things happened quickly after the security guard's call to the station. Though Priscilla had only been able to hear Dudley's side of the conversation, she assumed Gabrielle, or whoever was manning the front desk, let him know he didn't have suitable evidence for an arrest. A few minutes later, however, Priscilla's cell phone rang, with a request from Hank to drop by the station for questioning.

She'd agreed, of course. She didn't have anything to hide. She'd told her cousins to go home, that she could handle the matter herself, but Trudy insisted on coming with her. "As a form of moral support," she'd chirped. Priscilla had felt another rush of gratefulness for family. Joan and Gail had offered to stay behind to see if they could locate and question the owners of the cemetery.

Priscilla was aware that Trudy would have to wait in the main lobby of the police station while Priscilla was questioned, but at least her cousin would be a visual reminder to Hank that the Lathams had ties to the island as loyal and long-lasting as anyone.

So now she found herself tucked away in one of the station's interrogation rooms, waiting for an officer to come ask her questions about the sundial photos captured on her phone. The only bright spot was that she didn't have to make an extra phone call to let the police know Virginia's Cadillac had been spotted driving out of town on Saturday. Small comfort.

"Please, take a seat." Officer Terry Campos, a recent recruit for the West Tisbury Police Department, motioned for Priscilla to sit. He was young, and his short red hair and freckles only made him look more boyish. She'd almost expected him to break into a grin when he entered the room and tell her that this whole situation was an elaborate setup for some goofy TV show. But the officer's face, to her disappointment, was stern and unsmiling.

Officer Campos said, "Mrs. Grant, can you explain why you have multiple pictures of a stolen item on your cell phone?"

"Because I own the item. I bought the sundial at a local antique store over the weekend."

"And you didn't realize the item was stolen?"

"Of course I didn't realize it was stolen. Why would I purchase something I knew was stolen?"

Officer Campos shrugged. "It happens all the time. Pirated music and movies, hot designer clothing, you name it. If some-body thinks they're going to get a deal..." He sounded as though he were used to working the mean streets of an urban city instead of charming West Tisbury.

Priscilla continued. "If I stole something from a cemetery, why on earth would I confess my guilt by showing the guard a picture of the item I took?"

"You could have been trying to throw people off your trail. You know, like hiding in plain sight."

"That doesn't make any sense."

Officer Campos shrugged again. "Plenty of people act crazy and hope the authorities will think they're not smart enough to pull off the crime."

"Well, I'm not one of those people."

The officer smiled tightly. "I'm not saying you are, ma'am, but you've been suspected of theft before. I just need to ask you a few questions."

Priscilla pressed her lips together and didn't answer. He was referring to a situation involving a stolen painting last year. They'd found the real thief, and Priscilla's name had been cleared.

The officer continued. "You said you bought the sundial? Does that mean you still have it in your possession?"

"Yes, it's in my garden." Loosening her grip on her purse straps, Priscilla fished her phone from her bag and showed Officer Campos the photos she'd shown the security guard a few hours earlier.

"Mrs. Grant," Officer Campos said. "We don't have a formal warrant, but usually those who are innocent don't object to us searching their homes if we suspect they possess stolen goods."

Priscilla gritted her teeth at his words—*those who are innocent.* Of course she was innocent. It was as plain as the nose on her face, yet everyone was suddenly treating her like a criminal. She threw back her shoulders and met his gaze head on. "Certainly. You may check anything you'd like, though I don't know what it will prove. I didn't get a receipt from the antique shop. The proprietor told me they'd run out of register tape earlier in the day."

"And at which antique store did you buy the sundial?"

Priscilla paused. This was precisely the situation she had wanted to avoid earlier and the reason she'd gone to the cemetery first, instead of the police station. She didn't want to get Lucille Basham, stranger that she was, into trouble if she was somehow an innocent party too. "Acorn Antiques," she said finally.

"Thank you," said Officer Campos. He nodded toward the door. "You're free to go, Mrs. Grant. We'll call you before we stop by your house. Thank you for your time."

Priscilla headed out to the waiting area. The sight of Trudy sitting with her cheerful polka-dotted bag, so out of place in the somber police station, comforted her. Priscilla couldn't wait to get outside into the fresh air and warm sunshine, but first she stopped at Gabrielle's desk and asked her to let the chief know Virginia had been seen, and she was okay. Gabrielle took down the message and promised to pass it along.

"Ready to go?" Trudy said, jumping up.

Priscilla started to answer, but her cell buzzed inside her purse. She held up a finger to Trudy. "Just a minute?"

The phone had slid to the bottom of her purse, and in rooting around to find it, Priscilla failed to pick up before the call went to voice mail. She recognized the number that popped up on the screen though. Mildred, at the East Shore Historical Museum.

"Let's get out of here," she said at Trudy's questioning look. The two cousins left the station and slid into Priscilla's sun-warmed vehicle. Almost instantly, Priscilla felt herself start to sweat, though she wasn't sure whether the perspiration was a result of the temperature inside the car or trepidation at receiving a likely negative voice mail from Mildred. She blasted the AC and held the phone up to her ear to listen to the message.

"Hello, Priscilla, this is Mildred. I'm calling in hopes that you've recovered the Nancy Luce artifacts since our talk. All the items are due back in Boston at the end of this week, and the museum has already sent me an email asking for some photos from Virginia's lecture. I haven't answered them yet, and I certainly hope I don't have to inform them that the irreplaceable artifacts they lent us have vanished. Please call me back as soon as possible. Goodbye."

Priscilla grimaced and disconnected from voice mail.

At the expression on her face, Trudy frowned too. "That bad, huh?"

"Not good," Priscilla admitted.

The phone call was just what she had expected, but she still felt the pressure of it. Not only was she on the hook for the items' disappearance, but she was keenly aware of the effect such a loss would have on Mildred's reputation, and possible livelihood, as well.

"So where are we going now?" Trudy asked, buckling herself in.

"I don't know." Virginia had been seen driving her pink Cadillac around the island, so she wasn't missing, which meant the artifacts might not be either. Virginia had to be somewhere close by, and Priscilla had to find her. How, though? She and Trudy had already exhausted so many options, and for all Priscilla knew, they could be crossing paths with Virginia and not even know it, doubling back to places she had already been.

Trudy pulled out her phone. "Maybe Gail and Joan got some information from the local cemeteries."

"Good idea."

After a few minutes of chatting, Trudy hung up and shook her head. "They said they were able to reach the owners or managers of several cemeteries. It seems they've experienced a rash of grave ornaments being stolen lately, including some high-profile pieces, like that angel statue Joan mentioned, as well as your sundial. Nobody's reported any suspicious activity, but quite a few ornaments are missing."

Something was nagging at Priscilla. "They don't have security cameras at the cemetery?"

Trudy shook her head. "I don't know. Gail and Joan didn't mention anything about that. It would definitely be something to check out though. If they let us back in to investigate, that is."

The car had cooled considerably, so Priscilla switched the AC flow down a few notches as she turned the information over in her mind. Two mysteries. The missing artifacts and now these thefts. Were they connected somehow? Or was it just a coincidence that they had occurred at the same time?

Trudy continued. "It doesn't sound like the police have many leads on who's behind the thefts." She frowned at Priscilla. "Other than you, that is. What did Officer Campos want to ask you, anyway? Surely he knows you didn't have anything to do with any of this mess."

Priscilla sighed. "He mentioned that the police would like to check the cottage this afternoon and take a look at the sundial while they're there."

"Oh, your beautiful gift. I'm so sorry. If I hadn't been so impulsive—"

Priscilla cut her off as a familiar face drove by the idling SUV. "Trudy, did you see who that was?"

Trudy's eyes were wide. "I think we found our next suspect."

The woman who had driven by would know how to find Virginia if anyone could. A person who had kept close tabs on the writer for years. Virginia's rival, Eve Pennywhistle.

CHAPTER ELEVEN

Trudy yelped as Priscilla executed a U-turn and began to follow Eve. Priscilla looked over at her cousin. "Sorry. I don't want to lose her."

"Why? I mean, can't we just call and make an appointment to talk to her?"

"She could tell us no, Trudy. She's not the friendliest person, you know. She's a lot like Virginia." Priscilla frowned. "Every time I've spoken to her, she acts as if she knows something awful about me but she's too polite to tell me what it is."

Trudy laughed. "Oh, Priscilla. That's silly. What could she possibly know?"

Priscilla smiled. "I don't know, but I'd rather not find out."

The women both laughed, but in spite of the lighter moment, Priscilla never took her eyes off Eve's car. They were headed back into town. Priscilla checked her watch. It was almost four thirty. Since Eve lived in the other direction, she wondered if she was going to dinner. Sure enough, she pulled into the parking lot of the Little House Café. Priscilla slowed her car so Eve wouldn't see them. She waited until Eve got out of her car and went into the restaurant, then Priscilla pulled into a parking space on the other side of the lot.

"I take it we're having dinner here?" Trudy said dryly.

Priscilla glanced at her watch again. "The police haven't called yet, but when they do, we need to take off for my house."

"*We* do? When will you take me back to my car?"

Priscilla sighed. "Oh, Trudy. I'm sorry. I've been so selfish. Do you want me to drive back to the police station now?"

Trudy grinned at her. "Absolutely not. I want to see what happens next. Besides, I love this restaurant. I can almost taste their red Thai curry chicken kebabs."

"What about Dan? Do you need to call him?"

Trudy shook her head. "He's working. Again. I don't need to be home for a while."

"So, are you ready to see if we can get anything out of Eve?"

Trudy's eyebrows knit together. "What if she's having dinner with someone?"

"Well, I assume she is," Priscilla said. "We just have to be brave enough to talk to her anyway."

"Okay, if you say so." Trudy squared her shoulders. "I feel like we're Rizzoli and Isles."

"Oh, I loved that show."

"Me too." Trudy smiled. "Let's go."

The women got out of the car and entered the restaurant. Priscilla could almost taste their muffuletta pressed sandwich. As she slowly scanned the café, looking for Eve, her eyes stopped on a couple sitting in the corner. She felt the blood drain out of her face. For a moment, she felt dizzy.

As the hostess headed their way, Priscilla grabbed Trudy's arm and pulled her toward the door. Trudy tried to wrestle away, but Priscilla's grip was too strong.

When they got outside on the patio, Trudy disengaged her arm and stood in front of Priscilla. "What in the world was that about?" she demanded. "Have you lost your mind?" As she stared at her cousin, the indignation in her face turned to concern. "Are you okay, Priscilla? You look like you've seen a ghost."

"Let's get in the car," Priscilla said. Her legs felt like jelly, and she wasn't sure she could stand on them much longer.

Trudy, who obviously realized Priscilla was in trouble, took her arm and walked to the car with her. They got in and shut the doors. Priscilla started the engine so the air conditioner would keep them cool.

"Now tell me what's going on," Trudy said gently.

Priscilla took a deep breath to steady herself. "They were in there," she said, her voice trembling. She hated that she sounded so weak, but she was truly shaken.

"They? Who are you talking about?" Trudy asked. A couple of seconds after she asked the question, Trudy gasped. "Are you talking about Gerald and . . . and that . . . other woman? The blonde?"

All Priscilla could do was nod. Seeing them together one time could be explained away. But twice? No. Something was going on. Gerald was seeing another woman. It was as clear as glass.

"Look, Priscilla," Trudy said in a somber voice. "I don't care what you think you saw. That man is crazy in love with you. There has to be a reason he's been meeting with her. You've got to trust him." She reached over and put her hand on Priscilla's shoulder. "What does your heart tell you?"

As tears slipped down her face, Priscilla shook her head. "I . . . I don't know anymore. I truly believed he loved me. I know I love him. But how can I ignore this, Trudy? I've seen him with this woman twice now. In one day. If she were his cousin or something, why hasn't he mentioned her?"

"You haven't talked to him, Priscilla. You've got to ask him about this before you drive yourself crazy. I'm sure it's nothing."

Priscilla reached into her purse and took out a tissue to wipe her face. She had just put it back when Trudy squeaked out, "They're coming out."

Priscilla looked up to see Gerald holding the door of the restaurant open for the blond woman, who stepped out onto the patio. The two walked over to a black Escalade. The woman, who looked to be in her thirties, unlocked the door, and Gerald held it open for her. Priscilla's eyes were locked on the couple. Would Gerald kiss her? Instead he simply closed her door when she got inside, waved goodbye, and walked over to his own car. A couple of minutes later he drove off, going in the opposite direction the woman had gone.

"See?" Trudy said. "If they were together, they would have left in the same car." She grabbed the arm of Priscilla's jacket. "He didn't kiss her, Priscilla. He's definitely not interested in her."

"But why would they meet twice in one day?" Priscilla asked.

"It might have to do with work. Or maybe they're related, and she has to fly out tonight or in the morning. That's why they were together twice. It makes perfect sense."

"Maybe," Priscilla said slowly. Actually, Trudy's version of the incident gave her some hope. It did seem rather reasonable. She owed it to Gerald to let him offer an explanation before she assumed the worst. She gave Trudy a forced smile. "You might be right. Thanks. Do you want to go back in the restaurant and eat?"

As soon as the words left her mouth, her cell phone rang. Priscilla dug it out of her purse and answered. It was the police. After speaking to them, she hung up and looked at Trudy.

"I take it we're not eating?" Trudy asked.

"I'm so sorry, but I've got to go to the house. Do you want to ride with me or would you rather go by the station so you can get your car?"

"I'd rather pick up my car so I can drive home after the police leave. That way you won't have to get out again." She smiled at Priscilla. "I don't suppose there's any of your wonderful chicken salad sitting in your refrigerator."

Priscilla shook her head. "No, but I have some of the ham salad you love so much."

"Oh, my. I like your ham salad even more. Suddenly I'm glad we didn't eat at the café. Sounds wonderful."

Priscilla started the car and drove toward the police station.

"Aren't you going to call Mildred back?" Trudy asked.

"It's too late. The museum's closed now," Priscilla answered quickly.

"You waited until it was closed, didn't you?"

Priscilla sighed deeply. "I need something positive to tell her, and so far, we have nothing."

"But Priscilla, it might take a while for us to figure this out. I think you have to bite the bullet and call her."

Priscilla had to admit Trudy was right. Putting Mildred off only made things worse. "I'll call her tomorrow. I really will."

Trudy nodded. "Okay. I'm sure we'll find Virginia, Priscilla. I feel it in my bones."

"Well, I wish my bones were saying the same thing. Frankly, they just keep reminding me I'm not as young as I used to be. Some nights I can't wait to slip into a hot tub and soak for a while."

Trudy laughed. "I do the same thing. But one word of advice. You know that hot/cold cream that's supposed to make your joints feel better? Never rub that on right after you get out of the tub. Wow. The pain was just awful."

Priscilla looked at her cousin, her mouth open in surprise. "Trudy! Don't tell me you did that."

Trudy nodded. "I certainly did. I screamed so loud Dan came running into the bathroom. He thought I was being attacked."

Priscilla didn't want to laugh, but she couldn't help it. "Oh, Trudy. I'm so sorry. That must have really hurt."

"It burned like someone had set me on fire." She tried to keep a straight face, but two seconds later she giggled, which set Priscilla off again. The women were still laughing when Priscilla pulled into the parking lot of the police station.

"I really do feel bad for you," Priscilla said before Trudy got out of the car. "But thank you for making me laugh. I feel so much better now."

Trudy winked at her. "I'm glad my pain has amused you." She gave Priscilla a wide smile. "I'll follow you back to your house. See you soon."

As Priscilla drove away, she thanked God for Trudy. She had become more than just a relative. She was a true friend.

About twenty minutes later, Priscilla parked in the driveway of her cottage. Two police cars were already there. As she got out, Trudy pulled in behind her.

Hank got out of the first car, and two police officers from the second car joined him. They stood by Priscilla's front door.

Since this wasn't the first time the police had searched her cottage, she should be used to it, but she wasn't. It felt invasive, and she didn't like it. Trudy came up next to her. She followed Priscilla as she went up to the front door and unlocked it.

"Please wait here," she said, "while I put Jake on his leash."

"We don't want you going in first," one of the police officers said.

Priscilla realized it was Terry Campos. "I don't want you to frighten him," she said. "He doesn't know you."

"Go ahead, Priscilla," Hank said. He glared at Terry. "I'll tell her what she can and can't do, Officer."

Priscilla and Trudy went in first. Priscilla got Jake's leash and attached it to his collar. When she straightened up, she found Trudy looking at her.

"It will be all right, Priscilla," she said. "You have nothing to feel guilty about."

Priscilla nodded, but truth be told, having the police treat her like a criminal was discouraging.

She put on her brave face and opened the door.

CHAPTER TWELVE

Hank and the two officers searched Priscilla's house quickly but thoroughly. In thirty minutes, they'd pawed through every drawer and cabinet in the place and investigated every nook and cranny. They spent a little extra time in the attic and cellar. Then they combed the secret passageway that led to the beach. Priscilla had to admit, her home had a lot of good hiding places. But of course, the officers didn't find anything.

"See, I told you there was nothing here," Priscilla couldn't help but say, as Jake sat at her feet, leashed and quiet, with a look of doggy amusement on his face. He didn't seem to take the proceedings very seriously. Priscilla wished she could feel the same way.

"Humph." Officer Campos stalked from room to room, looking more like a kid playing cops and robbers than a real official. "We still need to sweep the garden."

Priscilla wondered for a fleeting moment if they were planning on digging up her yard, as though she were a pirate hiding buried treasure under the lilacs, but no. They made a beeline for the sundial. After checking a few photos and making a quick phone call, they hoisted the ornament into the trunk of the squad car. Priscilla noticed that it took both Terry and the other officer to lift it, when Gerald had muscled it into the garden on his own.

Gerald. She gulped, thinking of him. She had to trust him and believe that his motives were pure, but it was tough. After losing Gary, she'd wondered if she would ever be able to love a man again. And then she'd met Gerald, and they'd built a friendship, piece by piece. It had taken a long time to transition to a romantic relationship, to think about Gerald in a way separate from Gary. But she had come to that place, and now she was head over heels in love with him. The question was, did he truly feel the same about her?

Hank's voice broke into Priscilla's thoughts. "I'm afraid we're going to have to take the sundial as evidence." He motioned toward the empty dirt circle where the sundial had rested.

"Of course."

"I'm sorry about this, Priscilla," Hank said. "I know you're not a thief. I hope you understand we needed to be thorough." He shook his head and turned to face his officers. "All right, boys," he continued. "Let's get out of this lady's hair. She's been hassled enough by us. We'll leave you to some peace and quiet, Mrs. Grant."

He looked a little embarrassed as he walked out the door and pulled it shut behind him.

After the squad cars pulled out of the driveway, Priscilla unleashed Jake and sank into her armchair. Jake flopped on the floor at her feet.

Trudy sat on the couch with one foot tucked under her. "Quite a rough few days, huh?"

"I'll say." Priscilla sighed. "Not any I want to repeat, that's for sure."

"So, what now?" Trudy asked.

"Well, we need to keep looking for Virginia. We know she's still on the island. I don't feel like we're on as much of a wild goose chase as we were at first."

Trudy nodded. "We've searched a lot of places already. And met a lot of dead ends."

Priscilla chewed her lip thoughtfully. "One place we haven't checked is the library. It's possible Clara Lopez might be able to tell us a little more about Virginia's habits. Even if Virginia was a recluse, I know she was in contact with Clara for her research."

"That's a great idea. Do you want to go now?"

Priscilla's stomach grumbled. "Maybe we could eat first? I'm starving."

"Ooh, that sounds good. Your great ham salad. It's definitely worth the carbs. I can't wait."

"Give me a minute to make the sandwiches," Priscilla said. "How about some fresh fruit and iced tea to go with that?"

"That sounds perfect."

Priscilla got out the croissants she'd bought at Candy's, and in a short time, she had everything ready. The two cousins ate quickly before heading to the library.

"Thank goodness they have late hours tonight," Priscilla said, glancing at the gold placard hanging next to the public library's front door.

"Our taxpayer dollars hard at work." Trudy smiled.

They pushed through the front door and tracked down Clara, who was fiddling with the microfiche reader in the genealogy room.

"Priscilla! How are you?" Clara looked concerned. "I heard you haven't found the artifacts from the Boston Museum yet."

"Who told you?" Trudy blurted.

Clara didn't look ruffled at the outburst. "Mildred Pearson called here earlier today. She wanted to know if I'd heard from Virginia or from you, Priscilla."

Priscilla felt a pang of guilt that she'd avoided calling Mildred back earlier. Mildred had a lot at stake, and Priscilla knew all too well how panicky the older woman must feel. She felt a bit on edge herself.

"We haven't found anything yet. That's why we're here." Priscilla exchanged a glance with Trudy. "Trudy and I have been trying to find Virginia to see if she knows anything about where the artifacts might be. Supposedly she sent them back by courier to the museum, but they haven't shown up. We've checked with the local services, but they all deny receiving a call from her."

"Well, if you see her, let her know I have some books for her. She put a few special requests in by interlibrary loan last week, and I have to send them back if she doesn't claim them."

"So I guess that means you haven't seen Virginia either?" asked Trudy. "We've already searched half the island looking for her."

Clara shook her head. "No, I haven't seen her. I'm sorry."

"Do you have any guesses about where she could be? Any special places she used to go for research?" Priscilla asked.

Clara furrowed her brow in thought. "Hmm. She didn't really leave the house much, you know. I never saw her out and about in town. Why, after her nephew came to live with her, she didn't even run errands anymore. She used to send him to pick up her library books." She shook her head. "Such an odd fellow."

Trudy laughed. "He certainly is eccentric."

Clara raised her eyebrows, and Priscilla explained. "Trudy knows Douglas. She has a starring role in the summer play he's producing. *Murder by Moonlight.*"

"Oh, yes." A look of recognition came into Clara's eyes. "I do remember hearing about that." She paused for a moment. "As to where Virginia might be, have you all visited the West Tisbury Cemetery? That's where Nancy Luce is buried, and I know Virginia's spent quite a bit of time there talking to the caretakers and taking pictures of the grounds." She frowned. "I mean, she used to. Before she holed up at home."

You mean, before Joan went and called her a cosmetics dealer in front of half the town, Priscilla couldn't help thinking. The story was silly, and there was certainly nothing shameful about selling good cosmetics, but Virginia's pride in her life's work as a historian must have been wounded to the core to almost completely cut off communication with the outside world. Priscilla didn't know what she'd do without the relationships she'd cultivated on the island. Even having a few of them in limbo now made her heart ache.

"We've already been to the cemetery," Trudy jumped in. "We came across some interesting characters." She shivered, and Priscilla wondered if she was thinking about the eerie women in white. "But we didn't see Virginia."

Clara sighed and turned her attention back to the microfiche machine. "I'm afraid that's my only guess. I'm sorry I can't be of more help, but I do hope you find her."

"Thanks anyway, Clara," Priscilla said. "We appreciate it. I just hate that the lecture fell through."

Clara adjusted a knob on the reader. "Me too. It would have been good publicity. But all's well that ends well, I guess."

As Priscilla and Trudy headed out of the room, Trudy muttered under her breath, "Let's just hope all ends well."

Priscilla was about to murmur her agreement when a man stepped into their path, cutting off their exit.

"Excuse me, ladies. I couldn't help but hear you talking about Virginia. That wouldn't happen to be Virginia Lawrence, would it?" The man looked to be in his late forties or early fifties, with wire-rimmed glasses and puffy blond hair neatly parted to the side. Priscilla wondered if he was a visitor to the Vineyard. If he was a tourist, though, he didn't dress like one. Tourists usually wore beachy short-sleeve shirts and khaki shorts. This man wore a starchy suit, and by the determined set of his jaw, looked as if he were on a mission.

If the man had overhead them talking about Virginia, that meant he had been eavesdropping, a fact that made Priscilla uneasy. She didn't answer the man's question directly. "Do you know Virginia Lawrence?"

The man cleared his throat. "Well, I can't say that I've met her personally. But I certainly know of her. I came into town for her lecture last week and was disappointed when it was canceled. I was hoping to meet her face-to-face. I'd like to sit down with her and have a little chat."

"A little chat about what?" Trudy said.

"Oh, nothing, nothing." The man fidgeted with his hands. "I just need to know more about her, that's all. Would you describe Ms. Lawrence as a reckless sort of person? That is, does she often go missing?"

"Who said she was missing?" Priscilla asked, and then bit her lip. She hadn't meant to confirm that she and Trudy had been talking about Virginia at all, and now she'd gone and done just that. "She's doing research somewhere on the island. We haven't been able to get in contact with her."

"But no one has seen her, correct? So she is sort of missing."

"She's been spotted around the island a few times since Friday," Trudy said. "I'm sure we'll run into her sooner or later. Can't be too hard to spot a pink Cadillac."

"A pink Cadillac?" The man removed his glasses and wiped them before sliding them back onto his nose. "That is a distinctive vehicle. Perfect. That will help me track her down. Is there anything else you ladies can tell me about Ms. Lawrence?"

Priscilla couldn't dismiss her feelings of unease. The way the man maintained a laser-like focus on Virginia was unnerving.

"I'm sorry, sir, I don't mean to seem rude, but may I ask why you're looking for her?" Priscilla asked.

"I'm just— Let's just say I'm interested in her and her work. I'd like to talk to her about her work as a scholar of the island."

Priscilla narrowed her eyes at the man. "And your name? What did you say it was again?"

"I didn't," said the man, and as abruptly as he'd appeared, he turned on his heel and hurried out of the library.

CHAPTER THIRTEEN

The next morning Priscilla got up, ate breakfast, and fed Jake. After their walk, she called Trudy. Trudy had play rehearsal this morning and had asked Priscilla if she wanted to come by and watch for a bit. Priscilla accepted her invitation and suggested they drive to lunch together afterward. Joan had asked the cousins to meet at a Chinese restaurant that had recently opened. Priscilla loved Chinese food and was excited to try it.

She was looking forward to catching a glimpse of the play. She could hardly wait to see the opening on Saturday night. Trudy was a very effusive person who could be fairly dramatic. Priscilla thought she had the perfect personality for acting and expected her to be quite good.

When she arrived at the Playhouse in Vineyard Haven, she was struck by the clean lines and appealing exterior of the building. White clapboard with a bright red door and the American flag flying over the entrance. The Playhouse was one of the Vineyard's special jewels. The Martha's Vineyard Playhouse offered year-round live theater in a renovated historic building, a one-time Methodist meetinghouse built in 1833. Inside, the Patricia Neal stage hosted plays, musical events, and other performances. The lobby served as a venue for art openings and exhibits.

As she walked through the entrance to the theater itself, she smiled. It was beautiful inside. Rich wood beams and accents. Purple chairs and a bright red carpet that lined the stairs. Priscilla quietly took a seat to the side, hoping she wasn't disturbing the actors. They were in the middle of a scene. She recognized several of the people on stage. She spotted Cheryl Finnegan, who ran the children's ministry at Faith Fellowship; Elmer McBroom, a local retired insurance agent; and Willow Gibson, who owned Silver Willow Appraisals and Antiques in Vineyard Haven. Priscilla wished she'd shopped at Silver Willow instead of Acorn Antiques. Maybe she wouldn't have ended up with stolen property.

In the scene being rehearsed, a body was discovered. The actors were taken aback by their discovery, each one emoting shock and surprise. Then, from stage left, Trudy came out. Elmer told her to stay back, claiming she didn't want to see the body. It seemed to be someone Trudy's character cared about. Trudy insisted that he move out of the way, and she pushed past him. When she spotted the dead man—who, to Priscilla's amusement, appeared to still be breathing—Trudy screamed and collapsed to the floor. Her performance was really quite convincing.

From somewhere in front of the stage, a voice called out, "Cut!" Priscilla found it comical, since when she took drama in school, her teacher never used that word. For the most part, it was reserved for films and television. Maybe that's what Douglas was really hoping for someday.

She saw him stand up and approach the stage. After a thorough assessment of the scene, including a mild rebuke to Elmer for not projecting his voice loudly enough, he dismissed them for the day. Priscilla was surprised rehearsal had been cut so short. She was hoping to see more of the play.

Trudy, who seemed to have recovered from her faint, walked over to the edge of the stage, put her hand up to shade her eyes, and looked out into the theater. When she spotted Priscilla, she waved at her, then walked down the stairs at the side of the stage and came up to meet her.

"You were so good," Priscilla said, hugging her cousin. "I'm proud of you."

"Goodness gracious, Priscilla, any fool can scream and fall down." Trudy laughed. "I have scenes where I actually get to talk. Hopefully, you'll like those too."

"I'm sure I will. I still think you were very good. Your scream made the hair stand up on the back of my neck. Very believable."

"Thank you. Since we quit a little early, we have some extra time. Do you want to come backstage with me? You can see our props and dressing rooms."

"That would be very interesting," Priscilla said. She really did love the theater. Even going backstage was exciting. The thought crossed her mind that someday she might try out for a part in one of the local plays. High school drama classes were so long ago they probably wouldn't help her much now, but still, it could be a lot of fun.

She followed Trudy behind the stage. They entered a large room lined with clothes racks full of costumes. Priscilla was impressed.

"We have clothes from all kinds of periods," Trudy said. She pointed out one rack full of Victorian-styled costumes. Another rack held clothes that looked as if they could be from the forties or fifties.

Trudy took Priscilla's arm and pulled her over to a long table with lighted mirrors. Nearby, a large shelf held plastic boxes with labels, such as *beards, mustaches, wigs,* and *makeup.*

A young man walked past them. He smiled at Trudy. "See you tomorrow," he said.

"See you," Trudy called back.

After he walked out the door at the back of the room, Trudy said, "That's Jeff. He's playing an eighty-year-old man. You'll get to see him transformed. It's really something."

"Who does the makeup?" Priscilla asked.

"Douglas. He's a genius when it comes to changing people into the characters they're playing."

"And what will you look like on opening night?"

Trudy sighed. "Myself. I'm playing someone my age, so I won't look much different." She flashed Priscilla a quick smile. "I do get a beauty mark right here." She pointed to a spot near her mouth. "My character's kind of a floozy."

Priscilla fought back a giggle. Trudy's bleached-blond hair and her use of makeup made her a good choice for the role. Thankfully, however, Trudy wasn't a floozy or anything close to it.

"Let's go," Trudy said. She grabbed her purse. "We can leave by the back door."

When they got outside, Priscilla said, "We can take my car. I'll bring you back later to get yours."

"Sounds good. Are you hungry?" Trudy asked as she slid into the passenger seat.

"Starving. I've heard this new Chinese restaurant Joan suggested is very good."

"She's eaten there several times," Trudy said. "She highly recommends the Teriyaki chicken and the sesame shrimp."

"Mmm. Sesame shrimp for me," Priscilla said. "I love good shrimp."

"Maybe I'll order the chicken so we can try both dishes."

Priscilla nodded. Gerald did the same thing sometimes. Priscilla would tease him about eating her food. "If you want something, order your own," she would say. "Quit eating mine." He'd always laugh, but he still liked to sample her food. The truth was, she found the habit endearing. She smiled to herself, but there was sadness behind the memory. A few minutes later, they pulled into the parking lot of Song's House of Joy. Priscilla loved the name. The parking lot was almost full. That boded well for the restaurant. Residents of West Tisbury were sometimes slow in accepting new businesses.

Priscilla and Trudy got out and walked toward the restaurant. Priscilla spotted Joan's and Gail's cars parked a few spaces down. When they went inside, a smiling woman met them at the entrance.

"Welcome to Song's," she said. "I'm Amy Song. A table for how many?"

"Our party is already here," Priscilla said, pointing to the table where Joan and Gail sat, waving at them.

Amy got a couple of menus and asked Priscilla and Trudy to follow her. As they made their way through the crowded restaurant, Priscilla glanced around the room. She was grateful her cousins had arrived early and grabbed a spot. There didn't appear to be any other tables available.

"You're certainly busy," Priscilla said to Amy as she sat down at the table. "I've heard your food is delicious."

Amy grinned. "My parents love to cook. It's a miracle my brothers and I don't weigh five hundred pounds."

"Well, I guess we'll have to choose very wisely," Joan said, chuckling. "What do you recommend?"

"To be honest, it's all good," Amy said. "It depends on what kind of dishes you favor. Few vegetables? Lots of vegetables? I enjoy the sesame shrimp, but I also really like the Moo Goo Gai Pan. Whatever you do, don't miss the crab Rangoon. It's awesome."

Priscilla's mouth was already watering. She hadn't had any really good crab Rangoon in a long time.

"Your server will be with you shortly," Amy said, putting their menus on the table in front of them. "It was so nice to meet you. I hope you enjoy your meal."

"It was nice to meet you too, Amy," Trudy said. "And I'm sure we will."

Amy hurried back to the front of the restaurant where another couple waited for a table.

"It certainly smells good in here," Gail said, reaching for her glass.

"Yes, it does," Priscilla said. "I can hardly wait to try the food."

Priscilla checked out the interior of the restaurant. Red and black decorations with a few Chinese lanterns hung strategically around the room. The overall look was very classy and understated.

Their waitress, whose tag read *Missy*, took their drink orders and pointed at their menus. "Have you decided what you want?"

Priscilla ordered the crab Rangoon appetizer for the table. Then she and Trudy asked for the sesame shrimp. Joan ordered the Moo Goo Gai Pan, and Gail went with teriyaki chicken.

"Great choices," Missy said. "I'll get this out to you as soon as I can."

"So, are you okay?" Joan asked Priscilla when Missy walked away.

Priscilla had called Joan last night to tell her about the police searching her cottage. "I'm fine," she said with a sigh. "I guess I should be used to having my house searched, but I'm not."

"Well, it's just ridiculous," Gail said. "You'd think you were public enemy number one in West Tisbury."

Trudy giggled but quickly put her hand up over her mouth. "I'm sorry," she said, taking her hand down. "But I had a vision of Priscilla's face on a flyer in the post office."

"Oh, Trudy," Joan said sharply. "That's not funny."

A brief silence ensued before Joan snorted, and even Priscilla laughed. She was so glad to be with these women. They always made her feel better when there was a crisis.

"Did they take the sundial?" Gail asked.

Priscilla nodded. "I won't get it back. It's not mine. I'm just so sorry you spent money on it, Trudy. When the antique store refunds the money, I'll give it to you. "

"No, you won't. It was a gift from me. I won't take a penny from you."

Priscilla started to object, but just then Missy arrived with their crab Rangoon. She set the tray in front of them. They thanked her, and she left.

Priscilla reached out and took an appetizer from the tray. She bit into it. The sweet cream cheese mixture was stuffed with pieces of succulent crab, and the crispy fried wonton was perfectly crunchy.

"Oh my," Priscilla said after she swallowed the first bite. "I think this is the best crab Rangoon I've ever tasted."

Trudy picked one up and took a bite. Her smile made it clear she agreed with Priscilla's assessment. "Wonderful," she said after swallowing. "I'm so glad we came here."

"Me too," Joan said. She nodded at Priscilla. "Were you getting ready to say something?"

"I was going to argue with your sister about not allowing me to pay her back for the sundial. But I'd just be wasting my time, wouldn't I?"

Trudy swallowed the last bite of her appetizer. "You're finally learning," she said with a wink.

"Yes, just give up," Joan said. "No one's more stubborn than Trudy."

"Except maybe Virginia Lawrence," Priscilla said with a deep sigh.

A few minutes later, Missy came to the table carrying a large tray of food. After putting the dishes on the table and asking if anyone needed a refill on her drink, she hurried off.

"No one's seen Virginia yet?" Gail asked. "Are you sure she's okay?"

"Well, she was seen driving her car out of town," Priscilla replied as she picked up her fork. "So we know she's fine. We just can't figure out where she's staying." She pointed her fork at Trudy. "Which reminds me. I'd like to run by Virginia's house after we're done here."

Trudy frowned. "Why?"

Priscilla shrugged. "I don't know. Something's bothering me, but I can't figure out what it is. I just know I need to go by there."

"Okay..." Trudy said slowly. "We can do that."

"Are you sure you have time?" Priscilla asked.

Trudy nodded and rolled her eyes. "I barely have a husband anymore. As long as supper is on the table by seven o'clock, he doesn't care what I do."

"Oh, Trudy," Joan said. "That's a little dramatic. You know that's not true. Dan adores you."

"Well, if he does, he has a very strange way of showing it." She waved her hand. "Don't worry about me, Joan. You know I complain when I shouldn't."

The discussion moved back to where Virginia might be. Unfortunately, no one had an idea that pointed Priscilla in a promising direction.

After lunch, Trudy made them all promise to be in the audience Saturday night, as if any of them would miss her debut.

As Trudy and Priscilla drove to Virginia's, Priscilla said, "I hope Douglas isn't home, or this will be a short visit."

"You don't have to worry about that," Trudy said. "He said he was going out of town right after rehearsal today. Had some kind of important appointment."

Priscilla sighed with relief. "Good. I wouldn't want to explain what we're doing there. I probably couldn't come up with a believable excuse."

Even with Trudy's assurance that Douglas wouldn't be there, Priscilla was nervous as she turned onto the road that led to the large Victorian home. She pulled up into the circular drive, parked, and got out. Thankfully, Douglas's car was nowhere to be seen. Priscilla stood in front of the house with her arms crossed, staring.

"If you're waiting for the house to talk to you, you'll be waiting a long time," Trudy said.

"I know it sounds dumb, but there's something here. Something that keeps bothering me."

Trudy sighed. "Let's walk around the yard. Maybe it will help you figure out what's bugging you."

"Might as well."

Priscilla headed toward the garden, trying her best not to feel foolish. This was obviously a wild goose chase. Maybe she was so upset about Gerald she wasn't thinking straight. She was just about to tell Trudy they should leave when she looked down. She yelped in surprise.

Trudy came rushing up to her. "Are you all right?"

Priscilla nodded and pointed down. "That what's been bothering me. I've seen these stones before. They were in the cemetery. Trudy, these paver stones are stolen!"

CHAPTER FOURTEEN

Oh, Priscilla." Trudy's eyes were wide with surprise. "Do you think Virginia could have something to do with the cemetery thefts?"

"I don't know," Priscilla said slowly, as her mind raced. She gazed down at the pavers. They were the same design of abalone and shells she'd seen in the cemetery marking the edge of what she'd thought at the time to be an unfinished display. She didn't know what to think. Finding stolen items at Virginia's house, especially in light of the fact that Virginia also likely had the Nancy Luce artifacts in her possession, complicated matters. Were the two mysteries connected, or was it some huge coincidence?

"It certainly looks as if Virginia's guilty," Trudy said. "Zipping around the island in her car and cutting off communication with everybody. Right after the museum artifacts were taken..." Trudy stopped midsentence and gasped. "Priscilla! Virginia has been driving around the island to do research, right?"

"That's what we're hearing," Priscilla said.

"What if she's been behind these thefts all along? If anyone spotted her at a cemetery, they'd assume she was doing research. No one would give it a second thought." Trudy's expression held a hint of triumph with the thought she might have just cracked the case.

Priscilla smiled. "It's a good idea, Trudy. Virginia's definitely acting suspicious, but you're forgetting one thing."

"What's that?" Trudy asked.

"A Cadillac convertible doesn't have much trunk space. Maybe enough to store a few paver stones but not enough to transport the other, larger items that were stolen."

"Oh." Trudy's shoulders sank. "Then who do you think did it? Do you think Virginia was like you and innocently bought stuff that was stolen?"

"I'm not sure," said Priscilla. "Maybe." She chewed her bottom lip thoughtfully. "What about Douglas? Is he still a suspect in this thing? He certainly acts odd at times, like he's hiding something."

Trudy blew out a breath of air and laughed. "Douglas is just cut from some very unique cloth. He's an eccentric character all around. But a thief? I don't think so. He doesn't seem like he would be bold enough to break the law." She lowered her voice to a whisper, as though she were afraid Douglas was around and would hear her talking.

"He got confirmation this morning that a New York hotshot producer is going to attend opening night of the play. Douglas was a bundle of nerves. He said he needed to rewrite the ending to *Murder by Moonlight* because it wasn't good enough."

"Hmm." Priscilla filed away the information in her head. She might have to add Douglas to her list of suspects, even if Trudy was right. He didn't particularly seem like the criminal type, and he was so thoroughly absorbed with the play, it didn't seem as if he had time for anything else. Still, it wouldn't hurt to check him out some more, if she got the chance.

"Maybe we should keep our focus on Virginia," said Priscilla. "Not as a suspect, necessarily, but as a person of interest. And we should finally track down Eve Pennywhistle while we're at it. I have a feeling there's more to Virginia's disappearance than meets the eye."

"Do you want to head back to the library to look for Eve?" Trudy asked.

Priscilla shook her head. "No, I believe I should be more direct. I worried about her clamming up if I called, but she might be really suspicious if she thinks we're following her. I need to do something soon. We're running out of time."

"Because Mildred needs the artifacts back by the end of the week?"

Priscilla nodded. "I have to call Mildred back, as much as I dread it." She held one finger up in the air. "In fact, can you hold tight while I try to take care of that?"

"Sure," Trudy agreed and began snapping pictures of the paver stones with her cell phone.

Priscilla got into her car and dialed Mildred's number. Might as well get the toughest call over with first. After a few rings, Mildred picked up.

"Hello? This is Mildred Pearson of the East Shore Historical Museum."

"Mildred? Hello, it's Priscilla."

Priscilla heard Mildred take in a breath on the other end of the line. "I hope you're calling with good news for me."

"I wish I were."

"Priscilla." Mildred's voice was heavy. "I need those artifacts. Where are they?"

"I don't know yet, Mildred. I'm trying hard to find them."

Mildred continued. "But we are facing dire consequences if you don't find that diary and those letters. Do you have any idea what happened to them?"

"I'm not sure. Things have gotten complicated. Every time I start to get a handle on what's happened, the whole thing eludes me again."

"Please keep in touch with me," Mildred said. "I don't have to tell the Boston Museum anything definitive until the end of the week, but the clock is ticking."

Priscilla felt time slipping away from her all too keenly. "I will," she promised and hung up. She took a deep breath to steady herself before punching in Eve's number.

She expected the call to go directly to voice mail and was surprised when it didn't. "Hello, who is this?" a nasally sounding voice answered.

"Hello, Eve? This is Priscilla Latham Grant." Priscilla didn't normally throw in the "Latham" when introducing herself but figured it wouldn't hurt to remind Eve, as she'd reminded Hank, that she had bona fide connections to the island. Eve didn't hang up, so Priscilla considered that a good sign.

"Aren't you Marjorie Latham's niece?"

"I am. Just moved to the Vineyard two years ago. I love it here. It's home now." Priscilla watched as Trudy hovered over the paver stones, taking pictures from different angles.

"Martha's Vineyard is a unique location." Eve sounded friendlier now. "Are you interested in learning more about its history? Is that why you've called me?"

"I'd love to know more about the historic lighthouse on my property," Priscilla said. It certainly wouldn't hurt to appeal to Eve's scholarly side. "But I do have another matter—about a person, not a place—that I was hoping you could help me with."

Eve sounded guarded again, and there was a bitter edge to her words. "Is this about Virginia Lawrence dropping off the face of the earth? Because I don't know anything about the woman. Other than the fact she stole my research to use in her first book."

Another instance of Virginia stealing? Priscilla swallowed. "I don't know anything about that. I'm just trying to find Virginia because I think she may know something about the missing museum artifacts."

"The ones that were supposed to be at the Nancy Luce lecture?" Eve laughed, but it sounded more like a hoarse bark. "If you want my opinion, Virginia wanted to make sure she had the edge on everyone—meaning she wanted to make sure I wasn't any competition. She took off with those letters to make sure nobody had access to them but her."

"You really think Virginia would do something like that?"

Instead of answering the question, Eve changed the subject. "Do you know Candy's bakery?"

Priscilla almost laughed out loud. Did she know Candy's? She estimated she'd been there hundreds of times over the past couple of years. "I do."

"Why don't we meet there later today? Say, at three?"

Priscilla checked her watch. Even though she always had her cell phone on her, she couldn't break the habit of wearing a timepiece. Her wrist felt naked without it. It was one thirty now, so she and Trudy would have a little bit of time to kill before going to Candy's. But there was always some rabbit trail they could follow. Especially now that she suspected Virginia's garden featured stolen items. How many other yards on the island held the same?

"I'll be there at three." As she finished the conversation and disconnected the call, a noise caught Priscilla's attention. She strained to hear. It sounded like a car crunching into the driveway, though she couldn't be certain, as the thick trees blocked her view. It had to be Douglas, returning home. She wondered how she was going to explain to him why she and Trudy were snooping outside his aunt's house.

Priscilla waved to Trudy to jump into her car. A few seconds later, a pink Cadillac came into view. Virginia, wearing her distinctive red cape, hunched so low over the steering wheel that Priscilla couldn't even see her face. But Virginia obviously saw Priscilla. Virginia threw the car into Reverse and peeled out of the driveway so fast, tornados of gravel swirled in her wake.

"After her!" Trudy yelped and clicked on her seat belt.

Priscilla dropped her phone into the cup holder and gunned the engine.

Ahead of them, Virginia continued driving fast, kicking up clouds of dust that coated Priscilla's windshield. Trees swaying overhead threw shadows on the road in front of her, further obscuring her vision, but she kept Virginia's taillights in view.

"Watch the speed limit, Priscilla," Trudy cautioned. She gripped her hands in her lap. "The last thing you need right now is to get in more trouble with the authorities."

Priscilla set her lips in a tight line and pressed the gas pedal down a bit more. Thirty, forty, fifty. She watched the red line on the odometer creep up, bit by bit, and tightened her sweaty grip on the steering wheel. She turned left, then right, then left again, following Virginia in a maze of directions. Trudy alternately egged Priscilla on, and then shrieked at her to slow down.

Priscilla tried her best to keep up with Virginia, but the pastel car twisted and turned so rapidly on the wooded roads in front of them that she lost sight of it within a few miles. She found a clearing where she could pull over, and she put the vehicle in Park.

Trudy's eyes were like saucers. "I had no idea Virginia could drive that fast."

"She's like the little old lady from Pasadena," Priscilla agreed, trying to joke, though she was a bit in shock at Virginia's wild driving. If Virginia had taken a corner too sharply, she could have been flung from the open top of the vehicle and severely injured, if not killed.

Yet Virginia hadn't seemed afraid of getting hurt or wrecking her expensive car. She certainly hadn't seemed afraid of getting a speeding ticket.

Her fear seemed to be focused on meeting up with Trudy and Priscilla.

Priscilla had to wonder why.

CHAPTER FIFTEEN

Priscilla was shaken by Virginia's wild driving and left her car parked in the clearing until she could calm down. As she and Trudy sat there, it began to rain.

"So, Virginia is on the island," Trudy said. "But she's doing everything she can to hide from everyone."

"That's the thing that bothers me," Priscilla said, gazing out the front windshield. "She takes the Nancy Luce artifacts, and now she's stealing things from cemeteries?" She turned to look at Trudy. "Does that sound like someone who's as successful as Virginia? Someone who just sold her house? I realize she's funding Douglas's play, but surely she made a lot of money from her home."

Trudy shrugged. "What if she didn't? What if she has a mortgage and had to sell the house because she couldn't make the payments?"

"How would we find that out?" Priscilla asked.

Trudy winked at her. "I just happen to know her real estate agent. She goes to my church. Octavia Spoonmore loves to gossip." She frowned at Priscilla. "I know it's wrong, so don't lecture me. In this situation, though, it might be helpful."

Priscilla wanted to tell her cousin to forget it, but she kept quiet. She needed to understand Virginia's actions. Maybe finding out if she was in financial trouble would help to explain things.

"We have time before we have to be at Candy's," Priscilla said, ignoring Trudy's challenge about Octavia. "I'd like to drive by Virginia's house again. Just to make sure she hasn't gone home."

"But Douglas could be there by now," Trudy said. "He said he had to work on rewriting the play. If he's back in town, that's where he'd go to work. There's no way to drive up to the house without being seen."

Priscilla smiled at her. "We won't be seen if we're on foot."

Trudy's eyebrows shot up in surprise. "On foot?" She looked down at her shoes.

Priscilla smiled to herself. Her cousin loved high heels and wore them almost constantly. "You did notice it's raining, right?" Trudy asked.

Priscilla nodded. "Should help to hide us. If we stay off the road and walk through the trees, Douglas won't spot us. I've got to find out if the car's there." She reached over and put her hand on Trudy's shoulder. "If it is, we'll call Hank. We could actually catch her, Trudy. And get the artifacts back."

"Oh, Priscilla." Trudy sighed deeply. "It's going to be muddy. Besides, Virginia was headed the other way."

"Maybe she wanted us to think that." Priscilla started the car, turned on her windshield wipers, and carefully pulled out onto the road. "There's another road that leads to her house."

Trudy was quiet for a moment. "You mean the back road near the cliffs?"

Priscilla nodded. "She could have taken it and gotten home by now. You can stay in the car. I'm wearing sensible shoes. I didn't think about your heels."

Priscilla forced back a smile when she heard Trudy's next deep sigh. She knew her cousin well enough to know she wouldn't be satisfied sitting in the car while Priscilla was looking for Virginia. Sure enough, Trudy said, "I'm going with you. I can't let you catch Virginia by yourself. What kind of a lady detective would I be if I let a pair of high-heeled shoes hold me back?"

"Thanks, Trudy."

It took a few minutes to drive back to the road that led to Virginia's house. Priscilla didn't dare take the other way in the rain. It was a dirt road that turned especially treacherous when it was wet. But Virginia could have driven it before the rain started.

After a few minutes Priscilla pulled over next to the copse of trees that helped to hide the large house from prying eyes. "Are you sure you want to do this?" she asked Trudy.

"No, but I'm going anyway. It's possible I need to have my head examined."

"Well, I think you have a very pretty head."

"Flattery isn't necessary," Trudy said with a wry grin. "I already agreed to do this."

For a moment, Priscilla reconsidered her decision. Was this crazy? But what if they could actually find Virginia? She thought about Mildred and the Boston Museum. Priscilla took a deep breath and squared her shoulders. Then she stepped out into the rain. She had an umbrella in the trunk, but she didn't think it would work well with trees surrounding them. She hoped the branches would protect them somewhat from the rain.

Priscilla waited until Trudy got out of the car, then she locked it and put the keys in the pocket of her jeans. They began their trek through the trees, and Priscilla was surprised to find a path. It was muddy, but at least it would help get them safely through the thicket.

It wasn't far to the house. When they reached the edge of the tree line, Priscilla stopped and stared at the huge structure. Trudy came up behind her, mumbling about ruining her shoes and mourning the amount of money she'd spent on them.

"For goodness' sake, Trudy, I'll buy you a new pair of shoes," Priscilla whispered.

Trudy's rambling diatribe stopped. "I'm sorry. You don't have to buy me anything. We certainly are going to be a sight at Candy's with Eve. And why are you whispering? Are we afraid the squirrels will hear us?"

Priscilla gulped. They'd gone too far to go back now. She looked everywhere but didn't see Virginia's car. Douglas didn't seem to be there either. Of course, their cars could be in the garage.

"Stay here, Trudy," Priscilla hissed. "I'll be right back."

Trudy grabbed her arm. "Where are you going?"

"I need to look in the garage."

"You're not going without me," Trudy said. "Boy, I hope Douglas isn't looking out the window right now. If so, he's going to get a treat. Two drenched women, covered in mud and..." She looked at her sleeve. "Priscilla," she shrieked. "It's bird poop. I've been pooped on!"

Priscilla turned and shushed her. "Be quiet. Do you want Douglas to hear us?"

She watched as her cousin's lower lip began to quiver. "But...But it's bird doo doo. On my nice blouse."

"Oh, Trudy. It'll wash out. Just...just try not to think about it."

Trudy's eyebrows knit together as she glowered at Priscilla. "Sure. No big deal. Maybe I can find another bird and have matching sleeves."

"Trudy, will you please be quiet? You're going to ruin everything."

Her rebuke seemed to work. Trudy was silent, but her grumbling was replaced with an almost inaudible intermittent high-pitched squeak that escaped from between her tightly clamped lips.

"I'm going to check the garage," Priscilla said again. "Seriously. Just wait here." She carefully searched all the windows facing their way. No sign of Douglas. Priscilla took a deep breath and took off toward the large four car garage on the side of the house. She didn't need to wonder if Trudy was behind her. Her cousin's mud-soaked shoes made a sucking sound with every step.

When she reached the garage, she went around the side and peered into the window. Unfortunately, Douglas's car was there, but Virginia's wasn't.

Priscilla shook her head at Trudy and whispered, "Not here." She pointed toward the other side of the garage. The large driveway extended past the building and wasn't visible from their vantage point. It was the only other place Virginia's car could be. Priscilla scrunched down as she quickly made her way around the garage, but the pink Caddy wasn't there either. Once again, she shook her head and pointed toward the trees.

"We need to go back," she said softly to Trudy, whose eyes had grown wide and her face unearthly pale. Priscilla sighed with frustration. Surely getting a little wet and muddy didn't deserve this level of drama.

When she heard the sound of a man clearing his throat, she was certain Douglas had found them. She turned around slowly and was surprised to find herself staring into the face of the clearly irritated chief of police, Hank Westin.

CHAPTER SIXTEEN

H ank." Trudy's voice came out as a squeak. "What are you doing here?"

The chief looked disapproving. "I could ask you ladies the same thing. And I will. Why are you on the Lawrence property?"

Priscilla swallowed. As focused as she was on trying to clear her name, she just kept looking more suspicious. "We're still trying to find Virginia." She left out the part about the paver stones. No need to complicate matters unless she really knew what was going on.

"Oh, really?" Hank's eyebrows arched. "You think she took the museum items?"

Trudy jumped in. "We think it's a distinct possibility. We just haven't been able to talk to her."

"So you staked out her house?"

"Well, that wasn't our intention," Priscilla said.

"We saw Virginia in her pink Cadillac and tried to follow her, but—whew!" Trudy mimed wiping sweat from her forehead. "That woman has a bit of a lead foot."

Hank's frown deepened. "You saw the Cadillac? And Virginia was in it?"

"She was," Priscilla said. "Wild hair, red cape, and all." She paused. "This might seem insignificant, but—"

"Anything you could share would be helpful, Priscilla."

"I think we need to concentrate on Virginia. She drove as though she was afraid of us. Of Trudy and me. As if she was trying to escape, even if it meant being reckless. I have no idea why she would have that reaction unless she was trying to get away. It sounds to me like she's guilty of something."

"I have to admit that is odd." Hank rubbed the whiskers on his chin in a gesture of deep thought. "So Virginia was driving erratically. We've received several calls at the station from people who've seen her Cadillac, but by the time we're able to scout out the locations, we can't find her. It's like she vanishes into thin air. I decided to come by the house to see if she'd come back here."

"Douglas is the only one home right now," Trudy offered. "His car is here, but Virginia's isn't."

"So he's inside? You two are just one step ahead of me, aren't you?"

Trudy made a face and held up her sullied sleeve. "Be happy you were the second person on the scene. This is what one step ahead gets you."

Hank narrowed his eyes but was too professional, Priscilla imagined, to say anything. "I'm going to see if I can talk to Douglas." He kicked his boots, one at a time, against a tree to knock off some of the mud, and headed back to the house. Priscilla and Trudy followed him.

Hank pounded on the front door, but there was no answer. He waited and then knocked again. It was a while before they heard Douglas call out, "Coming, just a minute!" A few seconds later, he opened the door. He looked irritated and seemed rather jittery, but given his high-strung nature, that didn't surprise Priscilla.

"Chief Westin!" Douglas seemed surprised to see Hank, and his eyebrows arched even higher when he saw Priscilla and Trudy hovering in the background. "Can I help you with something?" Douglas swiped at the front of his wrinkled polo shirt, trying to brush off some copper-colored hairs. Douglas must have been spending time with Magnus. Jake's hairs stuck to Priscilla's clothes in exactly the same way. "Sorry it took me so long to open the door. I was just doing some gardening for my aunt. I want to surprise her when she gets back from her research trip."

"That's actually why I'm here," Hank said. "I received several calls to the station with reports of your aunt driving recklessly, even exceeding the speed limit. We were unable to locate her and thought we'd check here. Is she home?"

Douglas shook his head. "No, she's not here." He sighed. "I've been concerned about her driving, but she won't listen to me. Sometimes she drives like a maniac. I won't get in the car with her."

"Hmm, I see." Hank scratched his head. "Have you seen or talked to her lately?"

"As far as I know, she hasn't been home since she left that note. Of course, I've been really busy with the play I'm producing, you know. I haven't been home much. I could have missed her. I did talk to her on the phone last night though."

"I see," Hank said. "Where was she then?"

"Um, let me think." Douglas drummed his fingers together. "I think she said she was going to Edgartown to spend the night."

"Edgartown," Hank said slowly. "All right, Douglas. I'll pass that information along. We may be calling you again in the near future."

"Of course, of course. Anytime." Douglas swiped at his shirt again. "I'm happy to help."

"Thank you. We appreciate your cooperation." Hank turned to head back to his police cruiser, and Priscilla and Trudy made their way to Priscilla's SUV.

Priscilla looked at her watch and gasped. "Trudy, it's nearly three o'clock. We have to meet Eve."

Trudy looked in dismay at her mud-caked heels. "We're a mess. We can't get in your car like this. It still has that new car smell. We'll ruin it."

Priscilla's SUV was still pretty new, but she had more things to worry about than a bit of dirt on the carpets. "We'll just have to clean up as best we can." She found a stick and began scraping mud from her shoes. It fell to the ground in heavy clumps. A flash of movement at the front window of Virginia's house caught her attention, and Priscilla got a glimpse of Douglas spying on them before the blinds snapped shut. "But we don't have time to do it now," she continued. "Eve may be waiting on us."

Trudy nodded and tossed her stick to the ground.

"Just keep your feet on the floor mat, and we'll worry about freshening up at Candy's."

The two women climbed into the vehicle, and after obliterating the stash of disinfectant wipes Priscilla carried in her purse, they headed to Candy's.

The place was busy when they arrived, but luckily not as packed as Priscilla had expected. She tried to ignore stares from the other patrons at their bedraggled looks. At least Eve wasn't there yet, so Priscilla and Trudy scooted to the bathroom to clean up a bit more.

Priscilla waved her hands furiously in front of the motion-activated dispenser and grabbed handfuls of paper towels to wipe off her shoes. There was no way she'd be able to get them completely clean, but she could remove the worst of the mud.

"Trudy, did you think Douglas acted odd when Hank questioned him?"

Trudy looked up from intently scrubbing the sleeve of her blouse. "He always acts odd. You mean, more so than normal?"

"He seemed really nervous."

"He always is. You should have seen him when he got that call from the New York producer."

It was true. Douglas was wound a little tightly. Priscilla had noticed it before.

She smoothed her hair back into place and wiped a smudge of dirt from her cheek.

A woman entered the restroom, and both Priscilla and Trudy froze as if they'd been caught in a crime. Frankly, it did kind of look that way. The sinks blasted full force, the floor was caked in mud and discarded paper towels, and Priscilla had her shoes off, while Trudy had contorted to fit her entire body under the hand dryer.

"Hello," Trudy said cheerily as the dryer blew her platinum hair in a frenzy. "Just freshening up."

The woman paused a beat before turning around and heading back out to the bakery. Priscilla and Trudy dissolved into giggles.

"Did you see her face?"

"We are practically taking a shower in here, Trudy. We must look extremely odd."

Trudy sighed and stared down at her damp, but much more presentable, clothes. "I think this is as good as I'm going to get."

"Me too. Let's pick up our mess, so we don't cause poor Candy more work." They hurried to clean the floor and wipe down the sinks before rushing out to meet Eve.

Eve sat at a table by the window. She wore all black, and her hair swung around her face in a silver bob. She looked intimidating but in a different way than Virginia. Less eccentric, more calculating.

She gave Priscilla and Trudy a once-over as they sat down. "You two look like you've come from a barn raising."

Priscilla ignored the critical comment. "You said you wanted to talk about Virginia?"

"I wanted to tell you what I know about her, yes."

"And what is that?" Trudy asked.

"She's a criminal." Eve said the words clearly, as if she didn't care who heard them.

Trudy eyed her suspiciously. "What are you talking about?"

"She's a thief. Plain and simple." Eve lifted her coffee cup to her lips and took a sip. "She plagiarized my work. Just stole all my research and used it in her first book. She got all the acclaim. I received nothing."

"You mentioned that earlier," Priscilla said. "Are you certain?"

Eve snorted. "Am I certain? Of course I am. Virginia and I were research partners. We were planning on authoring the Martha's Vineyard book together, until Virginia got this idea in her head that she was doing more work than I was. She took off with our findings."

Priscilla had to admit that Eve's assertion didn't paint Virginia in a very flattering light. "What happened after that?"

"She stopped speaking to me. She holed up in that old house of hers and fell off the map. I don't know why everyone's so surprised she ditched the Nancy Luce lecture."

"You don't have any idea where she would be now, do you?" Trudy asked.

"You need to get those artifacts back, don't you?" Eve stared down Priscilla. "Well, you might as well kiss them goodbye. Virginia probably took you for a ride too. She always does what she wants to do. What other people want doesn't matter." Eve took another sip of her coffee and stood to leave without saying goodbye.

Priscilla didn't even have time to digest Eve's new information before Gerald walked in, still in his Coast Guard uniform. He saw her and waved. He looked so handsome that Priscilla's heart skipped a beat, but it was followed by a sinking feeling. If he came to their table, which she was sure he would, he'd know something was wrong between them. She'd managed to stay away from him for the past few days, but it would start looking suspicious if she avoided him much longer.

Gerald got in line to order, and Priscilla hissed to Trudy, "What am I supposed to do?"

"You have to talk to him, Priscilla. You have to confront this."

Priscilla had a knot in her stomach, but she knew her cousin was right.

Gerald sauntered over to their table and bent to give Priscilla a kiss on the cheek. "You look like you've seen a ghost. I was hoping for a happier reception than that."

"I'm sorry, Gerald." Priscilla stood up and slipped her arm around him. "I've just had a lot on my mind lately."

"I haven't seen you in a while. Please tell me you're free for dinner tonight?"

Priscilla started to make up an excuse to get out of his invitation, but Trudy cleared her throat and shot her a look.

"I . . . I guess I'm free. What time?"

Gerald named a time and place, and Priscilla made a mental note. She'd need all her courage and tact for this date. She prayed Gerald would have a reasonable explanation for meeting with the blond woman. Priscilla glanced down at her filthy shoes as Gerald walked away. Now she really needed to go get cleaned up.

Trudy's phone made a pinging noise, and she dug it out of her purse. After glancing at the screen for a minute, she smiled. "Guess what a little birdie just told me?"

"First, I want to know who the little birdie is."

"Octavia Spoonmore."

"When did you have time to call Octavia?" said Priscilla. "You just mentioned her before our trek through the woods, and you've been with me every second since then."

Trudy shrugged. "I sent a text while Hank was grilling Douglas. You were busy playing Sherlock." She took a deep breath, obviously excited about something. "Anyway, I found out something very interesting. Octavia said Virginia didn't have a mortgage on her house. She paid it off years ago. So, when she sold the property, she made a boatload of money."

"She's lived there a long time," Priscilla said. "I figured she might own it outright."

"Oh, but wait. It gets better."

Priscilla raised her eyebrows, and Trudy continued. "Our unassuming Virginia Lawrence?" Trudy paused a moment for effect. "She's a multimillionaire."

CHAPTER SEVENTEEN

It was a relief to be back home, surrounded by the four walls of her cozy cottage. From his position at Priscilla's feet, Jake wagged his tail, then rested his head on his paws to resume sleeping. Priscilla leaned down to give him a good scratch behind the ears. The last week had thrown some curveballs at her, and she wasn't sure what to think. Her mind swam with confusing information.

The suspect list for the two mysteries was out of control. Regarding the missing artifacts, Virginia seemed like the leading suspect, especially after the conversation with Eve. As unpleasant as Virginia was, though, Priscilla had trouble believing she was a thief. Virginia appeared to be someone who prided herself on truth-telling, even to a fault. Priscilla wondered how many budding friendships had been cut short by Virginia's sharp tongue.

But if she hadn't taken the Nancy Luce artifacts, why was she avoiding people? What was she running from? Priscilla still couldn't quite believe Virginia would steal anything belonging to Nancy Luce. She cared deeply for the so-called "Chicken Lady." Keeping Nancy's legacy from others didn't sound like something Virginia was capable of. Was it possible someone else showed up Friday night and took the artifacts, making Virginia think they were a qualified courier service? That was possible but rather unlikely.

Most people wouldn't be interested in a bunch of old papers and photos from someone who wasn't famous beyond the Vineyard.

Priscilla rubbed her temples. She just couldn't make sense out of Virginia's disappearance. One other possibility drifted into her mind. Was it possible the woman was afraid of someone? Had she been threatened in some way? Was she running because she felt she was in danger? But who could make her so fearful? Priscilla had no trouble coming up with people who disliked the elderly historian. Eve considered Virginia a thief and a coward. The women in white were furious at seeing Nancy Luce's memory besmirched. The strange man at the library was fixated on Virginia, for his own peculiar reasons. Douglas seemed protective of his aunt, but Priscilla wondered if he resented Virginia for selling her historic home. Maybe he had expected to inherit it, instead of seeing it sold to a stranger.

The missing grave ornaments were another matter. Someone stood to make quick money from selling the items on the black market, Priscilla was sure of that. She'd searched online and learned that several mainland towns had dealt with similar issues, finding statues and other various ornaments scattered several states away, months after the fact. Criminals found small-town cemeteries particularly easy targets, as they often had little in the way of official security.

Priscilla didn't know who to consider as suspects for the cemetery thefts. The women in white? The tourists she'd seen taking selfies? Maybe even Douglas or Virginia, though she supposed they could have been in the same boat as Priscilla and purchased the paver stones unknowingly at an antique shop.

Then there was the bombshell Octavia Spoonmore had dropped. Virginia Lawrence, a multimillionaire? Either Virginia had been incredibly thrifty with money all her life, or her house was worth more than Priscilla had realized. Another nagging thought tugged at Priscilla. Was it possible Virginia had come into money in a less lawful way? Priscilla was certain the distinctive paver stones outside her house were the same ones she'd seen at the West Tisbury cemetery.

Priscilla's shoulders felt tight, and she sensed the beginnings of a nasty tension headache brewing. Leaving Jake snoring on the rug, she went to the bathroom and washed a pain tablet down with water.

Enough thinking. She had another problem to deal with. Her date with Gerald. She knew she'd have to confront him about the blond woman.

She hoped she was wrong about the woman. Gerald had always seemed like such a good man, so trustworthy and reliable. He acted as though he cared for her deeply and only had eyes for her. Well, she'd find out the truth tonight.

Priscilla tried not to overthink her appearance too much, but the image of the beautiful, platinum-haired woman floated in her memory as she got ready. She shoved the thoughts aside and slipped into a pretty chiffon blouse, fresh slacks, and ballet flats. As a finishing touch, she added a slick of lipstick and a fluttery, turquoise silk scarf around her neck that brought out the blue-green of her eyes. Her hands shook only a little as she smoothed her hair into place around her face.

As she entered the living room, Jake raised his head and looked at her expectantly.

"I'm heading out for a bit, boy," Priscilla said. "You be a good pup while I'm gone." Mollified at her answer, Jake flopped back down. Priscilla tried not to think of how things might have changed by the time her date with Gerald was over. Either they would be closer than ever, or... The alternative made sudden tears spring to her eyes, and she blinked in a desperate attempt to hold them at bay. Would they still be together by the time she got home tonight? Only God knew the answer to that question.

The drive across town was a blur. Gerald had offered to pick her up at the cottage as usual, but Priscilla wanted to sit down at the restaurant for their talk. She didn't want to spill her concerns in the car on the way. He had to work later that night anyway, so she used the excuse that it would save them both time if she met him at the Inn, the restaurant he'd picked.

Gerald was waiting for her as she pulled into the parking lot. "Well, hello there." He grinned, and the sweetness of that boyish smile made Priscilla's knees weak. She gave him a hug and a small kiss, and they walked into the restaurant hand in hand. She hoped he couldn't tell how fast her heart was beating.

"Do you know why I suggested this place for our date tonight?" Gerald's eyes twinkled, looking more green than hazel in the low light. They settled into their chairs, and Priscilla noticed once again how broad Gerald's shoulders were and how appealingly his wavy hair fell onto his forehead. He stretched his hands over the table to clasp hers.

She shook her head in response to his question.

"This is our place, Priscilla." He paused and smiled. "We've had many special moments here."

She pulled her hands away from his and avoided eye contact. What should she say? How did she even bring up the woman she'd seen him with without seeming to accuse him of anything?

Gerald's smile faltered. "You're awfully quiet tonight. Is something wrong?"

Feeling like a mute puppet, Priscilla nodded again. The words felt too tight in her throat, and she didn't quite trust herself to speak. Maybe meeting Gerald in public had been a bad idea. She'd thought it would help keep her emotions in check, but it felt like the opposite was happening. She willed herself not to cry.

"I saw you the other day. At Little House Café. And Candy's before that."

"I know you saw me in Candy's. But I don't understand." Gerald looked curious. "You saw me at the café, but I didn't see you?"

"No. You didn't see me." Priscilla paused to take a sip of water. She took a deep breath in an attempt to steady her nerves. "You were with that woman again."

Gerald looked genuinely confused, and Priscilla continued.

"Is she related to you?" Priscilla sent up a silent prayer that Trudy's guess had been correct.

A flicker of recognition dawned in Gerald's eyes. He looked past her, as if trying to gather his thoughts. "No," he said finally. "She's not a relative."

Priscilla's heart sank. What other explanation could Gerald possibly have? She clutched her fingers together in her lap and waited. Instead of setting her mind at ease, Gerald reached for her hands again. Priscilla reluctantly put them into his. He looked her straight in the eyes.

"Priscilla, I cannot tell you why I was with that woman, but what I can tell you is that I love you. Very much. I would never be unfaithful to you. Do you believe that?"

"Yes." It was the truth. She did believe it. She just wasn't sure why he couldn't tell her the whole story. It wasn't like Gerald to not be forthcoming. It was one of the qualities she loved about him. He didn't beat around the bush. It made his silence now all the more unsettling. But maybe this really did have something to do with his job. It was the only thing that made sense.

What secret did he have, and why was he so intent on keeping it?

CHAPTER EIGHTEEN

On Wednesday morning, Priscilla woke to the sound of bells. Confused, she batted at the covers twisted around her legs and struggled to sit up. She'd slept poorly the night before, and if possible, felt more tired now than when she'd gone to bed.

She sat upright and listened. Jake was still snoozing, so the noise couldn't be too threatening. After a brief pause, the bells pealed again. Priscilla almost laughed when she realized the sound was coming from her cell phone. She had plugged it in to charge and set it on her bedside table last night.

She scooted to the edge of the bed to answer the call. It was Rachel. It would be good to hear her daughter's voice. Priscilla had been so absorbed with trying to solve mysteries that she hadn't spoken to Rachel since the weekend. She picked up the call. "Hello, darling."

"Hi, Mom." Rachel's voice was cheerful, and it warmed Priscilla's heart to hear it. It was such a particular joy to know your child was well and happy. Although she'd been pleased Rachel had made her own way in Kansas City, and then Boston, Priscilla couldn't help but feel a little thrill of excitement that she'd soon see Rachel for her wedding. Priscilla felt a thrill of pride at the wonderful young woman her daughter had become and couldn't wait to see Rachel get married.

"How are you, dear? How's wedding planning coming along?"

"Really well. I know a lot of people say wedding planning is stressful, but everything has gone smoothly so far."

Priscilla laughed. "It must be your superior planning skills. I'm sure you're dotting all the i's and crossing all the t's."

"I don't know about that, but A.J. and I are really excited. Maybe that's helped us stay ahead with the task list."

"And you should be excited. Getting married to the right person is such a blessing." Priscilla smiled as she thought of Gary. How her heart had soared when she walked down the aisle to be his bride. Her wedding had been a real-life fairytale, second only to the wonderful marriage that followed it. "You'll remember your wedding day for the rest of your life. I'm so happy I'm here to see it." Priscilla's eyes misted. She knew it had to bother Rachel that her father wouldn't be able to give her away.

Rachel's words broke into Priscilla's thoughts. "How about you, Mom? Did you find a dress to wear yet?"

Priscilla glanced at the skirt suit she'd purchased a few weeks ago. It was encased in plastic to protect it until the wedding, but she could imagine the beautiful brocade fabric and the elegant way it had skimmed over her hips when she tried it on in the store's dressing room. "I did find an outfit, and I think it will be just perfect. What I can't wait to see is you in your wedding dress." She paused, weighing her words. "I wish your dad was here to see you get married."

The other end of the line was silent, and Priscilla heard a few sniffling noises.

"Oh, darling, I didn't mean to upset you. I only meant he would have been so proud of you. And so happy to see you happy."

Rachel sniffled again, and Priscilla heard a rustling sound she imagined was a tissue. "No, it's okay. I miss Dad, but losing him doesn't hurt as much as it did at first. Mostly I just remember the fun times with him now." Rachel gave a small laugh. "Can you imagine how much he would have complained about having to dress up in a suit and tie?"

"He wouldn't have complained if it was for you, Rachel. You had him wrapped around your little finger from the moment you were born. That man was so smitten with you." Priscilla adjusted the phone. "And now you have another man who's smitten with you. I think a lot of A.J. And I know he really loves you."

"He does. He really does, and I love him too." Rachel's voice swung from thoughtful to teasing. "What about you, Mom?"

"What about me?"

"Are there wedding bells on the horizon for you and a certain handsome Coast Guard captain?"

"Oh, honey. I don't even know. Gerald and I care about each other very much, but let's not get ahead of ourselves." Priscilla's fears of Gerald dating another woman had been somewhat allayed after their dinner date, but she still wondered what he was hiding.

"All right." Rachel dropped the subject, but Priscilla suspected her daughter would bring it up again sometime soon.

"I need to get to work, Mom. I'll talk to you soon, okay?"

"Love you, darling."

"Love you."

Priscilla hung up and sighed. She felt a twinge of guilt at letting herself get so distracted by her puzzle-solving that Rachel's wedding had been relegated to the back burner. She committed to do better.

But first, to get ready for the day. She dressed simply and comfortably before taking Jake for his morning walk. Fresh air and sunshine were good cures for emotional woes, and Priscilla felt her mood lighten as she strolled with Jake. She took deep breaths of the cleansing, salty air and felt herself relax as she listened to the rhythmic waves crashing on the rocks. Jake barked at a few seagulls who dared get too close to him, and Priscilla laughed. The lighthouse, her lighthouse, stood tall and clean against the beautiful landscape, and she thought of how it lit up at night, throwing beams of light across the dark water to troubled sailors.

God always worked like that in her life. Just when she felt lost and adrift, His light would chase away her problems. Or at least make them easier to bear. More things than Rachel's wedding had been put on the back burner the past week. Lately Priscilla hadn't taken much time to read more than a few hurried lines of her Bible.

She had things to do this morning, yes, and mysteries to solve, but nothing more important than reconnecting with God. Maybe He would calm her anxious mind and help her figure out what to do next.

"Come on, boy." Priscilla slapped her leg and motioned for Jake to follow her inside. He ignored her and continued barking at anything moving in his path. Birds, squirrels, blades of grass. "I'll get you a treat." At the magic word, Jake's ears perked up, and he reluctantly tore himself away from the excitement of the shoreline.

Back in her cottage, with Jake's feet dried off from the early morning dew, Priscilla snuggled into her favorite armchair. She opened her Bible, and as she did when she felt particularly lost and in need of guidance, she flipped it open to a random spot.

Proverbs. Just the book when one was in need of practical advice on how to live life. Priscilla's eyes scanned chapter twelve but stopped when she hit verse nineteen. A verse that felt as if it were tailor-made for her predicament.

"Truthful lips endure forever, but a lying tongue lasts only a moment."

Waves of doubt had threatened to swallow her whole lately. She had been questioning her own abilities. Unsure of Gerald's true affection for her.

Yet, here was the truth in black and white. She wasn't seeing things as they truly were. Just like her lighthouse, dispelling the darkness with its shining beam, the truth would anchor her. The truth would cut through the darkness and whatever deception lay at the heart of the questions she asked.

She knew what she needed to do. Instead of letting doubt beat her down and wear her out, she needed to trust God. The truth would emerge from the lies in time. She only had to commit for the long haul and hold tight to her faith.

Refreshed, Priscilla rose with a newfound determination. She needed to start ruling out suspects. The women in white were first on her list, and she was pretty sure where she could find them. The cemetery.

CHAPTER NINETEEN

Not many people were out and about at the West Tisbury Cemetery, and thankfully, Dudley Farmer was nowhere to be seen. Instead, a new guard, one Priscilla hadn't met before, stood at his post. The man had his cap pulled down low over his eyes to shield his face from the sun.

His eyes never stopped scanning the grounds, even as Priscilla approached. She cleared her throat. "Excuse me?"

"Hmm?" The guard flicked a cursory glance at her. "Can I help you?"

"I hope so," Priscilla said. "This may seem like a silly question, but have you seen a group of ladies dressed in white gowns this morning?"

She thought the guard would laugh but instead he just grunted. "You mean those Nancy Luce kooks?"

As eccentric as the women in white acted, Priscilla didn't appreciate him calling them kooks. "I've seen them at Nancy Luce's gravesite, yes."

"Nope, I haven't fixed eyes on 'em this morning. They were here yesterday though. Leaving all kinds of trinkets all over the place." The guard shook his head. "Makes Mo's job tough."

"Mo? Is he another guard?"

"No, Mo's the guy who's been cutting the grass for us this summer. Poor fellow has a doozy of a time trying to trim around the stones with all the stuff people leave on them. A few weeks ago, he accidentally broke some ceramic chickens or some nonsense, and I thought those ladies in white were going to explode. They hollered at him until they were blue in the face. They even tried to get poor Mo fired."

Priscilla could imagine that would be the case. The women in white did seem obsessively protective of Luce, her memory, and anything attached to it. It wouldn't surprise Priscilla if they had somehow obtained the museum artifacts to set up their own private memorial.

Priscilla started to ask him another question, but a tall, silver-haired man stooping at a nearby plot caught her attention. The man pressed a bouquet of silk flowers into the ground at the base of Marian Sweetwater's gravestone. She'd met Marian's husband. Could this man be her brother? She felt a connection to the Sweetwaters so she asked the guard, "Sir, I'm sorry to keep bothering you, but can you tell me who that man is?"

"Him?" The guard lifted his cap to resettle it on his head. "That's Elias Sweetwater. Lives in Boston. Comes here a few times a year to leave flowers for his wife. He took her passing pretty hard."

Priscilla frowned. She'd talked to Mr. Sweetwater, the man who was so devoted to his wife. But he certainly wasn't tall and lanky like the gentleman currently paying his respects. The grieving widower she'd met had been short, with a gray mustache and a bowler hat.

"That's not Mr. Sweetwater," Priscilla blurted out.

The guard crossed him arms. "Oh, he's not?"

"No. I met Mr. Sweetwater a few days ago. I spoke with him. He looked nothing like that man." The silver-haired gentleman stood to his feet with difficulty and brushed dirt from the palms of his hands.

The guard narrowed his eyes at Priscilla and jabbed his thumb in the man's direction. "Look, lady, I met Elias Sweetwater." He cocked his head to the side. "See that couple over there? Used to be friends with the Sweetwaters before Mr. Sweetwater moved to Boston to live with their kids. Ask them who this man is if you don't believe me."

Priscilla clamped her mouth shut. Words from her morning's Bible study floated to the surface of her mind. *"Truthful lips endure forever, but a lying tongue lasts only a moment."*

Only one scenario was true. Either the tall, silver-haired man was Mr. Sweetwater or the short, mustached man was.

As Priscilla watched, the couple the guard had pointed out walked over to Mr. Sweetwater and began chatting. It was clear they all knew each other; they acted like lifelong friends, hugging and laughing together. Although it was possible the guard hadn't told the truth about who the widower was, it didn't make much sense. Why would he lie about something like that? And it was ridiculous to think the guard and the elderly couple were in on some kind of conspiracy.

So, it stood to reason that the short man Priscilla had met on Sunday was an imposter. But why would someone play the part of a grieving widower? What would he have to gain from that? At best, the charade seemed nonsensical. At worst, irreverent.

Maybe she could get some answers from Lucille Basham at Acorn Antiques. Priscilla's stolen sundial had come from there, so maybe other hot pieces had been sneaked past the proprietor.

"Thank you for your help," Priscilla told the guard. He grunted again in response. She started to walk toward her vehicle to leave.

"Ma'am! Excuse me, ma'am!" She was surprised to see the mysterious man with the puffy hair from the library hurrying across the grounds toward her. He was still wearing a stiff suit, though a different color and cut this time, and he looked as uncomfortable and overdressed in the summer heat as he had the last time she'd seen him.

Priscilla turned toward him as he struggled to catch up to her, the bottom of his jacket flapping in the wind as he ran.

"We met at the library a few evenings ago, didn't we?" he asked as he drew closer, gasping for air after his brief jog. "I'm afraid I don't know your name."

Priscilla immediately felt suspicious. The man had seemed so intent on finding Virginia, so single-minded. It had been odd. "I could say the same for you."

The man bent over as though it would help him catch his breath better, then straightened. "You're right," he said. "I'm sorry for being so mysterious. I'm Jackson Wither." He fished an ivory-colored business card from his wallet. "Here."

Priscilla took the card. *Herbert J. Wither. Associate of the East Boston Public Library.* The card looked legitimate, with gold lettering on a plain background.

"My first name's Herbert," the man said, as though Priscilla had asked. "Wouldn't you go by your middle name too?"

Priscilla felt herself relax a little and extended her hand. "I'm Priscilla Grant."

He shook her hand. "Nice to meet you. Officially, that is. I'm sorry I was so enigmatic at the library. I had my reasons for wanting to fly under the radar, but I didn't mean to alarm you."

Priscilla looked at the man's business card again. "You're here from the mainland?"

The man nodded. "I am."

"May I ask why?"

"I'm trying to locate Virginia Lawrence. I need to speak with her in person. Clara at the library told me I might find her here."

"Why do you need to find her?"

The man ignored her question. "Are you a friend of Virginia's, Mrs. Grant?"

Would she call herself a friend of Virginia's? Did Virginia really have friends? Or just followers? Priscilla didn't know, but she did find herself protective of the older woman. Virginia was grumpy and snappish, but she also seemed very alone, and that was never a good spot to find oneself in. "Yes, I'm a friend of hers," Priscilla found herself saying.

The man's glasses had slipped down his nose, and he pushed them back into place. "I'm with the Boston Library."

"So I saw from your card," Priscilla said. "What does the Boston Library have to do with Virginia?"

"Well, this isn't supposed to be public knowledge..." The man glanced around as though he expected to see spies lurking behind the trees and lowered his voice to barely above a whisper. "We at BPL are thinking about inviting Virginia to participate in our writer-in-residence program."

"Writer-in-residence? You mean she'd live in Boston?"

The man nodded. "Precisely. The library would fund her living expenses for a year, and of course, provide her with a generous stipend so she could fully devote her attention to her research on Martha's Vineyard. She has such a wealth of knowledge about an area of the country that isn't often highlighted." He scoffed. "People think of the island, and all they think about are presidents and celebrities. They miss out on the rich history of the common man."

"I don't know how in touch Virginia is with the common man," Priscilla said slowly.

"Oh?"

"She's been a recluse until recently. Her lecture the other night was supposed to be a kind of entrance back into society."

"Ah, yes. I was disappointed that was canceled." The man continued, "I've been very concerned about her disappearance. It confirmed that I was right to scout her out in the first place. We at the Boston Library want to be sure of the person we're inviting to be a resident." He smoothed down his tie. "It's a prestigious title, and no small amount of work on the part of the associates. If we invite someone into the program, we want to make sure they are reliable and steady. We want to make sure they are committed."

"Well, I don't presume to know Virginia well," Priscilla said, "but I know she is highly invested in her work." She didn't mention that, according to Eve, the majority of Virginia's research was stolen. She wasn't sure Eve was a reliable source. "She's out researching somewhere on the island right now, in fact. I'm not certain where she is, but I know her car has been seen by several people."

Jackson smiled. "Yes, yes, that pink Cadillac. That's pretty distinctive. I've been keeping my eyes open for it. I thought I saw it near Tisbury yesterday, out by that beautiful white lighthouse."

Priscilla realized with a shock that he might be talking about her lighthouse. "The white one with a black widow's walk and cupola?"

Jackson nodded. "Yes, it's just stunning. A beautiful example of coastal architecture. And the most charming little cottage beside it." He was definitely talking about her lighthouse. Why had Virginia driven by Priscilla's house? Jackson continued. "The car followed a road along the shore but then just disappeared. Like it vanished into the waves."

The image of Virginia's car steering into the ocean haunted Priscilla. Virginia had the whole world at her feet, it seemed. Millions of dollars, according to Octavia Spoonmore. Recognition with her research on Martha's Vineyard. A possible plum of a position with the Boston Public Library. Yet she had little in the way of true friendships, and the one person she might have been the closest to, Eve Pennywhistle, now viewed her as a bitter rival.

What was Virginia up to? Was she in danger? And more importantly, where was she now?

CHAPTER TWENTY

Priscilla said goodbye to Jackson and started driving toward Acorn Antiques. A perk of being out and about early in the day was being able to pull straight into a parking spot rather than having to parallel park. Priscilla crossed the street and pushed through the door to the antique store. She noticed the antique bikes and adorable picnic display still set up in the front window and wondered if Lucille Basham designed the arrangements herself. She hadn't met Lucille on her last visit to the store, so she had no idea if the woman would be willing to speak with her or if she'd be annoyed at Priscilla's questions. Well, there was only one way to find out.

Priscilla took a deep breath, wishing she had Trudy with her. Her cousin was once again at play practice though. Opening night for *Murder by Moonlight* was on Saturday, and since today was Wednesday, Priscilla was sure the entire cast and crew were in a flurry of last-minute activity. Trudy was nervous, Priscilla could tell, but also very excited. Her cousin had dreamed of being a leading lady on stage for years, and Priscilla was happy to see Trudy so content. When she wasn't dealing with Douglas's odd behavior, that is. Trudy had mentioned how erratic Douglas's whims were. "It's like he's the spoiled actor asking for only blue M&Ms in his dressing room," Trudy had quipped.

Priscilla imagined Douglas was just as nervous as Trudy. She was sure he had a lot invested in the play, not only his time, but probably some of his own money. She wondered how much Virginia had sunk into the production. With so much tied up in the success of *Murder by Moonlight*, Priscilla reasoned Douglas had the right to be a little jittery. Especially if that big-shot producer truly did show up.

A thought sprang to Priscilla's mind that she hadn't considered before. What if the play was picked up, and Douglas asked Trudy and all the other Vineyard actors to travel with the show? Would Trudy accept? Priscilla couldn't imagine Trudy leaving Dan for so long, and she worried it wouldn't be good for them, especially in light of their recent communication trouble. And what would Priscilla do if her cousin left? She'd come to count on Trudy's optimistic spirit and fun-loving attitude to brighten her day.

Priscilla shook her head to clear her thoughts. She was getting ahead of herself. The producer might not even show up, and he might not like the play enough to back it. Of course, she hoped, for Trudy's sake, the production would go off without a hitch. Even if the company went on tour, Trudy might not accept. No, Priscilla needed to focus on the present for now. Keep teasing out the strands of truth that had to be woven through the two converging mysteries she found herself tangled in.

"Welcome to Acorn Antiques. May I help you find anything in particular?" A soft-spoken woman with wavy hair and a long bohemian-style skirt stood at the counter.

Priscilla greeted her. "Are you Lucille?"

"I am." The woman stepped out from behind the oversized counter to shake Priscilla's hand. Her skirt swished softly around her ankles as she moved, and Priscilla noticed the glint of Lucille's tiny gold hoop earrings as the woman tucked her hair behind one ear.

"It's nice to meet you. I'm Priscilla Grant. My friend bought an item here over the weekend. A sundial?"

Lucille's gentle smile wavered. "If you're looking for more garden ornaments, I'm afraid I can't help. I had to get rid of my entire stock unexpectedly."

Priscilla glanced over her shoulder at the beautifully decorated booth she and Trudy had stopped at on their last visit to the store. Grapevines and twinkling lights still formed a makeshift pergola overhead, but the floor space was nearly empty. Gone were all the mosaic tiles, graceful statues, and birdbaths. The booth now featured a small wooden table with a few vintage books and knickknacks scattered across its top.

"I'll be getting more merchandise in soon," Lucille said as she motioned toward the bare space.

"To tell you the truth, the police took the sundial from me a couple of days ago."

To her surprise, Lucille's eyes filled with tears at Priscilla's innocent comment. "I'm so sorry. I hope you'll continue shopping here. I didn't know things weren't aboveboard. Why would I suspect the items would be stolen? And that nice old man...I just can't believe it."

"An old man? Is he the one who sold you the items?" Lucille was obviously upset, and Priscilla didn't want to make matters worse by prying, but she needed to know if the man who sold the stolen ornaments to Lucille fit the description of the Mr. Sweetwater she'd met at the cemetery.

Lucille took a deep breath. "Oh, I shouldn't say anything. I already told the police about him though, so I guess it's not a secret or anything. I just can't believe that charming old man could be a thief. He was so likeable."

"Do you remember what he looked like?"

Lucille pressed her lips together, as though she were trying to regain her composure. "Let's see. He was a short fellow with a mustache, I remember that. Sort of frail. He mentioned he was selling off his late wife's garden ornaments. He said he couldn't bear to look at them anymore without her around to tend the flowers in her garden. I felt sorry for him." Lucille sniffled. "At the time, I did wonder how such a fragile old man had managed to load all the pieces up. Some of them were incredibly heavy, and he made it sound as though he lived alone. I figured maybe he had some grown kids who helped him. I had to call in special help to get the pieces unloaded myself. Some of the statues were weighty enough they wouldn't slide on a dolly without digging grooves into the floor." Lucille pointed at the two parallel lines dug into the tile near the shop's door.

Lucille stepped back behind the counter and pulled out a handwritten coupon, which she handed to Priscilla. "Thankfully, the police have cleared me from any suspicion. You can be certain that in the future I'll screen my vendors more thoroughly. If you'd still consider being a customer here, I'd like to offer you a discount on any item you choose, no matter the price." She tucked her hair behind her ear again. "I assure you, nothing like this will ever happen again. I'm so sorry for any inconvenience we've caused you, Mrs. Grant, was it?"

Priscilla smiled. She liked Lucille. Instinctively, she felt the woman was telling the truth, and Priscilla felt sorry that the woman's tender, trusting nature had been taken advantage of by some ne'er-do-well. "Please, call me Priscilla."

Lucille looked relieved at Priscilla's smile. "Please tell your friend to come by so I can refund her money. Is there anything at all I can help you find today, Priscilla?"

"Actually, there is." Priscilla tucked the coupon into her purse. Rachel's wedding was drawing close, and she still hadn't found a replica of Gary's mom's cameo brooch. "When I was here the other day, I was looking for something specific. You didn't have anything that would work, but just in case something new has come in, I wanted to check with you." Priscilla briefly described the cameo, with its beautiful blue background carved from agate, but wasn't surprised when Lucille shook her head.

"I'm afraid we don't have anything quite like that," she said. "We do have a small selection of cameos, but they're the more common peach-colored carnelian background." Lucille showed Priscilla the display case where the cameos rested on a bed of velvet.

"Hmm," Priscilla said. "I really need the blue background, so if you get anything like what I'm looking for into the shop, maybe you could let me know." They walked back to the counter, and

Priscilla scribbled her name and phone number on a piece of paper. Lucille stuck the scrap in her address book and promised to contact Priscilla if she found anything that fit her description.

"This is just a thought," said Lucille, "but have you considered getting in touch with a local jeweler to see if someone would be interested in crafting a custom piece for you?"

Priscilla felt sheepish that she hadn't thought of that, but it certainly couldn't hurt to look into it. She got a few recommendations from Lucille of people to contact and left the store. The air smelled fresh and sweet after the musty, old-paper scent of the shop, and she took a few deep breaths.

She may not have found a cameo yet, but the day was delivering some surprises. She had likely ruled out Jackson Wither as a person of interest. She knew Virginia had been seen driving by her lighthouse. And she had a sneaking suspicion that the Sweetwater she'd met at the cemetery was mixed up in the theft of grave ornaments at the West Tisbury Cemetery. But how to find him? His real last name obviously wasn't Sweetwater, so it wasn't as if she could look him up in the phone book. Priscilla was sure if she saw the man again she'd recognize him, but the chances weren't likely she'd run into him by happenstance.

Not to mention the fact that he might not even be a year-round resident. He could be, and likely was, posing as a tourist while he pilfered items to sell for profit. For all Priscilla knew, the man could be long gone by now. After all, if the police hadn't tracked him down already, what chance did she have?

CHAPTER TWENTY-ONE

Priscilla's grumbling stomach warned her that she'd sleuthed through lunchtime. She needed to take a short break to drive home and grab a bite to eat. Then she could figure out what to do next.

She climbed into her SUV and headed in the direction of the cottage. Maybe she could call her cousins and see if anyone wanted to stop by for some conversation and a meal. She'd been eating out so much lately that she had a yummy assortment of restaurant leftovers in her fridge. As Priscilla drove through downtown though, she spied a familiar-looking vehicle parked smack-dab in front of Candy's.

Trudy. She must have finished play practice and stopped in for a pick-me-up coffee. Priscilla knew she was still on her low-carb eating plan and wondered how she was managing to stay away from all the delicious, sweet treats Candy had to offer. With Rachel's wedding coming up and the need to fit into that beautiful mother-of-the-bride outfit, Priscilla knew she should keep her sweet tooth in check too. Maybe she'd just stop in and have a coffee with her cousin for moral support. She could catch Trudy up on her new findings. Maybe she'd have some ideas about how to find the fake Elias Sweetwater.

Priscilla parked and headed toward the shop. A heavenly sugary aroma surrounded her as she stepped inside, and her decision to only have coffee wavered. Fine encourager she was. Poor Trudy had been exercising self-control for two weeks, and Priscilla couldn't keep her resolve from slipping for two seconds.

Priscilla saw Trudy's platinum-blond hair immediately as she entered. Her cousin's back was to the door, and she was surrounded by a group of laughing people, waving their hands around theatrically. Priscilla imagined they were the other *Murder by Moonlight* actors and actresses. Trudy had talked about her new friends a lot, though Priscilla hadn't officially met any of them. Maybe now she'd get a chance.

Trudy must have sensed Priscilla's movement behind her because as Priscilla drew close, Trudy turned to face her. In her hand was a plate filled with an assortment of pastries: a cinnamon-sugared doughnut oozing red jelly, a blueberry muffin, and one of Priscilla's favorites, a crème horn.

Trudy wiped her mouth and looked guilty. "Hi, Priscilla."

"Hi." Priscilla couldn't help but smile. "I stopped by to see if you wanted to swing by my house for a quick lunch, but I see you've already eaten."

Trudy pulled Priscilla to one side, away from her theater friends. "I know I shouldn't be guzzling sweets," she said, "but I am so stressed about this play."

"You're getting close to opening night. Maybe it's just nerves?"

"I'm sure some of it is, but mostly it's Douglas."

Trudy made a face, and Priscilla's mouth twitched with laughter. "Worse than usual?"

Trudy breathed out a frustrated sigh. "He's off his rocker. He's always been eccentric, but lately?" She put her hand on Priscilla's arm. "He's gone beyond the pale, Priscilla. We've been rehearsing overtime since he heard from that New York producer. Douglas is convinced this is his big break. He yells at us if we recite one word wrong or move a foot upstage when the script says downstage. He nitpicks everything, and it's driving us all crazy. We just needed to come here and blow off some steam, you know?"

Priscilla nodded. Her cousin's version of blowing off steam with cookies and muffins was probably a lot healthier than most vices. "I'm not the diet police. I understand. I'm a little stressed myself."

"Here. Take a crème horn. It'll help, trust me." Trudy handed Priscilla one from her plate, and Priscilla couldn't resist. She broke off a piece of the flaky, buttery pastry and popped it into her mouth.

Trudy tore off a tiny bit of blueberry muffin before setting her plate down on the edge of a nearby empty table. "So, enough about me and my silly woes," she said. "What in particular is stressing you out?"

Priscilla filled her cousin in on the details of her morning and all the new clues she'd received, including what Jackson Wither had told her.

Trudy's mouth fell open. "So that old man at the graveyard was a thief?"

"I don't know for sure, Trudy. I just know that the Sweetwater we met was not the real Elias Sweetwater. Not to mention the fact that the man we met might have also sold Lucille Basham hot property."

"Unbelievable." Trudy planted her fists on her hips. "How desperate for money would you have to be to steal items from a cemetery?"

"Pretty desperate," Priscilla agreed.

Trudy's eyes widened. "How do you find someone when you don't even know his real name? All we know is that he's short, has a mustache, and is old."

Priscilla shrugged. "It's certainly not much to go on."

Trudy sighed. "Back to square one."

"At least until we figure a few more things out," Priscilla agreed.

Trudy thought for a moment, mulling over the other information Priscilla had given her. "Well, if that mystery is at a temporary dead end, what about Virginia being spotted driving by the lighthouse? Maybe she was looking for you, Priscilla."

"I don't know," Priscilla said. "I can't figure out Virginia's part in this situation. She might have stolen the artifacts, or she might be a victim herself. Maybe someone blackmailed her. It doesn't hurt that she's a multimillionaire, if what Octavia said was true."

"I always say things that are true." As if on cue, Octavia Spoonmore strode toward them, her heels clicking forcefully on the floor as she did so.

"Trudy!" She made a big show out of hugging Trudy and giving air kisses. "And Priscilla, how are you?" She put her hands, with her elaborately manicured nails, on Priscilla's shoulders and looked her in the eyes. "I wondered how you were, poor thing."

Priscilla couldn't hide her confusion. "I'm just fine. Why wouldn't I be?"

Octavia clucked her tongue. "Look at you, putting on a brave face. You don't need to pretend with me, Priscilla. I'm on your side. You know, we girls have to stick together."

"I'm sorry? I don't think I understand."

"Well, are you putting your best foot forward, or could you be in denial? You're really committed to this, aren't you?" Octavia swatted at Priscilla's arm. "I'm talking about you and Gerald breaking up, silly. How are you doing?"

Priscilla felt her mouth drop open. Breaking up? "What gave you the idea Gerald and I weren't together anymore?"

Octavia's precisely filled-in eyebrows raised. "I didn't think you would be after he two-timed you. I saw him in here a few days ago with a beautiful blond woman. They seemed very excited about something."

Even though Priscilla held Gerald's promise close—*"I love you very much. I would never be unfaithful to you"*—her chest tightened. She straightened to her full height, which still wasn't quite as tall as Octavia in her towering heels, and cleared her throat. "I assure you, Octavia, Gerald is not dating anyone but me. Maybe you shouldn't assume things about other people."

"Well." Octavia's face puckered as if she had tasted one of Candy's sour lemon drop cookies. "I was only trying to help."

As gossipy as the real estate agent was, Priscilla didn't mean to actually hurt her feelings. She took a deep breath. "I'm sorry, Octavia. I have a lot on my mind lately, but that's no excuse to be rude. I apologize."

Octavia paused for a moment, as though considering whether or not Priscilla's response was sincere. Her pursed lips finally gave way to a small smile. "I accept your apology." She leaned closer to the two cousins. "I am actually quite glad I ran into you today. I wanted to know if you've heard from Virginia yet."

"No, we're still looking for her," said Trudy.

"Why?" asked Priscilla. "Have you talked to her?" If anyone would know what was going on in town, Priscilla figured Octavia would. Gossiping was a dangerous habit, but Priscilla wouldn't mind it so much if it could help them find Virginia. The image of her driving along the shore road and disappearing, as if she'd driven straight into the waves, really bothered Priscilla. She was sure the older woman was fine, but what if her suspicions were right? What if Virginia was truly in danger, and that's why she had left so abruptly before the lecture?

"Oh, that's disappointing," Octavia said as if she'd only heard Trudy's answer. "I had some last-minute paperwork I have to get filed, and I needed her signature. Silly me, I got the dimensions of her house wrong. These old houses are tricky. Between root cellars, turrets, and hidden rooms, I'm always running into some kind of discrepancy when it comes to accurate descriptions." She sighed. "So tough to get everything pinned down, you know?"

"Sorry," Trudy said, "but we'll contact you if we see her. She's a difficult lady to track down."

"I would be too, if I had as much moolah as she does. I'd be jet-setting every weekend." Octavia's phone buzzed from her bag, and she pulled it out and frowned. "Real estate emergency, ladies. Got to go. Let me know if you find Virginia."

Octavia clicked away on her spindly heels. As the door swung shut behind her, Trudy grabbed a napkin and wrapped up her remaining pastry.

"So what are we waiting for?" she asked, shoving the doughnut into her handbag.

"I don't know," said Priscilla. "More dessert?"

Trudy shook her head adamantly and patted her bag. "We've got fuel for the road. I mean, why are we hanging around here? We need to drive over to your house, Priscilla, and see if we can find any trace of Virginia. If she's really in trouble and looking for you, maybe she's left you a note or something."

"Great idea." Priscilla fished out her keys. "Let's head to my place."

CHAPTER TWENTY-TWO

When they walked into the cottage, Jake jumped up and hurried over to Trudy. He was always excited to see her. Trudy, who normally worried about her clothes and tried to protect herself from dog hair, put her arms around him and let him lick her face. Priscilla was glad that her cousins all loved Jake.

"I'll make coffee and see if I have something a little healthier than what we ate at Candy's."

"My stomach is a little upset by all the sweets," Trudy admitted. "If I keep eating like this, one of the scenes may include me busting out of that tight red dress they expect me to wear." She hugged Jake one more time, then walked over and sat down at the kitchen table. Jake followed her and lay down next to her feet.

Priscilla sliced some different kinds of cheese and put them on a platter, along with some grapes and chunks of watermelon. "How's this?" she asked Trudy.

"Looks great." Trudy picked up a piece of cheese and nibbled at it. Then she took a deep breath and exhaled slowly. "I'm so nervous about Saturday night. What was I thinking?" She looked at Priscilla, her eyes wide and shiny with tears. "What if I bomb, Priscilla? Will I ever be able to live it down?"

Priscilla sat down next to her cousin and took her hand. "You're not going to bomb, Trudy. You've got lots of natural talent. I have no doubt you'll be the hit of the show."

Trudy squeezed Priscilla's hand. "Thank you. What would I do without you?"

"Oh, Trudy. Joan and Gail would tell you exactly the same thing. You have a lot of support. I'm not the only one."

Trudy wiped her eyes with the back of her hand. "They've always been supportive. I guess I take it for granted. For some reason when you say it, it means more."

Priscilla laughed. "I'm not sure I understand why you feel that way, but I'm happy to know my opinion helps you." She'd put two forks and two small plates on the table, along with some napkins. She picked up one of the plates, grabbed a fork, and stabbed a piece of watermelon. "Dan will be there Saturday night, won't he?"

Trudy shrugged. "I don't know. I hope so. He's been working a lot of late nights. Some project at work...he says."

Priscilla heard something in Trudy's voice that concerned her. "You believe him, don't you?" she asked.

"I guess so," Trudy said softly. "The truth is, it's hard not to wonder..."

"Oh, Trudy," Priscilla said firmly. "Dan loves you. There's no way he'd ever cheat on you."

Trudy stared at her cousin. "How can you say that? You think Gerald might be dating someone else."

Priscilla immediately realized her own fears were causing her cousin doubt. She smiled at Trudy. "In your heart, you know Dan's trustworthy, right?"

Trudy appeared to be turning Priscilla's words over in her mind. Finally, she said, "Yeah. You're right. I really do trust him."

"And I trust Gerald. Let's both have a little faith and give our men the benefit of the doubt, okay?"

Trudy finally smiled. "Okay. Thanks."

"You're welcome."

"So, are we any closer to finding Virginia?" Trudy asked, steering the conversation back to the missing historian.

"I don't know," Priscilla said. "We know she's alive, since she's been seen around town, by us as well. I'm still a little worried about what Jackson Wither said."

"You're talking about that guy from the Boston Library?" Trudy leaned closer to her cousin. "What did he say that upset you?"

"Sorry. I told you he saw Virginia driving down that road near the beach yesterday, right? I forgot to tell you that she seemed to suddenly disappear."

Trudy gasped. "You don't mean..."

Priscilla waved her comment away. "I think she was probably driving fast, just like she was when we saw her. He just lost sight of her. I mean, if she really drove her car into the ocean, we'd know it. Someone would have seen it."

"Are you sure?"

Priscilla stared into her coffee cup. Was she certain? Maybe 80 percent. But not 100 percent. "I guess I should call Chief Westin. Just to be safe."

"It's probably a good idea." Trudy rested her chin on her fist. "Oh, Priscilla, surely Virginia wouldn't do something so...awful. I mean, she has a good life. A nephew who loves her, even if he is a little strange. Lots of money." Trudy was quiet for a moment, her blue eyes blinking. Finally, she put her arm down. "Wait a minute. She's been so excited about moving to Boston. That doesn't sound like someone who's planning to do herself in."

Priscilla nodded. "That's exactly what I was thinking. Why sell your house and make plans to move and then..." Priscilla couldn't even say it. She realized she really did need to notify Hank. Great. As if he wanted to hear from her again. She sighed. "I might as well get this over with." She got up, went to her phone, and called the police station. Gabrielle put her through to the police chief.

"This is Westin," he said gruffly.

Priscilla nervously cleared her throat. "Chief, this is Priscilla. I...I heard something this morning that I think you should know."

"Is this about the old man at the cemetery? We talked to the security guard not long after you left. We know about the man skulking around the cemetery. He's our prime suspect. You're off the hook."

Priscilla breathed a sigh of relief. "Oh. I'm so glad you talked to the guard. And I'm thrilled to be off your suspect list. But actually, there was something else I wanted to speak to you about."

"Go on."

She told him about Jackson Wither. "He said something toward the end of our conversation that really bothered me. You know that road along the shoreline?"

"Sure. It's not used much. Not in great shape."

"I know," Priscilla said. "But Jackson said he saw Virginia's pink Cadillac racing down that road. Then he said... Well, he said she suddenly disappeared from sight."

"When was this?" Hank asked.

"Yesterday. I'm not sure what time he saw the car but—"

Hank cut her off. "You have nothing to worry about. Someone saw Miss Lawrence early this morning in Edgartown."

Priscilla felt relief wash through her. "I'm so glad to hear that. I was really concerned."

"You know what bothers me?" Hank asked.

"What's that?"

"If Miss Lawrence is trying to hide out, why is it she isn't holed up somewhere? Why is she driving around in that car? It's as if she wants to be seen."

Priscilla pondered Hank's comment. He was right. It really didn't make much sense. Before she could let Hank know she agreed with him, he said, "I've got to go. If you find out anything helpful about Miss Lawrence, let me know. She needs to let us know where those museum pieces are. Since she was the last person to have them, if they're not returned soon, I'll have to charge her with Class C Theft. That exhibit is worth over two thousand dollars. She could be looking at five years in jail."

Priscilla's throat tightened. "But I really can't believe she took them. Her note said she gave them to a courier service."

"But that claim doesn't hold up. We've checked every courier service in town. I have to assume they're still in her possession, and she's refusing to return them. To me, that's theft, pure and simple. If you see her before I do, you should warn her. But to be honest, it's probably too late."

Before Priscilla could say anything else, Hank hung up. Priscilla stared at the phone. Five years in jail? Well, there went Virginia's writer-in-residence gig in Boston. Something she would probably love.

"What's wrong?" Trudy asked, as Priscilla put the phone down. "You look sick."

"The good news is I'm not a suspect anymore."

"That's great," Trudy said. "So why are you so upset?"

Priscilla came over to the table and sat down. She really did feel a little nauseated. "Well, this puts a new perspective on everything." She wrapped her arms around herself. "I guess I should have seen this coming..."

"What are you talking about?" Trudy said, her forehead wrinkled with concern.

"Hank says if Virginia doesn't bring the artifacts back soon, she'll be charged with theft." She looked into her cousin's eyes. "Trudy, she could go to prison. For five years."

Trudy's eyes widened, and her mouth dropped open. "But...But what if she's just...borrowing those things? For research, I mean? Or what if she called the wrong number and some unscrupulous person drove over to her house and took them?"

Priscilla shook her head. "Doesn't matter. Chief Westin says she was the last person to have them, so she's his main suspect." She rubbed the back of her neck. She could feel another tension headache trying to make an appearance. She wasn't sure why she was so worried about Virginia. She'd caused everyone so much trouble. But down deep inside, Priscilla just couldn't believe Virginia Lawrence would resort to thievery, no matter how much she liked Nancy Luce. She had too much respect for the history of the Vineyard and for Nancy Luce herself.

Yet no matter how she tried to explain away Virginia's actions, it seemed Hank Westin might be right. If he found Virginia, would she end up in jail? Priscilla needed to find her. And fast.

CHAPTER TWENTY-THREE

T hese crab cakes are divine." Gail took another bite of her lunch and sighed appreciatively. "I hope you didn't go to too much trouble on our account, Priscilla." Wednesday evening and Thursday morning had passed by uneventfully, and Priscilla had invited her cousins over for what she hoped would be a relaxing lunch.

Priscilla laughed. "No danger of that. I bought these frozen. All I did was heat them up in a skillet."

"You can't tell," said Joan. "They are delicious." She wiped her mouth with a napkin and added a second helping to her plate.

Priscilla spooned a little rémoulade sauce on her crab cake and took a bite. Her cousins were right. It was excellent, light and subtly sweet. The spicy, creamy sauce only elevated the wonderful flavor of the seafood. "Buying convenience food is still more expensive than making something myself, but cheaper than eating in a restaurant." Her pocketbook and her waist were starting to feel the effects of too many meals in the Vineyard's wonderful eateries.

"You've been preoccupied. You haven't had time for cooking," said Joan.

Priscilla nodded. She'd been consumed with the events of the last week, but today, it felt good to unwind for an hour in her little cottage with Gail and Joan. She'd clocked a lot of hours with Trudy lately, but she hadn't seen much of her other two cousins, and she had missed their company.

Gail finished her meal and carried her empty plate to the sink. "It's a shame Trudy wasn't here to enjoy lunch."

Joan looked at her watch. "Where is she anyway? We said we were meeting at one. It's almost half past now. It's not like her to be late."

Joan was right. It was highly unusual for Trudy to be late. Even on the day she and Priscilla had tromped through the muddy forest outside Virginia's house, they had still arrived on time for their meeting with Eve. Priscilla felt a small twinge of worry. She knew Dan and Trudy had been having some difficulties lately, but she hoped Trudy's delayed arrival wasn't a result of some marital tiff.

She didn't have to worry long. At that moment Trudy rushed in the cottage door, out of breath and looking frazzled. Priscilla breathed a sigh of relief.

"Where have you been? We were getting ready to send out a search party!"

Trudy didn't answer. She slung her purse straps over the chair back and sank into her seat. "Sorry I'm late. I'm so stressed out."

"About the play? You'll do great."

"I'm not worried about that. Well, not completely. I mean, I am a little nervous, but mostly because of Douglas."

"What's he done now?"

"He's had us practicing this play all summer, and then yesterday, he yanks it out from underneath us with this new ending he said he was working on. I'm so concerned I'm going to flub my lines."

Joan smiled at her younger sister. "I'm sure you'll be fine. And if you do flub them, at least you'll have some friendly faces in the audience. We'll all be there, and Dan too."

Trudy's frown deepened. "Actually, Dan said he has to work. Again. I can't believe he's going to miss the play. This is my big moment, you know? I thought he'd want to be there for it, but he just seems so inattentive. Anytime he's not working he's slouched in front of the TV with some kind of goofy sci-fi show that creeps me out." She huffed out a frustrated breath. "He's a scientist. You'd think he'd want to watch something logical and realistic."

Gail put her hand on Trudy's shoulder. "Oh, Trudy, I'm so sorry. I know that has to be a disappointment. Maybe he'll get off work last-minute and surprise you?"

"I doubt it," Trudy grumbled. Priscilla hated witnessing her cousin's negative attitude. Trudy was normally upbeat and cheerful. It wasn't like her to act melancholy. Then again, it wasn't like Priscilla to second-guess everything in her life, yet that's what she'd been doing lately. She was trying hard to give the situation with Gerald to God, but she was struggling. And she felt no closer to solving the two mysteries in front of her than before. Maybe that was something her cousins could help with, especially now that all three of them were here. Surely, if they put their heads together, they could find a way to put together some of the strange puzzle pieces that made up Virginia's actions and the thefts in the cemeteries to create a picture that made sense.

Priscilla cleared her throat. "I think a change of subject is in order."

"What do you have in mind?" asked Gail. "Something interesting, I hope?"

"Oh, it's interesting," said Priscilla. "Not to make you all sing for your supper, but how would you feel about playing detective for a few minutes?"

"I'm game," said Joan. "As long as we can sit on the couch where we can get comfy."

"I second that," said Gail. Trudy looked glum but nodded, so the group moved to the living room to settle in with their glasses of iced tea.

"So, do you have any new leads?" asked Gail. "Trudy mentioned you both followed Virginia on a wild goose chase the day before yesterday. She said Virginia drove like she was racing the Indy 500."

Priscilla shook her head, remembering Virginia's erratic driving. "It was amazing she didn't get in a wreck. One wrong turn on a curve, and that would be it." She shuddered to think about it.

"We didn't catch her though," said Trudy, the corners of her mouth still turned down. "So we didn't find out anything at all."

"That's not entirely true," said Priscilla. "We may not have gotten any information from Virginia, but we got plenty of other clues. We just don't know how they fit together."

"What did you discover?" asked Joan, reaching down to pet Jake as he pushed his head against her legs.

"Well," said Priscilla, "we found out from Octavia Spoonmore that Virginia is a lot wealthier than anybody realized. If what Octavia said is true, she's worth several million dollars."

Gail whistled through her teeth. "Wow. Now that *is* interesting. I bet there are a few people out there who would like to get their hands on all that money."

"Including Eve Pennywhistle," said Trudy, sitting up a bit and fluffing out her hair with her fingers. That looked more like the Trudy Priscilla knew, and she hoped her cousin's bad mood was starting to wear off.

"Eve? Was that the dour-looking woman at the library the night Virginia's lecture was supposed to happen?" said Gail.

Priscilla nodded. "And Eve thinks Virginia double-crossed her. She said she was Virginia's research partner, but Virginia stole her research and passed it off as her own. If it's true, Eve might feel that that money—assuming some of it was from the sale of Virginia's first book—should have been hers."

"We need to remember that Virginia has more than one enemy," said Trudy. She explained about seeing the women in white at the cemetery and how incensed they were over Virginia skipping the lecture.

"They're so creepy," Joan said. By now, Jake had wiggled his way onto her lap, and she scratched his back, oblivious to the dog hairs covering her sweater.

"We thought we had a suspect in Jackson Wither." Priscilla explained about the associate of the Boston Public Library. "But he turned out to be aboveboard. He was just trying to find information about Virginia to make sure she was a good candidate for their writer-in-residence program."

"What about Douglas?" Trudy jumped in. "Do you think he could've had a beef with Virginia? She did sell her house. Maybe he thought he was going to inherit it or something."

"I don't know," Priscilla said. "It's possible. She did give him some money for his play, though, so I would think that would smooth over any rough patches between them."

"So, basically," said Joan, "Virginia is still missing, and we still think she has the artifacts with her?"

"We're not sure, but it's looking more and more like it," said Priscilla.

"Well, what about the items stolen from the cemetery?" asked Gail. "Did you find out anything about that?"

"We discovered that Virginia might be tied to that case too," said Trudy. "The paver stones we saw at Virginia's house match some that are missing from the cemetery. What are the odds?"

"Do you think Virginia knew the items were stolen? Maybe she was an innocent bystander, like you were, Priscilla."

"Maybe," agreed Priscilla. "I have a hard time believing she knew, but that's just a hunch on my part. We did discover a person of interest who is likely behind the grave ornament thefts though." She filled her cousins in on her discovery that the Mr. Sweetwater she'd met at the West Tisbury Cemetery was not the true Elias Sweetwater. And that the imposter fit the description of the same man who sold Lucille Basham stolen antique garden ornaments.

"Wow," said Joan. "And he's out there, on the loose some-where. Did you tell the police?"

Priscilla started to tell her cousins that Hank had interviewed the same guard she'd talked to and was up to speed on the situation, but just then, her cell phone rang. Her chest tightened as she glanced down at the screen. It was the East Shore Historical Museum.

"It's Mildred." Priscilla grimaced. "I have to take this." She took a deep breath and stepped into the bedroom so she could have some privacy. "Hello?"

"Hello, Priscilla? This is Mildred." Even in the few words Mildred had spoken, Priscilla could tell the woman was beside herself. "Please tell me you've found the artifacts."

Priscilla let out a breath. "I don't have them yet, Mildred."

Mildred's voice shook. "The Boston Museum contacted me this morning. I had to tell them everything. They're considering pursuing legal action, Priscilla. This could shut down East Shore, not to mention what it would mean for me personally. And might I add, for you, as well. If you know anything that you're not telling me..."

"I don't." Priscilla rushed to explain, eager to calm Mildred's rattled nerves. She filled Mildred in about following Virginia's Cadillac. "We couldn't catch up with her, but Virginia is on the island. If we can just talk with her, we can get this whole mess sorted out. I know it's just some kind of misunderstanding. She may not have the museum pieces, but hopefully she can give us some information that might lead us to their location."

Priscilla's attempt to assure the rattled caretaker had little effect. After a brief, charged silence on the other end of the line, Mildred blurted, "I want Virginia arrested!"

Priscilla realized, with a sinking heart, that this was exactly where things were headed. Hank had already mentioned charging Virginia with Class C theft, and now Mildred was calling for her arrest as well. Priscilla just couldn't believe Virginia was guilty. It didn't add up that the woman would skip the library lecture when she'd seemed so committed to it. In fact, none of this made sense. Virginia didn't seem like the kind of person who would steal the artifacts—or leave her beloved pet behind. She'd seemed so devoted to Magnus.

Unless Priscilla could unravel the mysteries soon, Virginia Lawrence was going to jail.

CHAPTER TWENTY-FOUR

Priscilla spent Friday morning catching up on some tasks she needed to do at the cottage. A couple of hours of cleaning made a big difference. As she worked, she thought about her conversation with her cousins the day before. They hadn't come up with anything solid, but they'd raised several interesting questions. She'd hoped the result of their teamwork would steer her in the right direction, but that hadn't happened.

After she was done, she took Jake out for a leisurely walk. Even though it was June, it was a pleasant morning. Jake wasn't a fan of really warm weather. When their walks were finished, he'd usually head straight to his water bowl and nearly empty it. Of course, that meant another walk, but there was no way to reason with a dog about something like that.

Today, he was enjoying his time outside. They walked to the cliff and looked out over the ocean. Priscilla could spend hours watching the water lap up against the shore. The sound was so relaxing. It was one of the benefits of summer on Martha's Vineyard. You could open your windows and listen to the waves washing in while you drifted off to sleep.

As she gazed out on the water, she noticed the old road near the beach. It had been virtually abandoned. Frequent flooding had made it almost useless. Priscilla hadn't paid much attention to it because it was nearly invisible after being almost covered with sand. However, the tracks from a car, almost certainly Virginia's, were evident. Why would she choose to take this road?

Priscilla leaned over a little and looked up the beach. There were a few houses dotting the shoreline. Two of them were occupied year-round. One was a summer house, but the people who owned it came every year like clockwork. She wondered if any of them had seen the Cadillac. Maybe she should suggest that Hank talk to them. Even as the thought came, she dismissed it. She'd already told him about seeing Virginia's car. If she mentioned he should ask the owners of the houses if they'd noticed the Caddy, he would see it as interference. Besides, he'd probably already questioned them.

She was just straightening up when someone grabbed her from behind. She let out a small scream and turned around to see Gerald. "Why did you do that?" she asked, trying to catch her breath.

He pulled her back a few feet and pointed at the spot where she'd been standing. The recent rain had made the ground soft. As they watched, a large clump of dirt gave way and fell down the side of the cliff. It was the exact spot where Priscilla had been standing. She noticed Gerald's face was ghostly white. She put her arms around him.

"I'm okay," she said soothingly. "Thank you."

Jake, who'd been investigating the shoreline a few feet away, ran over to say hello. When he jumped up on Gerald's leg, trying to get his attention, Priscilla released Gerald. He bent down and scratched Jake behind the ears.

"Hey, what about all these stories where dogs save their masters?" she said accusingly to Jake. "Where were you?" Although she was teasing, she realized suddenly that if she'd fallen and hadn't let go of Jake's leash, he could have gone over the edge with her. The thought made her feel a little faint.

"When I saw you that close to the edge, it scared me," Gerald said. "But when I noticed the ground giving way..." He looked into Priscilla's eyes. "If something happened to you, I don't know what I'd do."

Priscilla grabbed his hand. "Nothing's going to happen to me. Come on in and have a cup of coffee."

Gerald glanced at his watch. "I don't have a lot of time, but I think I can work that in. I've got somewhere important I have to be in a little while."

Priscilla tugged on Jake's leash. "Let's go in, boy."

The three of them walked back to the cottage. By the time Priscilla brought Gerald his coffee, he seemed to have recovered from her near fall off the cliff. She couldn't help but reprimand herself for being so careless. She'd been living here long enough to know that sometimes after heavy rains, the cliff edge could be dangerous. Her curiosity had almost gotten her into serious trouble.

She put Gerald's cup on the table in front of him. He liked his coffee black, the stronger the better. Even though he hadn't asked for anything to eat, she put a plate out with scones she'd made, along with clotted cream and lemon curd. She'd never baked them before, but after tasting some at a church supper, she'd decided to give them a try. She was happy with the result. Gerald reached over and took one, putting it on the small dessert plate she'd placed on the table. He reached for the clotted cream and slathered it on his scone. Priscilla fetched her coffee and sat down next to him.

As she took a scone and smeared the luscious lemon curd on it, she asked, "I wasn't expecting you this morning. Did you stop by for a purpose?"

After swallowing a bit of his scone, he nodded. "Now that my heart's beating normally again, I wanted to ask you about the play tomorrow night."

Priscilla reached over and put her hand on his arm. "I'm so sorry. I really didn't mean to scare you."

"What were you doing?"

"I was looking at the road along the beach where Jackson Wither saw Virginia. There are some houses farther down the shoreline. I wanted to see them."

"You think she was headed to one of them?"

Priscilla shrugged. "I kind of doubt it. Virginia doesn't have many friends, but I'm certain Hank will check it out."

Gerald raised an eyebrow. "I'm surprised you aren't going to every house yourself, asking them if they've seen Virginia."

"I know I'm nosy, but sometimes I have to remind myself that Hank is a very capable police chief. He's also very patient with me. Most of the time anyway. I don't want to make him think I don't trust his ability to handle Virginia's disappearance." She put her scone down and sighed. "Virginia's being accused of theft now.

Hank wants to arrest her. The Boston Museum is also insisting she be found and prosecuted."

"And you're surprised by this?" Gerald said. "I'm not. Priscilla, she's disappeared with a rather valuable museum collection. I don't see how she could possibly expect to walk away without some consequences for her actions."

"I guess you're right. I just have a very hard time seeing her as a thief. I mean, she has a lot of money, and she respects the history of the Vineyard. What would be her motive to do something like this?"

"How do you know she's rich?" Gerald asked.

"Octavia Spoonmore. She told Trudy there wasn't a mortgage on Virginia's house. She made a bundle on it. And Octavia said she already had quite a bit before that."

"I'm not totally surprised. It usually costs a small fortune to buy a house on the island. Especially one as impressive as Virginia's."

Priscilla nodded her agreement. "I'm sorry. You said you wanted to talk about the play tomorrow night?"

"Yes, I did. I'd like us to go together, and then after it's over, I want to take you to the Inn for a late dinner."

"Well, I planned to hang around for a while to see if Trudy needs emotional support. I guess Dan won't be there. She's really nervous about her performance."

"Please, Priscilla. This is very important to me."

Priscilla was surprised by the pleading tone in Gerald's voice. "All right. I can talk to her on Sunday, I guess."

"Thank you. I'll pick you up around six thirty. The play starts at seven, right?"

"Yes. That sounds great."

Gerald hurriedly finished the rest of his scone, wiped his mouth, and stood up. "Thanks for the coffee and the pastry. It was delicious. I've got to run. Important appointment."

"You mentioned that. Care to share?"

Priscilla was surprised to see Gerald's face flush. "I'll tell you all about it later. I need to get going. I'll probably be late as it is."

Although his response bothered Priscilla a bit, she pushed the niggling feeling of doubt away. She'd promised herself not to be suspicious any longer, and she intended to keep that commitment.

"All right. I'll see you tomorrow night at six thirty." She walked him outside to his car and then waved as he drove away. Before she had the chance to go back inside, a car came speeding up the drive, headed right for her. She jumped out of the way seconds before the car screeched to a halt inches away from where she'd been standing.

CHAPTER TWENTY-FIVE

Priscilla grabbed one of the posts on her front porch, her heart beating a mile a minute. What was it about today? Two close calls within a couple of hours?

The car door opened, and Trudy bounced out. Priscilla had been so surprised by her dramatic entrance, she hadn't realized it was her cousin's vehicle.

"I'm so, so sorry," Trudy said breathlessly. "I didn't see you there."

"Well, what were you looking at?" Priscilla was a little peeved with her cousin. She drew a line at being run over. Even by a close relative.

Trudy hurried over and wrapped her arms around Priscilla. "I just wasn't paying attention. I'm so upset..."

Priscilla gently disengaged herself from Trudy's embrace. "Come inside. I have some scones and coffee. You can tell me what's bothering you." She was certain it was the play again. Douglas had scheduled a quick run-through that morning and a full dress rehearsal for the evening.

The women went into the cottage, and Priscilla guided Trudy over to the table. She held out a chair and waited until her cousin collapsed into it.

While Priscilla brewed a vanilla latte for Trudy, her cousin poured out the reason for her distracted mind.

"Why did he have to rewrite the ending this late in the game, Priscilla? The other ending was fine. Now...Well, it's okay, I guess. The bad guy..."

Priscilla held her hand up. "Stop right there," she said sharply. "Don't tell me the ending. You'll ruin the play for me."

"Oh, yeah. You're right. Sorry." She picked up a scone and scooted the lemon curd next to her, scooping up a big spoonful. "The new ending is fine, really. That's not the problem. It's trying to learn all the new lines in a couple of days. I got lost today, and Douglas yelled at me. In front of everyone." Trudy's eyes filled with tears. "It was so humiliating!"

Priscilla carried Trudy's coffee to the table. "Oh, honey. I'm so sorry. But I really believe you'll be fine. The dress rehearsal is tonight, right?"

She nodded. "I'd ask you to come, but I really don't want you to see the whole thing until tomorrow night."

"Are you sure you don't want me to come for a little while?"

Trudy sighed. "No, it's okay. I'm a grown woman. I need to do this on my own. No one else brings people to offer them emotional support."

Priscilla couldn't help but laugh. "I don't think there's anything wrong with a little help from your friends. Don't worry about it." She leaned over and looked her cousin in the eyes. "I'm going to tell you something my mother told me when I was in grade school and had a part in a school play. I was so nervous. She reminded me that everyone in the audience was on my side. They wanted me to succeed. She assured me there was absolutely nothing to be afraid of."

Trudy blinked several times as she digested this information. "You know what? You're right. For the most part, the audience will be made up of church friends and family." She reached over and grabbed Priscilla's arm as she wiped her tears with her other hand. "Oh, Priscilla. That's so helpful. Why have I been so afraid?"

"Because you forgot who your audience is. And also because of Douglas. Frankly, he should be more encouraging."

Trudy exhaled slowly. "Boy, is that the truth. I'm not the only one he's hard on. Remember Jeff?"

Priscilla shook her head. "I'm not sure..."

"The young guy playing an eighty-year-old man?"

"Oh yeah. I saw him the day I went backstage."

Trudy nodded. "Douglas is really critical of him. I thought a couple of times Jeff might walk out."

Priscilla frowned. "Maybe he should. Let Douglas play the part himself. In fact, let him play all the parts. Now that would be interesting."

In spite of herself, Trudy laughed. "He'd have a heart attack. All he cares about is that New York producer sitting in the audience." Once again, her eyes widened. "Oh, Priscilla. I forgot about him. What if I mess up in front of him and ruin everything for Douglas?"

"Trudy, who cares about that guy? You act for us. Your friends and family. Aren't we the ones you really care about?"

"Of course."

"Then play your part for us. Besides, that guy will be evaluating the play. He's not interested in the actors."

"Yeah, I guess you're right," Trudy said slowly.

"Of course I am. He knows you're not Hollywood celebrities. He just wants to hear the lines. Find out the plot. You don't need to worry about him at all."

"That makes sense."

"Yes, it does." Priscilla pushed the plate of scones toward Trudy. "Here, have another one. They'll cure anything."

Trudy smiled. "They are delicious."

"I told you about that new woman who started attending Faith Fellowship? Beatrix Cunningham?"

"Yes, I remember. I love her name."

"Well, you can love her even more. The scones are her recipe."

Trudy looked surprised. "I thought you got these from Candy's."

"No. I made them myself."

Trudy laughed. "Well, they're really good."

"I'm a little biased, but I believe you're right." Priscilla smiled. "Now are you feeling a little better?"

"Yes. I knew, somehow, you'd help center me. That's why I came here after the rehearsal."

"And almost ran me over."

"Good thing I didn't. I wouldn't have gotten any scones." Trudy giggled, and Priscilla slapped playfully at her arm.

"If you need support after dress rehearsal tonight, come by when you're done."

"I might. Truthfully, I should probably try to get a good night's sleep. I've had so much on my mind lately. Our mysteries. The play. Dan."

"I'm so sorry he can't come tomorrow night, Trudy," Priscilla said. She knew how much her cousin was hurt by Dan's lack of support.

Trudy shrugged. "He says this project is really important and thinks I should understand."

"But you don't."

Trudy picked up her coffee cup and stared into it. "I'm trying. He's going to be home tonight, but I won't be. Wouldn't you know it?"

"That's a shame. I'm sure you'll have more time when his project is completed."

"I hope so. I'm beginning to wonder if he even cares about me anymore."

"Oh, Trudy," Priscilla said curtly. "Now you know that's not the truth. Don't let thoughts like that in your head." She sighed deeply. "I remember doing the same thing with Gary when things on the farm got busy. I mean, I understood. But sometimes I felt he could have put some chores off so we could have a night out. He also missed several events that were important to Rachel. He didn't make it to her high school science fair. And she won a blue ribbon."

"Oh, Priscilla. How did Rachel handle that?"

"She was fine. I was the one who got angry."

Trudy took a sip of her coffee. "So how did you get over it? Or did you?"

Priscilla nodded. "I did. I finally realized Gary wanted to be there as much or more than we wanted him there. He was trying to be responsible. He felt taking care of his family financially was another way to show his love. And he was right."

"You think that's what Dan's thinking?" Trudy was quiet for a moment. "But I'd rather have more time with him than the money."

"I know that," Priscilla said softly. "But have you told Dan?"

Trudy clasped her hands together and stared down at the table. "No, I haven't."

"Why don't you have a talk with him? Tell him how you really feel?" Priscilla said.

"It will have to wait until after the play. I have rehearsal tonight, and tomorrow I guess he has meetings all day at work. On a Saturday, can you believe it?"

Priscilla smiled. "After the play will be fine. The important thing is that you share your heart with him. Men need encouragement too, you know. They need to know their wives still love them. Still admire them. They're no different in that respect from women."

"You're right." Trudy downed the rest of her coffee. "I need to get home. I have to go over my lines until I feel more comfortable for the dress rehearsal. Say a prayer for me, okay?"

"I will. I promise. But I know in my heart of hearts the play's going to be a great success and that you'll be wonderful."

Trudy stood up. "Thank you, Cuz. I feel so much better now. I don't know what I'd do without you."

Priscilla got up and gave Trudy a big hug. "I feel the same way. Thanks for tooling around town with me, trying to find Virginia. And trucking through the mud."

Trudy laughed. "Now that was an adventure. Let's not do that too often though, okay?"

"That's fine with me."

Priscilla walked Trudy to the door and said goodbye. Then she went back inside and sat down at the table to finish her second scone of the morning. A plan was percolating in her brain. It was a little daring. And it certainly could qualify for being nosy. But the more she thought about it, the more she became determined to see it through.

CHAPTER TWENTY-SIX

Priscilla knocked on the door of Trudy's house and waited breathlessly. She knew Trudy wouldn't be there, as her cousin had mentioned dress rehearsal for the play would run for at least three hours, with all the makeup and hair that would have to be done before and the fine-tuning that would happen afterward. So at least Priscilla felt confident Trudy wouldn't accidentally interrupt her as she talked to Dan.

When no one answered the door immediately, Priscilla actually felt a sense of relief. She wasn't sure she should be interfering in Trudy and Dan's marriage anyway, but she couldn't stand to see how much Trudy was suffering without trying to help. It was possible Dan wasn't even aware of what was going on. It didn't sound like Trudy had been very forthcoming with him. Dan certainly fit the stereotype of the distracted scientist to a *T*, often paying more attention to the minutiae of plankton than to the emotional landscape of his wife.

Maybe all it would take from Priscilla were a few direct comments explaining the situation, and all would be mended. That is, if Dan was even home. Trudy had mentioned he planned to be at the house while she was at rehearsal, but maybe he'd stepped out on a quick errand. Priscilla knocked again, this time a little louder.

After a few seconds, she heard muffled movement, and Dan opened the door, clad in rumpled khakis and his standby button-down shirt. It was a fitting uniform for a marine biologist. One he seemed to wear almost every day, no matter the occasion.

"Priscilla, what are you doing here?" Dan honestly looked as though he wouldn't have been more surprised to see flying frogs outside his door than he was to find Priscilla standing on his front porch. "If you're looking for Trudy, she's not here. She has play practice tonight."

"I know," said Priscilla. "I'm not here to see Trudy. I actually wanted to talk to you."

"Me?" said Dan, a look of bewilderment on his face. He wasn't a very outgoing person by nature, Priscilla knew, and though he had friends, she suspected they weren't the type to drop by unannounced to shoot the bull and watch the ball game. He was likely surprised to have a visitor asking for him instead of the effervescent Trudy, who drew people like moths to a bright flame.

"Yes." Priscilla took a deep breath. "I wanted to talk to you about Trudy, actually. She's struggling, Dan."

He wrinkled his brow. "She's feeling stressed over the play, I know. Is there anything else?" A sudden look of panic crossed his face.

The poor man appeared ready to jump out of his own skin at the thought of Trudy being upset enough for Priscilla to feel the need to address the situation. He obviously cared about her a great deal. Priscilla got the impression there was no serious marital discord between Trudy and Dan. They'd just started to take one another for granted, an easy thing to have happen in a marriage.

Dan seemed to realize Priscilla was still standing on the porch. "Where are my manners?" he said. "Would you like to come inside?"

Priscilla was grateful for the offer. She'd been on her feet a decent amount today, and her legs ached for a rest. She nodded, and Dan motioned for her to enter. Even if Priscilla didn't know which of her cousins lived here, she'd suspect Trudy right away. Traces of her bubbly cousin were everywhere, from the pretty cobalt-blue vases lining a shelf to the cheerful pops of accent color scattered throughout the décor. As Priscilla walked into the living room, she appreciated once again how airy and open it was. Late afternoon summer sunlight filtered through the large windows. Priscilla took a seat on the comfortable navy couch and hugged a bright yellow pillow to her chest.

"So, what's going on with my wife?" Dan perched on the edge of a chair, waiting for her to explain the reason for her visit.

How to launch into a conversation like this? Priscilla swallowed hard. She almost wished she could back out and make up another reason for talking to Dan. Something far less invasive than critiquing the state of his relationship with Trudy. Priscilla hoped she wasn't being a busybody. Her motives felt pure, but this was a sticky situation to be in. Diplomacy was essential.

Priscilla cleared her throat. "Trudy's feeling like second fiddle lately." Better to be direct than to beat around the bush. Dan was a no-nonsense sort of person, and she hoped he would appreciate a straightforward answer, rather than getting offended.

"To what? I've never looked at another woman. I wouldn't do that." Dan didn't seem offended, but he did look utterly perplexed.

"Not to another woman. To your work. Trudy says you've been clocking a lot of overtime lately, and I think she's been missing you."

"It's true," Dan said. "Several rush projects have come up at the lab. Trudy understands that though. She always has."

Priscilla smiled. "She might understand it, but it doesn't mean she likes it."

Dan breathed a deep sigh. "We haven't spent much time together this summer so far, but we have carved out space for each other in the evenings. We've been unwinding with *Bizarre Nation*. We're halfway through season one already."

Priscilla bit her lip. She assumed the show he mentioned was the creepy sci-fi program Trudy disliked. "That's another thing. First, I'm not sure if *Bizarre Nation* is Trudy's favorite show. And secondly, I don't think she feels watching television with you counts as quality time. I believe she feels like you're zoning out, not spending what extra time you have with her. You know Trudy. She's a people person. She needs to connect by talking. She wants to communicate with you. Tell you about her day. Find out about yours. Not sit in front of a TV."

Dan nodded slowly, and Priscilla continued. "She feels lonely, Dan. She's nervous about the play, and I know it would mean the world to her if you'd show up at the play tomorrow night."

"Oh, I can't do that," said Dan. "I would love to see Trudy act, but I have a meeting I'm required to attend tomorrow evening."

"I'm not trying to tell you what you have to do, Dan, but if there's any way at all to reschedule that meeting or take a rain check, I would do it. Trudy is feeling so alone right now, and that's a scary place to be in a marriage."

Dan paused for a moment and scratched his head. "Trudy's really bothered by me being gone lately, huh? I guess I wasn't paying attention. I was just focusing on getting things done. I wish she'd felt comfortable coming to me, though, instead of me having to find out through someone else."

"I think she wanted to talk to you. She just felt awkward. I know when Gary and I were married, he often had busy seasons on the farm where he had to work overtime. Rachel and I were kind of left to fend for ourselves. We understood, of course, and I never said anything to him because I knew he was just trying to be a good provider and a responsible man, but knowing that didn't make his absence any easier."

Dan sat quietly, as though he were trying to absorb the information Priscilla had just given him. "I'm not sure if I can get away for the play, but I'll try my best. Especially since I know now how much it means to Trudy. Thank you for letting me know, Priscilla. You're a good friend to Trudy…and to me."

Priscilla was relieved that Dan seemed to be taking her advice to heart. It lifted a weight from her shoulders. "Well, I'd better be going." Priscilla stood up and gathered her purse. "You're welcome to tell Trudy I came by. I don't want to force either of you to keep secrets from each other. That's never wise. But if you do tell her, please let her know I didn't mean to interfere. I just care about her, and I want good things for her." She smiled at Dan. "And for you. The older I get, the more I realize the importance of family."

Dan showed Priscilla out, and she climbed back into her vehicle. It was likely he would tell Trudy she'd stopped by. Priscilla could only hope Trudy wouldn't be angry. She knew if the tables were turned and Trudy had gone to Gerald with concerns over their relationship, Priscilla would have been embarrassed. She prayed Trudy wouldn't harbor any ill will toward her for interfering.

Tomorrow night would tell whether or not Dan had taken Priscilla's advice. She hoped, for her cousin's sake, that he would find a way to show Trudy how much he cared for her.

CHAPTER TWENTY-SEVEN

Priscilla got up early Saturday morning. She'd spent a restless night wondering where Virginia was. She couldn't stop worrying that the historian might be in some kind of danger—but if that were true, why was she tooling around the island? It didn't make sense. Priscilla was just starting to make breakfast when the phone rang. It was Joan.

"How about meeting your cousins for breakfast at Candy's?" she said as soon as Priscilla picked up.

Priscilla had been looking forward to a quiet morning at home. Besides, she was still trying to work off the two pounds she'd gained after her previous visits to Candy's. However, she couldn't ignore the tone of urgency in Joan's voice.

"Is everything all right?" Priscilla asked.

"I don't know. Trudy had a tough time last night, and I thought we could encourage her this morning. But there's something else. Something I think you should know."

"You can't tell me on the phone?"

Joan sighed. "I think it would be best if we talk about it in person."

Priscilla tensed. Could it be fallout from talking to Dan last night? Was Trudy angry with Priscilla about what she'd done? As the thought came, Priscilla rejected it. Trudy wasn't like that. If she got upset with a friend or family member, it never lasted long.

"All right. What time?"

"I've got a few things to do," Joan said. "How about ten?"

"I'll see you then." After Priscilla hung up, she looked down at Jake, who sat at her feet. He cocked his head and looked at her as if he was as confused as she was. "Any idea what's going on, Jake?" she asked.

He responded with a quick bark. It was clear he was focused on their morning walk—and not much else. She smiled down at him. "Let me change clothes, and we'll go, okay?"

It didn't take her long to dress. Soon, they were on their way toward the cliffs, although Priscilla had no intention of getting too close to the edge, since the ground was still wet. It was a cool, cloudy morning. Even though Priscilla loved the rain, she hoped it would stay away today. She didn't want the weather to keep anyone from the play tonight. She wondered if Dan would actually show up. She certainly hoped so.

After barking at the seagulls that swooped and cried overhead, Jake took care of business, and they headed back to the cottage. As they passed by the lighthouse, Priscilla remembered that Misty Harbor Tours was coming by today. Sometimes Priscilla greeted the bus when it arrived, but for the most part, Teresa Claybrook, who ran the tours, handled everything herself. Priscilla was proud to have her property be part of the tour. She and Gerald were working on the museum inside the lighthouse, but it was closed for now until she could update the collection. Gerald had mentioned some items he might like to include.

At the thought of Gerald, she couldn't help thinking about the woman he'd been meeting. She really did trust him, but they couldn't have secrets like that. It wasn't good for any relationship.

When she and Jake got inside, Priscilla made a cup of coffee and spent some time playing with him until it was time to leave. On her way to Candy's, she swung by the cemetery, just in case she could spot the old man who'd pretended to be Elias Sweetwater. Unfortunately, she didn't see him anywhere, though she was surprised to see the women in white gathered around Nancy's grave again. This time, they didn't pay any attention to her, and she drove away quickly, not wanting to spark another confrontation. They were so protective of Nancy Luce and anything that belonged to her. Were they looking for the artifacts? Could they have something to do with Virginia's strange behavior? Was it possible they'd threatened her in some way? Maybe Virginia was afraid to go home. But if she had been threatened, why not just go to the police for help?

Priscilla sighed and shook her head. No matter what angle she came up with, she couldn't get the puzzle pieces to fit together into a cohesive picture. There was something she wasn't seeing, and she had the distinct impression it was right in front of her face. She hated feeling this way. It had happened more times than she cared to admit. Although she'd been hailed as a capable sleuth, she wasn't sure she deserved the moniker. She was frustrated and confused. Of course, the situation with Gerald wasn't helping her concentration.

When she arrived at Candy's, everyone was already there. She glanced at her watch. She wasn't late. Why had her cousins arrived early? It seemed a little ominous. She got a cup of coffee and a cheese Danish, then she went to the table, feeling nervous.

As she sat down, she smiled at Trudy. Thankfully, Trudy smiled back. Perhaps she wasn't annoyed with her after all. "How did dress rehearsal go, Trudy?" Priscilla asked.

Her cousin rolled her eyes. "Just what you'd imagine. Douglas was almost manic. None of us could please him." She actually giggled, holding her hand over her mouth.

"What's so funny?" Priscilla asked.

Trudy put her hand down. "Some of us started making dumb mistakes just to drive him nuts. It was hysterical." She took a deep breath. "Until it wasn't. Jeff, you know, the young guy playing an old man in the play?"

Priscilla nodded.

"He purposely said the lines from the first ending. A lot of us went along with him. You know, like we'd forgotten the rewrites?"

"Oh, Trudy," Gail said sternly. "That's not very professional. Or even kind."

Trudy shrugged. "I know that, but it really did help to lighten things up some."

"For you and the other actors, but not for Douglas," Gail scolded.

"If you would've seen the way he was yelling at everyone, you would've cheered us on."

"I doubt it."

Trudy stuck her tongue out at Gail, who laughed. "You're incorrigible, you know that?"

Trudy granted her a wide smile. "It's my gift."

"So, how did things end up?" Joan asked.

"Well, Douglas went a little crazy when we acted like we didn't remember our lines. We had to apologize. Frankly, it was weird. Who really cares if the bad guy tries to kill someone by knifing them to death or making them drive off a cliff? It's ridiculous, really."

"He must have his reasons for believing the new ending is better," Gail said. "Isn't that New York producer coming to the play tonight?"

"Yeah, I think that's what's got him rattled," Trudy said. "But honestly, I'm tired of stressing out about this stupid play. I'm going to go out there tonight, do my best, and carry on with life." She sighed happily and gazed at the women sitting around the table. "After getting some very good advice from my family, I've settled down quite a bit."

"We're all so glad, Trudy," Priscilla said. "Now, can someone tell me what's going on? What's so important that you had to drag me down here and compel me to eat a cheese Danish, Joan?"

Her cousins burst out laughing.

"Yeah, that's why I got this cheesecake muffin," Trudy said with a wide smile. "Because Joan forced me to eat it."

Priscilla took another bite of her delicious Danish, then asked Joan, "Has there been another Virginia sighting?"

Joan shook her head. "I haven't seen her."

Gail and Trudy both chimed in that they hadn't spotted the runaway historian either.

"That's not it," Joan said. "Remember when you told us about that Jackson guy?"

Priscilla nodded. "Jackson Wither? From the Boston Library?"

Joan nodded. "Do you still have his card?"

Priscilla frowned. "I'm sure I do." She picked up her purse and riffled through it until she found Jackson's card.

She pulled it out and handed it to Joan, who looked at it and read, *"Herbert J. Wither. Associate of the East Boston Public Library."* Joan smiled widely and said, "Aha!"

"Aha what?" Priscilla asked.

"It occurred to me that you just accepted this guy's story. I mean, you believed he was legitimate, right?"

"I think he is," Priscilla said, frowning.

"Wasn't he very interested in the Nancy Luce artifacts?"

"Well, he asked about them," Priscilla said slowly. "I don't know if I'd call him *very* interested. Why?"

Joan leaned forward and lowered her voice as if someone might be listening. "Just to be thorough, I called the East Boston Library. They don't have a writer-in-residence program." With that, she sat back, looking like the cat that had swallowed the canary.

CHAPTER TWENTY-EIGHT

As Priscilla got dressed for the play and her date with Gerald, she kept running the information she'd gotten from Joan over and over in her mind. It was true that she'd never questioned Jackson Wither's claim that he was with the Boston Library. How could she have just taken his word for it? She should have investigated his claims, the way Joan had. She was grateful for her cousin's assistance, but she couldn't help but chide herself for her lack of follow-up.

She pulled on the dress she'd chosen for tonight. A satiny green dress with a light lace bodice. It brought out the green in her eyes. She pulled on matching heels and checked her image in the mirror. She'd curled her light brown hair with a curling iron. It looked pretty good, although she wasn't sure how long the curl would hold. She sprayed it lightly with hairspray. Hopefully, that would help.

She twirled in front of the mirror, feeling a little silly, but she wanted to look her best. She had no idea why Gerald felt tonight was so special, but she wanted to be ready for whatever he had in mind. No matter what, she fully intended to learn the identification of the woman he'd been meeting with behind her back. She sighed at her reflection. She'd made the decision to trust him, but she needed to finally hear the truth. Hopefully, by the time the night was over, everything would be all right again. She intended to give him a gentle talking-to about keeping secrets. From now on, she wanted to know what he was doing without having to find out accidentally or through local gossip.

When she felt she was ready, she checked the time and looked for her purse. Gerald should arrive any minute. Jake was lying in his dog bed, so she went over and stroked his soft head. "I'll be home late, boy," she said. He gave her a doggy smile and went back to sleep. Priscilla was grateful he didn't mind much anymore when she left. At first, he'd shown some stress when she was gone, but now, it didn't seem to bother him at all. He still got excited when she came home though. It made her feel good to have someone waiting for her who was happy to see her.

She saw Gerald's car drive up, so she grabbed her green-and-white pashmina. It looked great with her dress but would also help to keep away the chill should the night air turn cooler. She opened the door, and then closed and locked it behind her. Gerald was already out of the car and heading toward her door. He stopped when he saw her, his eyes wide.

"Wow, you look beautiful," he said. "No one will be watching the play. All eyes will be on you."

Priscilla knew he was teasing her, and she couldn't help laughing. "You don't look so bad yourself." He was wearing khakis with a dark blue jacket over a white polo shirt.

"Thank you, ma'am," he said with a wide smile. "Your coach awaits." He opened the car door for her, and she slipped inside.

Then he walked around to his side of the car, and they began the drive to the Playhouse. They'd just reached the road when Gerald asked, "So, how is Trudy doing? Is she nervous?"

"She was, but I think she's settled down. Either she's calmed herself, or she's catatonic. I'm not sure which one is true."

Gerald's hearty laugh filled the car. "Well, let's hope it's the former."

Priscilla sighed. "You know, I'm really looking forward to the play, but I'll also be very relieved when it's over. This has been so stressful for her. Douglas Lawrence has provided most of the tension."

"He is an odd duck," Gerald agreed.

"It's a good thing the play is only for one night," Priscilla said. "I don't know if the actors could take much more."

"Well, I intend to enjoy it. And our dinner afterward." He reached over with his free hand and took hers. "I love you, Scilla."

"And I love you too," she said.

As they continued on their way to the Playhouse, Priscilla couldn't stop wondering what he wanted to tell her at dinner. Did it have something to do with the attractive blond woman?

When they pulled into the Playhouse parking lot, Priscilla was thrilled to see it was almost full. Joan had offered to arrive early so she could save seats for Gerald and her. When they got inside, they found Joan quickly. She and Gail were near the front, in the third row. There were two empty seats next to them with playbills on them.

"Are these seats saved?" Priscilla quipped when they made their way down to where Joan and Gail waited.

Joan grabbed the playbills and motioned for them to sit down. She leaned over to Priscilla when she took the seat next to her. "Boy, you wouldn't believe the guff we got for saving seats. Theatergoers are vicious."

Priscilla laughed. "Oh, Joan. I doubt that's true." She glanced around and was surprised to see several people shooting her dirty looks. Priscilla felt a little guilty. Maybe she and Gerald should have gotten to the Playhouse earlier. Before she turned back around, one person caught her eye. Eve Pennywhistle was seated a few rows back, and her eyes were locked on Priscilla. If looks could kill, Priscilla would be breathing her last.

She quickly turned around and looked toward the stage. The curtain was still closed. She started to say something to Gerald, then she heard a man clear his throat. She glanced toward the aisle where Dan Gavin stood, a bouquet of red roses in his arms.

"Do you think they'd let me backstage?" he asked Priscilla.

"I'm sure they would," Priscilla said, grinning. She gestured toward one of the ushers, who came over to see what she wanted. "This is the husband of one of the actors in tonight's show. Can he take these roses to her before the play starts?"

The usher looked a little unsure. "Usually the actors receive flowers after the play."

Priscilla smiled at him. "But this actor needs to know her husband is here. It would mean a great deal to her."

The usher's hesitant expression melted, and he nodded. "I'm married. I understand completely." He turned to Dan. "You'll have to make it fast. The director is probably giving last-minute instructions."

"I won't take long, I promise." Before Dan walked away, he turned to Priscilla and said, "Thank you."

She watched as he followed the usher to a door at the side of the stage.

"Did you have something to do with that?" Gerald asked.

"Maybe a little," she admitted. "Trudy and Dan really love each other, but they'd started taking each other for granted. I just...steered Dan in the right direction."

Gerald laughed and put his arm around her. "If I ever do that, you have permission to set me in the right direction too."

"Oh, I will. Don't worry about it."

"You two aren't going to talk during the play, are you?" Joan asked with a grin. "I don't want to have to separate you."

Gerald shook his head and leaned toward Priscilla. "I'm confident nothing will ever separate us, so I'm not worried."

Joan chuckled and leaned back in her seat. As they all waited for the play to begin, Priscilla prayed his words would prove true. Was she being silly? Gerald seemed fine around her. So why was she worried that after tonight, everything could change?

CHAPTER TWENTY-NINE

As the theater lights dimmed and the curtain rose, Priscilla felt a little jolt of nerves. She'd never participated much in the theater herself, and right now, she was tucked away comfortably in her cushy seat, snuggled next to Gerald. She could still feel the hushed expectation of the audience and could imagine how the actors felt, singled out on stage. Priscilla offered up a silent prayer that Trudy wouldn't let jitters get the best of her. She so wanted her cousin to do well. She knew how much the play meant to her. Trudy had put so much time and effort into making the event a success, and Priscilla didn't want to see her disappointed.

She shouldn't have worried. Trudy swished onto the stage in her form-fitting red dress and delivered her opening lines perfectly. Her hair was piled on top of her head in a mess of blond curls, and her cheeks glowed prettily, though from rouge or from the roses from Dan, Priscilla had no idea.

Priscilla hadn't spent much time at Trudy's dress rehearsal, so she had only seen Trudy scream and fall down. She knew it was a murder mystery but had gathered very little information about the characters or the main direction of the plot. Now, as *Murder by Moonlight* unfolded, scene by scene, Priscilla cringed. She was aware that Douglas had started out as an actor and then had progressed to directing. As the play proceeded, she began to believe he may have made a regrettable career choice. The play was not particularly well-written, and certainly, in Priscilla's opinion, not of very high caliber. The storyline was flimsy at best and campy at worst, though the actors and actresses tried their best with the material they were given.

Priscilla could see why Trudy, in particular, had been so enamored with acting when she was younger. It was clear, seeing her strutting around as though she owned the stage, that Trudy had a real knack for acting. She knew precisely when to draw a line out for dramatic effect and when to deliver a funny phrase deadpan, making it hilarious. Decked out in sparkles and feathers, she looked as if she were in her element, soaking up the audience's laughs.

Intermission came, and the house lights turned on. People filed out of the rows to stretch their legs, but Gerald stayed seated. He reached over and took Priscilla's hand. "Enjoying the play so far?" His smile warmed her, and she realized how thoroughly she loved this man. She believed that he would do anything to protect her and make her happy. She let go of her concerns about the blond woman and squeezed his hand back. "I am. It's a blast seeing Trudy up there on stage. You can tell she's really enjoying herself."

"She's got a talent for the theater," Gerald agreed. "She's doing a great job."

"She is. I'm relieved. She was so nervous after she found out about the New York producer attending tonight." Priscilla sighed.

"Of course, it didn't help that Douglas put a lot of pressure on everyone."

"Douglas is a jittery sort," Gerald said. He looked around the crowded theater. "Can you spot the producer? Is he here?

Priscilla scanned the Playhouse, particularly searching the front row, where it was likely the producer would sit to capture the best view, but since she had no idea what he looked like, she couldn't know for certain. "I'm not sure. No one really sticks out, although there are a few people here I don't recognize. I guess we'll find out after the play. Trudy should know."

"If he is here and likes the play, what would that mean?" Gerald asked. "I mean, for Trudy? You mentioned the company might be invited to go on tour?"

"Possibly," said Priscilla. "I'm not sure how it all works, but it's possible."

Gerald squeezed Priscilla's hand. "That would be tough on you, wouldn't it? To have Trudy gone? You two ladies have been thick as thieves lately."

Priscilla laughed. "More like ladies trying to catch thieves."

"Any luck on that? The police aren't still bothering you about the sundial, are they?" The look of concern in Gerald's eyes melted Priscilla's heart. He truly cared about her. It was evident and plainly written on his face.

Priscilla sighed. "No. They know I'm innocent. I feel like I've uncovered so much information, but the truth just won't shake out. I can't seem to make any progress. Not with the theft in the cemeteries or what's going on with Virginia."

"Well, from what I hear through the grapevine, I don't think the police are doing very well with their investigation either." Gerald scratched his head. "What's your gut telling you? You know you've had hunches before in cases like this. Your instincts have often been right."

"Listen to you, Gerald O'Bannon." Priscilla playfully swatted him on the shoulder. "I think this is the first time you've been completely okay with me solving mysteries since I arrived in Martha's Vineyard."

"It's because I trust you," Gerald said simply. "I trust that you're going to do what you need to do—helping people—and that you'll keep yourself safe along the way. You have lots of people who love you, Priscilla. Me included." Priscilla didn't say anything, just put her head on Gerald's shoulder as he embraced her.

Their sentimental moment was cut short by an elegant dark-haired woman daintily maneuvering down their row. "Excuse me?" she said as she drew closer. The woman's hair was pinned into a classy chignon, and she wore pearl drop earrings that complemented her plum-colored pantsuit.

Priscilla tried her hardest not to flinch, but seriously? If this was another gorgeous woman approaching Gerald...Priscilla knew he was a catch, and lots of women loved a distinguished man in uniform, but this was getting ridiculous.

"Excuse me?" the woman repeated and looked right at Priscilla. "Aren't you Priscilla Grant?"

Priscilla felt a sense of relief. The woman wasn't interested in Gerald. "Yes," she said. "I'm Priscilla."

"I'm so sorry for interrupting your conversation," said the woman. "But I wanted to apologize for the other day."

"What?" Priscilla had no idea what the woman was talking about. She was fairly certain she'd never seen her before.

"I saw you at the West Tisbury Cemetery? I was with a group of friends?"

Priscilla's mind felt as blank as her face must look.

"You don't recognize me, do you?" The woman gestured at her outfit, a pearl bracelet glinting on her wrist as she did so. "I don't blame you. I am dressed a bit differently than when I saw you before."

Dressed differently? Who had Priscilla seen at the cemetery? The phony Elias Sweetwater. The tourists. The guards. And the women in white.

The women in white! A light bulb went off in Priscilla's head. Now she knew where she'd seen the lady before. This woman had been one of the ethereal gown-wearing women scolding her for losing the artifacts. It was ridiculous that she'd been intimidated by them. The woman standing in front of her now looked as if she was more likely to host a charity luncheon than to threaten anyone.

"No, pardon me," said Priscilla. "It took me a moment, but you were at Nancy Luce's grave, right?"

"Yes, that was me." The woman extended her hand. "I'm Gracie Linton."

"Priscilla Gra—" Priscilla started to introduce herself before realizing Gracie already knew who she was. She smiled sheepishly.

Gracie continued. "Anyway, I just wanted to apologize if my friends and I frightened you. We're just role-playing, you know.

Trying to keep the legend of the women in white alive. I've always loved acting and the theater. We might seem eccentric, but it's just a fun hobby."

Some hobby, thought Priscilla. She'd legitimately thought the women were certifiable. All she said, though, was, "Apology accepted."

Gracie looked relieved. "I hope you enjoy the rest of the play. What a riot your friend in the red dress is."

Priscilla realized Gracie was talking about Trudy. "That's my cousin Trudy. She's quite the theater aficionado too."

"Well, we have that in common, then," said Gracie, smiling. She wiggled her fingers goodbye as she maneuvered back down the aisle to her seat.

As soon as she was out of earshot, Gerald murmured, "Do you want to explain to me what all that was about?"

Priscilla started to answer, but she was cut off by the house lights flashing, signaling the end of intermission. "I'll tell you in a bit," she said, pressing a finger to her lips. Gerald raised his eyebrows as though he was preparing himself for a great story. Amid the softening din of the theater, everyone took their seats, and Priscilla prepared herself for the end of the play.

CHAPTER THIRTY

Unfortunately, the second half of the play wasn't much better than the first. Even so, the audience seemed enamored with Trudy. When she emoted her lines with theatrical fervor, there was laughter and a smattering of applause. Priscilla glanced over at Dan, who sat in a seat at the end of the row in front of them. She was tickled to see him beaming with pride. This time, her interference had turned out even better than she'd hoped. However, she chalked it up as a one-time thing. She knew it wasn't always wise to get between a wife and her husband.

She was still surprised by meeting Gracie Linton. So the women in white weren't really nuts; they were simply a group of women acting out the role of the infamous group that visited Nancy Luce's grave once a year. They'd certainly done a great job. Priscilla couldn't help but wish they'd come clean a little sooner. She was certain they really were concerned about the artifacts but not enough to try to steal them or to threaten Virginia. In her mind, Priscilla crossed them off her suspect list. So who did that leave?

Even as she asked herself that question, she realized her mind had wandered from the play. She could think about the artifacts and Virginia later. For now, she needed to concentrate on her cousin. She was certain Trudy would be asking questions about her performance later, and Priscilla didn't want to be caught without a proper response. Trudy was a very effusive and confident person most of the time, but she had some insecurity that needed to be allayed.

When Priscilla refocused, she became aware that the actors were trying to figure out who the murderer was. Jeff, who was playing the old man, was doing a great job. Something about him bothered Priscilla, but she couldn't put her finger on it. She tried hard to concentrate on the actors' dialogue, though she just couldn't shake the feeling that there was something important she was missing. What was it?

As she watched, Priscilla realized they were probably getting close to the scene she'd seen during rehearsal. Sure enough, the actors walked off. Then, the lights went down while the stage hands pushed a large mural of trees depicting a forest onto the rear of the stage. When the lights came back up, several actors were standing around a form lying on the ground. Trudy entered from the right. Some of the actors tried to hold her back, but she wriggled away from them and discovered the body. She produced an ear-piercing scream and fainted. A man playing a doctor knelt down next to the body and touched its neck.

"It's old Tom," the doctor declared. "He's dead." The doctor stood to his feet and pointed at the actors standing around. "One of you stabbed him to death. Who was it?"

Well, that was it for Jeff. He was probably glad to be free from the rest of the play. It would have been nice if one of the actors simply admitted to being the murderer so the audience could go home, but no one was that accommodating.

About thirty minutes later, everything was finally resolved. The murderer turned out to be the college professor trying to cover up the planned death of his mother so he could inherit her fortune. Priscilla had decided it was him during the first fifteen minutes of the play, so it wasn't a big surprise. It seemed that he killed several people so that when his mother was murdered, everyone would think there was a crazed serial killer on the loose, and her death would be lumped in with all the others. It was a pretty good plan, but when the professor tried to sneak his mother out of the old hotel where everyone was staying, Trudy's character saw him and called the police. His plan was to get her away secretly and stab her. But before he could carry out the evil deed, the police and Trudy showed up, the mother was saved, and the professor was arrested for all the murders.

Somehow, it seemed like a rather flat ending. Every other murder had been unique. It seemed unusual that the killer would repeat the old man's method of death with his mother. Trudy had mentioned the original ending once, but Priscilla couldn't remember it. She couldn't help but wonder if it might not have been better. Of course, it didn't matter now. The play was finally over, and the curtain came down.

The audience applauded enthusiastically, which wasn't surprising since many of them were related to the actors. When Trudy came out on stage, however, the applause exploded, and quite a few people stood to their feet, including Dan. Gerald and Priscilla stood with Gail and Joan. Trudy was obviously pleased by the response. She took her place next to the other actors. When everyone was on stage, they linked hands and bowed together. When the applause finally began to subside, the curtain came down for good.

"Well, that was…interesting," Gerald said as they stood to their feet.

"I think Trudy was wonderful," Priscilla said. "I'm going to concentrate on that."

"I agree," Joan said.

Gail leaned forward so she could see Priscilla. "Who was that woman who came up to you, Priscilla?" she asked. "I don't think I know her."

"I was wondering the same thing," Gerald said. "I didn't recognize her either."

Priscilla grinned. "Well, picture her with wild hair, wearing a long white dress."

Joan gasped. "Are you trying to tell me she's one of the women in white? How can that be?"

It was obvious other people in their row wanted out, so Priscilla said, "I'll tell you more about it later. I'm going backstage to see Trudy. Anyone else coming?"

Gerald nodded, and Gail and Joan held up their hands to show they wanted to come too. They all edged their way out of the row of seats and headed toward the stage. When they walked up the stairs, they passed several of the actors still in costume. They congratulated each one of them on the play and continued trying to find Trudy. They were on their way to the dressing room when

Priscilla noticed Trudy standing a few feet outside of the door talking to a man they didn't know. Dan came up behind them as they stood waiting for Trudy.

"That's the New York producer," he said. "Trudy pointed him out to me earlier."

"Really?" Priscilla said. "Why don't we wait for her in the dressing room? We shouldn't interrupt them."

"But what if people are changing clothes, Priscilla?' Gerald asked.

She smiled at him. "There are private dressing areas in the back. No one changes in the main room."

Assured they wouldn't stumble on a hapless actor in some stage of disrobing, the group headed to the dressing room. Priscilla caught Trudy's eye and pointed toward the room, letting her know where they'd be. She nodded that she understood.

When they entered, they found some of the actors sitting at the long tables in front of a large mirror that had been hung on the wall. They were removing their makeup. Priscilla spotted Jeff and went up to him. She introduced him to Gerald and her cousins. They all complimented him on his performance.

"Thanks," he said, "but I'm really glad it's over. Douglas shouldn't have changed the ending. It was better than this one." He sighed. "At least my costume was here. I wasn't sure I'd have it tonight. It kept disappearing from the costume rack."

Before anyone could respond, Trudy came hurrying into the dressing room. She was breathless, and her cheeks were flushed. At first, Priscilla thought it was just the makeup she wore, but when she got closer, it was obvious that wasn't the case.

"What's going on?" Joan asked her sister when she reached them.

"Come over here," she said, gesturing to a spot away from the other actors.

"Trudy, what in the world is going on?" Dan asked.

"That man is the producer Douglas was so excited about," she said, her voice high with excitement.

"He liked the play?" Priscilla asked, trying not to sound surprised.

"Oh, no. He hated it." Trudy took a deep breath before saying, "But he loved me. He offered me a spot in a play. It's a small role, but he said it could lead to bigger things."

Priscilla didn't know what to say. Everyone turned to look at Dan, whose mouth hung open.

"T-Trudy," he sputtered. "What did you tell him?"

She walked over and put her arm through his. "I told him thank you, but I have something here that means more to me than acting." She reached up and stroked Dan's face, then kissed him. This time, it was Dan who blushed. "I was just playing a part tonight, being someone I'm not, wearing a costume that isn't really me." She turned toward all of them. "The person I really am lives here, among all of you. With my Dan. That's good enough for me." She laughed. "But I'll always remember that someone from New York thought I was good enough to—"

"What did you say?" Priscilla interrupted her cousin, staring at her, slack-jawed.

Trudy frowned. "I'll always remember that someone from New York—"

"No," Priscilla said. "Before that. You mentioned wearing a costume that isn't really you." She turned her back on her cousins and went to where Jeff sat, still removing his makeup.

"You said your costume kept disappearing?" she asked him.

He looked confused by her question but said, "It was Douglas. He kept taking it, saying it needed mending. I never saw anything wrong with it."

Priscilla thanked him and hurried back to Gerald and her cousins, who looked confused by her abrupt actions. "Trudy, where is Douglas now?"

She frowned at Priscilla. "He left when he found out the producer didn't want his play. I think he went home."

Priscilla opened her purse and found her phone. "Then that's where we're going."

"What are you talking about, Priscilla?" Gerald asked, his eyebrows knit together in a frown. "We have a dinner reservation."

"I'm sorry, Gerald," she said as she phoned Hank. "But tonight, we're going to catch a thief."

CHAPTER THIRTY-ONE

G ail needed to get home since she cared for her elderly father. Joan had driven her, so they both left, while Gerald and Priscilla jumped in Gerald's SUV with Dan and Trudy following behind in Dan's car.

When they arrived at Douglas's house, the chief and a couple of other officers Priscilla didn't know were already there.

Priscilla and Gerald got out of his car and hurried over to meet Hank, who was leaning against his squad car.

"You haven't gone inside?" Priscilla asked when she reached him.

"No. We knocked. No one answered."

"But...but..." Priscilla sputtered.

"Don't get yourself in a tizzy," the chief said. "I called a local judge who's a friend of mine and asked him to sign a warrant. You're sure the clothes you saw tonight belonged to the old man in the cemetery?"

"Absolutely," Priscilla said. "The brown tweed jacket, the bow-tie, the bowler hat...I should have realized it right away. But Jeff is taller and built differently than the man I saw. Then Trudy said something that made me look again. Those are definitely the clothes worn by the old man in the cemetery."

Hank's phone rang, and he held up one finger. "Hold on. That could be the judge." He answered and listened for a few seconds. Then he said, "Thanks, Lyle. Appreciate it." He nodded to the other officers. "We're good. Let's go." He turned to Priscilla and pointed at her. "You stay here. At least until we're certain everything's secure."

"Sure," she said with a smile, having no plans to keep that promise.

Hank and the officers went up to the door and knocked. When no one answered, the chief tried the door. It was locked. He told one of the officers to go back to the car for a battering ram.

As Priscilla walked toward the porch, Gerald, Trudy, and Dan trailed behind. "Excuse me, Chief Westin."

"I thought I told you to stay back," he growled.

"I just wanted to tell you, before you break down that beautiful door, I think you ought to check under the doormat. It's possible Virginia hides a spare key so she won't get locked out."

Hank glared at her but leaned over to pull up the mat. Sure enough, there was a key. He waved the officer away who was approaching with the battering ram in his hands.

Hank opened the door, and once again, told all of them to stay where they were. The other officers entered behind him. A few minutes later, the chief came back to the door and motioned for them to come in.

"No one seems to be here," he said. He looked at Priscilla. "You've been in the house before?"

"Yes. The day I gave Virginia the Nancy Luce artifacts, and later that night when Virginia didn't come to the lecture."

Hank waved his arm around the room. "I'd like you to take a look and tell me if anything looks different. Maybe something out of place? Something that doesn't belong?" He scowled at all of them. "Keep your hands to yourself. We don't need to add your fingerprints to the mix."

Priscilla smiled at him. "We're really not the kind of people who go around handling other people's belongings, Chief. I don't think you need to worry."

Hank sighed, clearly frustrated. "Once again. Does everything look okay? See anything that concerns you?"

As she gazed around the room, Priscilla heard barking from somewhere in the back of the house. "That's Magnus," she said. "I met him when I delivered the Nancy Luce artifacts. I don't think Virginia would stay away from him this long. She adores that dog." She shook her head. "Can I check on him, please? I can't concentrate with all his barking."

"I'll send Paul back to see if he's okay," Hank said. He gestured to one of the officers, who left the room, heading toward the sound of Magnus's insistent barking.

Priscilla continued to scan the room. She walked over to the large window that looked out on the garden. The beautiful paving stones were gone.

"Here's something different," she said. "The pavers are gone. Probably because Douglas sold them."

"But we only have your word that they were there," Hank said. "That's not evidence."

"Well, that might not be, but one of them seems to have broken. I see pieces of it lying on the ground. Will that help?"

Hank came over and gazed out the window. "Yeah. That should do it."

"And I've got pictures of the stones on my phone," Trudy added.

Hank smiled. "That's great," he said. "I think we have all we need."

Priscilla smiled at Trudy, who gave her a triumphant thumbs-up. "You did it," she said.

"*We* did it," Priscilla said. She was getting ready to ask the chief what his next step would be when Magnus came bounding out of the back of the house. He ran straight to Priscilla and grabbed her hand with his mouth. At first she pulled away. He wasn't hurting her, but she couldn't understand what he wanted. She tried to pet him, but once again, he took her hand. This time, she let him lead her over to a spot on the wall across from them. Magnus released her hand and began to bark and scratch at the wall.

"What's gotten into that dog?" Hank asked.

"He's trying to tell you there's something behind that wall," Gerald said. "Sammy used to do the same thing." He walked over to Magnus and stroked his head. "Irish setters are very smart animals. You need to pay attention to him."

Priscilla knew how much Gerald missed Sammy. Seeing Magnus was probably hard on him.

"Well, unless Douglas Lawrence is hiding behind the wall," Hank said, "this dog isn't that smart."

"Wait a minute," Priscilla said. "I just remembered something Octavia said. About hidden rooms." She began looking for something that could open a secret door. After pushing and pulling everything she could, she finally noticed an odd spot next to a nearby built-in bookcase. She pushed it, and part of the wall opened a little bit. Gerald pulled it open until there was a space wide enough they could walk through. On the other side, they found a small room. Priscilla went inside with Hank and Gerald. Trudy and Dan stayed outside but peered in. In the middle of the room sat a chair where someone had obviously been tied up. Ropes lay around the legs of the chair.

Priscilla noticed a lot of red hairs on the floor. She was fairly sure Magnus hadn't been in here. She realized the hairs looked a lot like the ones she'd noticed on Douglas the day she'd called on him. She turned to stare at Magnus, who was sniffing the chair and the ropes.

Priscilla exhaled softly, horrified by what she realized had occurred in this room. "He...he had her here," she told Hank.

"Who had who here?" Hank asked.

"Douglas has been keeping Virginia here. That's who was tied up."

"Wait a minute, Priscilla," Trudy said. "We saw Virginia driving around town in her car."

Priscilla shook her head. "No, we didn't actually see Virginia, Trudy. We saw someone with a red wig wearing one of Virginia's capes."

"What do you mean?" Hank asked.

"We saw Douglas driving like a maniac, wanting to be seen so we'd all think Virginia was okay."

"So where is she now?" Gerald asked.

A sick feeling came over Priscilla. "Trudy, you said Douglas suddenly changed the last scene of the play. What was the original ending? I know you told me, but I just can't recall it."

"The bad guy put the victim in his car, put it in gear, and let it drive off a cliff," Trudy said.

Priscilla stood up. She swayed a bit, and Gerald reached out to catch her. "Chief Westin, we have to find Virginia's car. I think Douglas plans to get rid of his aunt for good. And it's happening right now."

CHAPTER THIRTY-TWO

The first thing the group did was check the garage. Priscilla hoped against hope that the pink Cadillac was parked inside, but a quick peek through the windows showed an abandoned, shadowy space. No Virginia. No vehicle. Priscilla's heart fell.

"So, Priscilla," Hank asked, "any idea where Virginia and her car might be?"

"I have an inkling," she said. "It's a shot in the dark, but if I'm right, we don't have a moment to lose." She had no idea of knowing how far Douglas had gotten ahead of them since the end of the play. It seemed he'd slipped out when Trudy was chatting with the producer. How long ago had it been? Fifteen minutes? Twenty? Douglas could have already taken Virginia to the cliffs and carried out her untimely death by now, especially with the way he drove. The thought made Priscilla's stomach churn like the ocean waves. She prayed they weren't too late.

She turned to face the group. "Where are the closest cliffs? A place where there's a road that will get you close to the edge?"

Hank scratched his head. "There's something about a mile away. A few beach houses farther down the road but not much else around the spot I'm thinking of. It's pretty isolated."

"He's right," Gerald piped in. "I've patrolled that section of water many times. I've busted more than a few people there, trying to smuggle out stolen goods or trade off illegal substances."

Priscilla squeezed her eyes shut, trying to block out the image of Virginia's car sailing off the edge of a precipice. "Lead the way, then," she said to Hank. She motioned to Gerald, Dan, and Trudy to hop in to Gerald's SUV.

There was little traffic on the roads by Virginia's house tonight, but Hank switched his siren and lights on anyway, the red and blue cutting through the dark of the tree-lined drive. As Gerald drove, Priscilla gripped her hands together so tightly her fingers ached. She sent up a silent prayer. *Dear God, please let Virginia be all right. You care about the sparrows of the air and the flowers of the field. I know that You care about her even more. Please tell me we're not too late.*

Priscilla was surprised to feel her eyes getting moist as they drove, Gerald hanging as close to Hank's bumper as was reasonably safe. She blinked back tears. In the little time Priscilla had known her, Virginia had offended, angered, and generally frustrated her. And it seemed likely most of the island felt the same way about the elderly historian. Virginia had few, if any, friends and more enemies than you could shake a stick at. Yet she was a valuable human being, despite her flaws. She was precious to God, and, Priscilla realized, to her as well.

Trudy leaned up from the back seat to rest a hand on Priscilla's shoulder. "Are you okay?"

"I am," Priscilla assured her. "We just have to get there before it's too late."

"We will." Gerald kept his eyes glued to the road, his jaw tight with determination. "Don't worry, Scilla," he said. Priscilla swallowed the lump in her throat as they followed Hank's police cruiser over the top of a hill. As they raced toward their destination, Priscilla saw the ocean spread out in front of them, sparkling in the moonlight. And before the ocean, the cliffs.

She scanned the horizon, looking for anything unusual. At first, the view seemed undisturbed. Peaceful. Calm. She spotted a few houses down the road with unlit windows. They sat like sleeping cats, unaware of the drama unfolding not far from them. No one was around. The only sound was the lulling, rhythmic lap of water against the shore.

But then Priscilla saw a glint of light on metal. Virginia's pink Cadillac, idling at the edge of the cliffs!

As they drove nearer, Priscilla could see what looked like an unmoving Virginia slouched in the driver's seat. Douglas stood at the open driver's door, fussing with something. Weighting down the gas pedal? Sticking the gear shift?

Not that it would matter. If he managed to push the car over the edge, the vehicle's controls would be useless. Gravity would override everything, and Virginia would be lost to the water, if not the rocks, below.

They only had seconds to spare.

Priscilla yelled at Gerald to stop. He jammed the SUV into Park, and Priscilla jumped out. "Douglas, don't do it!" At the sound of her voice, Douglas looked startled and quickly stood up, smacking the back of his head on the car's roof. His eyes grew wide as saucers when he glimpsed Priscilla.

"Stop right there!" Hank jumped out of the cruiser and bolted for the cliffs. "Put your hands above your head and keep them where I can see them!"

It was Hank's voice that propelled Douglas to action. He turned to face them fully, with his hands raised to show he carried no weapon. His look was innocent, but Priscilla could tell he was acting. She wondered how she hadn't seen through him before. The dripping concern for his aunt that was obviously a sham. His sugary charm as Elias Sweetwater. His panicked meltdowns over the producer, which she now suspected were linked to anxiety over his criminal plans unraveling before his eyes.

"Oh, thank goodness you're here! I hadn't heard from my aunt in a week, and I left right after the play to look for her. I found her out here, like this. I can't wake her up." He wrung his hands in the gesture of a concerned nephew.

"Save the playacting for the stage, Douglas," said Hank. "Besides, you told us you talked to Virginia on Tuesday. You said she was going to Edgartown."

"Uh, did I say a week?" stammered Douglas. "My mistake. I meant I hadn't talked to her yet today. A simple slip of the tongue, you know."

"Knock it off, Douglas," said Hank. "We have solid evidence against you. We found the hidden room where you held your aunt hostage. We also have your disguise. And there are those remnants of stolen paver stones on your property. You're going away for a long, long time."

"It was—it was all Virginia," stuttered Douglas, trying another tactic. "She's gone senile, I think. She's advanced in years and needs someone to look after her."

Douglas still thought he could throw them off the trail, with his dramatic illusions and covered-up truth. But Scripture proved right. Truthful words did stand the test of time, but lies were soon exposed. Douglas's lies had been unearthed all at once.

With Douglas still protesting, Hank cuffed him and loaded him into the cruiser. Gerald turned Virginia's car off and carefully checked her pulse.

"She's still breathing. Thank the good Lord for that," said Gerald. "We shouldn't move her though, in case she has some kind of neck injury or something else we don't know about. I contacted the hospital already. The ambulance should be here soon."

Trudy sidled up beside Priscilla. "Why is she unconscious? Did Douglas hit her in the head or something?" She sounded breathless, and Priscilla understood. She felt the same way.

"No. She doesn't have any wounds on her head that would indicate the use of blunt force," Gerald said, looking Virginia over closely. "I wonder if Douglas drugged her somehow. Gave her a sedative. It would have been easy enough, especially if he was bringing her food and drink while he kept her captive. I'm sure she willingly accepted everything he gave her. She'd fight to stay alive, not allow herself to die of hunger or thirst." Gerald steadied his hand on the side of the car. "From what I know of Virginia, she seems like a tough cookie. My money's on her. I think she'll recover and go back to driving everyone up the wall in a week or two."

Priscilla studied Virginia's sleeping face, her red wig askew and her normally clownish makeup worn off after what Priscilla assumed was the entire week locked in the Victorian house's hidden room. The wrinkles on the old woman's face were softened, and Priscilla shivered at the thought that they'd almost been too late. Douglas had nearly gotten away with his plan. And what was it all for? Money?

She guessed they'd find out soon, if he confessed.

In the distance, Priscilla could hear the wail of an ambulance drawing closer. Virginia was all right. Douglas had been captured. Two mysteries had been solved in one fell swoop.

Priscilla chuckled. It was amazing how the pieces of the puzzle had fallen together so neatly, when just a few moments before, the clues had felt as confusing and tangled as any case she'd ever encountered. Those waves of doubt she'd been feeling lately—with her friendships, with Gerald—had no place in her life. God had the situation well in control. He was the one she trusted with her faith and her future. Priscilla breathed a sigh of relief.

This confusing charade was finally drawing to an end.

CHAPTER THIRTY-THREE

Her bed had never felt so comfortable. Priscilla couldn't remember the last time she'd slept so deeply and soundly. She wasn't even sure if she'd moved from the position she initially fell asleep in. Pure exhaustion certainly led to a great night's rest.

She sighed contentedly as she rolled over and stretched. Sensing her movement, Jake loosed his jaws in a gigantic yawn and readjusted his sleeping position too. "We have to get up for church in a little bit, boy. At least I do." Priscilla laughed at the thought of Jake attending Faith Fellowship with her. He'd probably be more than happy to be around people who might offer treats or extra cuddles, but she had a feeling their new pastor wouldn't be too happy about his presence.

Priscilla laughed again to herself, making Jake perk up his ears in interest. "It's okay, boy. Go back to sleep." He obediently flopped back down and commenced snoring.

Priscilla sat up in bed and rolled her neck from side to side, working out the kinks. She hadn't realized how much tension she'd been holding in her body until the myriad of worries she'd been facing dissolved at Douglas's capture. Even though she'd been exhausted last night, she'd gone to the police station after the scene on the cliff and was happy to discover he was singing like a guilty bird. He'd given Hank a full confession.

It was amazing how all the pieces of the puzzle fell into place at precisely the proper moment. How ridiculous that she'd even once doubted things would work out. She'd lived long enough to learn that it was easy to trust God after the fact. The hard part was trusting when you were going through the storm. It was why the Israelites wandered the desert for forty years instead of taking the Promised Land right away. Priscilla resolved to be more committed in the future to casting her cares on the Lord, rather than letting worries weigh on her mind and heart.

Her cell rang on her bedside table, and she answered it.

"Priscilla, thank goodness you're up." Trudy's chipper voice sounded like sunshine. "I know you have church this morning, but I was talking to Gail and Joan a little bit ago, and we're just dying to know what happened after you and Gerald went to the police station last night. Did Douglas confess? Is Virginia all right? Why was she unconscious? Why didn't we—"

Priscilla cut off Trudy's laundry list of questions. "It's a long story, Trudy. Too long for a quick phone conversation before church."

"That's what I thought," Trudy responded. "So how about we meet up, the four of us, after service is done? Maybe Candy's?"

Goodness. Trudy was adrenaline-charged this morning. She should be worn out after her big night on the stage and all the excitement afterward, but that was Trudy. Her constant buoyancy was hard to get used to.

"Candy's again?" Priscilla said. She pinched the extra weight around her stomach. "I'm never going to get into that dress for the wedding."

Trudy sighed. "You know, Candy's has low-fat muffins and healthy smoothies. You don't have to eat crème horns, cheese Danish, or any other fattening treat."

"Isn't that the pot calling the kettle black?" Priscilla said. "What happened to your diet?"

A snicker came over the phone. "I was trying to lose weight for the play, but it's over now."

Priscilla laughed. "Okay, I give up, but this time I have to watch what I eat."

"I'm going to watch my food too," Trudy said. "As it disappears into my mouth."

"Oh, Trudy. You're a mess, you know that?"

"But I'm a lovable mess," she said, giggling.

"What time do I need to be there?"

"Around twelve thirty?" Trudy asked.

"Sounds great. See you then."

Priscilla hung up her phone. Then she brewed some coffee and got dressed for church. She fussed a little extra over her hair and makeup. Gerald still hadn't provided an explanation for the mysterious woman he'd been meeting with behind her back. With all the excitement the night before, they hadn't made it to dinner. Maybe he'd finally explain the matter when she saw him in church today. After all, they would be sharing space for at least an hour. More, if the pastor felt so inclined.

Priscilla still had two mysteries on her radar. Gerald's odd behavior and the location of the Nancy Luce artifacts. She couldn't talk to Virginia until she recovered from the drugs Douglas had given her. But she would see Gerald in just a little bit. Hopefully, today would bring the answers she'd been waiting for. She grabbed her purse and a light coat. After saying goodbye to Jake, she squared her shoulders, opened her door, and prayed that God would bring a resolution to the questions still weighing on her mind.

"Good morning," Gerald said as Priscilla slid into her seat next to him. "You don't look as bleary-eyed as I feel. What's your secret?"

"Now, now, a lady never reveals her tricks." Priscilla couldn't help but tease him. She was feeling some relief since Douglas had been arrested and Virginia had been found alive and safe.

"Well, whatever you're doing, it's working. You look lovely." Warmth spread through Priscilla at his adoring smile.

"I'm just happy," said Priscilla and tucked her hand in his. Then she paused and tipped her face up toward him.

Though she was silent, Gerald must have sensed she was holding something back. "I'm glad you're happy. But I sense an aside coming."

Priscilla shook her head. "No, it's nothing." She didn't want to force Gerald to tell her about the woman, yet it was the proverbial elephant in the room.

"This is about the woman I met with, isn't it?"

Priscilla sighed. "Yes, and I do still have to ask. Are you ever going to explain about her? I trust that everything was aboveboard, but it's only fair for me to know what's going on. Keeping secrets from each other isn't a good idea."

Gerald let out a breath. "You're precisely right. And I'm sorry. I don't want you to worry about me or my loyalty to you." He placed his hand on her cheek and looked her straight in the eyes. "I'll tell you right now if you want. It's been killing me to have you doubt my intentions, but..."

"But what?"

"If you would have the tiniest scrap of patience left for me, I promise to tell you at dinner tonight. It'll make more sense then."

Priscilla had no idea what Gerald was talking about, but she felt in her heart that he was being honest with her. Just as she'd finally been able to see through Douglas's lies, she knew that Gerald wasn't hiding anything negative or hurtful.

She pressed her lips together but then said, "Yes, I can wait until dinner."

Gerald smiled. "I promise it will be a pleasant surprise."

"I wouldn't expect anything less from you, Gerald O'Bannon."

After the church service, Gerald walked Priscilla out to the parking lot. After giving her a hug and a gentle kiss on the cheek, he held the door for her as she climbed into her SUV. Though Gary had been an excellent husband, he'd not been the sort of man to coddle her in the traditional ways. It hadn't bothered her then. She'd been proud of her role as the independent Kansas farm wife.

Somehow, though, Gerald's gentlemanly responses to her made her just as proud. His chivalry didn't make her feel overly dainty or high-maintenance. It just reassured her she was cared for. Cherished. Noticed.

She couldn't help feeling excited about tonight. What was the mysterious secret Gerald seemed so intent on keeping? Try as she might, she couldn't guess what it might be.

Priscilla drove to Candy's feeling better than she had in a while. She spied her cousins as soon as she walked in, tucked into a corner to the left of the entrance.

Trudy's eyes brightened when she saw Priscilla, and she hopped up from her seat to grab Priscilla's arm. Trudy steered her to the table, where Gail and Joan waited expectantly.

"So, dish out all the details," said Trudy. "We're dying to know how everyone's favorite neurotic director made the leap from writing murder to nearly committing it in real life."

CHAPTER THIRTY-FOUR

After getting a cup of Candy's low-fat French vanilla latte and two of her reduced-calorie cranberry muffins, Priscilla was ready to explain everything she could to her cousins. First, she took a bite of her muffin. She was surprised at how much it tasted like the regular muffin. She was thrilled to discover that she could have one of her favorite treats but still reduce the calories and fat. It was a happy discovery, and it made her smile. She took a deep breath and started with the thefts from the cemetery.

"You mean the old man you talked to was really Douglas Lawrence?" Gail asked.

Priscilla nodded. "He used the disguise to scope out items he could sell later. He'd flown through the money his aunt had given him, and he needed more. Some of those decorations are quite valuable."

"And where was Virginia all this time?" Joan asked.

"Locked up in a secret room!" Trudy interjected jubilantly.

Priscilla smiled and sipped her coffee. There wasn't much hope Trudy would stay silent while Priscilla revealed the truth behind the events of the last week.

"A secret room?" Joan said, her mouth hanging open.

After a quick glance at Trudy, Priscilla nodded. "Octavia mentioned that some of the old houses on the island have hidden rooms."

"But how did you find it?" Joan asked.

Priscilla laughed. "I didn't. Magnus did. He led us right to it. Started barking and scratching at the wall. Once I realized there had to be something there, it wasn't hard to find the release. Of course, when the door was opened, Virginia was gone."

"I can't imagine what that poor woman went through," Joan said. She frowned. "But the note? What about the note saying that a courier had picked up the Nancy Luce artifacts? Is that true? No one's been able to locate them."

Priscilla shrugged. "I'm not sure. I still don't have the answer to that question or know what happened to the artifacts. Hopefully, we'll find the truth soon. When I talked to the chief last night, he told me Douglas had no reason not to believe her about the courier. The scary thing is that she had a habit, he said, of thinking she was calling one number and dialing another. I guess any entry in the phone book that was near the one she looked up was good enough. She's tried to order Chinese food from a local cigar shop and flowers from a plumbing supply store."

"So she might have accidentally called someone else?" Gail asked. "Not a courier service?"

Priscilla nodded. "Exactly. I could see her telling whoever was on the line that she had a valuable collection that needed to be taken to the museum. The person who answered her call could have the artifacts. Maybe they even sold them by now."

"Maybe Douglas is lying about that," Joan said. "I'll bet he's the one who sold them."

"I hope not," Priscilla replied. "I mean, I'm glad Virginia's okay, but if those artifacts aren't found, it will be a great loss for the Boston Museum, and Mildred will be held responsible."

"So why keep Virginia locked up until last night?" Gail asked.

"He had to establish a believable story," Trudy blurted out. "He couldn't get rid of her right away. So, he—" She suddenly stopped and looked at Priscilla. "I'm sorry," she said, blushing. "You tell them."

Priscilla reached over and patted her cousin's arm. "You're doing fine. Go ahead." Priscilla didn't care if Trudy answered all the questions. It gave her more time to eat her muffins.

Trudy smiled and leaned closer to the table, her eyes sparkling. "He dressed like Virginia and drove around the island so people would think she was still here. And he drove recklessly on purpose so that when her car went off the cliff, everyone would assume her terrible driving led to an accident."

"But why?" Joan asked. "Was he in line to inherit her money?"

Priscilla nodded. "She made a lot of money on the sale of her house. With her other assets, he would have gotten millions. I believe he was planning to do away with her anyway, but then something happened that moved up his timeline."

"That's right," Trudy said. "There's another reason for why he originally locked her in that room," she said to her sister and cousin. "Do you want to hear it?"

Joan and Gail nodded, and Trudy gestured for Priscilla to continue the story.

"Douglas gave Virginia the paver stones as a birthday present. Since she's such a recluse, and no one ever visits her, Douglas never thought anyone would see the stones and realize they were stolen. But Virginia spends a lot of time in cemeteries doing research, and she recognized the stones Douglas stole from the West Tisbury cemetery," Priscilla said. "When she confronted him and threatened to call Hank, Douglas panicked. That's when he made her write that letter telling people she was too nervous to speak at the meeting and that she was going away for a while."

"One more question," Joan said. "How in the world did you think to check the cliffs for her?"

"That was all Priscilla," Trudy said. She turned to her cousin. "Tell them."

"It was really just a guess," Priscilla said. "Douglas suddenly changed the end of the play. When I watched it, the last scenes didn't flow well with the rest of the plot. That's when I wondered why he'd made the switch."

"Because it had given him an idea about how to get rid of her," Joan said, arching her eyebrow. "But it was too close to the truth, and he couldn't risk telegraphing his plans."

"Exactly," Priscilla said. "Actually, I took a wild guess. I could have been wrong."

"But you weren't," Trudy said. "You saved Virginia's life."

"Well, I'm not sure about that," Priscilla said. "I'm just grateful everything turned out all right."

Trudy picked up her cappuccino and shook her head. "When he found out the producer wasn't going to fund his play, he ran home to get rid of his aunt. He needed that inheritance as quickly as he could get it. I'll bet he would have started selling some of her things while he waited for the inheritance to come through."

At that moment, Priscilla's phone rang. It was Hank.

"Could you meet me at Virginia's?" he asked.

"I guess so," she said. "Can I ask why?"

"Virginia's home, and she'd like to see you."

"How is she?" Priscilla asked.

"Feisty," he said with a hint of frustration in his voice. "I guess that means she's fine. I've been talking to her, and she confirms everything Douglas said in his confession, but when I asked her about the stuff from the museum, she wouldn't tell me anything. She says she'll only answer my questions once you get here."

"Really?" Priscilla said. She was surprised, but she agreed to meet Hank after she finished having lunch with her cousins.

"The sooner the better," he mumbled. "She's quite a handful."

Priscilla chuckled. "I certainly agree." She said goodbye and hung up the phone.

"Who was that?" Trudy asked.

"Hank. I guess Virginia's home, and she wants to see me."

"Maybe she knows you saved her and wants to thank you," Joan said.

"Tell her a million dollars would be a great way to show her appreciation," Gail said wryly.

The women laughed.

"Now, if there are no more questions," Priscilla said, "I'm going to finish these wonderful muffins."

"I have one," Joan said softly. "Do you know who the blonde is yet?"

The light feeling that Gail's humor had created vanished like smoke in the wind. Priscilla shook her head. "Not yet, but Gerald said he'd tell me about her tonight."

Trudy reached over and took Priscilla's hand. "Everything will be fine, I just know it. That man loves you with all his heart, Priscilla."

"I have faith that you're right," Priscilla said.

Trudy let go of her hand and leaned back in her chair with a happy smile. "You helped Dan and me. Everything will turn out great for you too."

"Thanks," Priscilla said, "but I feel we need to establish some ground rules. No more secrets. It's not good for anyone trying to build a foundation of trust."

As the conversation went back to the events of the last week, Priscilla couldn't help but wonder why Virginia wanted to see her. Would she finally find out what had happened to the Nancy Luce artifacts?

CHAPTER THIRTY-FIVE

When Priscilla rang the doorbell at Virginia's, she was happy to be greeted by Magnus's enthusiastic barking. It seemed he was once again roaming free.

The door opened, and Hank ushered her inside. After greeting Magnus and getting a sloppy kiss on the face, Priscilla walked into the large living room where Virginia was propped up on the couch, covered with an afghan. Priscilla couldn't help but feel compassion for the woman. She'd been through a lot. Priscilla couldn't imagine being tied up and held hostage for several days. It was interesting to note that however tired or upset Virginia might be, she'd managed to put on all her makeup. Her wig was squarely in place as well.

When she saw Priscilla, Virginia gave her a rather weak smile and waved her over. She scooted up a bit, leaving a space at the end of the couch. "Sit," Virginia said.

Magnus immediately sat down, causing Priscilla to grin. It seemed she was meant to obey, just the way Magnus had done. She took her seat near Virginia's feet.

"I understand I have you to thank for freeing me," Virginia said. "I'm so grateful."

"Actually, it was a joint effort," Priscilla said. "My cousins helped, and so did Magnus. He actually led us to the hidden room."

As if he knew he'd just been praised, Magnus got up and came over to the couch, laying his head on Priscilla's lap. She gently stroked his head. He really was a special dog.

"Chief Westin has explained everything to me," Virginia said. "About how you figured out what Douglas was up to. I shudder to think what would have happened if you hadn't realized what he planned to do to me." Her voice caught, and Magnus moved over to be near his owner. He leaned up against her, and Virginia put her hand on his back. "Not sure what I would do without you either," she said gently to the beautiful Irish setter, who gazed at his owner with obvious adoration.

"There's something I'd like to ask you," Priscilla said slowly, not wanting to offend the woman by changing the subject.

"You want to know about the artifacts?"

Priscilla nodded.

"I asked her that too," Hank said, "but she wouldn't tell me until you arrived."

"I don't understand," Priscilla said to Virginia.

Virginia straightened up a bit more. "First of all, let's talk about my note."

"We couldn't find the courier service you contacted," Priscilla said.

Virginia laughed. "That's because I didn't call one. When Douglas forced me to write that note, I told him I was finished going over the artifacts and didn't want to be responsible to take them to the meeting that night. I told him I'd sent them back to the museum by courier."

"Why would you do that?"

Virginia smiled. "You were all looking for me, right?"

Priscilla leaned back on the arm of the couch. Virginia was a lot cagier than she'd given her credit for. "You did that on purpose."

"Of course. I have a bad habit of calling the wrong number when I pick businesses from the phone book. I knew Douglas would assume I'd done it again. At least he wouldn't be concerned about the artifacts. I wanted him to forget about them. If he thought I had them, he'd probably try to sell them. I couldn't let that happen."

"So you protected the artifacts, but you also realized that if we all thought they were missing, we wouldn't give up looking for them—and for you."

Virginia nodded, looking very pleased with herself. "Especially you, Priscilla. I know you have a reputation for solving mysteries. I was counting on your special talent to rescue me."

Priscilla smiled at the elderly woman. It was a lovely compliment, but she felt uneasy to think she was the one Virginia was counting on to solve the mysteries. What if something had gone wrong?

"Where are the artifacts then?" Priscilla asked finally, almost afraid to hear the answer.

Virginia threw back the covers and swung her legs over the side of the couch. She was wearing a purple silk lounger.

"Do you need help?" Hank asked.

Virginia sighed. "I've told you before, I don't need to be manhandled."

Hank rolled his eyes, and Priscilla fought back an urge to laugh. Maybe he was the one Priscilla should feel sorry for.

"Follow me," she told Priscilla as she stood up. She was just a bit wobbly, so Priscilla reached out to take her arm. Thankfully, she wasn't rebuked for *manhandling* her. Once Virginia seemed steady, Priscilla let go and followed her over to the wall. Virginia pushed the spot that opened the door to the hidden room. She grabbed the edge of the door and pulled it open.

Although he wasn't invited, Hank got up and stood behind them to watch. Virginia went into the room, knelt down on the floor, and pushed hard against one of the decorative wooden squares that made up the wall. A small door popped open. She reached inside and pulled out what Priscilla saw the artifacts. She sighed with relief.

"They're all here," she said. "When Douglas wasn't looking, I put them under my cape. Then I kept them safe by putting them in this hiding place. Thankfully, even though Douglas knew about the hidden room, I'd never told him about this special feature. I had to hide them quickly, while he was looking for rope to tie me up. He had no idea the artifacts were still in the house."

Priscilla smiled at the elderly woman and helped her to her feet. She started to reach down and pick up the artifacts when Hank cleared his throat.

"I'd rather you not touch evidence," he growled.

Virginia walked up to him and put her face a few inches from his. "How can they be evidence, you silly man? They weren't stolen." She turned back to look at Priscilla. "You take those back to Mildred. If everyone's still willing, I'd like to reschedule that talk at the library."

Priscilla glanced over at Hank to see his reaction. His face was flushed, and Priscilla was pretty sure he was biting his tongue, but he nodded at her. As Priscilla gathered everything up, Virginia went out to the living room and found a tote bag. "I don't know where the folder is that you originally had these in. Douglas must have done something with it." She handed the tote bag to Priscilla. "You can use this," she said. "But bring it back. I'm not made of money, you know."

"Yeah, I've heard girls are made of sugar and spice," Hank mumbled.

Priscilla laughed and put the artifacts in the bag. She could hardly wait to call Mildred.

"So it sounds like everything worked out okay," Gerald said.

Priscilla watched him from across the table, his handsome features illuminated by soft candlelight. They'd been on many dates to the Colonial Inn and Restaurant, but this time felt particularly special. The white tablecloths and glinting antique décor combined with the gentle murmur of other dining couples to create a cozy, romantic atmosphere.

"Yes, couldn't be better," she said. She smiled at Gerald, and he smiled back, not taking his eyes from her. Priscilla sighed happily and took a bite of her lobster bisque. The soup was delicious, the perfect indulgence after a week of stress and confusion.

"I called Mildred to tell her we had the artifacts," she continued. "Of course, she was overjoyed. The Boston Museum even allowed her to keep the pieces for an extra week so Virginia could reschedule her talk at the library."

Gerald's eyes sparkled. "You think she'll show up this time?"

"Yes, I'm sure she will. I expect we'll have a huge turnout. Do you remember Jackson Wither, that man from one of the Boston libraries?"

Gerald nodded. "I recall you talking about him."

"He invited Virginia to become their writer-in-residence for the next academic year, and she accepted. She was moving to the mainland anyway, and she seemed thrilled by the prospect of a new challenge and a new town."

"I thought you told me one of the cousins checked him out and discovered he was a phony."

Priscilla laughed. "Just a misunderstanding. When Jackson gave me his card, he handed me the one from the East Boston Library. That's where he used to work. They don't have a writer-in-residence program. But he moved from the East Library to the main library several months ago. He just forgot to put his new cards in his billfold."

"I hope this will be a good move for Virginia. That she'll get connected somewhere," Gerald said.

"Me too," agreed Priscilla. "I'm actually going to miss that eccentric old woman." Priscilla raised an eyebrow. "Enough about Virginia. You've kept me in suspense long enough, Gerald O'Bannon. If you make me wait until dessert..."

Gerald smiled. He suddenly looked shy, almost boyish, with that lock of hair falling across his forehead. "You're right. Thanks for being so patient." He put a hand on his heart. "I promise, after this, no more secrets. I will be an open book from now on—"

"Gerald! Just tell me already!"

"All right, all right." Gerald held up his hands in mock surrender, but he was smiling from ear to ear. He reached into his coat pocket and pulled out a small white box tied with a satin ribbon. "Do you remember telling me about a lost family heirloom you wanted Rachel to wear at the wedding? A brooch, I believe?" He slid the box across the table to Priscilla.

"Oh, Gerald. What have you done?" Priscilla could barely speak over the lump in her throat.

"Obviously, it's not the original. But it should look very similar."

With shaking hands, Priscilla untied the bow and lifted the box's lid. Nestled on a bed of white cotton batting was a cameo, the creamy white silhouette of a woman rising from a blue agate background. Priscilla gasped.

"The woman I was meeting with?" said Gerald. "She's a freelance jeweler. She created this piece for me."

"But how did you get the details right? The brooch is just perfect."

"Remember the night we had dinner here? You showed me a picture of Gary's mother wearing the brooch, and when you left to go to the ladies' room, I snapped a picture of the photo on my phone."

Priscilla thought back to that evening, how she'd felt the contents of her purse had been rearranged. It had been Gerald, hurriedly moving the photo back into what he thought was its original place. She was touched by the effort and expense he must have gone to, to have such a unique item crafted in such a short period of time.

Priscilla turned the piece over in her hands. She felt as if she were holding the original. What a gift Gerald had given her. Sudden tears flooded her eyes.

"Hey now, I didn't intend to make you cry," said Gerald, rising from his chair to wrap her in a warm embrace.

"They're happy tears," said Priscilla with a small laugh. "Oh, I'm a blubbering mess. I'm getting you all damp." She brushed at the dark spots now dotting Gerald's suit coat.

"Scilla." Gerald tipped her face up to his. "I don't mind."

They shared a sweet kiss, and he helped her fasten the brooch onto the front of her sweater. Priscilla couldn't stop gazing down at it. It was lovely, and the man across the table had thoroughly captured her affection. She hadn't been sure if she could love again after losing Gary, but, though it had taken a bit of time, Gerald O'Bannon had won her over.

As they enjoyed the rest of their meal, Priscilla couldn't imagine being happier. And she couldn't wait to give the lovely brooch to Rachel on her wedding day.

As she had many times before, she silently thanked God for leading her to Martha's Vineyard where her life had begun anew. A favorite Scripture whispered in her thoughts. A promise of beauty for ashes and the oil of joy for mourning. As she smiled at Gerald, she realized that God's words had certainly come true in her life.

LETTERS FROM THE AUTHORS

Dear Reader,

Like a lot of authors, my childhood dream was to be a writer. It was a dream I chased through high school essay contests, college majors, and many writing sessions squeezed in while taking care of my two rambunctious young boys. When I was given the opportunity to co-write this book with my wonderful mother-in-law, Nancy, for Guideposts, a company I've respected for years, I was ecstatic.

Until the doubt set in. I felt overwhelmed. Would I be up to the challenge? Or not? I chose to set aside those questions to press through and am thankful I did.

Like Priscilla moving across the country to start her life fresh, don't be afraid to step into the life you dream of. There may be seasons of doubt, but if you continue forward with your faith as an anchor, the world will open up before you.

Sincerly,
Shaen Layle

Dear Reader,

I've written quite a few books for Guideposts, but this one is very special. Being able to write with my beloved daughter-in-law added an element of joy that's hard to describe. She is the one who uncovered Nancy Luce, the "Chicken Lady." What a great element to add to our story!

I believe you'll not only love our Martha's Vineyard setting, but you'll also be captivated by Priscilla's search for the misplaced Nancy Luce artifacts as she and Trudy race around the island, chasing a reclusive, quirky historian who was the last person to have the items in her possession.

As for Shaen's doubts about being up to the task of writing a great book? I think you'll quickly see she had nothing to be concerned about. This is the first book I've ever co-written with anyone. I can hardly wait to do it again. And we will. Look for Guideposts' upcoming series, Mysteries of Lancaster County, where we'll write several more books together.

My deepest thanks to Guideposts, and to my incredible editor and deeply loved friend, Susan Downs, for allowing me to bring Shaen into the Guideposts family. There is no way Susan could ever be rewarded enough in this world for the blessings she's brought to my life. I believe with all my heart she will be repaid someday with many stars in her crown. In fact, the weight may make it difficult to wear—until we all throw our crowns at the feet of the Master.

Regards,

Nancy Mehl

ABOUT THE AUTHORS

Shaen Layle is a former librarian who writes every spare moment she's not helping her husband run his graphic design business or raising their two young boys. She is an avid reader and enjoys blogging about all things bookish at shaenlayle.com and discussing inspirational fiction in her Inspy Fiction Reading Challenge group on Facebook.

Nancy Mehl is a best-selling, award-winning author who lives in Missouri with her husband, Norman, and her Puggle, Watson. She's authored thirty books and is currently writing a new series for Bethany House Publishing. The Kaely Quinn Profiler series will kick off with book one, *Mind Games*, in December of 2018. In 2019 look for her books in The Mysteries of Lancaster County series, through Guideposts—also written with her daughter-in-law, Shaen Layle.

Readers can learn more about Nancy through her website: nancymehl.com. She is part of The Suspense Sisters, suspensesisters.blogspot.com, along with several other popular suspense authors. She is also very active on Facebook.

AN ARMCHAIR TOUR OF
MARTHA'S VINEYARD
Nancy Luce, "The Chicken Lady"

Martha's Vineyard is a beautiful, unique setting, and we enjoyed researching its history while preparing to write this book. One gem we stumbled upon was the story of historical figure Nancy Luce, affectionately known as "the Chicken Lady."

Nancy Luce was born in West Tisbury in 1814 and was the only child of Philip Luce and Anne Manter. She had a fairly ordinary childhood and adolescence, spent riding horses in the countryside and attending dances with her friends. When Nancy matured into young adulthood, however, she suffered health issues and became increasingly reclusive. After her mother and father died, Nancy continued living on their farmstead and withdrew from society even more, treating her chickens like children. She gave them fanciful names, such as Ada Queenie, Pondy Lily, Teeddla Toona, Levendy Ludandy, and Otte Opheto, and she fashioned elaborate tombstones for them when they died. She wrote pages of poems dedicated to her feathered friends—poems she later cunningly printed and sold as tourist trinkets to gawkers passing by on their way to the Methodist Campgrounds.

If you take a trip to the Vineyard, be sure to stop by Nancy Luce's grave at the West Tisbury cemetery. You can even leave a ceramic chicken in remembrance of the quirky woman some call the island's first female entrepreneur.

SOMETHING DELICIOUS FROM OUR SEASIDE FRIENDS

Priscilla's Perfect Ham Salad

1 stalk finely diced celery

2 tablespoons finely diced green onions

1 tablespoon finely diced red bell pepper

1 tablespoon lemon juice

½ teaspoon black pepper

1½ cups smoked ham, chopped in a food processor

2 hard-boiled eggs, chopped

⅓ cup Miracle Whip

2 teaspoons Dijon mustard

2 tablespoons sweet pickle relish

2 tablespoons real bacon bits

Stir together celery, green onions, and red bell pepper, then toss with lemon juice and black pepper. Combine veggie mixture with ham, eggs, Miracle Whip, Dijon mustard, pickle relish, and bacon bits in large bowl. Follow Priscilla and Trudy's lead and serve chilled ham salad on fresh croissants with a side of fruit.

Read on for a sneak peek of another exciting book
in the Mysteries of Martha's Vineyard series!

Lifeline
by Elizabeth Penney

Priscilla Latham Grant's heart skipped a beat as the noon ferry approached the dock, cutting through the waves with ease and authority. But the welcome sight of its arrival wasn't the reason for her butterflies. A certain someone on board was responsible for those.

Her daughter Rachel was getting married in a week, and she planned to stay at the lighthouse with Priscilla until then. They'd spend the remaining days before the wedding on last-minute preparations and hopefully have lots of girl time too. Pedicures, visits with the cousins, walks on the beach, and sharing Rachel's favorite meals were among the activities Priscilla had dreamed up. Probably enough to keep them busy for a month, she realized, smiling to herself.

For most of her life, Priscilla had lived in Kansas, where Rachel was also born and raised. But when Priscilla inherited a lighthouse and cottage shortly after her beloved husband died, she'd gathered up her courage and made the move. Martha's Vineyard was home now, and since Rachel, and her fiancé, A.J., now lived and worked in Boston, having the ceremony here made sense.

Passengers lined the upper deck, waving as the ferry drew closer. Priscilla waved back, trying to spot Rachel, but she couldn't find her among the double row of people. July was high season on Martha's Vineyard, and every ferry was packed. Everyone in the world wanted to be on the island, it seemed, and Priscilla was lucky enough to live here.

Her red and white Australian shepherd whined and tugged at his leash. "Hold on, Jake. They'll let her off in a few minutes." He always seemed to pick up on her moods, but Priscilla didn't doubt he knew exactly who was arriving. She'd only told him five or six times that morning.

The ferry slid into its berth, the smooth maneuver the result of much practice by the captain and crew. Shouts went up, the gang-planks went down, and people began to stream off the boat. Rachel was on foot, having decided not to bring her car. She really didn't need it, since she could borrow Priscilla's if need be.

Restraining her impatience, Priscilla remained standing near the tree she'd mentioned to Rachel. It would be too easy to get lost in this crowd, in the throng of people greeting each other with hugs and handshakes. Car doors and tailgates slammed as luggage was loaded. Engines roared. Now automobiles emerged out of the ferry's belly, one by one, moving at a crawl. Vans and Volvos and SUVs, even an ancient lime-green VW bug Priscilla had seen around town.

Anxiety tightened Priscilla's chest. *Where is she? Did she get on the ferry?* Priscilla pulled out her cell phone. Maybe she'd been mistaken about the time. No, there was the text from last night saying the noon boat. No missed calls or texts either. Should she—oh, why not? She punched in Rachel's speed dial code.

It rang and rang. Then she saw a tall, blond beauty striding in her direction, hair swinging loose, fresh and crisp in a white linen blouse, tan capris, and suede mules. A suitcase trailed behind, pulled by a handle, and she also held a large leather tote.

Priscilla's eyes burned with tears of relief and joy. "Oh, you're silly," she muttered to herself with a laugh. One might think they'd been separated for decades, not a matter of weeks. Blame it on the wedding. Everyone got emotional at weddings, right? Maybe even before they actually happened.

"Mom." Rachel's face creased in a huge smile. She stood the suitcase up, dropped the tote, and gathered her mother into her arms.

Priscilla squeezed, enjoying this all-too-rare opportunity to hold her daughter. Rachel smelled of vanilla and almonds, the aroma of her favorite shampoo. She was warm and solid and precious. Jake sat close, and Priscilla could feel his soft fur tickling her leg.

After a long moment, they disengaged with smiles. Rachel's face sobered. "I've got some news…an unexpected development."

"What is it?" Priscilla sagged, high spirits dashed.

Rachel laughed. "Don't look so serious. It's not that bad, well, I hope it won't be." She turned to one side and tipped her head at a young woman sitting on her tall suitcase a short distance away.

Priscilla hadn't noticed her until now, but she recognized her straight off. Marilee Montgomery, Rachel's future sister-in-law—and a royal pain.

A.J.'s sister gave her a little wave and a wry frown. "Hey, Mrs. Grant."

"Nice to see you," Priscilla said automatically. Meanwhile her mind was whirring, trying to figure out what to do about the unexpected visitor. True, she barely knew Marilee, but her first impression hadn't been positive. Snippy and pessimistic, the young woman was the complete opposite of her kind, calm brother. Priscilla felt exactly as if a rain cloud had moved over her sunny plans.

"I was thinking she could maybe stay with one of the cousins," Rachel was saying. "You don't have room at the cottage."

Marilee lifted a stubborn chin. "I brought my textbooks, so I've got plenty to do." Priscilla must have looked puzzled because she added, "I'm trying to get a jump on my advanced biology classes so I'll get into medical school."

"She's going to be in her senior year of college," Rachel explained, crossing her arms. "So, do you think Joan might want company?" Out of the three lovely Latham cousins Priscilla had met on the island, she was perhaps the closest to Joan Abernathy, a widow who lived alone.

"That might work," Priscilla said. "I'll give her a call." Wedding guests from Kansas were planning to stay with Joan, but they wouldn't arrive until next Thursday or Friday. Priscilla forced herself to smile. "We've got a great week planned, Marilee. Lots of girl time."

The response was a grunt. Marilee rested her chin in her hand and glumly stared at the asphalt, looking like she'd rather be anywhere else than Martha's Vineyard.

"I'll start loading our luggage while you call," Rachel said.

Priscilla pointed to where she was parked, then took a few steps away for privacy.

Thankfully Joan answered right off. "Hi, Priscilla. Did you pick up the blushing bride?" Joan and the other two cousins, Trudy and Gail, had been invaluable in helping with the wedding.

"I did." Priscilla's gaze rested on her daughter, who was hefting bags into the back of the SUV. "She brought a guest." A beat, then she said, "Marilee Montgomery, who needs a place to stay."

"Ohhh." Joan's drawn-out reply said it all. "Bring her here. I'll take her."

Relief shot through Priscilla. "Are you sure? She's, um, a little difficult. And when it comes to this wedding, she resembles a balky mule." The wedding dress shopping trip in Boston had been one to remember. Marilee had sneered at every dress, including the gorgeous confection Rachel chose.

Joan's laughter pealed out. "Don't worry. I've dealt with plenty of difficult young women in my day. It will be tight once the other relatives arrive, but we'll squeeze her in. And of course, after the wedding, you'll have room. If she's still here."

How long was Marilee staying? Priscilla made a mental note to find out. And also to ask Rachel why her future sister-in-law was here early. A.J.'s aunt and father were arriving on Friday. A.J. and Marilee's mother, unfortunately, had passed away, and Auntie Em had filled in as a maternal figure ever since.

"Thanks so much, Joan." Priscilla watched as Marilee hefted her bag into the back compartment. "I wasn't ready for this complication. We'll stop by in a few."

Joan sucked in air. "Can you wait until later? I have a doctor's appointment this afternoon, over on the mainland." She paused. "Come for dinner at seven. We'll grill something. Can you bring a side?"

"How about potato salad and corn on the cob from the farmer's market?" *As well as my unexpected baggage.*

"Perfect," Joan said. "I'm dying for fresh sweet corn."

After saying goodbye to Joan, Priscilla walked over to the SUV, forcing a happy expression onto her features. "You're all set, Marilee. My cousin Joan has invited you to stay with her. You'll love Joan."

Marilee muttered something, then gave a little shriek as Jake bounded up into the back seat—and onto her lap. He began licking her face, despite her protests and efforts to push him away.

"Jake, cut it out," Priscilla ordered. She reached in and pulled on his collar, tugging him away. "He likes you." The dog settled finally. If Priscilla didn't know better, she'd think he was grinning, the way his tongue was lolling in his open mouth.

The young woman scrubbed at her cheeks. "Ugh. That was disgusting."

Rachel's eyes met Priscilla's, and she mouthed, "Sorry." She foraged in her tote and found a pack of moist wipes. She handed them to Marilee. "Here you go."

Priscilla opened the driver-side door and climbed in, Rachel joining her in the front passenger seat. "I thought we'd go back to the lighthouse first, for lunch." Priscilla started the car, checking the mirrors before setting off. "Then what would you like to do?"

"I have to go to The Rocks," Rachel said. "There's some kind of issue with the appetizers." Rachel had decided to have the recently built upscale hotel host the reception after other plans fell apart. It didn't hurt that they'd gotten an excellent deal, since the place was trying to build its clientele.

Priscilla waited for another vehicle to go by before pulling out of the parking space. "You're still having surf-and-turf for the main course, right?" She'd thought the menu was perfect. Lobster suitable for the island location and steak as a nod to Kansas, known for its excellent beef.

"You bet." Rachel settled back in the seat with a sigh, her elbow propped on the open windowsill. "I'll probably be too excited to eat a bite, but I know our guests will be happy."

"I'm a vegetarian," came a remark from the back seat. "I can't eat steak, and I hate lobster."

Priscilla threw Rachel a look of pained amusement. "I'm sure there will be lots of salads and side dishes," she said. "We'll check on that, okay?" If Marilee were anyone but the groom's only sibling, she could make do with breath mints, as far as Priscilla was concerned. But the right thing to do for her brother's sake was to keep her happy.

Marilee didn't acknowledge Priscilla's accommodation. Instead she proceeded to share the dangers of a red-meat diet and the hazards often present in crustaceans.

"Seems to me budding medical students present a danger too," Rachel whispered under the cover of the rushing breeze, loud enough for only Priscilla to hear. "Of sucking the joy out of life."

Priscilla couldn't help but smile at this truthful observation. Then, feeling a pang of something—remorse, maybe even empathy—she added a silent prayer. *Please, Lord, give me the patience I need to deal with this young woman.* Then she amended it. *Not only patience, but love too. Help me love her, the way You do.* There was a prayer challenge, if she had ever lifted one.

Both passengers fell silent as Priscilla drove the familiar route toward home, along narrow lanes lined with historic clapboard and shingle-sided buildings. Flowers frothed in window boxes and garden beds, adding vivid color to a palette of gray and white. Overhead, arching trees in full leaf provided welcome shade from the strong midday sun.

"This place is wonderful," Rachel said with a huge exhale. "I'm finally starting to relax."

Priscilla glanced at her. "Good. I'm glad. Your wedding should be fun, not another source of stress." Young people today put so much pressure on themselves to make everything perfect so their lives could match the unattainable images plastered everywhere in the media. Real life didn't come with an editing program, she thought ruefully. She patted Rachel's hand. "Besides, it's going to be fantastic. You're marrying a wonderful man you love."

A sound of gagging came from the back seat, but then it turned into a cough. "Sorry," Marilee said. "My hay fever is acting up."

"I've heard stinging nettle tea is good for that," Priscilla couldn't resist saying. "I can brew you up a batch." The remedy was real, but as she hoped, the mention discouraged further discussion of seasonal allergies.

Even now, after a couple of years, Priscilla's heart gladdened when she pulled into her driveway. Straight ahead, the majestic white lighthouse rose high over the water, a beacon of safety for ships passing in the night. A sea-blue cottage with white shutters nestled at its base, small but cozy and charming.

Home. Priscilla pulled to a stop near the door so Rachel could easily unload her bags. The car doors opened, and they all piled out. Marilee stood to one side, arms folded, her head tilted back as she stared at the lighthouse, which was a beautiful sight against the deep blue sky.

Priscilla left her there while she unlocked the lemon-yellow door, Jake pushing against her legs, and let Rachel into the house. "Dump everything in here," she told her daughter, pushing wide the door to the spare bedroom, with its quilted bedspread and gingham curtains.

"Mom, I'm so sorry," Rachel said in almost a whisper. "But A.J. brought her to the boat while we were boarding. Auntie Em's water main broke, and they won't have water on her street for a week. What could I say?" Her laugh was helpless. "He thought she'd have more fun on the island."

Priscilla set her mouth firmly, determined to make the best of the situation. "You did the right thing. Not the easy thing, but the right thing."

A troubled expression shadowed Rachel's eyes. "I've tried to make friends with her, but she's resisted me all the way. In fact, it seems to me she's doing everything she can to spoil the wedding."

A NOTE FROM THE EDITORS

We hope you enjoyed Mysteries of Martha's Vineyard, published by the Books and Inspirational Media Division of Guideposts, a nonprofit organization that touches millions of lives every day through products and services that inspire, encourage, help you grow in your faith, and celebrate God's love.

Thank you for making a difference with your purchase of this book, which helps fund our many outreach programs to military personnel, prisons, hospitals, nursing homes, and educational institutions.

We also create many useful and uplifting online resources. Visit Guideposts.org to read true stories of hope and inspiration, access OurPrayer network, sign up for free newsletters, download free e-books, join our Facebook community, and follow our stimulating blogs.

To learn about other Guideposts publications, including the best-selling devotional *Daily Guideposts*, go to Guideposts.org/Shop, call (800) 932-2145, or write to Guideposts, PO Box 5815, Harlan, Iowa 51593.

Sign up for the
Guideposts Fiction Newsletter
and stay up-to-date on the books you love!

You'll get sneak peeks of new releases, recommendations from other Guideposts readers, and special offers just for you . . .
and it's FREE!

Just go to Guideposts.org/Newsletters today to sign up.

Find more inspiring fiction in these best-loved Guideposts series!

Secrets of Wayfarers Inn
Fall back in history with three retired schoolteachers who find themselves owners of an old warehouse-turned-inn that is filled with hidden passages, buried secrets and stunning surprises that will set them on a course to puzzling mysteries from the Underground Railroad.

Sugarcreek Amish Mysteries
Be intrigued by the suspense and joyful "aha" moments in these delightful stories. Each book in the series brings together two women of vastly different backgrounds and traditions, who realize there's much more to the "simple life" than meets the eye.

Tearoom Mysteries Series
Mix one stately Victorian home, a charming lakeside town in Maine, and two adventurous cousins with a passion for tea and hospitality. Add a large scoop of intriguing mystery and sprinkle generously with faith, family, and friends, and you have the recipe for *Tearoom Mysteries*.

Mysteries of Silver Peak
Escape to the historic mining town of Silver Peak, Colorado, and discover how one woman's love of antiques helps her solve mysteries buried deep in the town's checkered past.

**To learn more about these books,
visit Guideposts.org/Shop**